...avourite fantasy...

...highway robbery, swordplay, deep friendships, treachery, magic, piracy on the high seas, and romance' Robin Hobb

'Susan Dennard has worldbuilding after my own heart. It's so good it's intimidating' Victoria Aveyard

'A world you'll want to inhabit forever!'
Alexandra Bracken

'Featuring vibrant characters and an innovative system of magic, Susan Dennard's *Truthwitch* is a fast-paced adventure and a wonderful tribute to the power of the binding ties of friendship' Jacqueline Carey

'So, so, so great – epic fantasy, epic adventure, epic friendship'
Kate Elliott

'*Truthwitch* has it all, strong female characters, adventure, magic, romance, and non-stop action that will leave you breathless!' Maria V. Snyder

'Dynamic storytelling and a fully imagined magical world . . . Dennard's rich descriptions, insightful characterizations and breathtaking action sequences will keep readers on their toes'
Publishers Weekly

'Two devoted friends dreaming of independence contend with unfathomable magic and the schemes of empires in this action-packed series opener'
Kirkus

'It's great to read a fantasy book where sisterhood and no-nonsense women take the lead . . . triumphantly fun, *Truthwitch* casts off the current trend for gritty fantasy with a joyous laugh and a cheeky wink'
SFX

'A rollicking, swashbuckling adventure . . . Just the thing if you'd like to be swept away from real life for a while'
The Bookbag

Bloodwitch

Before she settled down as a full-time novelist and writing instructor, Susan Dennard travelled the world as a marine biologist. She is the author of the Something Strange and Deadly series as well as the Witchlands novels. When not writing, she can be found hiking with her dogs, exploring tidal pools, or earning bruises at the dojo.

To find out more about the Witchlands novels, please visit **thewitchlands.com**.

BY SUSAN DENNARD

The Witchlands series
Truthwitch
Windwitch
Bloodwitch

Bloodwitch

The Witchlands Series: Book Three

Susan Dennard

TOR

First published 2019 by Tom Doherty Associates, LLC

First published in the UK 2019 by Tor

This paperback edition published 2020 by Tor
an imprint of Pan Macmillan
The Smithson, 6 Briset Street, London EC1M 5NR
Associated companies throughout the world
www.panmacmillan.com

ISBN 978-1-4472-8886-2

1 3 5 7 9 8 6 4 2

A CIP catalogue record for this book is available from the British Library.

Typeset by Palimpsest Book Production Limited, Falkirk, Stirlingshire
Printed and bound by CPI Group (UK) Ltd, Croydon, CR0 4YY

MIX
Paper from
responsible sources
FSC® C116313

Visit www.panmacmillan.com to read more about all our books
and to buy them. You will also find features, author interviews and
news of any author events, and you can sign up for e-newsletters
so that you're always first to hear about our new releases.

FOR WHITNEY

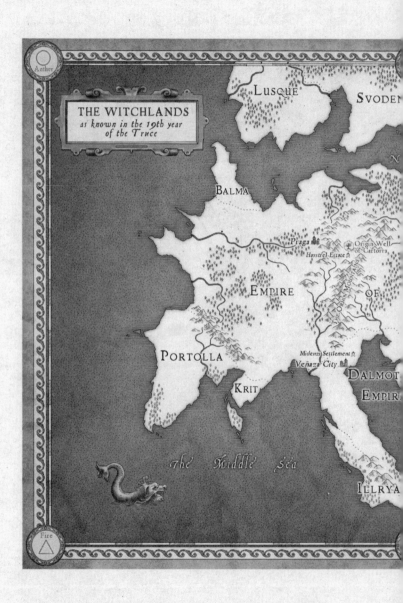

THE WITCHLANDS
as known in the 19th year
of the Truce

LUSQUE

SVODEN

BALMA

Praga
Hasstrel Estate

Origin Well
of Cartorra

EMPIRE

THE ORIGIN MOUNTAINS

OF

PORTOLLA

Midenzi Settlement
Veñaza City

DALMOT

KRIT

EMPIR

The Middle Sea

ILLRYA

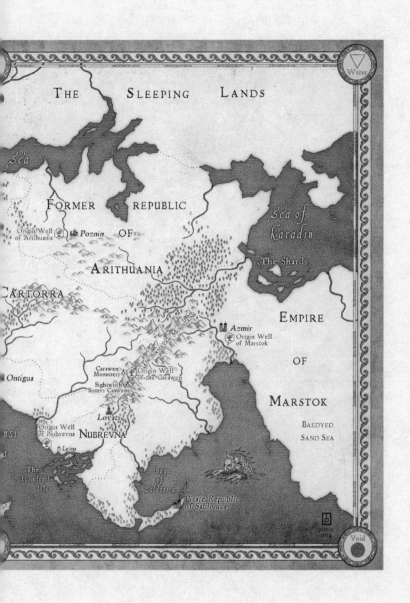

THE   SLEEPING   LANDS

Water

Sea

FORMER   REPUBLIC

Origin Well
of Arithuania

Poznin   OF

Sea of
Karadin

ARITHUANIA

The Shards

CARTORRA

EMPIRE

Azmir
Origin Well
of Marstok

THE SIRMAYA MOUNTAINS

OF

Carawen
Monastery
Origin Well
of the Carawen

Sightwitch
Sisters' Convent

MARSTOK

Ontigua

BAEDYED
SAND SEA

Lovats

Origin Well
of Nubrevna   NUBREVNA

nsi

Lejna

The
Hundred
Isles

Bay
of
Saldonica

a

Pirate Republic
of Saldonica

plane
zero

Void

That which is closest, she cannot see.
A strand fallen from the weave, cast adrift on
winds of flame.
A knife with two sides.
Blood on the snow.

—from "Eridysi's Lament"

Bloodwitch

THIRTEEN YEARS AGO

✳

Maybe today will be different.

For three peals of the chimes above the gatehouse, the boy has been playing with others. Six of them. Never has he been addressed by so many his age. Certainly, he has never been allowed in a game of fox and hen.

And certainly he has never smiled this much. His cheeks ache from the grinning, but he can't stop.

Lizl is catching up. She's the fox in this round, and the boy is the only hen left. She laughs. The boy laughs. It feels good, swelling in his chest. Bubbling up his throat like the spring behind the dormitories.

He can't remember if he's ever laughed before today. He hopes this game never ends.

Lizl catches up. She's older, longer-legged, and nimble in a way none of the other acolytes are. The boy overheard his mentor discussing yesterday that they might move her up to the next level of training.

Lizl's hand slams onto the boy's shoulder. "Caught you!" Her fingers dig into the loose linen of his Monastery tunic. She yanks back, forcing the boy to stop.

1

He laughs, a high, gleeful sound. Even the muscles in his stomach hurt now, and his cheeks—oh, his cheeks!

Which is why it takes him a moment to notice that Lizl is no longer moving. He's too happy for the monster inside to be waking up.

But then one of the other acolytes—Kerta, who'd been the first hen caught—calls, "Lizl? Are you all right?"

The boy realizes what's happening. Panic takes hold, his mind blanking out. His stomach shoveling low.

Let go, he tells himself. Let go, let go, let go. If he doesn't, Lizl is going to die, just like his dog died. But this is worse than losing Boots. This is a person. This is a girl he was playing with only moments ago. This is Lizl.

"What's wrong with her?" Kerta closes in, not yet alarmed. Merely confused.

Let go, let go, let go.

"Why isn't she moving?"

The boy stumbles back. "Please," he says to the monster inside. Or perhaps he's addressing Lizl. Or Kerta. Anyone who will make the girl's blood pump again.

If it doesn't, Lizl's brain will stop working. She will die.

Just like Boots.

Kerta notes the boy's terror now, and the other children start noticing too. "What did you do?" one boy demands.

"Did you hurt her?" another asks.

"Bloodwitch," declares the third, a bully named Natan, and that's when the boy sees it: the sudden understanding that flashes in their eyes. The collective hitching of their breaths and recoiling of their necks.

Now they know why the other children won't play with him.

2

Now they know why he's trained separately from other acolytes, alone with Monk Evrane.

It doesn't matter that seconds later Lizl coughs and crumples to the stones. It doesn't matter that she lives and the monster has gone. It doesn't matter that this was an accident, that the boy would never have hurt her on purpose.

The damage is done. The smiles are gone. The shouting, the fleeing, the hate—it's all starting again, as it always does.

They throw rocks after him as he races for the spring behind the dormitory. An old well no one uses anymore. It is overgrown with thorns that only he, with his wounds that always heal, can charge through.

Streaks of pain cut through his awareness. This shrub has fangs. It distracts, as does the drip-drip of blood once he reaches the water.

He sinks to his haunches on the stone shore, ashamed when more than blood splashes the cold waters. Crying, he knows, is not what monks do.

Worse than the tears, though, worse than the thorns' vicious bite and worse than the welts from the children's rocks, are the sore muscles in the boy's cheeks. A reminder of what he almost had. Of what he had had for a few perfect hours.

He was born a monster, he will die a monster, and monsters do not get to have friends.

3

ONE

✳

The blood looked fresh in the rain.

Weeping, oozing, even streaming in some places, the water from the storm hit wounds on corpses that had been stagnant for days. The granite bedrock would not accept the offering, and a river of blood slid downhill, following the terrain, gathering around Aeduan's boots. So many blood-scents to mingle against his magic, so many dead for his gaze to drag across.

This was the third massacre he'd found in two weeks. The third time he'd followed carnage on the air, the third time he'd smelled wet caves and white-knuckled grips amidst the slaughter. He was catching up to the attackers.

Catching up to his father's men.

The four stabs in Aeduan's abdomen spurted with each of his hunched breaths. He should have left the arrows where they'd hit, let the Threadwitch remove them with her careful hands instead of yanking them out as soon as they'd punched through his stomach wall. Twenty years of habit were hard to change in just two weeks, though.

He also hadn't expected the barbs.

Aeduan sucked in a ragged breath, rain coursing into his open mouth. There was nothing to keep him here, and the scent he'd hoped to find—the one he'd followed for two weeks, ever deeper into the Sirmayans—was not nearby. Oh, the summer heather and impossible choices that marked her blood had been here, but she had moved on. Before the attack, he assumed, or she too would now be numbered among the dead.

Before Aeduan could turn away from the corpses and limp for the evergreen forest whence he'd come, a new blood-scent tickled against his nose. Vaguely familiar, as if he had once met the owner and bothered to catalog the man's blood, but had never tucked it aside to remember forever.

The smell was sharp. Still alive.

Between one heartbeat and the next, Aeduan changed course. Thirty-four careful steps over gape-mouthed bodies. Rain sprayed into his eyes, forcing him to blink again and again. Then the stone expanse gave way to a mossy carpet stained to red. More bodies, all ages, all angles, covered the earth with a density that spoke of attempted escape. The square Nomatsi shields on their backs, though, had done nothing to stop the ambush from the front.

Blood, blood and empty eyes everywhere he looked.

Onward he picked across the bodies until at last he reached the swaying conifers. The scent he'd caught was thicker here, but the pine-needle floor was also slippery, dangerous from the storm. Aeduan had no desire to fall. He might heal from every scrape, every broken bone, but that did not mean it wouldn't hurt.

Or drain his magic further, which was the problem now. Stomach wounds were particularly unwieldy to repair.

Aeduan inhaled. Exhaled. Counting, waiting, watching as his blood dribbled out and the world fell away. He was not his mind. He was not his body.

He kept moving.

But then, over distant thunderclaps from the south, he heard a human groan. "Help." With that word, his senses sharpened, his spine straightened, and a new energy kicked in.

He strode faster. Rain splashed beneath his boots. Thunder rolled to the south. He followed a path through the spruce trees, their trunks creaking like ships at sea; he knew this was a Nomatsi road. He knew that traps like the one he'd triggered beside the morning glories likely waited ahead.

"Help."

The voice was weaker, but closer—as was the scent of the dying man's blood. A monk, Aeduan realized, when at last he crossed a dip in the path where a stream swelled with storm. Three steps up the rocky hill, a fallen white robe lay stained to rusty brown. And three steps beyond, with his back pressed against a fallen log, the robe's owner clutched at wounds in his belly.

Wounds like Aeduan's, that had come from traps meant to protect the Nomatsi tribe. Unlike Aeduan, though, this man had not removed the arrows.

For half a moment, Aeduan thought he could help the man. That he could use what remained of his own power to stop the man's bleeding. He had done it before with Evrane; he could do it again. The vast city of Tirla was no more than half a day away.

But even if Aeduan could sustain such power in his current

7

state, there could be no healing the sword gash on the monk's thigh. The femoral artery was split wide, and though rain fell hard enough to clear away blood, the artery gushed faster.

The man had only minutes left to live.

"Demon," the man burbled. Blood seeped from the edges of his mouth down his seamed chin, riding the rain. "I . . . remember you."

"Who did this?" Aeduan asked. There was no time to be wasted on names or useless memories. If anyone had been trained for death, it was the Carawens. And if anyone could help Aeduan make sense of this slaughter, it was the dying man before him.

"Purists."

Aeduan blinked. Rain splattered off his lashes. The Purists, though foul members of humanity, were not known for violence. Except . . .

Except when Purists were not Purists at all.

"Help," the man begged, clutching at the wound across his thigh.

At that sight, anger thickened in Aeduan's throat. Mercenary monks faced the Void's embrace without fear, without begging. To see desperation darken the man's eyes—it was wrong. All wrong.

Yet Aeduan still found his magic reaching out. Spiraling around the white fire and iron ore that made the monk who he was. A pointless endeavor, for there was so little blood left inside the man's veins it felt like trying to catch wind. No matter how tightly he grasped, his magic always came up empty.

"Why did you not use your stone?" Aeduan asked, and he

glared at the man's ear. At the Carawen opal that glistened there, waiting to summon other monks in case of an emergency.

The man shook his head, a bare trace of movement. "Sur . . . prise." The word came out choked with blood, his face paler and paler with each breath. "Trained . . . better."

Impossible, Aeduan wanted to say. *No one is trained better than a Carawen mercenary.* But then the man started coughing and reached for his mouth, and Aeduan realized he bore the burn-flecked hands of a blacksmith, the lopsided shoulders of a man who worked the forge.

An artisanal monk. The least combat-ready of all the Carawens. Why was this man here at all, away from the Monastery and away from his post?

Aeduan's lips parted to ask, but before the words could rise, the monk's final breath escaped from punctured lungs. His heart slowed to silence. All life vanished from his blood.

And Aeduan was left staring at yet another corpse rotting beneath the rain.

TWO

Iseult thought he might not be coming back. All night, she had waited—since dusk, when Aeduan had first strode off to inspect the path ahead.

The sun set, the moon rose, the rain came. The moon set, the rain subsided. Until at last, mist and dawn laid claim to the mountainside. Still, Aeduan did not appear.

Logically, Iseult knew it was unlikely that he would *never* return. After everything that they had been through together, why would he abandon her now? Two weeks, he had stayed by her side. Two weeks he had guided Owl and Iseult higher into the Sirmayans with neither payment nor prod to force him onward.

Viscerally, though, Iseult could find a thousand reasons the Bloodwitch would never return. A thousand excuses from coin to company for why he'd strode into the foggy forest at dusk and why he might never come back.

The story that shone brightest though, as the sun's first rays clambered over mountain peaks, was that he was kept away not by choice, but by captor. Or injury.

Or death.

That possibility sent her pacing on the gravel clearing beside their campsite. Ten steps one way. Pivot. Ten steps the other. Pivot. She never left sight of the narrow entrance leading to a dry, cozy cave of Owl's creation. Inside, the girl's mountain bat, Blueberry, curled fiercely around the child's sleeping form, leaving little space for anyone else.

Not that Iseult could have slept had she been in there too. Sleep had been her enemy for days now. Ever since the fire and the voice that controlled it had slithered into her dreams. *Burn them*, whispered a leering face consumed by flame. Each night he came to her. *Burn them all.*

She had tried to cleave him in her sleep. Tried to sever his Threads and corrupt his fire magic, just as she had done in her waking in the Contested Lands, but the man had only laughed while the flames swept higher. Flames that were all too real, as she'd learned that first night, when Aeduan had roused her. *A stray ember from the campfire,* he'd said, *and too much kindling nearby.*

Iseult had not bothered to contradict him. She also had not slept again, and that lack of sleep had left her with no means to speak to Esme about why this was happening. About *why* the Firewitch she had killed now seemed to live inside her.

No exhaustion burned in Iseult's eyes tonight, though. She wanted to leave—wanted to walk between those pines exactly as Aeduan had done at dusk and search every corner of the shadowy terrain, even if she knew it would be a fruitless hunt: Aeduan was too skilled to leave tracks behind.

Besides, she could hardly leave Owl.

Either Aeduan would return or he would not, and Iseult would keep marching back and forth until she had her answer.

11

Iseult heard him approach before she saw him. It was so unlike the ever-cautious Bloodwitch that she actually drew a cutlass from the sheath at her waist. There were bears in these woods. Mountain cats, too. And unlike humans, they bore no Threads—no colors to tendril and twirl above them, telling Iseult what they felt and to whom they were bound.

It was no Threadless animal that stumbled from the tree line, though, but the Threadless Bloodwitch instead. The instant she saw Aeduan's Carawen cloak brightening the shadows between the trees, cool relief crumbled through her. Until she realized something was wrong.

He limped from the forest, and his eyes, when they slid up to hers, were hooded and lost. "They're all dead." The proclamation came out hoarse and low. Aeduan swayed.

The relief in her belly splintered to horror. He was hurt. Badly.

Without another thought, Iseult shot toward him and swooped an arm behind his back—where her hand met rain-soaked fletching and arrows. Countless bolts erupted from him like the spines of a sea urchin, and now that she looked, his cloak was shredded and stained to brown.

Aeduan listed into her; his breath came in short gasps. His crystal eyes swirled red. Whatever was happening, he clearly would not stay upright much longer, and Iseult didn't want him passing out on top of her. Right where Owl could walk out and see him. The girl had a tendency to shatter the earth when she was upset.

There's a spring uphill, Iseult thought, a crude plan cobbling together. *I can clean him there without Owl finding us, and I can dry his clothes in the morning sun.* She just had to keep

12

Aeduan from slipping into unconsciousness before they reached the water.

With aching slowness, she guided Aeduan up the hillside. His eyelids fluttered, his feet dragged. Each step sent the ice in her belly knotting wider. As did each arrow she counted— seventeen in total. More than enough to kill a regular man, but Aeduan was no regular man.

Still, Iseult had seen him hit with double this many bolts before. There was something else happening here. Something deeply wrong. For some reason, he did not seem to be healing. His Bloodwitchery was not squelching or cleaning, it was not ejecting arrows and knitting him back together as she had seen it do before.

"Are you hurt somewhere else?" Iseult pitched the question into his ear. *Stay awake, stay awake.* "Is there a wound I cannot see?"

"Arrows." The answer slurred out. Useless.

She changed tactics. "Is this injury why you took so long to return?"

A grunt, a vague nod. Then: "Survivor."

Iseult tensed. "The woman from Owl's tribe?" Aeduan had followed the woman's scent for almost two weeks now. Twice, they had found these massacres, and twice, the woman's scent had continued on. This latest would mark the third instance. But when Iseult searched Aeduan's face for answers, all she got were pallid cheeks and harsh exhales.

"Was the woman there?" she pressed. Still no answer, though, so she let it go. They had reached the spring—thank the Moon Mother—and Iseult's exhaustion was catching up fast. Fear could only sustain a tired body for so long.

Iseult led Aeduan to a low boulder beside the spring's clear pool. The creek that trickled down the mountain had doubled in size overnight, thanks to the rain. With every muscle tensed, she eased Aeduan into a sitting position. A moan escaped his throat. Pain slashed across his face; she could hear his teeth grinding.

Even in the worst flames of the battlefield, even in the sea-swept moonlight beside a lighthouse, she had never seen him wear such suffering. Gripping his shoulder to keep him upright, she circled behind him. She would have to cut the cloak off if she wanted to keep this clean—

"Hurry," he said, and with that command, Iseult gave up any hope of avoiding a mess. There was no time to lose. She just hoped Owl would not wake soon.

She gripped the first arrow and yanked. Minuscule barbs shredded flesh, and blood sprayed. Aeduan hissed, head tipping back, as one by one, Iseult snapped the arrows from his flesh, and a pile of bloodied white feathers and cedar gathered by her ankles.

By the time she removed the last, his white cloak was streaked with fresh red. His spine slumped, and the only thing keeping him from falling headfirst into the water was Iseult's iron grip upon his collar. With the last arrowhead removed, she dug her heels into the gravel shore and towed him back. She wanted him to be upright so they could move away from the growing pool together.

Instead, Aeduan toppled backward. She barely caught him before he hit the earth and her knees buckled beneath his weight. Her bottom hit the rocks, pain barking through her seat bones. Her back hit a boulder, and her head cracked hard.

The spring wavered. Her eyes burned with sudden tears.

"Aeduan," she said, but her rasping words earned no response. His magic had finally dragged him into a sleep. He would not wake up until he was healed.

Meaning Iseult was trapped beneath him, while her chest swelled with . . . with *something*. "You're heavy," she said, trying to move him. But she had no energy left. Not enough to move his blood-slickened dead weight. His head, peaceful and still, rested on her shoulder.

He was so warm against her, even as the cold morning caressed her skin. Then there it was again, that swelling in her lungs. Warm. Fizzy. Until at last it burst forth in a shrill laugh that felt a thousand miles away. It was someone else's panicked amusement. Someone else's weary body and fire-kissed mind. Someone else's burgeoning headache and bloating scalp bruise.

Iseult was countless miles from her home, pinned to the rocks by a man who'd once been her enemy, while a wren chirruped from the waking forest nearby—and while a little Earthwitch and her mountain bat slept inside the hollow hill below.

If only Safi could see me now.

Unable to fight it any longer, Iseult's eyelids sank shut, and the world went quiet.

Heat roars. Wood cracks and embers fly.

"Run." Blood drips from his mother's mouth as she speaks.

It splatters his face.

With arms stained to red, she pushes herself up. She wants

15

him to crawl out from beneath her. She wants him to escape. "Run, my child, run."

He does not run. He does not move. He waits, as he always does, for the flames to overtake him and the world to burn alive.

Aeduan had been in this nightmare before. Trapped and bleeding while flames crowded closer. Heat fanned against him, smoke scorched his lungs. But instead of the fiery tent he was used to seeing, instead of the storm he knew would come coursing in, he found only blue sky and wispy clouds. Instead of the clotted stench of his mother's blood, he smelled only the faint reek of his own.

The pain in his chest was the same, though. Agony that did not want him to move, that argued with his mother's last words. *Run, my child, run.*

Aeduan tried to turn, as he always did in the dream to no avail. Except this time, his head swiveled easily. The arrows and death that usually pinned him down were not stacked atop him. Instead, he realized with a jolt of confusion, *he* was pinning down another.

He gaped, his fire-flecked vision swimming and swaying. A head rested upon his shoulder, and he found he knew this face. He knew this profile—but what was the Threadwitch doing in his dream? It was as if she'd been holding him while he slept, and the oddness of that thought sent all his usual dream terror funneling away.

Orange flame and black smoke flickered, giving color to her ice-white skin. She was so close; he could see the ash gathering on her eyelashes and the frizz that heat and rain had lifted from her fine black hair. She had changed so much since he'd met her: the teardrop scar from the Poisonwitch acid by her left eye, the frayed, uneven edge to her hair from the fires of the Contested Lands.

Aeduan found himself unable to look away. How much more damage would he cause her? This Threadwitch who was not a Threadwitch at all?

She should not be here, he thought. If she stayed in his dream, then she would die like he did. Over and over until the rain came and Evrane with it.

He did not want her to die. In his dream or in real life. Unlike him, she was not a monster. She would not heal from the flames. She would not revive.

"Iseult," he tried to say, and to his surprise, the name actually tumbled from his tongue. Soft vowels. Hard consonants. A sound and taste that fit her so perfectly.

She stirred. Her hands, which were draped against Aeduan's sides, furled inward. Her fingers dug into his hipbones.

And at that touch, his stomach froze over. His lungs tightened with cold. Fire might consume them, but her touch was made of winter.

"Aeduan," she exhaled, and with that sigh, the flames around them shrank back. Then they shivered out completely, revealing a pond. A spring that Aeduan knew, surrounded by evergreens and boulders.

The ice inside him froze harder. No longer a comfort, but murderous in its intent.

This was no nightmare. Iseult truly held him; she truly breathed his name in sleep; they had truly been surrounded by flame.

17

Too much. It was too much for his pain-racked mind or body to handle, to comprehend. Iseult so near. Iseult's fingers still pressed into his hipbones. Iseult razing the earth to ash.

Against his most desperate, frantic desire—against every instinct that screamed at him to awaken fully—Aeduan's eyelids fell shut. A moan slipped over his tongue.

Then the darkness took hold, and the flames of his nightmare carried him away once more.

THREE

✳

This was why Adders wore black.

Safiya fon Hasstrel understood now. Black did not show blood the way the white floors did.

The ease and speed of it all stunned her the most. One moment, she had been staring at the nobleman's long, horse-like face, still attached to his body. The next moment, it was on the floor, bleeding, eyes blinking.

Vaness had invited the man to her throne room, as was proper when relatives visited. Cousin, second cousin, great-great-aunt's wife—they were all met in the imperial throne room. This man was a third cousin on Vaness's mother's side.

After kneeling before the Empress, his purple robe rustling with the movement, he'd been so bold as to plant a sandaled foot on the lowest step of the marble dais. Mere paces from where Safi stood, dressed in a perfect sleeveless white gown exactly like the Empress's.

He looked her up, he looked her down, obviously knowing exactly what Safi was. Vaness hadn't kept her Truthwitch secret.

Clearly, though, the man also did not *believe* in Safi's powers. His confident foot on the dais. The smile creasing

19

through his jowled face, and even the unrushed nature of his bow, all belied skepticism.

Most people Safi had met in Azmir had been this way: so certain a Truthwitch was impossible. A story. A legend. Not a flesh-and-blood nineteen-year-old with the muscles and scars of a soldier.

Or perhaps the cousin had simply believed that, even if his lies were caught, the Empress of Marstok wouldn't actually hurt him. Family relations and all that.

"This is my cousin Bayrum of the Shards," Vaness said in that inflectionless, heavy way she had of speaking when at court. As if each word were carefully selected to not only express *precisely* what she intended, but also to convey how much thought she had put into the utterance.

Actually, now that Safi considered it, it wasn't only at court that Vaness spoke this way.

Vaness sat upon an iron stool. No cushion, no decorative additions. Very simple, really, for a woman with as many titles as she held—Empress of the Flame Children, Chosen Daughter of the Fire Well, the Most Worshipped of the Marstoks, the Destroyer of Kendura Pass, and likely several more that Safi had forgotten.

White adorned the throne room, as it did most of the palace, and the iron sconces upon the walls held neither candles nor Firewitch flame. The domed glass ceiling overhead, crafted by Azmir's famed Glasswitches, filled the room with more than enough morning light to see by.

A single wave of Vaness's hand, and every iron fixture could shoot off the wall, molding into whatever shape the Empress might need.

Not that Vaness would need to defend herself with her Adders nearby. Twelve of them flanked the dais at all times, clad in black so dark it seemed to suck in the sunlight. Gloves, headscarves, and soft, silent boots—the only skin Adders ever showed was the narrowest streak of their eyes.

The black sentries were never far from their Empress, and these days, never far from Safi either. One in particular, named Rokesh, had been appointed the lead guard for Safi. He followed her everywhere, though to protect her or to keep her in line, Safi wasn't entirely sure. She had taken to calling him Nursemaid, and surprisingly, he chuckled every time.

Safi had been exceptionally well behaved since arriving in Azmir two weeks ago. She went where she was told to go; she listened when she was told to listen; she searched for lies when she was told to search for lies. And when noblemen eyed her up and down as openly as Bayrum of the Shards was doing, then she offered a polite curtsy in return—even though she *wanted* to break their arms.

Habim would be very impressed by her self-control.

"How do you do?" she asked.

The man only waved her greeting aside before swiveling toward Vaness and launching into a long-winded description of his travels. How he had crossed the Sea of Karadin in a storm, how flame hawks now nested on the mainland shores, how bandits lay in wait amidst the cotton farms beside the river.

As the man continued to list off the trials of his journey, each one more impressive than the last, Safi stared him down. Bayrum of the Shards was a liar—that much was obvious. His love for subterfuge and deception frizzled down her spine, scratching at her insides in a way that only an untrustworthy soul could.

Safi would have expected no less from a nobleman, though. At court, everyone lied. It did not matter what nation, what government, what people. Uncle Eron had once told her that when power was at play, lies grew thick as weeds and the liars beneath them flourished.

It had proved true in Cartorra, in Dalmotti, and now again in Marstok. Like weeds, though, lies were not a symptom of corruption in the soul, and truth was not a symptom of its purity. Nations could not run without blackmail or false promises or money exchanging hands, especially not nations as vast as the Marstoki Empire.

What Safi needed to know, though, was if this cousin was a part of the plot to overthrow Empress Vaness. It wasn't a plot that Safi believed existed. Yes, there had been explosions and attacks across the city. And yes, there was a current of . . . of *wrong* and of *rot* shivering through Azmir, but that was connected to the Baedyed Pirates' rebellion. Safi was certain of it. After all, those pirates had made their betrayal known in Saldonica, and they had already tried to kill Vaness once.

Vaness remained unconvinced, however, for one simple reason: the recent attacks had not included cries of *For the Sand Sea! For the Sand Sea!* This, she insisted, was the way of the Baedyeds. This, she insisted, was why another plot must be at work.

Now Safi was forced to meet every Sultanate minister, every military officer, and every backwoods imperial relation in Marstok, not to mention the massive gathering of basically *everyone* in the empire who had come to the city for the Empress's birthday celebration tomorrow.

It had been almost fun at first. A novelty. New faces, a chance to put all her training to the test while she sieved out the pure from the wicked. The first day, she had taken her duties very seriously, listening with great care to anyone who crossed the Empress's path. But soon, all the words, all the truths and the lies, had blended into an endless cascade of meaningless nothing.

By the second day, Safi focused less. By the fifth, she had stopped listening at all. The words mattered little. If there was rot within this court, she would have to spot it another way. Her solution became three questions—very simple questions that eliminated any chance for an adept liar or devout believer to somehow trick her magic. For the reality was that Safi's witchery was easily confused. Her power tricked by strong faith. Her magic duped by rumors or ancient mistruths.

When Bayrum of the Shards finally paused for a breath between tales of a daring escape from raiders, Safi pounced. "Are you aware of the peace treaty with the Baedyeds?"

The reaction was immediate, although to the man's credit, he showed no panic on his face. No muscle twitched, no eyelid fluttered. "Yes. I heard Her Imperial Majesty was negotiating such an accord."

True, Safi's magic hummed. It caught her by surprise. Many knew of the treaty, but they usually lied about it. No one wanted to admit to partaking in gossip.

"And," she continued, "have you heard of a plot to overthrow the Empress and claim the throne?"

"Nothing specific." A dismissive shrug. "But such rumors always abound. Wherever there is power, flies will clot." He smiled at Vaness, and though the expression rang false, his words rang true.

"And," Safi asked lastly, each word carefully spaced, "did you know of the explosion on the Empress's ship—"

"Everyone knows of it!"

"—*before* the attack occurred?" Safi had to pitch her voice louder to be heard, but the effect was instantaneous.

A pause, a blink. Then a slow "Of course not. What a ridiculous question."

The lie dragged down Safi's neck. Scratched over her skull like fingernails. The nobleman had indeed known, and such a thing was only possible if he had been involved in the plot.

A vast pit opened in Safi's gut. Her toes tapped a descant against the tiles. Here was a man responsible for almost killing her two weeks ago. She and Vaness had survived; the Adders and crew had not been so lucky.

Safi glanced at the Empress of Marstok. Vaness had already rooted her dark eyes on Safi's face. She arched a single eyebrow, seemingly disinterested in whatever word might fall from Safi's tongue.

Yet just as Safi could feel the cousin's lies, she could spot Vaness's too. The Empress was the coiled asp, waiting for an answer and ready to act.

Safi bowed her head. "False. He knew of the attack."

A snap from Vaness's fingers. A cry from the cousin. Then the man's hands were rising, his sleeves falling back to expose pale wrists and forearms.

In a blur of gray speed, iron shot from the shackles at

Vaness's wrists, wound into a disc, and sliced through the man's neck.

His head hit the tiles. His body slumped next, blood spurting and oozing and gathering in the grout. Great pools of red that spidered and spread.

What poor servant will have to clean this? Safi wondered vaguely—also wondering why there was still no sound coming from her throat. Or why she was so calmly smoothing at her white dress. Or why she was fixating on the three spots on her hem, already drying to brown.

Somehow she kept her legs from rubbering out beneath her. Somehow she managed to speak to Rokesh when he cut into her path as she stepped off the dais a few moments later and aimed for the door.

"I'm ill," Safi told him. Her voice sounded so very far away. Her breakfast, however, felt very near and rising fast.

"She may go," Vaness said curtly from behind.

At a clap from Rokesh, seven more Adders marched into a square formation around Safi. If she extended her arms, she'd brush their black shoulders. They aimed for the door, clearly knowing Safi intended to get away from this place. Away from that body.

For some reason, the unlucky servant tasked with getting the blood off the white floor was all that fed through Safi's mind, though. She didn't want to add to the mess by stepping through the red. She didn't want metallic, sticky blood on her white slippers, and she didn't want to track prints across the marble tiles or into the sandstone halls.

Around would be easier. *Around, around, around.*

But she couldn't go around. Not with the Adders beside

her. They stepped through the blood, and she had to step with them. It splashed and spread, and Safi tracked it out the other side.

At the wide throne room doors, Safi pushed into a jog. The Adders did too. Down the seven endless sandstone hallways they ran, aiming for the Empress's personal living wing. Safi had sprawling quarters of her own next to Vaness's. Next to a private library too, which no one but the Empress and now Safi were allowed to use. So aside from the ever-present Adders stationed at every door, Safi had a sliver of privacy in her room.

Privacy for vomiting alone.

She almost made it too. Thirty paces from the ornately carved oak door, Safi's sickness reached a head. There were few decorations in the halls, only the occasional lemon trees, sconces, and dangling iron wind chimes. Nowhere for assassins to hide. Nowhere for a sick young woman to hurl up her breakfast.

Safi had no choice but to skid to a halt and double over in the hall. Acid and bile spewed out, chunky where the chancellor's blood had been liquid. Erratic where the blood had slithered so smooth.

More mess for the servants.

As she retched, the Adders stayed firmly planted in their square around Safi. Even when bits of bile splattered on Rokesh's boots, none of them reacted. Nor made any move to help. A reminder that they were soldiers. That Rokesh was *not* a nursemaid, and he was most certainly not a friend.

Well, Safi was as disgusted with herself as the Adders no doubt were. She had killed someone. That man's life—that man's *death*—were on her now. And though she had seen death before, grim, violent, bloody, she had never been the cause of it.

Safi wiped her mouth with the collar of her dress and hauled herself upright. The world swayed, and she briefly wished at least one of the Adders would meet her gaze. Then Rokesh finally did.

"This isn't what I wanted," she told him, even though she knew he did not care. Still, she felt the need to make him understand. So she repeated, louder and with a throat burned raw, "This isn't what I wanted."

Then Safi stumbled the rest of the way to her room, blood and sickness trailing behind.

FOUR

✳

Beside a towering waterfall, Merik Nihar picked his way up a cliffside. Spindrift misted his sun-soaked face.

"Another hour," Ryber had said at the bottom of the cliff. "Then we'll reach the Sightwitch Sister Convent, and I'll guide you through the glamour that protects it."

Always, Ryber had guided Merik and Cam, steady and true. Since leaving Lovats two weeks ago, she had led them through the Sirmayans, ever closer to her childhood home—the long-lost Sightwitch Sister Convent, a place Merik hadn't known existed. And he certainly hadn't known that Ryber was a Sister from their ranks.

Water caressed Merik's face. He was tired, he was parched— so parched, he'd already imagined dumping his face into the waterfall and gulping whatever he could before it dragged him down.

He glanced at Cam behind him. Then glanced again.

"I'm fine, sir," the boy groused. He had to shout to be heard above the falls. "Stop looking at me like that."

"I'll stop looking," Merik countered, "when your hand is fully healed." He knew Cam was sick of the fretting.

Overprotective hen was his phrase, but Cam also couldn't see how pale his brown, dappled skin had become since leaving Lovats. Since the Nines had cut off his pinkie.

"At the top," Merik called, "let's stop and change the bandages."

"Fine, fine, sir. If you ins—"

A great rip tore through the earth, stealing Cam's words and tossing Merik against the cliff face.

It tossed Cam right off.

Without thought, Merik's magic snapped free. A whip of winds to snatch the boy before he hit the rapids. A coil of air to launch him straight into Merik's arms.

Then he clutched the boy close while aftershocks rumbled through the stone. While they panted and heaved and hung on. It felt an eternity before the quake fully faded, leaving dust and water thick in the air.

"Sir," Cam breathed against him, eyes bulging and terrified. "You used your magic."

"I know," he said at the same time Ryber coughed out, "Everyone all right?" Her umber black skin was streaked with dust from the tremor as she clung to the ledge above.

"Hye," Merik called, even though that might not be true. Two weeks, he had stayed so diligent against his witchery's call. Against the Nihar rage too, for they were connected. He could not stop his winds when the anger took hold.

And he could not stop Kullen when the winds awoke.

"Just a bit farther," Ryber said. She scrabbled down slightly and grabbed hold of Cam's good hand. Then, with Merik to push, they got Cam onto a higher ledge.

"Maybe," Cam called as he climbed, "the first mate didn't notice the magic."

29

Not the first mate, Merik thought, wishing yet again that Cam would stop calling Kullen that. The first mate was gone. Kullen was gone. He had cleaved in Lejna. His magic had reached a breaking point, then it had burned through him and turned him into a monster. Yet unlike other Cleaved, who died in minutes from the boil of corrupted power, Kullen had stayed alive.

And somehow, Kullen's mind had been replaced by a shadow beast that called himself the Fury.

Merik was just about to resume his own ascent when a voice split his skull: *THERE YOU ARE.*

Merik clutched at his head.

I AM COMING.

"Sir?" Cam blinked down at him. "Is it the first mate?"

"Hye," he gritted out. "*Move.*"

This time, Merik did not resist his magic. Kullen had found them; they were already damned. He drew in his breath, clogged as it was with dust off the mountain, and let the hot air spiral close. Fragile strands, but enough to push them faster. Enough to send him, Cam, and Ryber skipping straight up to the top of the cliff.

When at last they reached the final ledge, they scrabbled to their feet and ran. No one looked back. They could hear the storm approaching, sense the cold on its way.

Fast, impossibly fast with all that dark, wretched power coursing through it. A journey that had taken days for Merik, Cam, and Ryber would take mere minutes for the Fury to complete.

They ran faster. Or they tried to, but waves of dizziness crushed against Merik—and Cam, judging by the boy's yelps of alarm.

"Ignore it," Ryber commanded. "It's part of the glamour's magic. You just have to trust me and keep going." She took hold of Cam's forearm, and Cam took hold of Merik's. They ran on.

They reached a forest. Trunks striped past, prison bars to hold them in and nowhere to go but forward. Green needles bled into red bark and melted into hard earth. Everything spun and swung.

Ryber never slowed, though, so Merik and Cam never slowed either.

Then the creatures of the forest began to flee. Spiders rained down and tangled in Merik's short hair. Then came the moths—a great cloud racing not toward the sky but simply ahead. Away from the Fury.

I never thought you would leave Nubrevna, the Fury crooned in Merik's mind. *All this time, I thought you would return to the Nihar lands. After all, do you not care about your own people?*

Birds launched past Merik. Mice and rats and squirrels too.

"Faster," Merik urged, summoning more winds. Cold winds. The world might be unstable, but if he had to, he would fight.

"We're almost there!" Ryber shouted from the fore, while beneath their pounding feet, the earth quaked yet again. Merik couldn't help but imagine each lurch as one of Kullen's steps booming ever closer.

"Where are we even going?" Cam panted. "If he can follow us through the glamour—"

"He can't."

"He already did." As Merik uttered those words, he slowed to a stop and looked back. Black snaked across the forest floor. So fast, there was no outrunning it. So fast that before he had even turned forward once more, the darkness swept across him.

He still had hold of Cam, and Cam still had hold of Ryber. They kept running.

Soon, no sunlight penetrated. The darkness moved and shifted around them and Merik had never known there could be so many shades of gray. Then hoarfrost raced across the forest, a crackling that froze creatures as they fled.

Where are you, Merik? Where has my Heart-Thread taken you?

Merik couldn't answer, even if he wanted to. The dregs of the glamour's magic fought to disorient him ...

Until he saw it: a haze of gray stone amidst the shadows. Hewn from the mountain itself, a chapel coalesced before them, its high doorway blocked by saplings and sedge.

Ryber slowed, releasing Cam and grabbing for the knife at her hip. There was no time to hack through the brush, though, so Merik thrust his winds straight at the overgrowth. Raging air ripped the plants up by the roots.

A dark doorway yawned before them.

In moments, they were inside, and what little light they'd had vanished entirely. The chaos followed, though. As did the bellowing of winds, charging ever faster their way.

"*Ignite!*" Ryber shouted, and a weak torch lit among the endless shadows.

Merik and Cam skidded to a stop. "Keep your hand elevated, Cam!" He didn't know why holding Cam's bloodied hand aloft seemed the most important thing when death chased from behind.

Ahead, Ryber's hands slammed against a stone wall. "Why

is this here?" she screamed. "Why are you closed to me? I am Ryber Fortiza, the last Sightwitch Sister—*why have you closed to me?*" She smacked her hands harder against the granite. "I've only been gone a year! Open up! You *must* open up!"

Nothing happened, and she jerked back toward Cam and Merik. "This shouldn't be closed. I've *never* seen it closed!" Her hands clutched at her heart, at her face. Then back to her heart again. "It must be because he follows—" She broke off as the hoarfrost slithered into the chapel's space.

The pale lantern light guttered out.

The Fury had arrived.

Merik shoved Cam behind him. "Stay with Ryber," he ordered, and to his vast relief, the boy actually obeyed. Then Merik stepped back through the door and advanced on the shadows.

"Let them go!" His voice sounded stretched, as if cold had sapped it of all dimension. "It's me you want, isn't it?"

"*No.*" The word whispered against Merik's face, plucking at his skin. Then the Fury stepped from the shadows. A thousand dark ripples moved around him; the evergreens crashed and waved. Somehow, though, Kullen looked as he always had. Tall, pale haired, paler skinned. Only his eyes had changed: black with small lines radiating along the temples.

Black lines like Merik wore across his chest. The foul taint of the Cleaved.

A bolt of pity cut through Merik. Ryber loved Kullen as much as Merik did. But unlike Merik, she had not yet seen this monster Kullen had become, and he hoped she would never have to. He hoped she would not turn back this way.

As if following Merik's thoughts, Kullen smiled—a taut,

inhuman thing that stretched at his lips but did not reach his eyes. "I know my Heart-Thread is with you." He sang the words, and his steps bounced closer, almost jaunty. "And is that also young Leeri I see following?" The smile spread wider. "He always was so loyal. But *no one* is as loyal as I am, Merik."

Wind burst out, a wall to knock Merik back. He hit the ground. Pain tore through him and Kullen laughed and stalked closer.

But Merik drew in the Fury's own winds, enough to attack, enough to distract. Then he charged upright, and as he flew, he swung out a leg and aimed for his Threadbrother's knees.

Kullen was already skipping back by the time he reached him, but it was enough. They had moved away from the door, and Merik had—for a flicker of a moment—gained the advantage. He unsheathed his cutlass; he swung. No magic, just brute force. It was the one thing he had always done better than Kullen: swordplay. And though Kullen tried to sweep at Merik with magic, his attempts were dull. Halfhearted.

For of course, they were bound by cleaving magic and Threads. If Merik died, then Kullen died with him. And while Merik might not understand how, there was no denying that truth he had faced in Lovats two weeks before.

He was faced with it again now as Kullen skipped and slid, avoiding Merik's blade yet scarcely fighting back. "You won't kill me," Kullen declared, spinning left.

"I will." Merik darted, his blade aimed for Kullen's neck. "I would gladly die if it meant saving the people you've abandoned."

"Always so brave, our Prince Merik. Always so *holy*. But remember: the holiest have the farthest to fall."

34

"*SIR!*" Cam shrieked, tinny and distant. "The door!"

Kullen heard those words too. As one, he and Merik turned. As one, they flew for the chapel. It was no different from the hundreds of races they'd held as children in Nihar, and just like in those days, Kullen was faster. Yet Merik had meant what he'd said: he would die to protect Cam and Ryber.

As the chapel zoomed in close, Merik swung one last time at Kullen. He missed Kullen's neck, but not Kullen's ear. The top sliced off. Kullen screamed, a sound that exploded in Merik's brain. Mental fists that punched away all thought, all consciousness.

The shadows roared over Merik. He fell.

Merik awoke in the middle of a storm.

He tried to stand—wriggling left and right, straining to rise as dark rain flayed his skin. *I'm bound,* he realized at the same instant that lightning pierced the skies. Thunder crashed, against his skin and inside his skull.

Merik rolled left. Mud slid over his cheek. Grass swept and writhed around him, and rainwater pooled. If he did not at least sit up, the water would rise. He would drown.

That wasn't what frightened him most, though. No, *that* was Kullen's voice cracking through the storm, buzzing in Merik's brain.

Just in time, Threadbrother. You will get to see exactly what I came here for.

Digging his shoulder into the sodden soil, Merik drew in his knees. His wrists were tied behind his back, and his ankles looped tight. But with several grunts, groans, and popped joints, he managed to get his legs beneath him. He managed to sit up.

A meadow surrounded him, broken up by eight massive stones in three rows. Crudely shaped columns, they towered twice as high as a man, twice as wide, and over the nearest one, Kullen flew. Lightning sizzled into him, winds spun and flew.

A thousand years, these have stood. A thousand years, the Sightwitches have hidden their treasures from the world. But no longer. Once this glamour falls, I will lead the Raider King's forces to this place. Electricity ruptured outward, blinding in its brightness. *And we will claim the sleeping mountain.*

Just before Merik's eyes seared shut, unable to fight the heat or the light or the noise, he saw the magicked lightning hit one of the stones. It fractured, a sound that ripped across the sky, ripped into Merik's exposed skin.

A *boom* of energy tore through the earth. It dragged Merik down, back into the mud, where rain hammered against him and shadows took hold once more.

FIVE

oday was the day.

Two weeks of preparation, of cleaning and assembling, of organizing and arranging and pestering the High Council for help, donations, people—*anything* really, the stingy bastards—and now the underground city was finally ready for refugees.

Vivia Nihar, however, Queen-in-Waiting to the Nubrevnan throne, was not ready at all.

Her heart seemed to have gotten stuck somewhere behind her esophagus, and she had rubbed so much at her left coat cuff that she'd actually snapped off the gold button.

Whoever found it would be very happy, indeed.

Vivia stood before the Pin's Keep main entrance, crowds thick before her. Squalling babes and frantic fathers; lone, lost teenagers; and coughing grandmothers, too. But none were the faces Vivia wanted—the two faces she'd expected to see when the chimes had rung in the ninth hour.

Come on, Stix, come on. This wasn't like her. Stacia Sotar, Vivia's former first mate—now elevated to full captain—was always on time, always *early*. Yet nowhere in the thicket of hungry faces did Vivia spot Stix's white hair, so bright against her black skin.

Nor did she spot the man Stix and five other guards were meant to escort: her father, Serafin Nihar, former King and former King Regent.

"You're *sure* they aren't inside?" Vivia asked her own nearest guard for the fourth time since the chimes had clanged. And for the fourth time, the woman shook her head. "There's no one inside Pin's Keep, Highness. As ordered."

The shelter had been completely cleared out. All its volunteers now waited in the cellar where the tunnel to the under-city began, or else they waited in the under-city itself. Fifty soldiers also stood sentry, while another two hundred were dispersed throughout Lovats, as insisted upon by Vizers Quihar and Eltar. *Riots are a possibility*, they kept chorusing, and loath as Vivia was to admit that they were right . . .

Well, they were right. Vivia's lottery system might have worked thus far without protest, but once families saw others being escorted into a new, underground home, such reactions might shift like a fickle tide.

And Vivia could hardly blame them. Lovats had been in shambles since the seafire attack two weeks ago, and it had hardly been pristine or whole before that. Which was why Vivia had had her Pin's Keep volunteers spend a week telling any and every person they met that this lottery system was *Only step one in a much larger, longer-term plan to house the city!*

Admittedly, Vivia had yet to sort out the rest of her plan, and the sudden ending of the Twenty Year Truce—as well as the resuming war that the Truce had paused—now kept the High Council too distracted to help her. Once her coronation *finally* came, though, and once she *finally* wore the crown that was hers by birth, then she could take matters into her own hands. She wouldn't need the approval of a bunch of men who never agreed on anything.

Vivia cleared her throat. She couldn't wait any longer; Stix and her father would just have to miss the opening. She gave a final swipe against her shirt front. Then patted the edges of her face. A movement she had done so often as a child, and had *thought* she'd grown out of as an adult.

Until two weeks ago, when they'd named her Queen-in-Waiting.

When you are with others, her mother always used to say, *the Little Fox must become a bear. Now, is your mask on, Vivia?*

Yes, Mother, Vivia thought. *It's on.* Her lips parted, and the crowds nearest her quieted—

Then there they were. Stix at the fore, shoving through the fray and half a head taller than the rest. Behind her, surrounded by soldiers in the same navy uniforms Stix wore, marched Serafin.

And Vivia realized the people hadn't quieted for her at all. They recognized the former King; they gawped and whispered and waved. Serafin waved back, grinning. His cheeks bore more color than Vivia had seen him wear in almost a year.

She should be happy about that. And she was—she really was. Yet there was something else knotting in her belly. Something she didn't like that she wished would stop immediately. And it did stop the instant her eyes met Stix's. The instant Stix smiled, dazzling and bright.

Heat fanned up Vivia's neck onto her face, an inescapable blush that happened every time she saw her best friend, and

39

likely would continue until Vivia finally worked up the courage to mention the kiss from the under-city.

Nothing had been the same since that kiss—a mere brush of Stix's lips on Vivia's cheek. And nothing had been the same since Vivia had been labeled Queen-in-Waiting . . . yet not truly labeled at all, because although the power might have passed from her father to her, the "waiting" part seemed more important to the High Council than the "queen" part.

"So sorry, Your Highness," Stix murmured, hurrying into position on Vivia's left side. "A message came in that needed immediate processing. *But*," she added, glancing at Serafin, "I wasn't sure he should see it."

"What could be—"

Stix waved her off. "We can deal with it after this."

Right. *This.* The unveiling of Vivia's under-city. The reason all these hundreds of families had lined up, and these thousands of people had piled into the Skulks to ogle her.

And the reason Vivia's guts had punched holes through her other organs.

"Vivia," her father declared, a bass boom that could silence an entire city—and did. It was good to hear him so strong after months of fragile whispers. It was, it *was*. "Shall we begin?" Serafin moved to Vivia's other side.

"Hye," she breathed, and hastily, she tapped once more at the edges of her face. *Yes, Mother, it's on.* Then she sucked in her breath, matched her father's fierce expression, and—

"*The empires*," Serafin bellowed, "*have resumed the war*."

Vivia's teeth clacked shut.

"*We did not ask for this, and we never have.*"

Her father was speaking. Why was he speaking?

"Always, they try to cow us and displace us. Always they try to crush us beneath their boot heels, and always, Nubrevna has stood strong."

What was her father doing? This was supposed to be her speech. Vivia had spent three days writing it.

"This city and its people have stood for centuries." He opened his arms wide, body hale and voice relentless. *"And we will stand for centuries more. Today marks a new era for us. A new beginning that we will not let the empires steal away."*

He pumped a fist to the sky, and the crowds broke loose like a thunderstorm. Noise slammed against Vivia, charged and alive.

"Today," he went on, somehow pitching his voice even louder, *"we open the Lovats under-city and begin moving families into its homes—we begin moving you. We have worked hard for two weeks to prepare this space. We have worked hard for you."*

More stamping, more screaming, and Vivia *knew* she should be stamping and screaming too. Not just because the under-city was ready, but because this was the Serafin she remembered. This was the force she had grown up with, the ruler she'd tried to be.

But she was too stunned to do anything. He was saying *her* speech before the people *she* had worked to house. Hye, he had always told her, *Share the glory, share the blame.* But this . . . this felt bigger than that.

A hand gripped Vivia's forearm. She stiffened, knowing Stix meant only to comfort her. Or maybe her friend meant it as a sign of solidarity—a sign that someone else in this rapturous mayhem knew Serafin was claiming glory he hadn't earned.

As he trumpeted on, reciting words *Vivia* had written and

words *Vivia* had practiced in the mirror, she found her shoulders rising toward her ears. Found her fingers curling into aching, throbbing fists at her sides.

One should not need credit, Jana always used to say, *so long as the job gets done.* And the job was getting done. It was getting done well—Vivia had seen to that. And her father looked healthier than he had in ages. She should be happy. She *should* be happy.

"And today," her father finished, "*we prove to ourselves and to the empires that though we cannot always see the blessing in the loss . . .*"

"*Strength is the gift of our Lady Baile,*" finished the people, a refrain to shake the city's ancient stones, "*and she will never abandon us.*"

"Vivia?" Serafin turned to his daughter, beaming and victorious. "Open the doors."

And Vivia's throat closed up. Tears seared along the backs of her eyeballs, for of course, those were supposed to be her words. She was supposed to turn to Stix and say them. *Captain? Open the doors.*

Instead, her father had said them. Instead, the Queen-in-Waiting was the one turning toward the entrance. And instead, the Queen-in-Waiting, who had failed thoroughly to be a bear or a Nihar or anything impressive at all, was the one laying gloved hands upon an iron latch while her father basked in the city's love.

Behind Vivia, the entire city of Lovats quaked with joy, with excitement, with anticipation—and all of it was focused on Serafin Nihar. A man who had never even set foot in the under-city.

Vivia shoved open the entrance doors. A groan of hinges and wood that the crowd's din swallowed whole. Then she stepped inside, and thanked Noden that the hallway was empty.

Because this way, no one could see her cry.

Vivia led the way into the under-city. The family behind her, a mother and two sons, uttered not a word the entire way through Pin's Keep, nor into the cellar, nor down the tunnel leading underground. Torches flickered, smokeless and Firewitched. An expense Vivia had insisted on in a space where smoke could be deadly.

She wished the family would speak. Somehow, the silence was worse than the crowd's cacophony outside.

This morning, when Vivia had imagined this moment, triumph had foamed in her chest. She'd felt so full with happiness and pride that she'd wanted to laugh into her breakfast. She *had* laughed into her breakfast.

Now, her chest felt bludgeoned. Over and over, a staccato explosion that made her lungs billow double-time. That crushed her ribs in a vise and made her heart feel so heavy, so flattened it was hard to breathe.

She wanted to break something. She wanted to scream. She wanted to curl in a ball and cry. But this wasn't rage. This wasn't grief. It was something skittery and aflame. Something shameful and unforgiving.

One should not need credit, she shouted inwardly. *One should not need credit!* She wasn't even fully Queen, yet already she was a terrible one, exactly what her mother had trained her *not* to be.

And an unfaithful daughter too.

It didn't help that her left shoulder ached. The gash from a raider blade two weeks ago had healed well thanks to salves and tonics. Time in the underground lake had helped too, but the wound wasn't fully gone yet.

When at last Vivia reached the tunnel's end, six faces framed a doorway hewn from the limestone: the Hagfishes, smoothed away by time and foxfire.

Two weeks ago, Vivia had come here with Stix. For the first time, she had pushed this door wide and discovered the forgotten under-city—just as her mother had always described it would be. Now, when Vivia shoved back the limestone, light rumbled over her. Laughter too, from her volunteers and soldiers.

She wished it would all go away.

"Welcome," Vivia wheezed without glancing at the family. She needed to leave here. She needed to go somewhere alone and face this bludgeoning in private.

The mother crept into the under-city first, eyes as wide as her two boys'. "Thank you, Your Majesty," she said, hesitant but real.

"Not *Your Majesty*," Vivia gruffed out. "Just *Your Highness*." Instantly she wished she hadn't said that. Rude, rude, rude—she *knew* she was being rude, yet rather than apologize or simply say *You're welcome*, like a normal human would do, Vivia kept staring into the middle distance.

Then Varrmin—thank the Hagfishes—appeared. He worked in the Pin's Keep kitchens, jovial, warm, and all the things Vivia had never been. The instant he was near enough for Vivia to see the gray scruff in his beard, she spun on her heel and fled.

There was another exit from the under-city that fed into the Cisterns, and she aimed for that. She wanted to feel the Tidewitched waters of those tunnels—and she wanted to reach them before any guards could form rank around her.

She wasn't fast enough to evade Stix, though. Vivia didn't know where the woman came from, but suddenly she was there, falling into step beside Vivia, her long legs easily keeping Vivia's frantic pace.

"How is it," Stix asked, "that men always seem to claim victory over the triumphs earned by women?"

Vivia didn't answer that question. She hadn't answered it two months before, either, when Merik had been appointed Admiral with absolutely no qualifications to recommend him except his gender.

Instead, Vivia stomped faster. The empty, lantern-lit houses she had worked so hard to clean now glowered down at her.

"I'm sorry he did that," Stix went on. "I know you wrote that speech."

"One should not need credit," Vivia murmured, "as long as it gets the job done."

"Wait." Stix reached for her. "Your Highness."

Your Highness. No more calling her *Sir* or *Vivia.* For two weeks, it had been this way, and Vivia didn't know if it was because of the kiss or her new title. Either way, she hated it. She wanted the old Stix back.

"Please," Vivia said at last, wishing her voice wasn't so shrill. "Please, just call me 'Viv.'"

No reaction. Instead, Stix offered a rolled-up missive

stamped with the Royal Voicewitch seal. "This came for you, but I didn't think . . . That is to say, I thought you should see it before your father did."

Vivia knew she ought to reprimand Stix for hiding this from Serafin. He might not be King or King Regent, but he was still Vivia's first and foremost adviser. She said nothing, though, because for the first time since leaving the crowds outside Pin's Keep, Vivia's heart felt a bit less flattened. Her lungs felt a bit less crushed.

She slowed at an intersection and unfurled the message. Foxfire flared brighter than lamps here, casting the paper in green.

It was from the Empress of Marstok.

Now that true negotiations for trade have begun, I wish to invite you to Azmir. Some decisions are best made face-to-face. As are some apologies, particularly for the treaty terms my ambassadors attempted to make before my return.

I have alerted all soldiers to allow Nubrevnan Wind transport into the city, should you decide to come. All I ask is for several hours' advance warning.

Vivia blinked. Then read the message again, a new sensation winding through her muscles and lungs. A hot, tightening sensation that was a thousand times preferable to the frenzied panic from before.

On the third read-through, a laugh choked up from her belly. For *surely* the Empress could not be serious. "Tell Her *Majesty*," Vivia said at last, crumpling the missive and shoving it into Stix's waiting hands, "that she can come to me if she really wants to negotiate. And that all I ask is for '*several hours'* *advance warning.*'"

Stix chuckled at that, but it was a taut, nervous sound. And when Vivia launched back into a march, she followed more sedately behind.

"Who the hell-waters does she think she is?" Vivia demanded.

"Well," Stix said, "she *probably* thinks she's the Empress of the Flame Children, Chosen Daughter of the Fire Well, the Most Worshipped of the Marstoks, Destroyer of Kendura Pass—"

"And?"

"And she's used to people doing her bidding."

Vivia scoffed. "I could have just as many titles too, if I wanted them."

"Of course you could, Your Highness."

Your Highness. There it was again, and just like that, it was too much. Vivia didn't need Stix's pity; she didn't need Stix's condescension. And above all, she didn't need credit or titles or the adoration of a city she worked so hard for.

She didn't, she *didn't.*

They were almost to the exit now. The wooden barricade built to keep unsuspecting refugees out of the dangerous tunnels glimmered in the green light, and the waters of the Cisterns rumbled in Vivia's chest. They called to her magic as they barreled past, uneven and weak since the attack two weeks ago.

Before Vivia could tow out the key that would allow her through the barricade, Stix pushed in front of her. "Wait. Please," she began. "Just hear me out, Your Highness."

"Why?" Rude, rude—there she went again, being rude. "What is it you need to say?"

"I think you should go to Azmir."

It was not what Vivia expected, and it was also not what Vivia wanted.

But Stix wasn't finished. "Believe it or not, the city will not collapse if you're gone for a day, and the chance to trade with Marstok . . . Can we really risk passing that up?"

"I don't have time," Vivia snapped. She pulled out the key. "Please move aside, Captain."

Stix didn't move. She just folded her arms across her chest, a pose Vivia had seen her make a thousand times, usually relaxed and smiling while her nearsighted eyes squinted.

Now, there was no smile. Now, Stix's lips were pinched tight. "Why don't you have time? The operation with the under-city is complete, and you have soldiers across the city to see that it runs smoothly. The High Council doesn't meet until tomorrow, and you have *me* to make sure the dam repairs proceed as planned. If anything, today is the perfect day for you to go."

"But my father—" Vivia began.

"Has nothing to do with you. He stole your speech. He stole the applause and recognition that should have been yours. *You* are Queen-in-Waiting. Not him. And how many times have we said that Noden and the Hagfishes ought to bend to a woman's rule?

"Please," Stix added, straightening off the barricade. "The Hasstrels only sent us that one shipment of grains, and now they aren't answering our Voicewitches. We *need* this. So do it for you, and do it for Nubrevna. You might not have all

48

the titles the Empress has, but that doesn't make you any less than her. And *you* are Queen-in-Waiting, Viv. Not your father."

Ah. *Viv.* The one thing Vivia had wanted her best friend to say for the last two weeks, and now it was offered alongside a plea.

The bludgeoning returned, twice as strong. Twice as vicious. Vivia had to get away before her chest burst. She *had* to be alone.

"I'll consider it," she said, stunned when the words sounded crisp and normal. Then she pushed past Stix, unlocked the barricade, and hurried into the tunnels beyond as fast as her bungling feet would carry her.

And when the Cistern's tides barreled toward her, she did not try to stop them. She did not use her magic to take control or ease their impact. Instead, she let the waters of her city drag her down and carry her far away.

SIX

Stacia Sotar ran her fingers over the carvings in the limestone. Her skin glowed green beneath the foxfire. A hundred tiny boxes, each with diagonal lines to intersect, framed a rectangle as tall as she. It was as if someone had intended to build a door here, had even begun the process and then abandoned it before actually hollowing out a passage.

Or maybe the door only travels one way.

For some reason, Stix kept thinking that this morning. That maybe, somehow, by some magic she did not understand, there was indeed a doorway here.

A doorway that only traveled one way.

Stix's hand fell away from the carvings. She eased back two steps, head shaking as it did every time she'd come here. The urge to talk to Vivia swelled in her chest. She wanted to ask Vivia what she thought this door might be, tucked off the edge of the under-city, and above all, she wanted to know if Vivia heard the voices that trickled out from the stone.

The truth was, though, that Stix would never . . . she *could* never speak of this to Vivia. The Queen-in-Waiting had enough burdens as it was—too many, actually, and Stix refused to add to that heap.

It didn't help that things had been stretched so thin between her and Vivia since the kiss they never spoke of. It was so odd—had always been so odd—that Stix could be so near to her best friend, yet somehow a thousand leagues away. She caught glimpses of the real Vivia from time to time, but that was all she ever got. Tiny peeks that never seemed to last.

After the kiss, Stix thought she'd finally earned that raw honesty. That she'd earned Vivia's true face she so adored. But then the promise of the crown had been laid atop Vivia's head, and with it, a thousand tasks needed to rebuild a city scarred. Vivia had retreated behind her masks and her duties.

Leaving Stix to face the whispers all alone.

Besides, what could Stix even say? *I know the underground city too well, Viv. I find secret corners and hidden streets that I should not be able to find.*

Or, *I feel anxious every moment I'm away from the city. But as soon as I'm back inside its walls, I feel as if I can breathe again.*

Or, the one that scared Stix the most, the one she couldn't even voice aloud to herself: *There are whispers in the back of my skull, Viv. They talk all day, all night, and I am slowly losing my mind to them.*

The whispers only spoke when Stix was aboveground, out of the under-city. They only screamed when she was far away from this door. When she was here with it, though, they were quiet.

It had started with dreams two weeks ago. Darkness and

51

screaming and a pain in her neck that woke her in the night. She found her sheets soaked, sweat sliding off her in thick rivulets.

A week after that, the shadows had started coming during the day. Little flickers of movement that made her fear her already weak vision might be getting worse. The shadows only lasted a few days, though. Then they vanished and the whispers began.

The whispers were the worst part yet, because she could never *quite* hear them. It reminded her of a cadet she'd trained, who, no matter how much she told him to speak up, never got his voice above a squeak. The majority of what he said went forever unheard, forever lost to the din around him.

These whispers were like that.

At times, Stix thought them a hundred different voices speaking inside her brain. Other times she thought them only one, as if all those separate sounds and languages were blended together like a vast orchestra playing a single tune.

One voice or many, it did not change the fact that none of the words made sense. It was a language—or languages —she did not know.

Worse yet, the low, inaudible murmur of the voices never ceased. All day, all night, they followed Stix. Always incomprehensible, always angry, and they expected Stix to do something about it.

But I can't hear you! she had mentally screamed a thousand times in the past two weeks. Twice, she had even slipped up and barked it aloud.

Her only relief came from Pin's Keep. The boisterous bustle of the crowded main room, where the homeless and hungry came for food. Where all that noise could, for a time, drown out the maddening whispers. But only in the under-city did Stix feel truly at home.

There, the whispers shifted from furious to cajoling. *Come,* they seemed to say in words that had no meaning. *Come this way, keep coming.*

Every night Stix followed, knowing tomorrow she would regret it. Tomorrow, she would be exhausted with her head pounding and the whispers returned. But the call of the city was always stronger, and every night, she gave in.

Even now, when Stix should have been helping families move in or overseeing dam reconstruction, she wasn't. It was her father's birthday too, and she'd promised him a trip to the Cleaved Man. Instead, here she was, standing in front of this door to nowhere. *Again.* But there were no more answers here than there had been last night or any other night before it. Only the faint hum of *Come this way, keep coming.*

"I can't," Stix told them. Then she rubbed her eyes—by the Twelve, they burned—and turned away.

Stix was in the Cisterns, tracing the same path Vivia would have taken to reach the surface, when she passed a marking on the limestone wall. It wasn't new; she'd seen it a hundred times before today.

For some reason, though, *today* it gave her pause. For some reason, even though water thundered this way through the tunnel, Stix's feet slowed. Her gaze raked up and down the image.

It was a relief of Lady Baile, patron saint of change, seasons, and crossroads. In one hand, she held a trout, and in the other, wheat. The limestone saint stood as tall as Stix, so worn by time that her fox-shaped mask was missing. Actually, most of the head was missing.

But not the eyes, and it was the eyes that had hooked Stix's attention. It was the eyes that were causing the voices to rustle and churn.

This time, though, they spoke in a language she knew—and this time, they were telling her where to go. Telling her how to come and keep coming.

"Hye," she said, the sound lost to the waters rushing this way. "I'll be there soon."

Abruptly, the choir in her skull silenced. Then the Cistern tide reached her. Frothy, violent, and bound to the magic singing in Stix's veins. She let it carry her away, because there was no reason to retrace Vivia's steps now. No reason to return to Queen's Hill or travel to the dam.

Stix needed to go south.

Come this way, keep coming.

SEVEN

✳

Aeduan awoke, confused. There had been pain and fire and impossible dreams—dreams he could not quite remember. Iseult had been there, though, while they slept within a pyre beside a spring.

When his eyelids scratched up, soft light seared into them. He was in the cave that Owl had made, where the mountain bat's stink overpowered all other smells. But not his magic. He sensed Owl nearby, the rosewater-and-wool-wrapped lullabies that thrummed inside her veins. And if she was still here, then Iseult must still be here too. Not just in dreams but in waking.

He had no explanation for why Iseult had remained, nor could he deny the relief seeping through him that she had.

Clearing his throat, Aeduan twisted sideways—only to find Owl squatting beside him, her big, teardrop eyes unblinking.

"Breakfast," she declared, thrusting a wooden bowl at Aeduan's face. Earthworms wriggled within, and it took all Aeduan's self-control not to recoil. Instead, he sat up. His blanket fell back; cold air swept against him. For some reason, he was missing his shirt.

"Blueberry's favorite," Owl explained, and as if to prove the point, the beast ducked out from the back of the cave, where shadows reigned. The musty bat stench rolled over Aeduan. His breath steamed into Aeduan's face.

The worms continued to writhe.

Owl shoved the bowl in closer. "Eat."

Aeduan accepted the bowl, which set Blueberry to snuffing right in his ear. Hot, damp snuffs. He waved Blueberry back and glanced toward the sliver of daylight that marked the entrance. "I . . . need water first, Owl."

The girl seemed satisfied with this, and after watching Aeduan stumble to his feet, she snuggled into the still-warm blankets and Blueberry settled down behind her.

Rock scraped Aeduan's chest as he slid outside. Gooseflesh prickled down his exposed skin. The air here was much colder, even with sunlight to warm the midmorning fog. He shivered and forced his feet to move away from the cave and to the edge of the evergreens. Once there, where undergrowth and moss clotted thick, he dumped the bowl of worms. Three days since Owl had started speaking again, and already she'd become a wealth of trouble.

Aeduan placed the empty bowl atop a stone for later retrieval, yet as he stood there crouched over, an ache stung at his chest—like a dagger between the ribs. Without warning, he coughed. And coughed. And *coughed*. The onslaught would not subside, until eventually, a soft hand came to his back. Cautious. Concerned. Startling enough to give him pause. Then the Threadwitch's inscrutable face swung down to peer into his. "Are you all right?"

Aeduan did not try to straighten. Shadows crossed his vision.

Frustration throbbed in his chest. What was this weakness? What was this ailment? His magic should have healed him by now. "What . . . happened?" he asked from a throat made of acid.

"I was going to ask you the same." She helped him rise. Her hands were warm against his skin. "Do you not remember returning?"

"No," he admitted. Iseult was near enough for him to spot streaks of green in her eyes. To spot how cold had colored her nose to pink. It reminded him of his dream with gentle flames and serenity on her face. She had uttered his name, her eyes never opening, and her fingers had gripped at his hips and stolen his breath.

She stole his breath now, and he had no breath to spare.

He jerked away from her. The conifers dipped and bled. "Where is my shirt?"

A flush swept up her cheeks. She motioned vaguely up the hill. "It's drying. I-I . . . washed it."

"Oh." He forced himself to straighten fully. It made everything hurt. "I will get it then." He shifted as if to stride away, but either the movement was too quick or his body was truly too weak, for the black rushed in once more. With it came coughing. Then the Threadwitch's fingers were upon him once more, and when she guided him toward a low campfire and helped him to sit, he did not protest.

He *could* not protest.

A pot sat beside the dying fire, a damp cloth dangling from one side. Iseult scooped water into a cup. "Drink."

He complied, and though the warm liquid felt like broken glass against his throat, he welcomed the pain. It sent the black scampering away. The coughing too.

57

"If you had let me come with you," Iseult said while he drank, "then I could have helped you navigate the path." It was an argument they'd had three times before: should Iseult join him or should she stay with Owl? If she came, then she could read the Nomatsi road and help Aeduan reach the slaughter sites uninjured. If she remained, she could prevent Owl and Blueberry from generating inevitable trouble.

"The traps were mostly triggered when I arrived," he said. A lie. Although there had been several corpses, dressed in what he now realized was Purist gray, the bulk of the road had been navigated without triggering any protections.

Aeduan could only assume that the men who attacked knew what they were doing. The Nomatsi tribe had been killed without warning, just as the previous two had been.

He finished the water before saying: "It was the largest tribe yet. All dead."

"Oh." A mere sigh of sound, of resignation, even as Iseult's face stayed impassive. "But if the traps were triggered, how did you get hit with so many arrows?"

"I found someone still alive. A monk. But he was not trained to fight. I . . . had to deal with him."

Iseult's eyes widened. A fraction of a movement, yet enough for Aeduan to catch. Enough for him to add, "I did not kill him," even if he did not know why he wanted to clarify. "He was wounded when I found him, and after he died, I stayed to bury him. That was when I triggered the traps."

Another soft sigh. Then she sank into a cross-legged position beside him. "Did he see who attacked them?"

Aeduan nodded, though instantly wished he hadn't. The

world spun. "The monk," he forced out, eyes wincing shut, "said it was the Purists."

"Not raiders then?"

"I do not know." Again, a lie, but he saw no reason to tell Iseult that he knew of Purists working with the Raider King. That he knew of one Purist in particular, working with his father.

"Corlant," she said, filling in one of the gaps on her own. "He was there, wasn't he?" Without waiting for a reply, she tugged something from her coat pockets, then opened her hands for Aeduan to see.

Two arrowheads shone black against her pale palms. Both bits of iron were bloodstained, but only one gave off any blood-scent—Aeduan's own.

"This one injured me in Dalmotti." She furled her left fingers into a fist. "And this one I pulled from you at dawn. I think they're cursed. No," she amended, head shaking, "I *know* they are. Owl called it 'bad earth.'"

Bad earth. He glanced down at his chest, at the six old scars that marked his flesh and the four new puckers on his belly—puckers that should not be there at all, just as the seventeen holes in his back should not be there either. He'd had more than enough time to heal.

"Corlant," Iseult continued, "can do that. He . . ." She tapped at her right biceps. "He almost killed me with a cursed arrow in Dalmotti." There was a strain to her voice now, like a fiddle pulled too tight. "I was unconscious for a long time. I-I almost died."

"That cannot happen to me. I am a Bloodwitch."

She shrugged as if to say *How can you be so sure?* Aloud,

though, she said: "Why was he with this tribe? The Midenzis are on the other side of the Jadansi. Unless ..." She trailed off, a tiny frown wrinkling her brow.

Aeduan offered no reply. Lying did not come naturally to him, and he had already pushed his limits. Silence seemed his best option now.

For a long moment, Iseult gazed at him, unblinking. As inscrutable as all Threadwitches were trained to be. Behind her, the fire popped, and a final burst of flame guttered upward. Smoke gathered. A soft breeze pitched across Aeduan's bare skin.

He wanted his shirt back.

"We need a proper healer," Iseult said at last, giving a pointed glance to Aeduan's stomach. "We need better healing supplies, too, and we're out of lanolin for our blades."

We, Aeduan thought, and before he could argue—before he could ask *Why we?* or even *Why did you wait the whole night instead of leaving?*—Iseult was on her feet and circling behind him. Trails from the movement streaked across his vision. Smoke and flesh and flame.

"You're bleeding again," she murmured. Then her fingers were on him once more, warm and sure while she pressed the damp cloth to his back. He hadn't even seen her pick it up.

"No." He reached around to take the cloth from her hand. "I can do it," he tried to say, but the twisting in his ribs, the stretching of the wounds down his back, set his lungs to spasming once more.

This time, the coughing would not abate. Even after two cups of water, he could not suck in enough air. So when Iseult tried a second time to dab away the blood that never stopped falling, he did not protest.

Nor did he protest when she said, "We should go to Tirla, Aeduan. I know it is a Marstoki stronghold, but we can find a healer in a city that size. And we can get fresh supplies too."

We, we, we.

The damp cloth felt like razors against his skin. Everything hurt in ways that it should not, and his shredded throat would soon bleed if he did not stop this coughing. He was weak; he hated it. Carawen monks were meant to be prepared for anything, and Aeduan had always prided himself on being doubly so. Yet over the last two weeks, he'd been ill-equipped and constantly unsteady.

It didn't help that Aeduan had never worked for free before. It was a nagging pressure along the back of his neck. Like words tickling: *You should be getting paid. Each moment that passes is another coin lost.* It was also another moment in which he had not contacted his father or pursued the coins owed to him.

Two weeks ago, Aeduan would have followed the scent of clear lakes and frozen winters—the ghost who had stolen his coins and aided Prince Leopold in Nubrevna. Two weeks ago, he would have also returned to Lejna and claimed those coins from where Iseult said they were hidden. And two weeks ago, he would have looked at each passing massacre and felt nothing. After all, death was inevitable in wartime, and as his father always said: *Life is the price of justice.*

But two weeks ago, he had not found Owl, bound and drugged by raiders claiming his father's banner. Two weeks ago, he had not encountered dead Nomatsi tribes and recognized the scents of his father's men amidst the slaughter.

And two weeks ago, he had not been traveling with a woman to whom he owed more life-debts than he could keep track of, and with more life-debts stacking between them each day.

Like right now. She tended him, and Aeduan did not know why—nor did he know how to tally such ministrations. He simply knew he was indebted. He simply knew he could not leave until he had paid her back.

And there was still the problem of Owl's missing tribe. Of the scent like summer heather and impossible choices, still alive. Still somewhere in the mountains ahead.

"Yes," Aeduan agreed at last, a ragged sound between coughs. "Let us go to Tirla."

It had been raining on the day Aeduan learned his father still lived. Aeduan had gone to a Monastery outpost in Tirla for his next Carawen assignment. So many had requested him specifically in those days, and this time was no different. One mission, however, had caught his attention above the rest.

He could remember the words exactly.

> *Bloodwitch monk needed to find a hound named Boots*
> *Meet at farmstead north of Tirla, blue wind-flags above the gate*

Aeduan's childhood dog had been named Boots. He had killed that dog; maybe he could save this one.

Except that when he reached the dilapidated farmstead,

there was only a man waiting to see him in a small house with a thatched roof.

Aeduan drew a knife before entering. He did not sheathe it for many hours, even though the man seated on the stool beside the hearth was an unmistakable reflection of Aeduan— except for the lines around hazel eyes and a gray fringe that brightened his hair.

"It is you," the man had said in a gravelly voice that hummed deep in Aeduan's chest. A voice that still told the story of the monster and the honey in Aeduan's dreams.

Aeduan did not put away his knife. He did not react at all, even as the man rose. Even as he said, "Aeduan, my son."

Ghosts, after all, did not return from the dead.

"You're alive." The man spoke Nomatsi, a language Aeduan had not used in over a decade. "I . . . thought you were dead."

Aeduan had thought the same. He said nothing, though, and neither man sat. Both men stared.

"Your mother," the man began, a question in his tone.

But Aeduan shook his head. A single hard snap. Dysi had not survived. Aeduan would not say so aloud.

A pained inhale from the man, before he gave a curt, almost businesslike nod. "Twice I have loved," he said. "Twice empires have taken everything from me." Then he swallowed. He frowned, and for the first time in many, many years, Aeduan recalled that yes, his father *had* had another family. Daughters and a wife that had died.

"So you must see," the man continued, "why having my son returned to me . . . It is more than I ever dared hope." He spoke so simply, as if commenting on the weather. As if describing how best to evade an enemy's blow.

63

Such flat tones for such desperate words, yet somehow, this made their meaning cut deeper, and for the first time since entering the thatched-roof house, Aeduan spoke.

"Tell me where you have been."

His father complied.

Aeduan learned that in the fifteen years since the attack on their tribe, Ragnor had moved to Arithuania, following Nomatsis on the run and witches cast out by their empires. He learned his father had built an army meant to end imperial tyranny once and for all.

And he learned that his father had a place for him at his side, if Aeduan was willing to take it.

Aeduan was.

In the end, the blood-scent had convinced him that this man was indeed his father. It had changed in fifteen years, though—the bloodied iron and sleeping ice might still remain, but gone were the nighttime songs and the loving hounds that he remembered. Now there was fire. Now there was inconsolable loss. It stained every piece of Ragnor's blood. It gave his eyes a weight that no one else could understand.

No one but Aeduan, who had been there on the day everything had been taken away from them.

In the end, it was Ragnor's words that had convinced Aeduan to actually join him. And since that day in the thatched-roof house, his course had been so clear. Aeduan had never second-guessed. He had never hesitated. Coin and the cause. Coin and the cause. No space for personal wants, and no desire for them either. He had given up hope so very long ago. There was only action, only moving forward. Coin and the cause. Coin and the cause.

Until two weeks ago.

Now everything was muddied. Now Aeduan felt trapped between duty and life-debts. Between his father and a child. He could not fully serve Ragnor while also searching for Owl's tribe. He could not find Owl a home—or repay Iseult what he owed—while also remaining committed to coin and the cause.

He was caught, like the man from the tale who wanted to feed his family during a blizzard but could not bear to kill the lamb. In the end, everyone died of starvation, including the lamb.

For Lady Fate makes all men choose eventually. Even Bloodwitches.

EIGHT

Somehow, Iseult had become the one in charge. She didn't like it. Not one bit. First of all, she had never been to Tirla, and "follow the signs" was the only advice Aeduan had been able to give in his current condition.

Second of all, Owl simply would not listen to her. Like her namesake, she was a fighter. If Iseult asked the girl to do anything—from washing up at night to simply staying within sight while they trekked onward—the girl instantly dug in her heels and refused. Or she just pretended she couldn't hear Iseult at all.

If Aeduan, however, asked her to do the exact same thing... oh, *then* Owl obeyed in a heartbeat. The sunset Threads stretching from her toward Aeduan sinewed stronger each day. Aeduan might not have Threads, but Owl was undoubtedly bound to him.

Over their two weeks of travel, it had not been an issue. An annoyance, certainly, but Aeduan had always been there to sweep in and take charge of any stubborn situations. Now, with Aeduan barely clinging to consciousness and all of his focus on getting one foot in front of the other, Iseult had to control Owl all on her own.

It wasn't going well. In fact, since that morning when Owl had thrown their trout breakfast on the fire, Iseult had decided she hated the girl. She knew it wasn't a good look, hating children, but Iseult was also convinced that even Safi, who had an actual knack for handling little ones, would call this child a "thrice-damned demon from beyond the hell-gates."

Owl argued with *everything*. Breakfast. Washing up. Wearing shoes. Staying on the path. And at any hint of sharp words from Iseult, she would scuttle into the nearest branches and hide among the trees. Or, when no trees were near, the stones served just as well.

One moment, she'd be storming off. The next, she'd have vanished entirely, as if the earth had sucked her right in. Then before Iseult could try to find the girl, Blueberry would trundle over, nostrils huffing vast plumes of fetid air while his silvery Threads flashed bright with distaste for Iseult.

The feeling was mutual.

The closer they got to Tirla, the more people clotted the roadways, their mules and wagons churning the earth to mud. Nestled in the middle of the mountains, Tirla connected three borders, and with war coming after nineteen years of peace, people moved. Families fled the growing raider threat; soldiers mobilized to stop it; traders hoped to make coin off them all. At the first hint of one such artery leading to the city, Iseult had called a halt. She did not want to go traipsing into humanity with a mountain bat in tow.

Aeduan, coughing heavily, had instantly dropped to the

earth beside the stream Iseult had chosen for their break. Its shore was thick with blackberries, yet Aeduan had swept aside the thorns, no thought for blood or pain, and then gulped back water until his attack subsided. He was of absolutely no use in the argument that followed.

"I do not like it either," Iseult said to a pile of rocks that was vaguely girl-shaped and bore hateful gray Threads overtop. "But you have to tell Blueberry to stay hidden. We'll soon be with other people, and if they see him, they'll try to hurt him."

"Can't hurt," the stones insisted, a small mouth appearing amidst the pile. "He's bigger."

"Yes," Iseult was forced to agree. "And that's the problem. If they attack him, he'll attack right back."

Pink acceptance swirled up the stones' Threads, as if Owl thought this was perfectly reasonable.

"And," Iseult went on, "we cannot have that. Owl, we need to get into Tirla to help Aeduan. Don't you care about Aeduan?" As if on cue, the Bloodwitch started coughing once more.

Actually, it *was* on cue, for when she glanced his way, she found the faintest smile brushing his tired lips.

"Owl," he said between dramatic hacks, "tell . . . Blueberry . . . to stay here. I promise we will not be away from him long." Aeduan's voice was in tatters and his posture pained, but still he sent a weary gaze to Iseult and mouthed: *What else?*

And, Iseult mouthed back, *no magic*.

A nod, but he did not speak right away. Instead, he wiped water from his mouth and motioned stiffly toward the trees.

In gruff Dalmotti, he murmured, "It might be best if you leave. I do not think . . . That is to say, it is simpler with only two people."

"You mean she hates me." Unwelcome heat rushed to Iseult's face, but she did as suggested, and without a backward glance, she hauled up their packs—roped together so she could carry them both—and strode into the forest, aiming for the nearest road.

She didn't make it far before Blueberry materialized from the trees, as silent as a true bat and with Threads burning disdainfully. It was as if he thought it entirely Iseult's fault that he could not join them in Tirla. As if he thought it *Iseult's* fault that Owl was upset or Aeduan had been badly injured.

Iseult couldn't help it. In complete abandonment of all her Threadwitch training, she fixed the massive beast with a sneer—and goddess, it felt good. The way her eyes narrowed and her nose wrinkled. The way her teeth bared and heat plowed through her lungs.

Burn him. Heat flickered in her fingertips. *Burn his furry flesh and then burn the little girl too.*

Instantly, Iseult's expression fell. Cold scoured through.

This was not her temper. This was not her fire. And this was *not* her voice. She had been trained to keep her body cool when it ought to be hot, her fingers still when they ought to be trembling. She was trained to ignore the feelings that drove everyone else, yet here she was: driven. *Dragged* by emotions she could not control.

By a fire she could not control.

For half a seemingly endless breath, Iseult was overcome by guilt. By how much she hated herself and her magic and what she had done to that Firewitch. He wasn't even the first person she had killed. All those soldiers and Adders in Lejna that Esme had cleaved . . .

That had been Iseult's doing. The Puppeteer had used *Iseult's* mind to find out where Iseult was. Then Esme had used *Iseult's* mind to ultimately make her attack.

Iseult clutched her temples and stumbled away from Blueberry. Away from Owl or Aeduan.

"Stasis," she hissed at herself, thinking of ice, ice, and only ice. "Stasis in your fingers and in your toes."

Branches smacked against her. Mud from last night's rain churned beneath her boot heels. The pack jangled and bounced with each step. No amount of moving had outrun the demons so far, though, and no amount of running had evaded the Firewitch. There was no reason to believe it would suddenly start working now.

She would just have to be more vigilant then. No more flashes of anger. And *absolutely* no more sleep. She'd started a fire this morning when the blow to her head had pulled her under—thank the Moon Mother, only gravel had surrounded her and Aeduan.

Tirla, she was certain, would be much more flammable.

Iseult finally slowed at the first signs of people. Threads thick as a quilt wafted along the periphery of her magical range. Every type of emotion was covered, from iron pain to scarlet Heart-Threads, but needling through them all was one commonality: the green focus of people on a journey.

Here Iseult waited, the minutes skipping past and her magic readjusting to so many people, so many Threads. The stasis that had eluded her earlier now anchored into place, comforted by rules she was accustomed to. She had grown up around people; she had lived many years in a crowded city: detachment and logic were easier when one was always on the outside looking in.

With Aeduan, there had been no Threads. There had been no outside.

Eventually, the Bloodwitch hobbled to her side. He clutched Owl's hand in his, and though a pouty red rattled across the girl's Threads, at least she was moving again—and Blueberry was nowhere to be seen.

Aeduan fixed Iseult with his ice-blue stare, questioning. As if he wondered why she had jogged so far away. As if he wanted to know that she was well.

She pretended not to notice. The flames were her problem and her problem alone. There was nothing he could do to help her. There was only moving forward and slogging on.

Goddess, she wished Safi were here, though.

"Think like Iseult," Safi whispered. It had been her prayer for the last two hours while she'd sat on the edge of her bed in these beautiful white quarters—wearing the same beautiful white dress the man had bled on.

White, white, white. Everywhere Safi's eyes landed was white, from the walls to the tiles. The first day, Safi had admired her quarters. Soothing and bright. Now, she saw it for the truly terrible shade it was. White showed blood too easily, and once that blood was dried, there was no erasing it.

The footprints she'd tracked in were still on the ground, mottled to rusty brown. An inescapable reminder of what

Safi had done. What Safi had caused—because the memories branded in her brain were not enough. The detached head, with its still-blinking eyes and spurting arteries. The man's last words: *What a ridiculous question.*

The thirteenth chimes clanged outside; the sun beamed down, though only a gauzy gray light filtered through the iron shutters over Safi's lone window. A small courtyard garden bloomed out there, and at this hour, katydids clicked and clattered.

She wrapped her fingers around the Threadstone at her collarbone and rested her head on her knees. This stone had been a gift from Iseult, and it—like the matching one Iseult had—lit up when either girl was in danger.

"Think like Iseult. Think like Iseult." Safi's Threadsister would see some solution out of this disaster. Cool, logical Iseult would work through it like a knot in a fragile necklace, plying Safi with questions and coaxing out the facts of the situation.

The facts were that twice in her life now, Safi had carved her own path, had played her own cards—with no one to guide her—and *this* was where her choices had led. She had become Truthwitch for Empress Vaness in exchange for trade with the starving nation of Nubrevna. Then she had made a similar choice in Saldonica. The mark on her thumb was a reminder of that.

A day after her duel with Admiral Kahina and her resulting agreement with the woman, a thin red line had appeared *right* where Kahina wore her jade ring. The ring had flashed when Safi had promised to give Kahina whatever she wanted; Safi suspected that meant the deal was far more binding than mere

72

words. Like everything else here, though, she tried not to think about it. Her choice had saved her, and it had saved Vaness and the Hell-Bards too.

Of course, the Hell-Bards were gone now. The Marstoki Sultanate had opposed having any more Cartorrans than Safi in the palace, as had the generals, admirals, nobility, and Adders. The uproar that the Hell-Bards had caused as Safi's guards and companions—it hadn't been safe. For them or for Safi.

Which left Safi with another fact: she was all alone in the imperial palace, surrounded by Lake Scarza waters on all sides, the Kenduran foothills beyond that, and thousands of local enemies who wanted her dead. A thousand more foreign enemies too.

She knew Rokesh and the other Adders would protect her, but while she and Vaness might have become allies in Saldonica, even friends, if it became a choice between Safi's life and the empire's future . . .

One life for the sake of many was a truth Safi understood all too well.

Perhaps the most important fact of all, though, was that the Truthwitchery Safi had hidden her entire life was now public knowledge. The one thing she *never* wanted to be, that she had run from for nineteen years . . . It had all come to pass. She was a tool for an empire, a knife for Lady Fate, and men would die because of her magic.

True, purred Safi's power, an unwelcome warmth in her chest. She squeezed her eyelids all the tighter. She wanted to leave. She wanted to abandon this post she had chosen, and she wanted to run as fast and as far as she could go.

73

Safi wasn't so foolish, though. If she tried to escape, she would end up in chains, and chains would keep her from *ever* leaving Marstok. Chains would keep her from ever finding Iseult—the only thing in all the Witchlands that mattered.

Iseult now traveled with a Bloodwitch. With *the* Bloodwitch who had hunted them across the Jadansi, and though Iseult might have claimed she trusted him, Safi did not believe her. She *couldn't*. Both times the girls had spoken in Safi's dreams, something had been wrong. Something had made Iseult's thoughts skitter and her words fret with lies.

Safi feared Iseult did not travel with that Bloodwitch monster by choice—and she had no way to find out. Iseult hadn't come to her dreams again in a week and a half.

Safi groaned. The knot in her chain of thoughts had led her back to the beginning: trapped in court with Iseult far, far away. She was no good at this. She *needed* Iseult to help her isolate the best course of action.

As she sat there, toes tapping on the tiles, a squawk tore through the room. Her gaze snapped up, and she found a crow staring at her from the garden door. An old crow, if the white around its beak meant anything.

Its head cocked sideways, eyes eerily sentient.

"I don't have food," Safi said, rising. "Go on, crow." She shooed at the creature. A halfhearted gesture at best. "Leave before I call the Adders on you."

The bird looked thoroughly unimpressed. Though it did hop backward when Safi approached, its wings fluttering.

"Go on," she said, a bit more forcefully this time, her own hands sweeping like wings. "Get out before a poisoned dart finds you . . ." She trailed off as the crow kicked up and flapped onto a telescope at the heart of her small garden.

It had been a gift from the Empress, purchased in Veñaza City during the Truce Summit. Constellations had guided Safi and Vaness on their travels though the Contested Lands, so Vaness had thought Safi might enjoy having the telescope to "view the heavens more closely."

Safi knew Vaness had meant the gift kindly, yet it had felt more like a cruel reminder that Safi was trapped behind walls, with stars as her only escape.

The bird perched on the telescope's edge. Its wings stretched wide, feathers glimmering in the sunlight. It wasn't the crow she stared at, though—it was what the crow had trapped in its beak: a chunk of rose quartz. At first Safi thought it was a Painstone, except it wasn't glowing. Besides, why would a crow have one?

But then the bird dropped the stone, gave another urgent squawk, and flapped away—although not before leaving a glorious splatter of shit on the brass telescope's casing.

"Thanks," Safi muttered, although she *was* grateful he hadn't shit on her head instead.

Curiosity propelled her into the hot garden, the nearest insects quieted. Her stained slippers crunched on yellow gravel.

It *was* a Painstone. She couldn't believe it. The magic was clearly drained, but the shape and size were right. And when she crouched to pick it up, she spotted a hole at the top where string was meant to go through.

For several breaths, Safi remained kneeling, staring at the stone while the knot in her mind unwound. Cautiously, she tugged at the idea-chain. Gently, she traced it around,

around, around, all while a small smile towed at the edge of her lips.

Then there it was: a plan that might save her. Simple, clear, and one that Iseult would like too. It would require tools and books. And tomorrow, when the grouchy Earthwitch healer came to check on her foot and nose—neither injury had healed quite right—she would pester the woman with questions. Because if other witches could apply their magic to stones and salves and locks and drums, why couldn't Safi?

If she could make a *Truthstone* then Vaness wouldn't need her here at all. It wouldn't be Safi's words consigning traitors to death anymore, and best of all, she could go after Iseult without delay.

Lungs suddenly brimming, Safi snatched up the dead Painstone and stood. She had a task, she had a plan, and it felt *good*. Enough standing still inside a palace. Enough waiting for the corruption to come to her. Enough being someone else's tool.

Safi got to work.

Vivia stood barefoot at the edge of the underground lake. Shadows played across the rippling surface, cast by the lantern she had left on the shore. She'd left her boots there too, as she always did when she came here.

This was the heart of Lovats, fed by miles of underground rivers and aquifers long forgotten. It was Vivia's heart too, and the only place she could go when the panic became too much. Here she could breathe. Here she could be Vivia. Just Vivia.

This is the source of our power, Little Fox, Jana had told her. *The reason our family rules Nubrevna and others do not. This water knows us. This water chose us.*

"Extinguish," Vivia whispered to her lantern, and darkness draped the cavern. After three rib-bowing breaths, her eyes adjusted to reveal sprinkles and sprays of luminescent foxfire. Six spokes that crawled across the cavern's ceiling.

Two weeks ago, there had only been three spokes, because two weeks ago, the city had almost fallen. But Vivia and Merik had fended off the raiders and the monster called the Fury. They had repaired the dam, and shortly thereafter, the foxfire had returned.

Two weeks ago, Serrit Linday had also called this place an Origin Well.

Ever since that seed had been planted in Vivia's head, she'd been unable to stop its roots from spreading. There was one elemental Well unaccounted for in the Witchlands, and though Vivia's magic wasn't bound to the Void, there was no denying that this lake was more than just a pool where water collected.

Of course, if she really did have the Void Well hiding beneath her city, then what did that even mean? It was one more problem, one more question to add to her ever-growing list.

Before her lungs could cinch with panic at that thought, Vivia darted into the waves. The lake embraced her, warm and welcome. Shivering and alive. Grounding in a way that true ground never was.

This water didn't care about fathers or mothers or distant best friends. This water didn't care about messages from empresses or speeches stolen away. The water cared only for this moment and this place. It flowed where the land allowed it. It changed as the seasons demanded. And it never fretted if it couldn't be what others wanted.

Vivia's eyes fell shut. Her magic skipped outward, greeting the fish and the salamanders, skating past boulders and roots, through fissures and over grooves. Her senses moved upstream, they moved down, and she felt and *reached* for anything that might be out of place, for anything that wasn't right inside the plateau.

Yet all was well, just as it had been since she and Merik had saved the city two weeks ago, and second by slippery second, Vivia returned to her body. Gone was her panic, replaced by the power of tides and the strength of storms.

She was Vivia Nihar, Queen-in-Waiting of Nubrevna—chosen and bound to these eternal waters. She could face down entire navies, she could ride a waterfall from mountain peak to valley's end. She could battle almost any man or woman and be named victor.

And Stix was right: it *was* time that Noden and the Hagfishes bent to a woman's rule.

So Vivia made her decision. She would travel to Azmir. Today, just as Stix had suggested, and she would negotiate trade with the Empress of Marstok.

And Vivia would do it for herself, she would do it for Nubrevna.

NINE

The fifteenth chimes were singing by the time Iseult, Aeduan, and Owl reached Tirla. *City of a Thousand Names*, they called it, for every few decades, a new nation or empire laid claim to its sharp roofs and crooked streets. Since Marstok had conquered it, they had named it Tirla, after the long lake beside which it rested.

A setting sun canted down, turning whitewashed buildings to gold. Iseult would have found it beautiful were she not drowning beneath the children's shouts, the merchants' calls, the donkey brays and endless hammer of hooves—not to mention the soldiers' barks or the blacksmiths' bellows or the *creak-creak-creak* of wagon wheels. The din buffeted her from every direction.

For every noise, there were just as many people. Bodies, bodies, bodies everywhere she turned, and each moving beneath their own distinct Threads, their own erratic, emotional lives. Iseult's relief at the presence of humanity had quickly been overwhelmed, and now she wished she could just *stop*. Close her eyes for a single moment and enjoy at least one less sensory onslaught.

But that was not an option. Not yet.

For the final mile into the city, she had walked with her arm underneath Aeduan. Owl hadn't liked that. Aeduan had liked it even less, and Iseult had liked it least of all. It took so much of her focus to keep him upright and to keep Owl from wandering off—not to mention ensuring she and Owl were properly hidden beneath hoods and scarves. She knew the laws in Marstok were more forgiving than others when it came to Nomatsis, but that did not mean she wanted to test them.

Legal protection could not eliminate centuries of hate.

As it was, Iseult veered out of the crowds at the first inn she saw. A dangling sign declared *The White Alder*, and a second sign below claimed *Vacancies*. Even better, the inn was built mostly of tiny white bricks and terra-cotta tiling. As far as Iseult was concerned, the less wood, the better.

As Lady Fate would have it, though, once inside the crowded stable yard, she came face-to-face with a long-dead, sun-bleached alder standing majestically at the heart. She eyed it warily as she passed. She also paused at the front door to check that . . . yes, yes, her hood was firmly pulled down across her face. She turned to Owl. The girl's lips puckered into a scowl, her glare even fiercer than Blueberry's had been, but Owl did not resist when Iseult tightened her scarf. Nor did she argue when Iseult murmured, "Stay close to Aeduan, and do not speak."

A hum of clay red annoyance twined through the girl's Threads, and with it came a flash of pale contempt, as if she were thinking *I rarely speak, foolish woman.*

Iseult supposed she had a point.

They ducked beneath a low entrance into a noisy dining

space that was, to Iseult's relief, also white stone. Oak tables with matching chairs filled the space, and though she couldn't see it, she sensed a small fireplace at the end of the room. It tugged against her, like a lodestar to a magnet. Heat itched up and down her fingers.

Cool as a Threadwitch, she reminded herself before striding purposefully for the nearest expanse of bar counter. Here a woman with black hair piled high atop her head carefully carved a ham. She did not glance up at Iseult's approach.

Nor did she shift her attention when Iseult said, "We need a room for the night." She merely continued cutting the ham, juices oozing with each slice and her Threads a focused green.

So Iseult coughed. Then tried again, more loudly. "We need a room for the ni—"

"I heard you." No pause in the woman's cautious shave. No shift in her Threads. "We're full."

"Your sign says otherwise."

"Well, the sign is wrong."

Iseult's nose twitched. She'd so rarely had to do this without Safi at her side, and she doubted her usual threat of chopping off the woman's ears and feeding them to the rats was going to work in this situation.

Then again, Iseult's mentor Mathew always said, *Money is a language all men speak.*

"I can pay," she began.

"Not enough." The woman's carving did not miss a beat. Her Threads, however, fluttered with irritated red. "We're an expensive establishment."

"How expensive?"

"Fifty cleques a night."

Iseult didn't need Safi's magic to know *that* was a lie. The woman was marking up the price; her Threads made it clear she wanted Iseult to leave. But Iseult had something to prove now, and Moon Mother save her, she was about to waste a lot of coin just to make a point. Just to defend her own people.

Safi would be proud.

From the folds of her coat, she eased out a silver taler and slid it onto the counter. Then she offered her best attempt at a smile. "How about twice that?"

Instantly, the woman's Threads erupted with suspicion. She straightened, knife rising—not quite a threat, but not *not* a threat either. "Did you steal that?"

"No." Iseult's voice was perfectly still, her expression perfectly blank. She was Threadwitch calm through and through. "It was payment for . . . sewing."

"Oh?" The suspicion in the woman's Threads spread wider. "I thought sewing was a man's work for the 'Matsis."

Ah. Well, *that* was unexpected. Of all the innkeepers for Iseult to encounter, she had to find the one who actually knew something about Nomatsi culture.

"It is," she said as evenly as she could. *Give her what she expects to see. Give her what she expects to see.* "I . . . learned the skill from my father. But my father was killed by raiders, and now my family and I"—she motioned to Aeduan and Owl—"are just looking for a place to stay a few nights. We'll leave soon, I promise."

A thoughtful grunt, and slowly the woman's Threads melted. First into the bright cyan of understanding, but tinged with midnight blue grief. Then at last, a wave of pink acceptance.

Iseult's good fortune scarcely lasted a heartbeat, though, before Aeduan started coughing. A great explosion of air and sound that sent nearby patrons spinning toward him, a blanket of horrified Threads.

The same horror rushed over the innkeeper's Threads, and her face sank into a scowl. The knife tilted back to its threatening slant. "No plague."

"It's *not* the plague." Iseult pitched those words loud enough for the innkeeper and the nearest patrons to hear. She even rolled her eyes in the most Safi-like way she could manage. "If he were sick, then my sister and I would be sick too. That's how disease works, you know."

The woman did not like Iseult's tone, but she also didn't argue.

"He was injured in the raider attack," Iseult went on, "and the wound hasn't healed well. In fact, if you could point me to a healing clinic, I would be grateful."

After a moment of consideration, the woman's Threads blurred back to acceptance. A curt nod, and she finally set down the knife in exchange for the silver taler still gleaming on the dark counter.

"There's a clinic a few blocks east of here," she said, crooking down to grab a key. "But it's unlikely you'll find anyone to help. Almost all our healers have been pressed into service and sent to the border." When she stood again, the dark sorrow was back in her Threads. "I know what it's like to lose someone to raider violence. Here." She offered Iseult the key, and also a pile of bronze coins. "Room thirteen. Third floor, third door on the left."

"Thank you." The word fluttered out, softer than Iseult

intended. No act, no Threadwitch control. The woman had charged her far less than fifty cleques, and for that she was grateful.

"A word of advice." The woman's chin tipped up. "Keep you and your family hidden. People are saying the Nomatsis have moved to the Raider King's banner. They aren't welcome in Tirla because of it."

Iseult blinked, stunned. "But that's not true. He has been killing *us*."

The woman did not look impressed. "It doesn't have to be true for people to believe it, so stay out of sight and don't make trouble." A bounce of the woman's eyebrows, and before Iseult could even nod, the innkeeper was back to carving her ham.

Sharing a room, Aeduan discovered, was vastly different than sharing a forest.

Through the torture that pulsed within his skull, he could not sort out *why* the walls made a difference—he was technically no closer to the Threadwitch or Owl here than he had been in their little cave the night before. Yet, somehow this space felt a hundred times smaller. A hundred times more crowded.

A low bed sagged beneath a single window, its green coverlet finely made, if well worn. A chipped washbasin with cobalt leaves around the edge rested atop a table near the door, and there was even a warped mirror hanging above it.

Owl was immediately fascinated by the mirror, and Aeduan was grateful to have her distracted. Pain thumped in every organ, every limb, and it banged harder with each passing minute. He could barely keep the coughing at bay. Then there was the blood, an endless seep from not only his old scars, but now the twenty-one new ones. The shirt Iseult had gone to the trouble of cleaning was now stiff and red once more.

At least, he thought as Iseult helped him sit, *I did not get any of my blood on her.* "Thank you," he tried to say as he sank onto the bed, but all that came out was a harsh sigh.

The wood groaned beneath him. The dark-paneled room listed sharply. Then the Threadwitch moved in front of him, a hazy vision of pursed lips and green-golden eyes. Her hands moved to his throat, gentle as always, and it took him a moment to realize she was removing his cloak.

He stiffened. She hesitated. A faint lift of color reached her cheeks. "May I? We need to tend your wounds."

There was that *we* again.

He nodded, and as she eased off the cloak, he realized the problem was not that the room felt too small. No, the problem was that Iseult felt too big. She filled every space in his vision. Every touch, every word, every breath. There was no escaping her.

She folded Aeduan's cloak, acting as if it were not filthy and pocked with holes, before carefully placing it on the floor. Brows drawn in concentration, she twisted back to him. Her fingers reached for the edge of his shirt, as if she intended to tug it from his pants. As if she intended to peel it up over his bare, bleeding chest.

It was too much.

His hands shot to hers. He stilled her fingers where they rested at his hips. "No" was all he said. A mere exhale of a word, but enough. The color on her cheeks fanned brighter. She snatched back her hands. Then pulled her whole body away, angling toward Owl. A split second later, and Iseult was scrabbling away from Aeduan entirely.

"Leave it!" she cried. "That mirror is not for you to pull apart—Owl, *leave it!*"

And Aeduan found a frayed exhale scraping from his lungs. He was more relieved than he cared to admit that Owl was making trouble. The sentiment was short-lived, though, for the actual act of removing his own shirt turned out to be an impossibility—and if he was honest, no longer a priority.

Every muscle in his body screamed. Shadows fringed his sight, and he simply had nothing left to fight them with anymore.

A man is not his mind, he tried to tell himself. The first lesson every monk learned. *A man is not his body. They are merely tools so that a man may fight onward.*

Aeduan's attempts didn't work—and he could no longer deny that Iseult was probably right: the arrows that had struck him had been cursed.

This, he supposed, must be what dying felt like.

"Apparently she can control glass too," Iseult muttered in Dalmotti, twisting back to Aeduan. "Because this child wasn't tiresome enough already . . . Aeduan?" Her face dipped in close. "Aeduan, stay awake—just a little longer. Can you do that?"

"Hmm," he agreed, and though it took monumental effort, he forced his eyelids to stretch high. Forced his spine to straighten.

Iseult's and Owl's wide eyes met his.

"I'll go find a healer now," Iseult went on. "And buy supplies for the road."

"No ..." He swallowed. "There is an outpost for the Monastery in Tirla. I can ... get supplies ... there."

Disbelief widened her eyes. "I thought you were a monk no longer."

He *had* told her that, hadn't he? And he had meant it too, even if the *why* of it from two weeks ago now seemed muddled in his mind.

"You can barely speak," Iseult went on, "much less walk."

"I ... must, though," he argued, wondering why she insisted. Why she cared. "The dead monk ... he requires closure."

"Then I will go report the man's death for you."

For several long moments, Aeduan stared at her, considering. Always, she perplexed him. He had no idea what she might say next. What she might do next. At times, it angered him—she had no right to care. But at other times ...

Well, he did not know precisely. He just knew that he was glad he'd not yet abandoned this course and returned to his father. Glad he had not gone to Lejna or hunted the ghost that smelled of clear lake waters.

"Only monks may enter," he said at last, voice hoarse. Body shamefully frail.

Iseult's nose wiggled. "Fine," she said. "You can visit the outpost later, once you've healed. Rest for now, though. And Owl"—she fixed a stern eye on the girl—"lock the door behind me, and *no* tampering with the mirror while I'm gone."

Several pained breaths later, Iseult left the room. As promised, Owl locked the door with a pointed glance from across the room. The tumbler clicked into place, and Owl crawled onto the bed. She settled cross-legged beside Aeduan, expression expectant. "Story," she said.

It took Aeduan a moment to even comprehend that word: *story*. It was not as if people went around saying it to him often. Or *ever*, really. And it was not as if he knew many to tell six-year-old Earthwitches.

"Monster and the honey," she specified, more insistent now, and this time, she poked him in the biceps.

It hurt. The blackness advanced. He would pass out if he did not do something, and as useless as he was, he did not want to leave the girl all alone in a strange inn where mirrors were begging to be melted apart and remade.

But the monster and the honey . . . It was a tale his father had woven a hundred times when Aeduan was a child—and it was a tale Aeduan refused to ever tell. After all, stories like it were dangerous. They made the hopeless hope and the forgotten dream of being remembered. But the truth was that monsters could never be changed into men, no matter how much honey they might gather.

So Aeduan swallowed, throat aflame, and began a different story. A harmless story. One his mother had told him many times, all those years ago, about a dirty cat trapped in a thunderstorm and the little girl who saved him.

TEN

✳

I t was a song that saved Merik from the shadows. A voice so perfect, he thought surely he must be dead. That this must be the hall of Noden; this must be the chant of His most hallowed lost.

But there was warmth on Merik's face, and when his eyes briefly cracked wide, sunlight pierced in. He instantly screwed them shut again.

Still the voice sang on. Tripping, trilling, soprano words to fill his ears with a language he did not recognize, yet loved all the same. He was the cat in a perfect beam of sunlight. He was warm, he was loved, and he never wanted this music to end. If he was a dead man, then this was the song that would save him.

Shadows skated across the sun, flickering the light behind Merik's eyelids, and a gentle *scritch-scritch-scritch* nudged beneath the music. A familiar sound that brought to mind a similar sunshine, a similar morning breeze kissing his face. And a similar steady beat of footsteps as Aunt Evrane paced her workshop in Nihar, grinding away at a mortar and pestle.

He could almost hear her old rebuke, bouncing on this new singer's song:

> The Fury never forgets
> Whatever you have done
> Will come back to you tenfold,
> And it will haunt you
> Until you make amends.

Dark words, he thought, forcing his eyes open once more. Dark words for such a lovely tune and this lovely warmth surrounding him.

It was not warmth that met his opened eyes, though, nor sunshine, but a tiny, glassless window set high atop a dark, damp stone wall. The sun was still there, but with clouds knotted before it, there was no glare to hide the uneven gray bricks framing the window. No glare to hide the moss fuzzing along the rim, or the bits of braided, beaded yarn—green, yellow, pink, and blue—dangling from above.

Ivy crept along the ceiling, while painted red poppies curled and crawled along the crumbling walls. *Ancient things made new again*, he thought, and with it came the first bolt of panic amidst the song.

Cam. Ryber. The Fury.

Where the hell-waters was he?

Merik tried to jolt up. It hurt—a flashing, skittering pain in his ribs, his stomach, his spine. He instantly gave up and sank back down, but when his neck hit the rough floor, something heavy and hard clacked against it. He jerked upright again, despite the pain, despite the dizziness, and found that a smooth wooden collar encircled his neck. Hanging from an iron latch was an iron lock, and from that lock was a loose-woven iron chain that spooled to the ground before snaking to a hook on the wall.

The world spun. His muscles ached. Merik yanked at that lock—yanked and yanked again.

"That will not work."

So distracted was Merik, he had not noticed the singer had stopped her singing. He had not noticed her approaching from behind. Only now that her words hung in the air beside him did he realize he was no longer alone.

He whirled toward the sound, chain scraping. Distantly, he realized that the walls were curved, that the whole space was rounded, and he was in a small alcove. A tower, he decided. Then he found the speaker's face, and all time, all panic trickled to a stop like the final grains of sand in an hourglass.

She was as beautiful as her voice. Nomatsi, he thought, for she was too unnaturally pale to be Fareastern, but unlike most Nomatsi women, her hair ran down to her waist and was plaited through with bright bits of colorful felt, glistening beads, and even stalks of dried purple heather tucked behind her ear.

"Only I can remove the collar," she said, sweeping into a crouch before him. Her spruce gown swished, the mortar and pestle clanked as she set them beside her feet, and for several endless moments, Merik was caught up in her burning golden eyes. They were not a young woman's eyes.

Ancient things made new again.

It took Merik a moment to realize she spoke in Arithuanian. He wasn't good with that tongue. He could understand it well enough, thanks to Kullen's mother using it when they were young, but actually finding words and forming sentences . . .

"Where?" he wheezed out. It was the best he could do.

But the young woman understood. "You are in my home, Prince Merik Nihar. In Poznin."

Poznin. Impossible. He had been on the other side of the Witchlands only . . . yesterday? Or had it been longer? And what about Cam and Ryber—were they safe?

At Merik's gathering distress, the young woman laughed. A beautiful sound, but . . . *wrong*. Like a shark shouting or a fish crying, this was not meant to tumble from her throat. And the dimple in her right cheek only made it worse.

"I do not need my Loom to read your thoughts, Prince Merik. I can see them as easily as if they were written in your Threads. You are wondering how you got here, yes? That is easily answered." She pushed to her feet, sweeping up the mortar and pestle as she rose. A plume of pale dust trailed behind. "Your friend brought you here. The one who used to be called Kullen before *I* awoke the Fury inside." Another laugh, another chill down Merik's spine.

"The bond you share with him is so strong that you were pulled into the same Cleaved half-life as him—and now, like him, you are *very* hard to kill . . . Though it is not impossible. Which is why you must remain here, Prince. We need the Fury to lead raiders inside the Sleeper's mountain, and we cannot risk you suddenly dying and ruining everything."

That sounded vaguely familiar. On the journey to the Convent, Ryber had said something about a Sleeper . . . and a mountain . . . And *something* about doors and different ways inside.

92

By the Hagfishes, Merik prayed Ryber was all right. Cam too. *Please, Noden. Please.*

"You," Merik tried to say. "Who?"

"My name is Esme, and it is thanks to me that you are still alive. And *this* . . ." She bent forward to tap at the wood screwed around his neck. More dust puffed from the mortar's bowl. "It blocks your magic, so there is no need to try your witchery. On me, or on anyone else."

At those words, the hourglass of Merik's panic snapped around. Sand toppled and spun. He inhaled as deeply as he could, lungs bowing against screaming ribs, and he *pulled* at the power that always lived there. At the air, at the winds, at the currents in the world around him.

He came back with nothing. Nothing but dust from the mortar wafting up his nose. He coughed—which earned more laughter as the young woman skipped away. She returned with a porcelain cup three coughs later.

"Drink," she commanded, and Merik obeyed.

The water, though strongly sulfuric, was perfection against his spasming throat. While he drank, Esme sauntered across the room to a desk heaped with books. Unlit candles in varying states of decay slouched on every available space: the desk, the floor, on stones pushing free from the wall, and on the sill of a larger window overlooking the cloud-spun sky.

An evening sky, he guessed. Still, though, he summoned the words from his thick skull: "What . . . day is it?"

"On the Nomatsi calendar, it is the twenty-seventh day beneath the Eight Moon. On the first people's calendar—the ones who lived here a thousand years ago—we are on the twenty-seventh day of Storms." Esme peeked back at Merik, a sly smile on her lips. "But I imagine, simple as you are, Prince, that you wish to know the day on the 'common' calendar." She rolled her eyes. "Such a word implies ease and choice, doesn't it? But in truth the *common* calendar was forced upon us with whips and chains."

Throughout this long speech, Merik said nothing. Showed nothing on his face beyond the truth of pain in his ribs and spine. Even his unfocused gaze he kept pointed toward Esme, so that she would not sense how he took note of every space in the tower, every possible weapon or potential tool. She had referred to Threads, so she must be some kind of Threadwitch— which would also explain the assortment of stones piled on a low table beneath the main window.

She had also mentioned awakening the Fury inside Kullen. *That* was a question Merik would have to poke at later, though.

"On the *common* calendar," Esme finished, "we are on the two hundred and forty-third day in the nineteenth year since the signing of the Twenty Year Truce."

So Merik had lost only a few hours, then. Kullen must have flown his unconscious body directly here after destroying that stone, which meant he had not attempted to hunt down Ryber or Cam. One small boon amidst this maddening storm.

After draining the final sips of water, Merik cleared his throat. "They . . . will have to start again."

At Esme's puzzled look, Merik wondered if perhaps he had chosen the wrong words or conjugated improperly. But then the young woman's expression cleared, and her delighted, spine-twisting laugh skipped out once more. She even plunked down her mortar and pestle to clap her hands.

"You mean the calendar! They will have to start it

again—yes, yes, they will, for the Truce has ended. *Oh*, how fun. You actually have a brain, Prince. I would never have guessed it to look at you, but you are not like my other Cleaved, are you?" Another clap, and this time she hopped to her feet to prance toward a stack of books at the opposite wall.

My other Cleaved. With that phrase, a thousand questions clamored to life in Merik's brain. Who this woman was, why she possessed Cleaved—or for that matter, *how* she possessed Cleaved . . . And why she'd spoken of Merik as if he were one of them.

More troubling, though, was the fact that Merik felt no alarm. No panic like before. Only a gathering warmth behind his lungs and a slow dissipation of the pain.

"It makes sense, I suppose," she went on, snagging a worn tome off the pile. "You are not directly bound to my Loom, and I did not cleave you intentionally like the rest of my servants. Nor did I fully cleave your Threadbrother. I *tried* to." She flipped open the book, her sigh brushing atop flapping pages. "But he is made of so many people and so many ancient Threads, it was not as simple as I had thought it would be. Ah, but now that *you* are here, Prince . . ."

She spun toward Merik, eyes wide and finger tapping at some page he could not see. Though he thought he should be able to. She was not so far away. He blinked. The room blurred.

"Now that you are here, Prince, I shall fill in all the gaps that this diary failed to explain. Magic is not what it was when Eridysi first ran her experiments. Your collar, my Loom—I have had to modify and adjust everything. But now that you are here ... *Ah,* there is so much for us to explore. I wish I had not added the sleeping draught to your water! For then we could have started right away."

Ah, Merik thought as cozy sleep charged in, pulling him to the ground in a clank of wood and chains. *She drugged me. How nice.*

ELEVEN

※

Never had Vivia seen a city so large.

Though tens of leagues away, Azmir consumed the horizon like wildfire across the plains. City of the Golden Spires, City of Eternal Flame. This city—and the enormous, expanding canyon around it—had as many absurd titles as its empress. And all of them, she had to admit, were deserved. From the striped canyon walls that ascended into the Kendura Hills to the whitecapped Sirmayans beyond, from the crowded wharves that clustered halfway across Lake Scarza to the Floating Palace on its red-earthed island at the center, Vivia had never seen or imagined any place like this.

As the six Windwitches carried Vivia ever closer to the imperial capital, the hard angles of its towers came into bright focus under the sun. It was ten times the size of Lovats—twenty times, even, and with a hundred smaller villages to dot the surrounding hills. Yet it was not the scale that stunned Vivia. Fresh, clean, *standing*, Azmir looked as if it had been built only a year before, even though she knew it to be centuries old.

As the Floating Palace rushed in closer, a white wonder

of towers broken up by bursts of green, Vivia's stomach snagged. She tried to blame her spinning vision and wobbling knees on the descent, but once she landed, she still felt like hurling. Like charging for the nearest cypress trees and hiding far from sight.

For there was nothing, *nothing* that this lush, vibrant empire could possibly want from Vivia or Nubrevna. When it came to trade or treaties, Marstok had all of the advantages and none of the shames.

No regrets. Keep moving. She was here; she had power; she would not waste this trip.

Vivia smoothed at her silver coat before yanking off her goggles and attempting to tame her hair. It did not comply.

Meanwhile, sixteen women and men in green uniforms now marched toward her. None carried more than a single sword at their hips, and most carried no weapon at all. Which meant these guards were purely ceremonial—no show of threat, nor even a show of power. This was a polite welcoming party, and the Empress did not wish to scare Vivia away.

It wasn't working.

"Your Highness," said a woman at the fore, and in absolute coordination, the soldiers bowed low. "Her Imperial Majesty awaits you in her personal quarters."

Personal quarters, Vivia thought as she beckoned for her own people to follow. The Empress was truly going out of her way to keep Vivia at ease.

And Vivia *truly* did not like it. She felt like the crab lured into the kitchen pot. The waters might start out cool and blissful, but outside the copper, flames were cranking higher.

Vivia's sense of unease only increased as she followed the

soldiers through a garden brimming with rhododendrons (that should have stopped blooming months ago), between two marble columns delicately carved to look like tree trunks, and finally into the actual palace.

They encountered none of the imperial bodyguards known as Adders in the stark, marble halls, nor any more soldiers than the ones leading Vivia. Only servants passed by, and they were quick to duck aside and bow.

Perhaps most unsettling of all were the frequent clay basins filled with water. Twelve of them, actually, at every turn in the hall or every intersection. There were no lilies or fish within the basins, and the clay did not match the iron decor everywhere else—the iron planters for the lemon trees, the iron sconces for Firewitched flame, the iron wind chimes with no wind to ever hit them.

Once again, it was as if Empress Vaness were saying, *Look! I have given you water for your witchery. You are safe! Relax!*

Vivia did not think she could be any less relaxed, and as a curved doorway appeared at the end of the hall, framed with Adders and two more clay basins, Vivia had to concentrate on simply keeping her feet moving forward.

She should not have come here. Oh, Noden, *why* had she come here? This was a terrible idea, and those sad little buckets of water were not enough to save her from anything.

Ten paces before the door, the welcome guard split into two perfect rows. They said nothing as Vivia and her Windwitches strode past, so Vivia did not slow.

Clack, clack, clack. Her boots drummed out a funeral dirge. Though the Marstoks watched her, she couldn't help but brush

99

at her coat, tug at her cuffs, and lastly, pat along the edges of her face until the Nihar frown that Merik wore so easily had settled into place.

When Vivia was almost to the Empress's door, it swung open, so silently it must have been oiled yesterday. Or maybe it was oiled every day in a place as wealthy as this one.

Beyond, afternoon sunlight streamed. Beyond, waited the Empress of Marstok. And beyond, Vivia *prayed*, was not proof that she should never have come here.

She crossed the threshold.

Once, as a child, Vivia's aunt had shown her a music box. From Dalmotti, the thing had been bewitched to only open at Evrane's touch. At the time, it was the most beautiful thing Vivia had ever seen—white with gold edges—and when the box's lid had cranked up and the tune had twinkled out, she'd felt transported to another world. A world where she did not need masks, and where no one would ever try to hurt her or steal what wasn't theirs.

For a brief instant, as the sunlight caressed her, as the white simplicity of the space settled into her vision and wind chimes rang from a terrace across the room, Vivia felt that same sense of beauty. Of safety and peace. Here the little fox could be the little fox forever.

Yet just as Evrane had snapped shut the music box and scolded Vivia for holding it too long, as soon as Vaness swept into Vivia's view, the world—that perfect, untouchable world—gusted away.

"Your Highness," Vaness said as she entered from the terrace. Her black silk gown floated around her, a simple dress with a high neck, capped sleeves, and skirts just short enough to expose slippered feet. She bobbed her head, and Vivia matched the movement, if awkwardly.

Hell-waters, the Empress was smaller than she remembered. Vivia suddenly felt as large as a sea fox and a hundred times less graceful.

"Your officers may wait here, if that is acceptable." The Empress spoke in smooth, if thickly accented Nubrevnan. She motioned to several white-cushioned chairs against the wall. Orchids dangled between them, and at Vivia's nod, her people stiffly took seats.

They looked absurd. Navy uniforms and wind-blustered hair against the gossamer elegance of the palace.

"Let us speak on the terrace," the Empress suggested. Then she walked purposefully away, leaving Vivia time to murmur, "Wait here. You know what to do if anything goes wrong."

Subtle salutes followed, and Vivia found her lips quirking. Good officers, these Windwitches. Though she missed having Stix at her side, she didn't doubt for a second that each of these soldiers was reliable.

On the terrace, Vivia found two iron chairs and an iron table set with sugared figs and a pitcher of water. Nothing elaborate, and no servants or Adders in sight. In fact, the only view was of a tall clay wall around the terrace, and cypress trees clustered within an herb garden that filled the air with sage and lavender.

Vaness made no move to sit, and as the moments trickled by, she openly studied Vivia. Inspected her from top to bottom, no embarrassment in her gaze, and no judgment either.

Vivia let her. She even went so far as to clasp her hands behind her back and stare right back. The truth was that acting like two bitches sniffing bottoms in an alley was much easier than the polite diplomatic nothings Vivia's mother had taught her.

"You have . . . grown," Vaness said eventually. "I believe the last I saw you, you had not yet developed."

"You had," Vivia replied, and it was true. The single time she and Vaness had encountered each other—ten years ago—Vivia had still been a girl, but Vaness had been a woman grown.

She had been stunning, even at age seventeen, and she was even more stunning now. Especially as a slight smile toyed across her lips.

"Let us sit." Vaness eased onto the iron chair, her posture perfect. "We have much to discuss."

"Hye," Vivia agreed, and for half a breath, she debated mimicking the Empress's grace. Everything felt so soft, so dainty, so far removed from everything that Vivia was . . . and yet somehow, everything Vivia wanted to be.

But no, she was not here to be cowed. She was not here to be manipulated. She was here for Nubrevna, and nothing more. So as she sat with the same brusqueness she would use around any of her soldiers, and as she patted once more at the edges of her face, she summoned her inner bear. "We *do* have much to discuss," she declared. "Such as, first and foremost, what exactly in Noden's watery Hell am I doing here?"

Tucked within a hollowed-out wall, Safi watched the Empress of Marstok face off with the newly named Queen-in-Waiting of Nubrevna.

Until this morning, Safi had thought she preferred the throne room for this sort of work. Her legs might grow stiff from standing, but at least she was in the open. At least sunlight and fresh air could wash against her skin. Now she realized that darkness was better. The heat and the walls and the lack of anyone to look at her or await a declaration of *true* or *false*—that was better. That was safer.

Every day since arriving in Azmir, Safi had spent at least an hour in a stifling space somewhere. There was this one, a second in the imperial dining room, and a third in the vast amphitheater where the Sultanate met each day to handle the infrastructural and economic problems of the empire.

Normally, there were too many voices to keep up with. Normally, Safi had to rely on her gut to sense decay in the room. Of course, until today, there had been no decay, and although Bayrum of the Shards might have been the first, Safi was sure he wouldn't be the last.

So, as long as Safi was in this wall, then she did not have to fear her magic. She did not have to fear another sudden death. She could listen, she could evaluate, and she could choose her words carefully. Perhaps best of all, though, was that in the darkness, Safi could work.

She had already taken twelve books from the Empress's personal library, and she had even taken *notes* on one of them. Iseult would have been wildly impressed. The book, *Crafting Painstones*, had seemed a logical starting point, and the text covered Painstones as well as bewitched tonics and tinctures. Healers, Safi had learned, embedded their power into the act of creation itself.

And that had given her an idea: if she could hold a piece

of quartz while using her own powers, maybe she too could *embed* her power into the rock.

Vaness had kindly provided her with a fresh wedge of rose quartz as well as a handful of other gemstones—no questions asked, thank the gods—and now Safi was setting her plan in motion. She let her magic swell to the surface as she watched on.

And what Safi saw was utterly enthralling. In fact, she had no idea how she had *ever* considered Vaness boring. Now, she was anything but the Empress of Insipid.

Never in Safi's life had she seen two such women competing for space in a room. She'd seen plenty of men do it, clucking about like roosters in a yard. And she had seen men try—and fail—to bend women whose spines were made of steel.

This was something else entirely. It was two women a thousandfold stronger than any man, each with agendas all their own and witcheries that could slay. They stood like rivals in a Cartorran pugilist's ring, but instead of tile and sand to cloak the earth between them, an iron table and water carafes waited. Weapons for the taking.

The wind chimes twinkled, a soft prelude to what would certainly be a symphonic explosion. To compound the tension of it all, Safi's magic trembled as truth and lie crashed against her in unison. Both women rang with honest clarity; both women grated with practiced falsehood.

The symphony began.

"The reason you are in my 'blighted city,'" Vaness declared, "is because the last time I saw you, you were stealing one of my ships."

104

"And the last time I saw you," Vivia countered, "you had sabotaged one of your ships so that I would steal it."

"A distraction." Vaness flipped up a hand. "I wanted the cargo your brother carried. It was worth the price of those weapons."

True, murmured Safi's magic—and she imagined pouring that truth straight into her quartz.

Vivia seemed to also sense Vaness's honesty, for she stiffened, briefly, as if surprised. "You mean it was worth losing your weapons to claim this Truthwitch you supposedly have. Let us see her then, if she is so special."

"So that you can steal *her* from me too?"

"Perhaps." A casual shrug from the Queen-in-Waiting. "Tell me: was she worth the cost of war?"

"Tell me: were my weapons?" The Empress's eyebrows bounced high. "Your actions were the first to risk the Twenty Year Truce. It was pure chance that the magic in the document deemed *my* act the greater crime."

"I stole a ship. You landed on Nubrevnan soil with soldiers. I think the magic gauged properly."

"Says the woman who turned her own navy into pirates."

"Says the woman who freed my Foxes from a Saldonican prison." Vivia thrust out her chin. "Why did you do that?"

"Because the Truthwitch asked me to." Vaness plucked an invisible hair off her gown. "*I* would have left them to rot."

"And why would *she* have asked you to do it?" Vivia pressed. "Why would she care?"

"For the same reason she asked me to negotiate a treaty with Nubrevna in exchange for her peaceful surrender. Something, or perhaps *someone*, connects her to your homeland."

"Merik," Vivia said, and with that name, Safi forgot all about her plan. All about her magic or her stone.

In the two weeks since she had learned of Merik's death, there were moments—like right now—when his face would bubble to the surface. The way he'd looked at her on that moonlit cliff in Nubrevna, part longing, part awe ... and even part regret, for their short time together had seen them pitted as enemies. It was only as they were parting ways that they seemed to realize they were better off as friends.

Or perhaps as *more* than friends.

But now Merik was gone, and Safi would never know what might have been.

"I have brought you here," Vaness said, "to finish my bargain with the Truthwitch."

"What's in that for you?"

"Nothing is in it for me, but I made a promise to her, and I never break my promises."

"I see." Vivia spread her hands wide. "Originally, you would only treat with my brother. Now he is dead, so you are forced to treat with me—even though we both know that you and I will ultimately negotiate nothing. You will still come out with clean hands, because, after all, you *tried*."

"Absolutely not." Vaness bristled, a reaction so true it caught Safi by surprise. Never did the Empress let her mask slip.

And suddenly Safi remembered her plan once more. She focused on her magic; she focused on the quartz; she focused on the conversation.

"Surely Nubrevnans possess something," Vaness said, "that is worth trading for."

"You know my nation has nothing to offer."

"No, I do not know that." Vaness sucked in a long breath, examining the Queen-in-Waiting. "You are a fascinating case study," she said. "It takes a great deal of audacity to make a move such as piracy."

"More like desperation."

A soft chuckle from Vaness—again, humming with truth in a way that threw Safi off guard. "I appreciate," Vaness continued, "that you do not try to hide the reality of your circumstances from me. No attempts to inflate what you have."

"What would be the point?" Vivia shrugged. "You know the true state of Nubrevna. You have spies."

"Not as many as you might think," Vaness countered. "Your house is difficult to infiltrate. You instill an incredible amount of loyalty among your people."

"Perhaps. When they are willing to look past my gender." Vivia glanced toward the door, beyond which her officers waited. Impatience shivered off her. She tugged at her coat collar and adjusted her cuffs.

Right as she directed her gaze once more to the Empress, though, Rokesh materialized from the cypress trees. He stalked into the sunlight.

Before Safi could even blink, two ropes of water had lashed from the carafe and were racing toward the Adder.

"*Stop*," Vaness barked.

The water stopped. And Rokesh stopped too, dropping to one knee—though out of respect or to avoid the attacks, Safi could not say.

"What game are you playing?" Vivia snarled, her water whips steady.

"No game," Vaness snapped. Then to Rokesh: "Why do you interrupt?"

"My apologies, Empress." Rokesh bent his head to his knee. "There is an emergency that requires Safiya."

Ah. Safi straightened inside the wall, fingers crushing around the quartz. It would seem she was needed elsewhere. *Please don't be the throne room. Please don't be someone corrupted.*

"We have a guest," Rokesh explained, "and I presume you will want to assess him for untruths."

"Who is it?" Impatience steamed off the Empress. "No family was meant to arrive today."

"This man is not family. He is a former Firewitch general, and it seems he has decided to end his retirement." Rokesh glanced in Safi's direction, his eyes briefly catching hers through the spyhole. "Habim Fashayit awaits you in the library, Your Imperial Majesty, and he claims he is here to help us win the war."

TWELVE

※

Iseult was glad to be away from the inn. Glad to be away from Aeduan and the girl who never listened.

That room was much too small for them. The nearness of Aeduan . . . and Owl too . . . had addled her mind. Or maybe it was the cleaved Firewitch that steeped her blood with his flames. Or maybe it was simply exhaustion or the sudden, unsettling need to keep her face hidden.

No matter the cause for her idiocy, Iseult was still scolding herself by the time she reached the healer's packed clinic. She could not *believe* she had thought to remove Aeduan's shirt. It was one thing to pull off a man's clothes and tend his wounds when he was unconscious. It was quite another when he stared back at you, breath catching and eyes blazing.

Something had wrestled in her chest at the sight of him like that. His hands resting over hers. Something she didn't recognize, at once fiery and frozen.

It *still* wrestled. Goddess, what had she been thinking?

Iseult practically ran through the streets of Tirla, shame chasing fast at her heels, and haggling over healing supplies was a welcome distraction. She bought salves and tinctures, bandages and gauze, and unlike the innkeeper, the harried attendants had no problem with Iseult's silver taler. Unfortunately, though, an extra silver taler would not get her name moved up on the fourteen-page list for a healer's visit. She scribbled her name at the end anyway, though the odds were not in Aeduan's favor that the lone healer would come before they departed.

Hopefully their new supplies would be enough to keep the curse away. At least until a better solution presented itself.

As Iseult ducked back into the tangling traffic of the day, she was struck by a tightness behind her ribs. A sharp pang that skittered atop her heartbeat. *Regret*, she decided after a moment. But no, that wasn't quite it. This was a softer pain, laced with something almost like . . . like hunger.

It wasn't until Iseult passed a Purist holding a *Repent!* sign that she finally pinpointed the feeling. *Homesickness*. Tirla was so much like Veñaza City. Cleaner certainly. Colder too, and with green-clad soldiers to thicken the crowds, but it still felt like home. A few hours here and already she'd found her weft inside the city's weave. The noise was no longer a bother but instead a comfort, as reliable as the tides, and checking her hood was once again second nature.

What if, what if, what if—for the past month, that question had come to her at least once a day while her fingers clung white-knuckled to her Threadstone. Always it hit in the lulls between chaos, when no threat hounded Iseult's heels. When there was too much time for her brain to flitter to the past and catalog all she had left behind. When there was nothing to keep her mind from wishing—and wondering—what might have happened if she and Safi had never pulled that roadside heist north of Veñaza City.

What if, what if, what if. A useless refrain with no satisfying answers. For without the misfired holdup, Iseult and Safi would never have drawn Aeduan's mercenary attention—and without that, she would never have returned home to the Midenzi tribe. Then she would never have been cursed and fled for Nubrevna, where she would never have encountered the Origin Well . . .

And she would never have learned that she might be half of the Cahr Awen. That she and Safi might be the mythical pair of legend meant to heal the Origin Wells and cleanse the world of evil.

Iseult would never have made a bargain with Aeduan—whose Carawen order was meant to protect the Cahr Awen—and they would never have saved Owl from the Red Sail pirates. Then she would not be here now, chest hollowed out while she towed healing supplies through a foreign city that did not feel so foreign at all.

In fact, if Iseult let her gaze drop to the cobblestones, let her awareness settle back and her witchery guide her through the throngs, she could almost pretend she was on her way to meet Safi. That at any moment, her Threadsister would shove in close, grumbling about the crowds, and they'd head for Mathew's shop. Why, that storefront over there looked just like his, right down to the sign declaring *Real Marstoki Coffee, Best in Tirla*.

Iseult halted midstride, heart punching into her throat. It couldn't be. It *couldn't* be. Surely she would not be so lucky as to find one of Mathew's coffee shops here. She had lived for over six years in Mathew's shop in Veñaza City, training with the Wordwitch confidence man—and with his Heart-Thread Habim too.

Hugging her sack close, Iseult cut across the street and in a flurry of speed—of desperation, even—she shoved through the shop's front door. It was like coming home. First came the smell of coffee, rich and rounded against her nostrils. Then the color hit her eyes, the rugs, the tapestries, and the pillows all arranged exactly as they were in Veñaza City. Even the people lounging on sofas and low stools looked the same. Even the porcelain cups from which they drank *looked the same*.

This was his. This was Mathew's, and that meant she could contact him. Oh, Iseult could not believe her good fortune—the Moon Mother had blessed her today indeed. She hurried toward a high counter at the back of the room, where a young woman with skin as dark as the coffee she ground and Threads an attentive green glanced up at Iseult's approach.

"Would you like to order?" she asked, her Marstoki accented like Habim's was—which meant she was from the capital. "You can order a full carafe or by the cup."

Iseult slowed to a stop before the counter. Excitement was making her tongue fat. She had to swallow. Then swallow again before she could say, "I-is Mathew fitz Leaux in?"

A beat passed. The woman's Threads stretched taut with turquoise surprise. Then tan wariness. Then finally a shuddering mixture of the two. She set down her cylindrical grinder and scooted aside the bowl in which the grounds had been gathering, all while her gaze swept up Iseult. Down.

"It's . . . you." She spoke in Marstoki, but then she hastily shifted to accented Dalmotti. "Welcome. It is good to see you, Iseult det Midenzi."

Now it was Iseult's turn to feel surprise and wariness. Only

112

years of training kept her from reeling back. "You . . . know me?"

"Of course! Every shop has been told to look for you. Though I will admit, I did not think you would walk into mine. But, oh—wait here!" The woman's hands flung up, beseeching. "I have a message for you." She spun in a cloud of saffron skirts and disappeared into a back room.

The woman returned in less time than it took the nearest patron to drain his cup, and excited streaks of color had gathered on her cheeks and in her Threads. Iseult could only assume there was some kind of reward for finding her.

She liked the idea of that. It made warmth chuckle in her chest and a grin play along her lips. When she caught sight of Mathew's familiar handwriting on a slip of beige paper, she let the grin rush in. Full force, ear to ear, not worthy of a Threadwitch, and she didn't care.

Seeing her name in Mathew's scrawl was nice. So, *so* nice.

> *Iseult,*
> *Stay put. Wherever you are, I will send one of our people to meet you. They will then guide you to where you need to be.*
> *I am sorry things went awry in Veñaza City.*
> *Much love,*
> *Mathew*

After reading the letter once, Iseult's smile faltered. After two reads, it withered away entirely. And on the third read-through, she found her cheeks had scrunched into a frown. Surely this was not all he had to say. *Surely* there was a coded message hidden within the words—a common trick of Mathew's—or ... or perhaps some implied message tucked away. *Say one thing and mean another.* It had been a favorite game for Iseult and Safi.

Yet when, after the sixth reading, Iseult still found nothing, she was forced to accept that this was the entirety of the message. *This* was all Mathew had felt he needed to share.

Lightning gathered in Iseult's shoulders as she read it for the seventh time. *Things have gone awry? That is the best description a Wordwitch can find?* Things had gone so much worse than awry—and he hadn't even mentioned the spectacular mayhem that had crashed upon her since Lejna. Yet now Mathew expected Iseult to simply "stay put" and wait for one of his "people" to meet her. Well, they had told her to do the same in Veñaza City, then again in Lejna, and look how well her waiting had turned out.

"'Guide you to where you need to be,'" she whispered to herself, the squall now pushing up her neck. As far as she could see, where she needed to be was tending Aeduan. She *needed* to be helping him find Owl's family, as they had agreed, and after that, where she *needed* to be was at Safi's side.

Iseult loved Mathew and Habim. Fiercely. They were her Thread-family, and nothing in this world mattered more than Thread-family. But she was tired of being treated like some Fool card in the taro deck, to be tossed into the game whenever it was needed. Safi too had been played against her will, and now she was trapped in Marstok while Iseult was an impossible distance away.

With a long inhale, Iseult screwed her Threadwitch calm back into place. At least on the surface—at least for this young lady to see. "I am staying at the White Alder," she said, words smooth as a sandy shore at low tide. "Room thirteen. If someone needs to find me, they can look there. However," she added, arching an eyebrow in her best imitation of Safi, "they had better hurry. I leave Tirla soon, and I have no plans to 'stay put' longer than that."

The first hints of sunset greeted Iseult by the time she left Mathew's shop. Dusk came early in the mountains, and ringing chimes heralded the seventeenth hour as she returned to the White Alder.

Twelve beats in, Iseult realized she was being followed.

The first thing Habim had drilled into Iseult when she'd begun training six and a half years ago was to constantly—*constantly*—make note of who was around her. Every few heartbeats, she would sink into her magic and sense the weave of the city. The placement of its Threads.

Clang, clang. No one was following her. *Clang, clang.* Someone was. They were clever about it, though. Subtle and sly, staying just far enough back that if Iseult were to turn her head, she would see nothing out of the ordinary. But there was no hiding Threads, and this person's were unmistakable.

They gleamed more brightly than anyone else's on the street, like a flame burning in a field of wheat. Except this flame was dark green. This person was focused, and this person was hunting.

Learn your opponents. Learn your terrain. Choose your battle-fields when you can. Habim's second lesson tickled in Iseult's ear as if her mentor stood right beside her. Iseult didn't know

115

this city, though, so learning her terrain and choosing a battle-field was impossible. For now, simple escape would have to be her aim.

Rather than calm her, though, having a plan seemed to stir her blood faster. There was only one person who had any desire to hunt her—and he had already hired men to do so. Likely, he was near Tirla too, since his arrows had cursed Aeduan only yesterday.

Corlant. This person following Iseult might not be that Purist priest, but she had no doubt her pursuer worked for him.

No, no, *no.* He had not gotten her at the Midenzi tribe. He had not gotten her in the Contested Lands. He would not get her now.

With a sudden twist, Iseult ducked down a side street. Wind-flags whipped overhead. As she'd expected, the man's Threads gave pursuit. Three steps, and her pursuer turned too—but Iseult did not run. She did not shove at the crowds. Soldiers lurked on every corner in Tirla, and their uniforms mottled the evening traffic to green.

Her skin, her hair . . . she couldn't risk drawing attention.

She reached another street and spun around a wagon of cabbages, then hurried—faster, faster—across a blacksmith's front stoop. Heat billowed out from the open double doors. A woman shouted at her to come see her wares.

That shout—it reminded Iseult of a different chase in a different city. She had leaped from boat to boat to escape Aeduan that day. Perhaps she could do something similar now. No canals here, but there were carriages. And though she could not hop across them, she *could* use them for escape.

Red-topped carriage to the left. Too fine. *Chicken cart to the right.* Too foul. *Refugee caravan coming behind.* Perfect. It had three covered wagons, drawn by mules. Only the second and third wagons, though, had people crowded inside. Their Threads were almost colorless. A sign that loss and grief had numbed them to feeling.

Iseult slowed her pace, veering right so she could fall into step beside the caravan. Seconds plodded past; her pulse boomed inside her skull. *Threads still following. Almost here, almost here—*

The mules reached her, ambling and tired, and Iseult made her move. She circled behind the first wagon. A lift of a canvas flap, and she scrambled inside. Everything these people could carry had been stuffed inside the wagon, leaving Iseult's body to bulge against the canvas. But the driver of the caravan could not see her, and her hunter did not either.

The person's Threads had stopped at the edge of the intersection, and tawny confusion was rapidly taking hold. Red frustration too. Then they moved. Then stopped. Then moved. Then spun.

Iseult couldn't help but grin, her fingers moving to her Threadstone. Safi would have been proud of her. Habim too, although he might have scolded her for not getting a better look at her opponent. *Never rely on magic or weapons,* he used to say. *They can always be taken away.*

Fine, fine, she thought, and ever so carefully, she peeled back the canvas and found Threads bright as sunshine.

Their owner was as bright as sunshine too, his skin and curling hair a gleaming gold that Safi would have fallen boots over brains for.

Trickster. The name flitted across Iseult's mind—the Moon Mother's youngest, most devious brother, with the coloring of the sun but lucent shimmer of the moon. Like this young man, Trickster always wore pale gray. The color of dawn, of dusk, of the dappled forests in which he hid.

In the stories, Trickster was the most dangerous of the family, his loyalties as fickle as the breezes he loved to ride. Luckily, those were just stories, though—while this man was very real.

Iseult let the flap fall back into place. She would remember that man's face. She would remember his Threads too.

If they ever met again, she would be ready.

THIRTEEN

✳

Habim Fashayit.

General Habim Fashayit.

Uncle Eron's man-at-arms, the mentor who had trained Safi to fight and raised her like a father. Who had taught her to be a wolf in a world of rabbits. He was here in Azmir. Here in the imperial palace. And he was a general.

Safi had always known Habim must have been an officer of some kind for the Marstoki armed forces. When, after years of badgering, neither Habim nor Eron nor even Mathew had ever opened up about Habim's specific past, though—or about how he'd ended up in the employ of a Cartorran dom— Safi had eventually stopped wondering and simply accepted Habim as he was: stern, implacable, a skilled fighter, an even more skilled tactician, and prone to assigning *far* too many essays on the history of warfare.

Between one heartbeat and the next, all of Safi's childhood questions blazed back to life, a thousand times hotter than they'd ever been ten years ago. Her whole chest felt aflame. She wanted to laugh, she wanted to skip, she wanted to grab her Threadstone and scream at Iseult, wherever she might be,

119

that Habim Fashayit was here! *General* Habim Fashayit was here in Azmir! In the imperial palace!

Never had Safi been so glad for shadows and solitude. For a moment to react in private before anyone saw her face.

The tiny trapdoor that led into the wall clicked behind Safi. Afternoon air twined against her. She gulped it in, smoothing her face into the same expression she always wore around Rokesh and the Empress: dutiful focus, blank disinterest. After a quick check that her attempted Truthstone was tucked into a pocket, she swiveled toward the Adder.

He said nothing, so she said nothing, and once she was out of the wall, the remainder of her Adder guards stepped into tight formation around her. They crossed into the main garden. Sunshine poured over Safi's face, and the midday breeze carried the scent of roses, lilac, and honeysuckle. Insects whirred while birds chirruped from the bushes and the trees.

Situated upon three terraced levels, the imperial gardens overlooked Lake Scarza's glittering blue waters, offering a full view of crowded Azmir on the sunlit shore. Usually, Safi savored these walks—a chance to be outside in the open. Right now, though, she only had space for Habim.

Goat tits, she wished the Adders would walk faster. Habim was so near. *Move, Nursemaid, move.*

Finally, after crossing the top level, they reached a familiar marble terrace where a fountain bubbled and wind chimes rang. Then they were to the sloping entrance into Vaness's private library, where Safi had come only a few hours before.

No pause, no break in stride while the Adders—and Safi—coasted inside. Shelves lined the walls, every spine bound in matching garnet leather. Books lay stacked upon desks and honey satin chairs. And of course, iron adorned every spare inch: in the sconces, on the table legs, and around the shelf frames. It was a library fit for an empress, for an Ironwitch.

Two doors led out of the library. One made of oak carved with sunbursts that fed into Safi's and Vaness's quarters. Safi knew this door; she had used it. The *other*, a simple door barely large enough to duck through, led to the Empress's personal office. It was a space Safi had been expressly forbidden to enter. Guest status, it would seem, only carried one so far.

It was to this door they now marched, and excitement wound hotter in Safi's belly. Her hands were sweating too. *Stasis*, she told herself, just as Iseult always did. *Stasis in your fingers and in your toes.*

Rokesh moved to the lead, and after he pushed open the simple door and slunk through, Safi was able to follow inside.

It was not what she expected. Where the rest of the Floating Palace was marble or sandstone tile with wide windows to stream in light, this room was paneled with oak stained almost black—and with no windows at all. Candle chandeliers hung from an arched ceiling, their waxes and wicks all perfectly sized and burning with smokeless Firewitched flame.

Then Safi glimpsed Habim across the room, straight-backed and staring at her from familiar line-seamed eyes. He stood opposite a long table, its surface covered by an intricate relief of the Witchlands.

Habim did not meet Safi's gaze. Instead he strode around the table and declared, "This is not the Empress."

Safi's eyes prickled at the sound of his gravelly voice. Gods below, it was good to hear it. *Stasis. Do what Iz would do.*

"The Empress is detained." Rokesh bowed low. Then he sidestepped and motioned to Safi.

Habim gave her an appraising glance. "You must be the Truthwitch, then."

"Yes," Safi said, though her voice almost cracked. His scrutiny, his eyes raking up, raking down. It was so customary, so *Habim*. The grim slant to his lips, the slight pucker between his brows. Her whole life, he had looked at her to assess her weaknesses. Right now, though, she felt he was assessing her strengths. Her health, her safety.

No doubt he wondered why she had new scars above her eyebrow and on her thumb. Or why her hair only reached her shoulders—or why she clearly favored standing on one leg instead of the stable, even stance he'd raised her with. And there was no missing how his eyes caught on the iron belt at her waist and steel chain around her neck.

Habim had come to Azmir for Safi. That truth swelled inside her chest, and suddenly, Safi's eyes burned even more. She forced herself to pull back her shoulders and puff out her chest.

"I am the Truthwitch," she said, louder. Full of the domna training *he* had instilled in her. "May I ask who you are?"

Habim sniffed, angling back to Rokesh. "This child's presence means you do not trust me. I expected a better welcome, Adder."

Rokesh opened his gloved hands. Part apology, part shrug. "Nineteen years in retirement is a long time, General."

"And it would have been longer if the Twenty Year Truce

had not ended so suddenly." He snapped a hand toward miniature troops, ships, and supply chains placed across the table. "I had thought Her Imperial Majesty possessed a steadier head than her parents, yet breaking the Truce to claim a young woman who is rumored to be a Truthwitch . . ." His chest expanded with a deep inhale, as if he were tamping down the urge to shout.

A lie, though. It was all a *lie*, and inwardly, Safi beamed.

Then his breath hissed out from clenched teeth, and he added: "Let us hope you were worth it, child."

Child. Safi didn't have to fake her eye roll at that.

Rokesh, however, only laughed. His eyes crinkled in his shroud. "Ask him your questions, Truthwitch, and let the general see your full worth."

Just like that, Safi's breath snagged in her throat, for asking those questions was the last thing she wanted to do. Suddenly her hands shook. Suddenly she saw blood and bile and stains along a floor.

She wiped her palms against her thighs, and beside her, Rokesh's shoulders sank ever so slightly. He eased nearer, until his veiled face was mere inches from hers. "I can ask the questions," he murmured. "If that would make it easier."

Safi bit her lip. It *would* make it easier, but there would also be no point. If she couldn't do this with Habim—with one of the only men in all the Witchlands she truly trusted—then she would never be able to do it again. And she *had* to do it again. It was why she was here; it was the only way she could leave.

Unless I can make a Truthstone.

She slipped a shivering hand into her pocket and pinched the quartz between thumb and forefinger. She *could* embed her magic into this rock. And she *could* ask Habim her three questions.

Gradually, her lungs relaxed. "Thank you, Nursemaid," she said at last, "but I can manage."

There it was again, that smile to crease in Rokesh's eyes. Then he nodded and backed away.

Safi turned to Habim. She turned to her mentor.

"Are you aware of the peace treaty with the Baedyeds?" The words lobbed out, controlled, and a thousand miles away. Mathew had trained her for this. She wouldn't let him or Habim down.

"Yes," Habim answered simply. "I heard rumors from officers with whom I still correspond, and then I heard confirmation of this treaty when I reached the capital."

To Safi's surprise, all of these statements rang with honesty. Habim *had* heard, and he *had* been in contact with other officers.

Habim wasn't finished yet, though. "The entire thing was poorly handled." He directed this to Rokesh. "It was badly negotiated, with no bounds for enforcement. We destroyed the Baedyed way of life. When they would not live in our settlements, we killed their horses. When they would not abide by our rules, we stole their children. They have no reason to work with us, and every reason to hate us. The Empress was a fool to believe otherwise, and the Baedyeds were right to abandon the agreement in favor of a better one."

No reaction from Rokesh beyond a smooth "You may tell the Empress that yourself."

"I intend to." Habim cut his hawkish attention back to Safi. "Next question, Truthwitch?"

Safi notched her chin higher. "Have you heard of a plot to overthrow the Empress and claim her throne?"

Habim sighed, an annoyed sound Safi knew so well—except this time, it was a lie. The falseness fretted down her skin and gathered at the base of her spine.

"No," Habim snipped. "Next question."

And the lie strummed harder.

Safi tensed. For half a moment, she thought her magic responded incorrectly. That it reacted to his fake posture and fake expressions . . . Except there was no truth to buzz with the lies. There were *only* lies. Which meant he did indeed know of a plot to overthrow the empire.

Bayrum of the Shards had known too, though. *Such rumors always abound*, he'd said before Vaness's iron disc severed through him. *Wherever there is power, flies will clot.*

Safi gulped. Whatever Habim had heard, he was not the source of the plots. He had come to Azmir for Safi; not for Empress Vaness.

So she pressed on. "And, General Fashayit," she finished, "did you know of the explosion on the Empress's ship before the attack occurred?"

"No. Next question."

True. Safi's shoulders relaxed. Fingers she hadn't realized were fisted now uncurled. "That was the last question."

"And?" Rokesh asked. "Did the general pass?"

Even if Habim had not passed, there was only one thing Safi would say. But he *had* passed, so it was easy to speak with conviction. "Yes, the general spoke the truth."

"Good," Habim replied before Rokesh could open his mouth. Already Habim twisted toward the table, dismissing

125

Safi and the Adders. Like a chime-piece wound too tightly, he moved to the next second, to the next order of business, and didn't wait for the world to catch up.

"I will see the Empress now, thank you." He waved to a contingent of troops along the Marstoki borders. "Tell her there is much to be discussed, and if *this* is her imperial strategy, then it will be a very short war, indeed."

Vivia's pulse hammered in her ears. Her magic surged in her veins, and beside her, two streams of water hung ready.

"You may lower your water," Vaness said with a graceful wave.

"Oh may I? I'm so glad to have your permission."

Vaness huffed a weary, if overdone sigh and swept to a seat. "If I had wanted to kill you, then you would already be dead. Besides, you do not truly feel threatened, or you would have called your officers."

Ah, the Empress was too sharp. So, with a brazen smile to spread across her mask—what else could Vivia use to keep control?—she eased the water back into its carafe. A slow, slinking coil of power with nary a drip to splatter free.

"If you are needed elsewhere," Vivia drawled, "then I presume our meeting has come to a close."

"I apologize." A bob of Vaness's dark head. "This was unexpected, and," she admitted, "unwanted. Here. Before you go." She slid a rolled paper across the table.

Vivia took it, careful to keep her expression bored while she untied the golden ribbon that bound the thick vellum page.

126

"There's nothing here." The paper was completely blank.

"Not yet." Vaness pulled a second rolled paper from her gown, and in seconds she had it stretched over the table—although a pencil toppled out and clattered to the floor.

And for the first time ever, Vivia watched the Empress of Marstok flush. Then, to Vivia's even greater awe, the Empress's grace briefly failed her. With an embarrassed, almost agitated speed, she snatched the sheepskin-wrapped graphite off the floor.

Her bracelets clanked, her cheeks burned brighter, and Vivia was forced to admit that Vaness might just be the most beautiful woman who had ever lived. It was almost . . . well, *laughable* that anyone could be that pretty.

Vaness regained her poise mere heartbeats later, bending over the table with the same air of purpose she always wore. "These pages are Wordwitched. When I write on one, like so . . ." She scribbled something and straightened.

"Now, look at your letter."

Vivia did so, only to find her eyes immediately widening. *This is my handwriting* was written across the top in smooth, compact Nubrevnan letters.

"You may respond." Vaness offered Vivia the pencil.

Vivia made no move to take it. "What," she began slowly, "am I meant to do with this?"

"*Respond.*" She wagged the pencil at Vivia.

"Why?"

"I would have thought it obvious. You are a busy woman, I am a busy woman. With this, we can negotiate a treaty from afar. When we reach the end of the page, it will clear itself, and we may start our conversation anew."

"How will I know it's you?"

"Because that is my script. I can write several more sentences if that would help—"

"No." Vivia laid the paper on the table. "I have no need for you or your ... Or your ..." Her eyes met Vaness's.

And suddenly, just like that, Vivia was too tired to even go on.

Always, she played the part of anger. Always, she maintained the role of power and control, of impatient Nihar rage. Always, she stormed in, she stormed out. She yelled loudest, fought hardest, and kept others—be they friends, be they empires—at bay. Why, though? In all her years of doing this, of mimicking her father and wearing the mask of a bear, it had never served her well.

The High Council wouldn't hold her coronation, Stix didn't want to be near her, and scarcely seven hours ago, her father had stolen the triumph she had worked so hard to earn.

Now, the Empress of Marstok, with her eight million fancy titles, was offering Vivia a chance. *Vivia*, not her father. And fool though she was, Vivia had believed Vaness when the woman had said she was impressed by the Foxes.

No matter how Vivia looked at this, she could see no reason to refuse.

"All right." The words fell from Vivia's tongue like water from an ancient faucet: rusty and strained. "All right," she tried again, less stilted, and this time forcing herself to nod. "Please write a few more words, and I will do the same."

Vaness smiled. A real, rich thing that scrunched her eyes and relaxed the muscles in her jaw. *Far too beautiful.*

Several minutes passed with only the gentle scratch of the pencil to fill the air between them. Vivia watched as what Vaness wrote appeared in real time upon her paper.

This is my handwriting. I am Vaness, the only daughter of Rishra and Alalm and the Empress of Marstok. I look forward to negotiating with Nubrevna.

She passed the pencil off to Vivia. The sheepskin grip was warm to the touch. *This is my handwriting,* Vivia wrote. *I am Vivia, the only daughter of Jana and Serafin, and the Queen-in-Waiting of Nubrevna. I hope you do not screw me over.*

This earned her a chuckle, and as Vivia handed back the pencil, Vaness waved it aside. "Keep the pencil," she urged. "I have others."

"As do I." Vivia set it on the table. "We are not *that* poor, Empress."

Another chuckle, another smile, and moments later the meeting ended.

This time, when Vivia crossed the Empress's quarters, the imperial wing, and finally departed the palace entirely, she found there was a different spring in her step. She wasn't so foolish a little fox as to think that anything productive would come out of this talk, but maybe, just *maybe*, she could get away with a little hope.

FOURTEEN

*

*I*t is overcast on the day the monster wakes up.

The boy and his black-furred terrier—a gift from his father six months ago, named Boots—play outside the family tent. Their tribe has set up camp in a hot corner of the Contested Lands.

Boots pants and pants, even though the sun hides behind grim clouds, so the boy takes him to the swampy river nearby. They will swim, he decides, and he tells himself it is for the dog's sake that he wants to go.

Dogs do not sweat, his mother once told him. They cannot cool off as we do. The boy thinks he is being charitable, considering his dog's comfort as he does. It will only be an exciting side benefit if he also happens to see the crocodiles in the water that Alma told him about.

For hours, he and Boots splash with the fat, slippery catfishes that make their home among the reeds. They hunt grasshoppers as big as the boy's hands. He tries to catch them; he fails. He tries to teach Boots to catch them, but Boots only stirs up the water and frightens away the bugs.

The clouds part. The boy forgets entirely about crocodiles.

Eventually, he hears his mother calling that it is time for supper. He tromps dutifully back to shore.

He is halfway there, the water barely to his thighs, when sunlight glints on two specks nearby. Then the reeds begin to move, and the boy realizes something approaches. Something larger than he is. Something that skates and slithers across the water as easily as the quicksilver in his mother's timepiece.

Boots starts barking. That high-pitched yip his father says the boy ought never to ignore. The boy doesn't ignore it. He also doesn't move, though. There's nowhere for him to go. The crocodile's yellow scales coalesce within the reeds—sharper, sharper by the second. Directly between the boy and the shore.

Before he can formulate a scream, Boots lunges.

And the crocodile's jaws snap. Boots yips. The crocodile spins. Water churns, and Boots is trapped within the beast's jaws. No barking now, only water, thrashing and wild.

Blood dyes the brown marsh red. So dark. So thick. Even the foam riled up by the attack is red, red, red.

And the sight of it does something to the boy. It pinches at the thumping in his chest. It sends cold walking down his spine. For some reason, his eyes feel hot, and his muscles feel strong. Even his lungs feel different—hollower and bigger than they did only a moment before.

He inhales.

And he smells . . . Freedom. Pure and rich and alive. And alongside the freedom is . . . Loyalty. Somehow, he knows this scent belongs to Boots. Just as he somehow knows the other scent—the freedom and the ancient, eternal hunger—belongs to the crocodile.

Without thinking, without even understanding what he does,

131

the boy walks into the fray. His fingers graze the crocodile's spinning scales. Water thunders around him.

Stop, he tells the beast. Stop.

And the crocodile stops.

Release Boots, he commands, and yet again, the creature obeys. Blood, so much blood—but the freedom and the loyalty somehow still burn strong.

Hold on, the boy tells Boots, and with a strength he didn't know he had until right now, he scoops up his bloodied, whimpering best friend.

Then he aims for shore, and this time, he remembers how to scream.

When Iseult finally returned to the White Alder, a precious scene awaited her. Owl asleep on the bed, Aeduan asleep on the floor beside her—seated, his head lolled back on the mattress.

The evil Bloodwitch did not look so evil with sunset to warm his sleeping face. Even the demon-child looked sweet in this light. Neither awoke when Iseult crept in with her satchel full of supplies. Nor when she eased down the items and grabbed the pitcher beside the washbasin. Nor even when she left the room to fill said pitcher at the Waterwitched faucet at the end of the hall.

A man was already there, water splashing as he filled his room's pitcher and three canteens. His bored Threads shifted to grassy interest at the sight of Iseult. He saw a feminine shape; he was keen. Iseult checked her hood, her sleeves, then she slouched as far back against the wall as she could without risking losing her place in line, should anyone else arrive.

This was a mistake. It only increased the man's curiosity. It was so predictable: a man feeling entitled to a woman's attention. He craned, he rocked, he stretched—all subtle at first, and all with the intent of peeking under her hood. He gave up on subtlety once he had finished getting water, and when he shuffled by, he darted in close, jutting his head low and peering straight into Iseult's face.

The result was instant. Iron gray hostility hit his Threads. His face crumpled into a sneer. At least he was blessedly silent as he left, offering no slurs or threats. Yet Iseult didn't like how she could still sense his Threads, even once he had entered his room—or how the two other sets of Threads with him shivered into aggressive hate. She did not bother filling her pitcher all the way before hurrying back to Aeduan and Owl. And once ensconced in their room again, she checked and double-checked the lock.

On the bright side, she supposed, Trickster was nowhere near.

Quietly as she could, Iseult poured the freshly retrieved water into the basin, but when a small cry broke the silence, she snapped toward the bed.

No one had awoken, though. The cry had come from Aeduan. He flinched and flinched, as if being hit. Over and over. *Flinch. Flinch. Flinch.* His face . . .

Iseult blinked. This was not the curse that struck Aeduan. This was grief. It was despair, as if the one thing he loved most in the world had been taken away from him.

And it was horrible to watch. Iseult wanted to stop it. She

wanted to rush to him and jolt him awake. Wanted to cup his face and tell him it was going to be all right and that whatever ghosts haunted him had now passed. It was a visceral desire, not a logical one, and she crossed the room in two long steps.

She knelt, reaching for his face. Heat curled off his skin, strong as an inferno. *Flinch, flinch, flinch*. Sweat shone on his brow.

A fever, she thought distantly, glad she had bought a tonic against that.

Then Aeduan stopped flinching.

And Iseult froze, her fingers a hairsbreadth from his jaw. Her breath held. Heartbeat by thudding heartbeat, the lines on his face smoothed away, slipping once more into the innocence of dreamless sleep. Part of her wanted to keep going. A tiny secret corner of her chest, tucked just in front of her left lung—*it* wanted to keep going, to feel the edges of his jaw and watch as he woke up.

But that was a part of her she refused to acknowledge, for as long as she pretended it wasn't there, then she didn't have to consider what it might mean.

She drew back her hands. For some reason, they were shaking, as if she had never done this before. As if she had not hovered beside an unconscious Aeduan only yesterday, observing the high curve of his cheeks and the thick frill of his lashes. In sleep, he was so easy to touch. To tend. No crystal eyes to bore into her. In waking . . .

This room is too hot. She was the one sweating now, she was the one feeling feverish. And it was not the heat of the Firewitch, either, but something else. Something that made her stomach cinch and her rib cage feel too small.

134

Quiet as a cat, just like Habim had taught her, Iseult backed away until she was to the washbasin once more. If she was lucky, Aeduan would not awaken until she had laid out everything he needed to tend his wounds. Then she could tiptoe from the room, and perhaps find a shadowy spot to hide in the common room below. Somewhere she could mull over what had happened with Trickster, somewhere she could order food for Aeduan and Owl without being seen by other guests.

And without being seen by Aeduan. His command from before still scoured against her ears. *No.* He did not want her help. *No.* He did not want her touch. Yet fanciful fool that she was, she had almost done exactly that . . .

And still wanted to.

She could only imagine the horror on his face if he had woken to find her fingers on him. It would have been so much worse than earlier.

No.

But the Moon Mother, it turned out, was against Iseult tonight. While Iseult managed to place clean linen strips, two different Earthwitch healer salves, a Firewitch healer powder, *and* the Waterwitch healer tonic beside Aeduan without disturbing him, when she tried to carry the full washbasin over, water sloshed onto his leg.

His eyes snapped wide. So blue. So lost. "You are back." Hoarse words. Scarcely a whisper.

The temperature in the room doubled. Iseult's tongue doubled too. "S-sorry to wake you." She scooted away.

Or she tried to. Aeduan latched onto her wrist, his grip surprisingly strong. "Stay," he breathed, and there was that

135

penetrating stare. The one that made her whole world fall away.

Moments trickled past. His grip weakened; his gaze did not. Iseult could pull free if she wanted to. An easy move, an easy twist.

She didn't.

"Scar," he said at last.

She had no idea what he meant. "I don't—" she began.

"Scar," he repeated, more emphatic, and though his gaze didn't move, his thumb did. It grazed—slightly, slightly—over her wrist. Then onto her palm to where, yes, there *was* a faint scar. Earned from a fisherman's hook in Veñaza City.

"My fault."

"Yes," she agreed.

His thumb moved, back up her palm toward her wrist. His skin was rough. His touch was not.

And Iseult's entire body shut down. There was no other way to describe it. No other words for how still everything inside of her went. No breath, no heartbeat, no vision beyond Aeduan's thumb tracing along her hand.

"Why?" he murmured eventually, finger finally slowing at her pulse point.

"Why . . . what?" She had no idea how she got those words out.

Aeduan swallowed, the muscles of his neck, his throat strong, even if his body was weak. "Why are you still here?"

She blinked, surprise briefly shrinking her tongue. Briefly calming her mind. "Where else would I go? Did . . . did you need me to get something else for you?"

"No. Not that—" He broke off, coughing, and his fingers

136

finally released Iseult. Suddenly, the skin around her wrist felt too cold. At odds with the rest of her body, which was blistering from the inside out.

"With Owl," Aeduan rasped once the coughing had passed. "And . . . me. Why do you stay?"

"Oh." It was the last thing she expected him to ask, and for half a skittering moment, Iseult feared he had somehow seen the note from Mathew in her pocket. Somehow he knew that she had other options before her. Except that this was impossible—she had only just received the message. There was no way Aeduan could know that someone was coming for her.

And why do you care if he does know? her brain demanded. *He knows that you seek your Threadsister. He knows that you have Thread-family and that you cannot stay beside him forever.*

Well, he may know that, whispered the tiny secret corner above her lung. *But do you?*

"I . . . owe you life-debts," Iseult offered eventually. It was the only explanation she had ever put into words for herself. "Many of them. Why? D-*do* you want me to leave?"

So hard to squeeze out those words, and Aeduan offered no response. Instead, he simply stared at her, unblinking and inescapable, and with each passing second, his eyes shed more sleep. Awareness hardened in his gaze.

All while the room grew hotter and hotter and Iseult's tongue grew fatter and fatter. Now she realized her heart had never stopped, her lungs had never paused. It was just that they'd been hidden behind the expanse of him. Of his eyes, of his fingers, of his touch.

Beside her, Aeduan heaved himself into a sitting position.

A moan of pain, a spasm of agony, yet Iseult made no move to help him. *No.* Instead, she simply watched as the seconds ground past and internally chanted, *Stasis.* A futile refrain really, for once Aeduan had straightened fully and set to removing his shirt, it became too frustrating for Iseult to endure. His pain shivered in the air between them. The urge to yank off his shirt for him—it made her fingers flex against her thighs.

She was a pot about to boil over.

Iseult pushed upright. A bit frantic, a bit loud, but no movement came from the bed, no shift in Owl's Threads as Iseult returned to the now barren table. She gripped its edges, then forced her gaze to the mirror. To her own reflection, where hazel eyes glinted in the lantern light.

Stasis, stasis, stasis. How many times had Iseult's mother made her stare in a mirror, forcing her to master her Threadwitch calm? How many times had Gretchya made Iseult observe her own face for every tic, every twitch, every failure to maintain smooth perfection? Iseult had hated it growing up. Now, though, in a room made of flames, she sank into the forgiveness of a cold, methodical lesson from the past.

She could master her face, and then true tranquility would follow.

"I could find no clothes," she murmured at last, no stammer. No inflection. No more Aeduan to devour her senses. "I will try again tomorrow, when shops might be open."

"I can get clothes . . ." A grunt of pain behind her. A savage exhale. Then, "At the Monastery outpost. I can get more clothes."

"You still intend to go there?"

"I . . . must."

Iseult swallowed a sigh, even as her reflection stayed still. She wanted to argue, but knew it to be pointless. This was not the first time she'd encountered behavior that contradicted a story told aloud. Aeduan claimed he disliked the Carawens, that he was not even part of their ranks anymore, yet he'd remained so scrupulous to their rules over the past two weeks of travel. He had meditated upon waking, he had kept his Carawen cloak fastened and clean, and he had regularly recited prayers at dusk.

Safi had been no different. She had always claimed to despise her uncle, yet she'd also gone out of her way to impress him. Finding reasons to show off her fighting prowess, dropping her latest history lessons into conversation, and twice even pulling heists while he watched on.

Iseult supposed it was as simple as rejecting that which might reject us. It hurt less when you were the one to act first.

She turned away from the mirror, stronger now. Cool, cool all the way through, and she found Aeduan dabbing at the wounds on his belly. Clumsy movements that splattered water to the floor.

Stubborn fool. It was a wonder Owl slept through all that splashing.

He dunked. He cleaned. He dunked. He cleaned. He dunked . . . he fumbled. The linen fell into the washbasin. It sank, and his dull fingers could not get it out again.

Silently, stoically, Iseult returned to his side and retrieved the linen. She wrung it out before offering it to him. But when his fingers curled around the cloth, she did not let go.

"Is it truly so awful to let me help you?" The words knifed

139

out louder than she'd intended. Almost petulant in her ears. She wanted an answer, though, so she held on.

Water dripped to the floor.

"Your . . . touch," he said eventually, "is . . . too much."

Too much? she wanted to repeat. *Too much what?* There were so many ways that phrase could be taken. Logic, of course, told her that he referred to pain, except one look at the mess around them told her that couldn't be true. Her touch was defter than his, her fingers gentler.

Iseult released the linen, released his hand. He had given her an answer; she would press no further—even if that tiny secret corner wanted her to. Even if it nagged her while she returned to the mirror: *It is not too much pain that bothers him. It is too much of something else entirely. The same too much that makes your tongue fat and your face hot. The same too much that makes your body shut down.*

And Iseult hated how much she wished that tiny secret corner spoke true.

FIFTEEN

※

The shadows were not kind to Merik. They taunted in a voice that was not Kullen's. That was amused and probing and in a language he scarcely understood. They pulsed, they boomed, they grasped and coiled—and always, always, they laughed.

Twice, he managed to drag open his eyes. Twice, he saw a crisp, blue sky overhead and felt damp winds scrape against his face. Twice, he hovered into awareness firmly enough to sense that he was moving, being carried by someone with strong arms and a relentless grip.

That was all Merik saw before the laughing shadows returned.

When at last the shadows cleared entirely, the sky was no longer blue. Sunset was creeping in, a great slanting of the world against a sky painted pink. A chill air frosted Merik's face, and as he shoved himself upright, he realized he was wet.

He was shivering, too.

A forest materialized around him, growing firmer with each breath as the final remnants of poison smudged away.

141

Fog crept and curved around alders, their pale trunks speckled with black. Churned-up mud trailed out from the nearest trees, showing an oft-trod pathway across sodden grass.

It led to a towering slab mere paces from where Merik lay. It was like the standing stone Merik had seen Kullen destroy, except this one was carved with elaborate whorls. In some places, the marks had smoothed away to nothing. In others, pale lichen crusted overtop.

Whatever this stone was, it was ancient and it was revered. Trinkets and tributes covered the grass, some placed today and others left long ago to rot beneath the cold Arithuanian sun. Between a loaf of bread molded to black and a doll whose painted face had faded to nothing, three pears gleamed. Perfectly ripe, their green curves flared to red like the sunset beginning to gather above.

Merik's mouth watered. It had been so long since he'd eaten, and the only water he'd had was the poisoned tincture Esme had given him.

Esme. With her name came the memories of where he was and how he'd gotten there—hundreds of leagues away from the Sightwitch Sister Convent. Hundreds of leagues away from Cam or Ryber or anyone he knew, and now someone had dumped him onto a shrine in the middle of a wet forest.

Had that someone been friend or foe? As far as Merik could see, there was no one here now, and his winds told him nothing. The collar still hung at his neck, and no amount of breathing deeply offered any connection to his power.

He was alone in a forest with no magic and no help.

Which meant there was also no one to stop him. In a dizzying burst of speed, Merik pushed to his feet and bolted for the forest. His heart jumped to maximum speed in moments; his lungs felt instantly drained. Alders whipped past, ocher leaves bright amidst the fog. The ground sucked at his plodding footfalls. He thundered on anyway, and he did not slow. He was going to get away from here. He was going to find people to help him, and then he would somehow get back to the Convent, to Cam and Ryber.

Merik had just reached firmer soil, where the forest shifted to beeches and firs, when pain lanced through him.

It was as if he were trapped on his exploding ship all over again—fire, fire everywhere. In his veins, beneath his skin, scratching at the backs of his eyeballs. A strangled cry tore from his throat before his knees gave way. He collapsed to the cold earth.

Black writhed under the skin on his hands.

You are going the wrong way. Esme's voice slithered up from his chest and into his skull, glass shards and nightmares. *Surely you would not try to run away from me, Prince. Surely this was all a mistake, and now you will turn around and come back.*

"No," Merik gritted out, fighting to crawl onward.

Yes, and the pain ignited a thousand times hotter. It stole his sight, his hearing, and screams erupted through the trees. His own screams, a thousand miles away and agonizing.

Turn around, Prince, or I will make this worse. And yes, I can make it worse.

Merik did not know how it was possible, but he believed the woman called Esme—and he believed that any more pain would crack him in two.

Stop. He did not know if he shrieked the word or simply thought it, but it took hold of every space inside him. *Stop,*

143

stop, stop. He clawed himself around, still on all fours, and dragged himself back the way he'd come.

It took four mind-scorching paces before the flames finally reared back. Cold nothing rushed in. Merik collapsed to the ground, shaking.

Good, Esme trilled. *Now walk back to the shrine, Prince, and we shall begin again.*

"Yes," he forced out, though he could do nothing but stare up at the amber leaves of a beech and try to breathe. Pain still cinched in his chest, moving in time to his staggering heart. Screams still rang in his ears.

He lifted his trembling hands up. Even backlit by sunset, he could see lines pumping beneath the skin. Esme had cleaved him—or started to—and she had spoken of other Cleaved back in the tower. She had called them her own, as if she had done this to them. As if she had done it to Merik.

Puppeteer.

There'd been rumors of a woman with the Raider King who could control the Cleaved. There had been tales that she *created* them, but Merik had dismissed them as lies—as impossibilities meant to frighten the empires and Nubrevna too. He had blamed the other leaders at the Truce Summit for ignoring a threat in Arithuania, yet it would seem he had done no better.

It was one more thing he had refused to see in all his holy conceit, and now everything he had done would haunt him until he made amends.

Though right now, all that mattered was obeying Esme. It shamed him that he could be so weak, but there was the truth: he would do *anything* she told him if it would keep the fire away.

Merik set off, his gait stumbling and uneven through the

forest. His attention remained planted on the ground before him, his mind focused on simply staying upright. No space for thought, no space for fear, no space to notice the cold fog seeping around him.

He reached the shrine right as the sun was dipping beyond the horizon. This time, when he saw the pears, he ate them without hesitation. Juice slid down his face and over his fingers, and nothing—*nothing*—had ever tasted so sweet.

It wasn't until the third fruit that Esme's voice returned. *Do you know what this place is?* The words jolted Merik from his pleasure. Reality thudded into him, hard enough that he choked. Pear chunks splattered on a silver-plated bowl nearby.

"No," he croaked eventually, wiping fruit off his sticky mouth.

This is a shrine that was built thousands of years ago, before the time of witches.

Merik hadn't known there was a time before witches.

No one remembers the past, unless it is written down. And the ones who did *write it down have all been forgotten. The past is so easily erased, Prince, and only the Sleeper knows what god or force of nature this shrine was originally built to honor.*

There was a strange ache to those words, as if Esme longed for the past to return. As if she mourned the loss of history and knowledge.

Now the silly Nomatsi tribes use it to revere a god who never lived, the Moon Mother's middle sister, whom they believe takes the form of a barn swallow. Superstitious fools. Venom thickened Esme's words. *There is no Swallow, and there never was. Although,* she added, almost as a smirking afterthought, *they do leave nice gifts for her, and it is these gifts I want you to take. Do you see any gemstones? Most will be rough and uncut.*

145

Merik nodded. There were many scattered around. Then he realized she might not sense his movement, so he added a gruff, "*Onga.*" Arithuanian for *yes*. He felt stronger now, thanks to the fruit. More awake, more alert.

Ah! A squealing sensation filled his mind, almost like wasps buzzing, and he sensed his response had made her very happy. *You are perfection, Prince! None of my other Cleaved have their minds left, you see? I can move them as I wish, and I can make them do simple tasks, like attack or defend or carry a helpless prince into the woods. But it requires all my focus. I must hold their leashes and direct them precisely where I want them to go. Even then, I cannot easily see through their eyes, so when I've needed to collect things, I have had to do it myself.*

Until right now, that is. If you can see the gemstones, Prince, then you can pick them up for me. And, oh, I have so many more gems—and other items too—that I need collected. You could not have been more perfect if I had designed you myself.

The buzzing returned. Merik thought she must be laughing.

Now take the gems, Prince, and return to me.

"How will I know where to go?"

Oh, that is easy. Simply follow the pain. With that declaration, agony ruptured through him.

He screamed.

Grab the gemstones to make it stop!

He grabbed them—and other items too. Anything that looked like a rock, anything small or round or within grabbing distance, he stuffed into his pockets. He could scarcely see. He certainly couldn't think, and every nerve inside him was aflame.

Good boy, she crooned once his pockets were full. *Now walk.*

Merik walked.

SIXTEEN

※

The walk through Tirla was a tedious hike. Though Iseult's salves and tinctures had eased some of Aeduan's pain, they were slow to act—and most would need several days of application to have any effect. At least, that was what Aeduan assumed according to how normal people healed.

How strange. He never thought he would be lumped with normal people. When he was young, it had been all he'd wanted. Now, he hated it.

Winds hastened around him, driving him faster. Clouds scudded in. A storm would break before he could complete this errand if he didn't hurry.

When at last the lake's front came into view, waves choppy, Aeduan steeled his spine. Inhaled, exhaled. *Not my mind, not my body.* Then he rounded onto the main quay, crowded even at sunset, and approached the outpost with as sure-footed a stride as he could manage.

The tall building wedged between a public stable and a mapmaker's shop had changed little in the last two years. It bore the same weather-stained limestone front, the same rook-and-tree sigil over the entrance, smoothed away to a featureless oval form, and the same heavy oaken door with no latch on the outside.

He knocked once. An eye-level slat hissed wide. Dark eyes peered through, flicking first to Aeduan's face, then to the opal in Aeduan's left ear.

"Good enough," came a muffled voice from the other side, and in a squeal of hinges—also unchanged—the door swung open to reveal the monk on the other side. Unfamiliar but typically wizened. Outpost guard assignments were comfortable, well paid, and perfect for mercenary monks well past their prime.

"You look like shit," the man said.

"I feel like shit," Aeduan replied, earning a bark of laughter as he limped into the cloister beyond. Acolytes, their white cowls turned to gray beneath the gathering storm, tended neat rows of cabbage, beets, and carrots. Lucky bastards. Aeduan had applied six times for a remote training position. Anything to get away from the Monastery.

He had never been approved, and in hindsight, he supposed it was to be expected. No one trusted a Bloodwitch. No one trusted a demon.

Aiming right, he circled the garden until he reached the requisitions shop. The beet and carrot leaves thrashed in the wind. Thunder hummed in the distance.

"You," came a surprised voice as Aeduan stepped inside the store—also unchanged, with its low counter at the back and a wall filled with cubbyholes. The Marstoki woman on the other side who ran this outpost, however, *had* changed: a few more gray hairs around the crown, a few more wrinkles around the eyes.

"It has been a while, Monk," she said. "And you looked much better back then."

"Two years." Aeduan approached the counter. Pain dogged each step, but he could not show it. This woman might have been one of the only monks to ever tolerate him, yet he had no illusions she liked him. He had brought in a great deal of coin for her outpost; monsters were useful like that.

"I was in Dalmotti," he explained. "On a tier seven. Only just returned."

"A tier seven. That would explain all the blood, then." At Aeduan's confused expression, her thick eyebrows notched up. "Or do you mean it was an *old* tier seven?"

He shook his head. "I don't know what you mean."

Incredulity sent her brows even higher. "Have you not heard of the new Abbot's changes? Assignments are rated by coin now, not length of contract."

New Abbot. This was the first Aeduan had heard of that.

A startled laugh split the woman's lips. Aeduan must be doing a poor job of controlling his expressions.

"When was the last time you visited an outpost, Monk?" She leaned onto the counter. "The Elders chose Natan fon Leid as the old man's replacement over a month ago."

Aeduan's head tipped sideways as he chewed on these words. He had not visited an outpost in over two months. The monks in Veñaza City had not been as welcoming as this woman here.

Logical, then, that he had heard nothing of a new Abbot or rating system—and part of him wished he had not learned it now. Natan fon Leid had always been egocentric, even for a Cartorran, and his lust for power had been insatiable

149

growing up. Qualities perfectly suited to the role of Carawen Abbot, but not qualities Aeduan particularly appreciated.

Another laugh from the woman, and she straightened. "Not an admirer, I see?"

"Hmm," he offered in reply, annoyed his face seemed beyond control. It was taking all his effort to simply remain standing. Managing expressions too . . . He had no idea how the Threadwitch did it.

"Do you have Painstones?" he asked.

"A few." The woman craned toward a cubby on her left. "The Marstoks are diverting all supply to the border skirmishes, though, so I've had to raise the price on them . . . Wait." She froze mid-reach, gaze leaping back to Aeduan. "Why do *you* need a Painstone?"

"It is not for me," he lied.

She did not look as if she believed him, but she also did not press further. Several breaths later, a small satchel dropped onto the counter. "That's a tier four by the new rules. Expensive," she clarified. "Are you sure you want it?"

All supplies in the Monastery had to be paid for through service, but Aeduan did not care if the cost of this stone was a tier four or a tier ten. He needed something to keep him strong until he could meet with a healer witch, and he would take whatever he could get.

"Yes," was all he said in reply, snatching it off the counter and depositing it in a pocket. Now he just had to finish this errand. Then he could slip off somewhere and don it. "I also need a new uniform for myself. Black."

Black, he had decided, would cover these recurring blood-stains.

"Do you want a new cloak too?" She eyed the shredded, filthy fabric. "I have plenty. The cost is only a tier one."

Aeduan shook his head. His cloak possessed modifications he could not purchase here: salamander fibers against flame, a fire flap against smoke. Even pocked with holes and streaked with blood as it was, he would rather wear this old cloak than any piece of cloth that might be new.

After confirming his size had not changed—and agreeing that a tier one assignment seemed fair payment, even if Aeduan was not sure what that meant anymore—he moved to the next item on the list.

"I need travel clothes for a girl. About six or seven years old. Small for her age."

"Oh?" The woman clearly itched to ask why he needed this, but it was against the rules to inquire. Assignments were private; monks were discreet. "Well, Lady Fate favors you today, then. I just received . . ." Reach, grab, and drop. "These last week. Not new, but clean and well made."

She was right. The wool tunic and breeches, a gray-brown shade like bark on a beech tree, looked a bit large, but better too large than too small. And the pine green cloak was just the right size.

Aeduan nodded. He would take them.

"Those will be another tier one," the woman said. "Anything else?"

"More travel clothes." He swallowed. Then swallowed again. "For a woman about your size."

"Ah, for grown women, we have many options." The monk opened her arms, gesturing to an entire column of shelves. "What quality do you need? What climate of travel? I have embroidered silk all the way from Dalmotti, if your woman is a wealthy one."

"Not my woman." His fingers flexed.

"Or I have more sturdy fare, cotton and wool. There are other options in between as well—and do you want a gown or breeches?" Without waiting for an answer, the monk began stacking items atop the counter. From silk to wool to velvet to homespun, all colors and fabrics were represented.

And Aeduan had no idea what to choose. Iseult had not actually specified that she wanted new clothes. In fact, the longer he stared at the growing piles, the more he wondered if she might be angry he would presume to know what she liked. Or would she be angry if he did not make a choice? Surely she would want new clothing to replace her current tatters, if for no other reason than new clothes would be warmer in the growing mountain cold. So perhaps that brown wool suit on the end would do . . .

Aeduan stared at it, his brain sluggish as spring thaw as he tried to catalog the advantages. *Good for camouflage. Good against snow, and also movable in a fight.*

And also, he had to admit, hideous.

Then, there was that midnight blue velvet beside it. A popular style in the mountains, a pretty color, and it looked movable as well. The fox fur on the collar was a nice touch. Or there was the gray suit beside it. Or the black one beyond that, or the teal-trimmed mustard beyond that.

It was not until he had moved through twelve different outfits that he realized the monk was grinning. An amused twitch of lips as if she knew something he didn't.

Heat flared on Aeduan's cheeks. His molars gritted in his

ears. This decision was a trivial one; he was letting pain cloud his judgment. It did not matter what he got Iseult. He did not care if she liked it. She would take it, no matter what it was, and that would be that.

"Black," he gruffed out, jerking a finger toward a suit he'd already passed.

"Are you sure?" The woman's smile widened.

Aeduan glared. "Black," he repeated, and outside, thunder boomed.

By the time the woman had stuffed his purchases in a homespun satchel and tallied up what he owed on the assignment ledger—two tier ones, a tier two, and a tier four—rain beat down outside.

He did not say good-bye when he left.

Aeduan changed into his new uniform in the outpost baths. Breeches, undershirt, brigandine, belt and baldric, and finally, the Painstone dangling from a leather thong. Not until he tucked it beneath his clothes and it touched his chest did he feel the effects of the magic.

Between one heartbeat and the next, rain and storm and shouts from the outpost battered against him. The world sharpened, a flood of color and light. And the pain—it fled back like rain sucked into sand. Aeduan could breathe. He could see, and it crashed into him so fast, he almost fell against the nearest wall.

By the Wells, he was reborn.

Hands braced on the bricks, Aeduan inhaled until his lungs pressed against his ribs. Only now could he truly comprehend how much pain there had been. How much his spine had furled since last night. How much he had stumbled and slurred and fought to stay conscious.

He exhaled, savoring how free the air felt, how easily his muscles now moved. Then he inhaled once more, and this time, he summoned his magic. It roared to life, no skips or skitters. Monk and acolyte blood-scents clamored against him, each as unique and distinctive as the bodies and minds they belonged to.

Back through the cloister, now empty, he trekked. Rain pelted the crops. Mist clogged the covered walkway, and by the time he entered the crowded common room, where available assignments were nailed to the wall, lightning splintered overhead.

In the back of his mind, it occurred to Aeduan that this was an unseasonable thunderstorm. Particularly since Tirla so rarely saw them.

Inside the common room, the plank walls were divided into ten sections. Directly to Aeduan's left was tier one, and slips of paper covered every surface—not so different from the old way. Short-term contracts, he supposed, would also pay the least. Tiers two and three were almost as heavily papered, yet rather than the typical cluster of monks poring over assignments at these lower levels, every monk in the room was glued to the right side.

Tier ten.

White cloaks, some dripping, some dry, blended together as each person leaned in close, craning to read an assignment staked to the wood. Whatever it was, it must be worth a lot of money. In the past, Aeduan would have marched straight for it, shoving aside the others and pleased when they glared and called him *demon*. Today, though, he simply aimed for the left.

Two tier ones, a tier two, and a tier four. As he scanned the scraps of paper, written in all hands and varied languages, he found his wrists had started rolling. Round and round and round again. Standing here, choosing from assignments—reading about overdue debts and missing livestock, about seafire requisitions or short-term guard postings near the border—was exactly why he had taken that position with Guildmaster Yotiluzzi two years ago. He had wanted the coin; he had wanted to leave.

You could leave now, his mind nudged. *Take the items and never pay.* After all, he had no loyalty to the Monastery. No plans to ever return. But . . . there were uses to the opal in his ear. To the cloak upon his back. There were uses to these outposts too, and if he did not pay his debts, those uses would be denied.

He plucked two tier ones off the wall. Both were near the city; both could be handled before tomorrow's dawn even brightened the sky.

"You surprise me, Bloodwitch."

Aeduan's jaw ticced. He did not need to turn to know who now stood beside him. *Speed and daisy chains, mother's kisses and sharpened steel.*

"Not going for the tier ten?"

Slowly, Aeduan turned to face Lizl. Her amber brown skin glistened with rainwater. Her white cloak dripped to the floor. She was tall, but he refused to lift his chin to meet her eyes. He simply rolled his gaze upward, expression flat, and said, "No."

"Why not?" She offered a smug grin, arms folding casually.

155

Her posture was misleading in its ease. She was the best mercenary monk out of the hundreds at the Monastery.

Except for Aeduan. He still had her beat.

"Ten thousand talers." She counted off a single finger. Then a second and a third finger as she added, "Plus twenty thousand piestras *and* twenty-five thousand cleques. That's enough money to buy a kingdom, and it's an open assignment, too."

Open assignments meant anyone could try to complete them, and they remained open until they were done. There had never been one in all of Aeduan's years of mercenary work. Nor had he ever heard of one with such a high price attached.

It did not change his mind, though.

"I have no interest."

"Good. Because I intend to do it."

"I do not care."

"You should." She laughed, a sound like breaking glass. "So beware, Bloodwitch, because if you cross my path again, I will destroy you." With a parting smirk she spun around—cloak spraying Aeduan with rain—and stalked from the common room.

Aeduan did not watch her go. Like everything else around here, she had not changed at all in two years. Never mind that he had not crossed her path on purpose, that he had no interest in the tier ten, and never mind that she could not destroy him even if she wanted to. Lizl hated him; she had always hated him; she always would.

In a flurry of speed, Aeduan grabbed the first assignments he saw on the tier two and tier four walls. Then he left the common room and its huddled monks to finish what he had come here to do: he went to the Shrine of the Fallen.

Underground, as all Carawen shrines were, rain dripped down the steps leading from the cloister. A puddle splashed at the bottom. Thunder chased behind. Aeduan followed a tunnel deeper into the earth, until at last he reached the stone room, a miniature version of the massive underground catacombs at the Monastery. Low, vaulted ceilings flickered with candlelight, while the black marble hexagon at the heart of the room absorbed all light.

As wide as Aeduan was tall, the marble slab reached his mid-thigh. Four monks knelt around it, each reciting their vows at their own speed. Aeduan had no plans to join them. He had not known the man who had died. He wanted this errand complete.

A fifth monk stepped from the shadows. It was required that all monks serve at a Shrine of the Fallen for a year, and most waited until old age before fulfilling the duty. This monk, though, was young. Perhaps no more than a decade past Aeduan.

"Are you here to pay your respects?" she asked. "Or report?"

"Report." He withdrew the dead man's opal from his pocket. "I do not know the monk's name. I found him a day south of Tirla. An artisanal monk, caught in a battle."

The woman sighed, a sound laden with regret, and plucked the opal from Aeduan's palm. "It is the tier ten." She frowned at the gem. "It is taking our lives one by one. A hundred of us have fallen trying to finish it." Her gaze cut back to Aeduan's. Piercing. Desperate, even. "No fortune is worth one's life, Monk. Remember that."

Then she bowed her head respectfully and melted once more into the shadows.

*

Aeduan returned to the common room. Curiosity propelled him. Curiosity and something harder—something almost like certainty, though he could not say how he knew.

It roiled in his gut. It made his strides slice long against the rain.

He had to shove through the monks clustered before the wall. Some snarled, some glared, just like the old days—and just like the old days, they all withdrew when they saw the blood swirling across Aeduan's eyes.

Bloodwitch, they whispered. *A demon from the Void.*

Then Aeduan reached the lone paper staked to the planks. Such a simple beige sheet for such important words, and nailed above it were two more papers listing payments, as if the bounty had been increased not once but twice since first arriving.

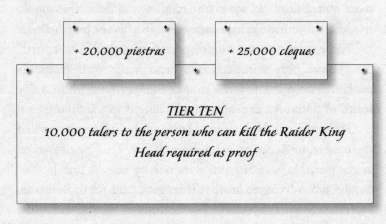

+ 20,000 *piestras*

+ 25,000 *cleques*

TIER TEN
10,000 talers to the person who can kill the Raider King
Head required as proof

SEVENTEEN

✳

The early-evening sun bore down while Safi trailed the Empress of Marstok and Habim beside Lake Scarza. Naval ships groaned against their tethers and white sails floated for as far as the eye could see. Thousands of boats, yet still only a fraction of the full Marstoki forces. Most, Safi had learned, were moored on the southern coast or already at sea.

After Vivia Nihar's departure, Safi and Vaness had traveled with Habim to the northernmost tip of the lake, where the navy kept their main headquarters. Safi had changed into an Adder uniform: black tunic, loose black pants, and supple black ankle boots. The only difference between Safi's uniform and the other Adders' was that the iron belt at her waist carried no weapons, and she did not have to wear the head-scarf. Yet.

Rokesh and eleven other Adders moved around the group, spaced wide enough apart to allow Vaness to move unimpeded along the wide sandstone bulwark that overlooked the main docks.

"The Cartorrans want your Truthwitch," Habim said matter-of-factly. Hands clasped behind his back, he examined sailors no differently than he had examined Safi and Iseult growing up. "Emperor Henrick grows bolder each day, Your Majesty. He taunts us, trying to see how close he can get before we attack."

"And when they do get too close," Vaness responded, no change in her iron stride, "then we will kill them."

True, true, true.

"No," Habim countered, "we will not." He slowed to a stop, forcing Safi and the Adders to slow as well. "If we escalate the conflict, it will only give Cartorra—and Dalmotti—a reason to escalate as well. We are not ready for that, Your Majesty. We may be large, well organized, and well supplied, but that does not mean we will win.

"The bulk of your troops are Children of the Truce. They have no grasp of what war looks like, no understanding of what's at stake, and little reason to care."

Safi's chest frizzed with the truth in that assertion—and it brought to mind a similar statement made on a similar evening only a month before. *You have no idea what war is like,* Uncle Eron had said.

And he had been right. Safi saw that now. She too was also a Child of the Truce.

As if on cue, an officer marched by on a lower parapet. He barked orders to a flag-bearer toting the standard. A *young* flag-bearer, not old enough to yet have whiskers. Not old enough to have even grown into his feet.

Safi winced at the sight of him; Habim simply sniffed; Vaness showed no reaction at all.

Moments later, they resumed walking, so Safi resumed following. They now discussed ground forces and supply chains, river routes and highway checkpoints. All subjects Safi had been forced to study—under Habim's tutelage, no less—but for which Iseult had always been the better student.

Safi had known Habim her entire life, yet the man she trod solemnly behind was not the man she'd grown up with.

There were similarities, of course. The impatience that always cropped his words or the stillness on his face when he was displeased—*that* was Habim through and through. But everything else was new to Safi, from the stiff green-coated uniform with gold tassels to the way everyone bowed low at him. Above all, it was the references he made to places and past events that Safi had never heard of, but that resonated with trembling truth.

Was there any part of Safi's life that had not been a lie? And how had she, the only Truthwitch on the entire continent, never once suspected?

At a warship with gleaming gold decks and scrabbling sailors in green, Habim and Vaness paused. In less time than it took Safi to wipe the sweat off her brow, two pages rushed in with a table and set it between Habim and the Empress. Then they scurried away while Habim removed a paper from his coat. After plunking two stones on either side to weigh it down, he motioned Vaness closer.

"This is a map of northwestern Marstok and the Sirmayan Mountains," he explained. "Here you can see the main watch-towers. These three mountain passes must be better protected. A loss of any one of these towers will cut off supplies to Tirla. The city would fall within a week."

Heat splintered in Safi's shoulder blades. A warning of

duplicity, and suddenly she was very alert and very keen to join this conversation. Neck craning, she tried to glimpse the lines and Xs Habim traced for the Empress. Yet all she saw was the map, exactly as described.

Except . . . the longer she stared, the more her vision seemed to blur. She scrubbed her eyes before squinting once more at the page.

And her magic blared hotter, scratching over her skull now. *False, false, false.* Then the map vanished entirely.

Somehow, Safi managed not to react. Somehow, she kept a bored, tired expression tacked in place. Her mind, however, was alight. And her heels—*oh,* how her heels suddenly wanted to bounce and carry her closer to the table.

Instead, she yawned. A great stretching of her jaw that would have earned a scolding as a child. She pretended to hide it. Pretended to turn away from the Empress, all while swishing just a few inches sideways. Then a few inches nearer to the table. Another yawn, another stretch.

Now the map was fully in view, and *now* she could see that it was no map at all.

It was a message.

Do nothing. We have a plan.

That was all it said. Safi read it three more times, but there was nothing else. In Mathew's familiar scrawl—on a document clearly Wordwitched—there were only six words: *Do nothing. We have a plan.*

Hell-ruttin' weasel pies. Safi couldn't decide if she ought to laugh or cry at the message. Because really, Habim? He was *really* telling her to keep doing what she had already been doing, and he *really* expected her to just wait around for some unknown plan?

Safi had followed her uncle's plan in Veñaza City, and it hadn't ended well. Twenty years in the making, a scheme that spanned the Witchlands, that was meant to stop the war from resuming and bring permanent peace to the empires—Safi had ruined it all in one night. Oh, she had done as ordered and followed the plan across the Jadansi on Merik Nihar's ship, but then circumstances had forced her to deviate. Namely, her uncle's ridiculous, unfair treaty with Nubrevna. And that deviation had landed her here, in Marstok.

It wasn't her fault, though. It was the fault of a shoddy scheme with too many moving parts, as well as the fact that *no one* ever told her what in damnation was going on.

And Safi especially wanted to know about Iseult. Safi wanted to know where in the Witchlands her Threadsister was. She wanted to know if Iseult was safe. And above all, she wanted to know how Habim intended to get her and Safi together again.

"Nomatsis," she said, but Vaness and Habim only ignored her, continuing their discussion of winter snows and transport. So Safi repeated a bit louder and more emphatically, "*Nomatsis.*"

This time, Vaness broke off. "What is the problem?" She offered the faintest glare Safi's way. "What about Nomatsis?"

"You currently provide space for their tribes to congregate outside cities." Without asking for permission, Safi strutted to the table, chin high. Her shadow stretched across the map, and she tapped where she *thought* Tirla had been. "Where

163

will they go in the war, Your Majesty? What will you do to ensure that they are not targets of the empires?"

Vaness regarded Safi. The iron shackles at her wrists slithered and spun. The breeze off Lake Scarza wisped against her hair.

"Many Nomatsi tribes," she said eventually, "have moved to the Raider King's banner. They need no protection from me, Safi. If anything, this makes them the enemy."

"But not all tribes," she countered. "And perhaps they wouldn't go to him if they felt they were safer here to begin with."

"Hmmm." The iron shackles slowed. Then she twisted back to Habim. "She makes a valid point, General. Have you accounted for Nomatsi tribes? How do you intend to protect them?"

Safi had to fight off a grin. *Yes, have you accounted for Nomatsis, Habim? Have you accounted for Iseult?*

His nostrils flared. "Twenty years ago, I protected their tribes and everyone else within our borders. I will protect them again, and it insults me that you would assume otherwise." Habim's focus never left Vaness as he said this, but his words sparkled in Safi's rib cage—as true as true could be.

"Does the Truthwitch"—now Habim looked at Safi with daggers in his eyes—"have any other questions?"

"No." She bared her toothiest grin. "I think your strategy is a sound one, General."

He visibly bristled, weight shifting, lips puckering. And relief chuckled through Safi that even as Firewitch general and court Truthwitch, Habim still found her insufferable.

"It is good to know that farm life has not softened you,

General." Vaness offered these words calmly. Almost lightly, as if she joked.

Habim, however, did not take them that way. "Farm life," he snapped, "is as difficult as soldiering, Your Majesty, and it would do well for an empress to remember that."

Before Safi could blink, the iron at Vaness's wrists shot to the general's throat. Two crescent blades against his neck. In that same instant, the Adders unsheathed their blowguns and took aim.

Then everyone waited. Officers patrolling the lower levels gaped upward. The page boys ogled with slack jaws. Even the sails and the masts and the creaking, moaning warships seemed to hold their collective breaths.

"It would do better," Vaness said with all the force of her title and her magic behind her words, "for a general to remember his station."

Habim swallowed. "Forgive me, Your Majesty. Farm life *has* softened me, it seems."

"See that you harden yourself quickly then, or next time my blades will see just how soft you have become."

With that promise to linger between them, the blades slithered back to Vaness's wrists. Then she left the table and her general behind, offering no good-bye nor acknowledgment of Habim's low bow.

In seconds, blowguns still ready, the Adders closed in tightly around Vaness and Safi, and in seconds, the mentor Safi had never truly known was out of sight.

EIGHTEEN

✳

It was not the first time Iseult had been alone with Owl. It was, however, the first time they had been alone without Blueberry there to distract the girl. It was also the first time she had been alone with her in a crowded place, and Iseult was keen to obey the innkeeper's orders: *Don't make any trouble.*

It didn't help that Owl made no attempt to pretend she felt anything other than disdain for Iseult, and Iseult was not particularly skilled at pretending *she* felt anything other than disdain for the little girl. Oh, she could keep her face blank easily enough, but then her words tended to snap. And if she managed to keep her voice calm, then her face sank into a frown.

Currently, though, they were in a standoff. Iseult wanted Owl to bathe. Owl wanted nothing of the sort. Her ancient gown had once been sage, now it was pure brown. Her skin fared no better.

"We're all dirty," Iseult explained. "Look." She pointed to the washbasin, swirling with filth. "I just washed all of that off of me."

Owl glowered at the basin, Threads gray with stubborn hate.

"I'll get clean water for you, of course," Iseult added. "Just like I got for me after Aeduan left. Don't you want to be clean too, Owl? Remove all that dirt?"

"Dirt is good." Owl stomped her foot.

And Iseult sighed. Of course an Earthwitch would say that, and at this point, Iseult was too tired to keep arguing about it. Let Aeduan deal with her when he got back.

When Owl realized she had won the argument, triumphant pink flew up her Threads. She even flung an arrogant smirk Iseult's way before scrambling from the bed to the window.

Goddess, she was awful. A demon-child to the core—and this truth was only proven all the more several minutes later. Iseult had just finished sopping stray water off the floor, when Owl suddenly smacked her palm against the window.

"*Dead*," she snarled.

Iseult flung toward her, alarmed.

"Dead," the girl said again, smacking harder at the glass. Loud enough to draw stares from the courtyard below. "Dead, dead, dead—"

"Enough!" Iseult scooted across the room, but Owl jumped off the bed and darted to the center of the room. Then she began to stomp.

"Dead." Stomp. "Dead." Stomp. "*Dead*." With each stomp, the room shook. The mirror, the washbasin, the window— they all rattled in time to her feet. And with each stomp, her Threads grew more frenzied, jumping between shades of fiery fury and tan confusion, of slate fear and purple want. There were even strands of blue sadness to twine between it all.

It made no sense, and it also was *not* going to work. It must sound like an earthquake in the room below, and if Iseult couldn't get Owl to settle down, there might be an actual earthquake to contend with soon. Or at least a lot of angry soldiers at the door.

"Stop." She lifted her hands, palms out. "Owl, stop—you have to stop. You're snagging the weave!" She approached cautiously, hands never dropping, and this time, when she reached for her, Owl did not pull away. Instead, she gave a final stomp, pointed a finger at the window, and declared, "Dead."

For several long breaths, Iseult did not move. She reached out with her magic, breath held, sensing for any Threads approaching. But the Moon Mother favored her, for no one near seemed to have noticed Owl's tantrum. In fact, it sounded like a storm was rolling in, so perhaps people thought Owl's stomping had been nothing more than thunder on the horizon.

"Outside," Owl said, the first word that was not *dead* in several minutes, so Iseult took the hint. She clambered over the bed and peered outside. Darkness had moved in, forcing her to squint against the brightness of the room glaring on the glass.

Sure enough, at the heart of the square below, the dead alder thrust up toward the sky. Raindrops speckled its pale trunk, one by gathering one. "That was here when we arrived," Iseult said. "Why does it bother you now?"

"Danger," Owl explained, and a bolt of fear briefly shimmered up her Threads.

Iseult's lips pursed. She could see them puckering in the glass. *A Threadwitch does not frown.*

168

"I suppose the storm *could* knock it into the inn," she offered, schooling her face. "Is that what you're worried about? Surely after all these years it would have fallen if . . ." She trailed off. A figure had appeared beside the tree. A man in a beige hood with Threads that shone bright as sunshine.

Trickster.

He paused on the near side of the tree, head dipping back as if to look up. To glance Iseult's way—

She jerked away from the window and twirled around on the bed until her back was against the wall. Her heart thudded behind her rib cage. Her eyes met Owl's.

The girl nodded.

Iseult *had* lost Trickster, though, hadn't she? Yes, yes, she absolutely had, so how in the Moon Mother's great weave had he found her again?

She stretched her magic wide, grasping, reaching—*there*. His Threads scissored into her awareness. He was entering the inn by the front entrance, yet he had veered right into the main room. *Maybe he doesn't know I'm here. Maybe he isn't looking for me at all. Maybe he just needs a place to stay.*

Unlikely, she decided, and not worth risking. She needed to end this situation before it could even begin—and the last thing she wanted was to get trapped in this tiny, claustrophobic room. Or worse, for Owl to get trapped in here, panic, and destroy the inn outright.

Burn him, suggested the Firewitch, but Iseult tamped that down. She was logic, she was focus, and there would be no flames. There would be no emotion at all.

The hall outside is dimly lit. The faucet at the end is beside a back stairwell. Unlit. Iseult could wait in those stairs, watch from the shadows. If the man approached, she could head him off before he reached their door.

"Owl," she said, easing back over the bed. Calm, casual, nothing to see here. "I am going out into the hall for a moment. Lock the door behind me and stay quiet. Can you do that?"

To her vast relief, Owl nodded and sank to the floor. She must have sensed Iseult's urgency—and how could she not? Despite Iseult's cool words, she *was* creeping toward the door, hunched practically in half to avoid the window. She paused at the hook where her cutlass and belt hung, but no. Even if Marstoks allowed Nomatsis to carry weapons in public, tensions were too high. It was not worth the risk.

Besides, Iseult could fell a man barehanded if she had to.

"I'll be back soon," she whispered. Then she slipped into the hall. The lock clinked into place behind her.

Twelve careful steps carried Iseult to the end of the hall. The faucet dripped as she passed, then she was to the stairwell. It was perfect for hiding. Iseult dipped into the shadows, magic casting outward once more . . .

The man was ascending the stairs, his Threads shot through with the green concentration of someone on the hunt. He moved fluidly. One step, two step, three—all the way up until he prowled into the third-floor hall. Slower now, he approached the door on the balls of his feet. Well trained and silent in this growing storm.

If Iseult did not have her witchery, she never would have sensed him coming.

As it was, this close, his Threads burned bright as a full moon. And the longer she stared, the more she sensed a charge crackling beneath the surface. Like a river in winter, where a riptide of dark currents churned at the slow, icy heart.

Trickster, she thought again. Then a heartbeat later, *Danger*.

The man aimed straight for room thirteen, no hesitation, no pause—and any lingering doubts Iseult had that he was here for her were gone in an instant. He sank to a crouch before the door, then he shrugged his cloak off one shoulder.

A one-shot Firewitched pistol rested in a holster at his hip.

The man's Threads shrank in tightly, pulled taut by single-minded intensity. And in that moment, as his arm stretched long overhead and his wrist cocked back as if to knock—at a normal height, so that anyone who opened the door would be taken by surprise—Iseult realized she had not told Owl what to do. She had not said, *Do not answer if you hear a knock.*

Owl would open the door. The man would attack.

Iseult moved. No stealth, only speed, she charged from the staircase into the hall. She reached the man right as startled turquoise ignited his Threads. Right as he angled toward her and grabbed for the pistol.

A front kick to his arm. The pistol flew. Then she pivoted and drove her knee into the back of his neck. He snapped forward, a shout breaking loose. His face hit the door.

But Iseult wasn't done. *Burn him, burn him, burn him.* His hood had slipped back, revealing pale hair. She grabbed it, yanking his face toward her. Then she kneed him again—this time in the temple. Over and over and over, until his body went limp. His Threads hazed into unconsciousness.

For several seconds, Iseult stood there, planted above him and staring down. Her pulse boomed in her ears, her breath came in panting gasps. She needed to move. Needed to get out of the hallway before anyone saw her here. Already, curious Threads were moving toward doorways in the rooms nearby. Any moment now, someone would arrive. She was Nomatsi; he looked Cartorran. This would not go over well.

Except Iseult also couldn't simply leave this man here. He would wake up eventually, and then he would attack again.

Burn him, burn him, burn him.

Her nose twitched. Threads approached from downstairs. No time, no time.

"Owl?" she called. "Open the door, please."

Immediately, the door swooshed back, as if the little girl had been waiting there all along. Iseult pushed inside, grabbed the man by the shoulders, and dragged.

She had no idea how she moved him all on her own. He was not a large man, but dead weight was dead weight. Thank the goddess for the storm outside, hiding the scraping, scratching, *heaving* sound his body made across the floorboards.

All the while, Owl watched on, her Threads curious and, for some reason Iseult did *not* want to consider, thoroughly delighted.

Iseult got the man mostly inside. She dropped his shoulders, dove for his feet, and then curled his legs up. Right as she got his boots in far enough to shut the door, a person stepped into the hall.

It was the man from the faucet, his Threads now alight with horror.

"He drank too much," Iseult said. Then she slammed the door and fell to her knees.

172

NINETEEN

✳

Aeduan stared at the tier ten, unmoving. Unblinking. The room, the monks, their voices and their blood-scents—it all melted back into distant nothing. Elbows jostled, eyes glared, but Aeduan did not leave. He did not look away.

Ten thousand talers for his father's head.

A king's ransom indeed.

Two weeks ago, Aeduan would have taken the assignment without hesitation. He would have updated his father immediately via Voicewitch, and then he would have found a way to collect all that coin.

So, so much coin.

He would have had no qualms about faking the bounty. His father's cause mattered more than the crude morality of the Monastery. Nor would Aeduan have cared if more monks died along the way, trying to win the coin for themselves.

Life was the price of justice, and Ragnor's cause was a righteous one. The time to end imperial tyranny was now. Two weeks ago, Aeduan had believed that without question. No cracks in the stone, no weakness in his foundation. He

173

was the son of Ragnor the Raider King, and his sole job was to raise coin for the cause.

Which was why he should take this tier ten. He should take it right now and then find a Voicewitch.

Instead, Aeduan turned away from the wall. The paper and its words smeared into nothing. He left the common room.

Rain beat down in the cloister, the storm having risen to full force. Clouds blocked out the sunset, darkening dusk to a false midnight. Aeduan walked along the covered edge, staring at leaves bent by raindrops.

He left the outpost, where his gaze skimmed with unseeing eyes over water splashing on the quay. Frothy with dirt, it pooled fast. He might have left the monks behind, he might be striding beside Lake Tirla while rain soaked him through, but he was not moving forward.

He was pulled in three directions. The inn was one way. His father was another, and the Monastery assignments another too, leaving Aeduan well and truly caught now. No different from the man with the lamb in the story—and also like that man, Aeduan knew he could not evade Lady Fate's gaze forever.

She would find him; she would make him choose.

The people pulled Aeduan from his thoughts. They fled past, racing from the docks and sprinting for buildings beside the quay—and that was when he noticed the waves crashing up from the lake. Ships teetered and tottered, slamming against one another with wood-crunching force.

Rain slashed harder and harder with each passing second. The wind slashed harder too.

The animals, though, were what set Aeduan to running. Dogs, cats, and rats by the hundreds poured out of structures and flooded the street. They circled the lake, leaving the city. Had Aeduan been alone in Tirla, he would have followed. Had he been the Aeduan of two weeks ago, he would have abandoned the city and left it to the storm.

He was not that Aeduan, though. This Aeduan was caught between starvation and the slaughter. This Aeduan was not yet ready to choose.

Wind and rain howled loud as a nightmare. Street signs vanished behind the rain, building fronts faded into gusting darkness. Only his familiarity with the city kept him moving onward in the right direction.

And the Painstone. Without it, he would have been trapped at the outpost, possibly even unconscious by now. He certainly would not have been able to face the hail. Small rocks that kicked off the cobblestones, spraying water and slamming into Aeduan's legs, chest. They expanded the farther he jogged, soon growing as large as his fists. These shattered, explosive shards that smashed through awnings, carriages, and soon, if he wasn't careful, would smash through his skull too.

Aeduan veered left. The crowded roofs above this street gave some respite from the hail. Short-lived, though, for the road soon ended and he was on another wide artery aiming uphill. He covered his head with the satchel of clothes and ran faster.

Then lightning shredded down. It wiped away Aeduan's sight and blanked out his hearing—and the thundercrack that followed almost toppled him. It was only the beginning, though. Again, again, the lightning thrashed, and the city quaked beneath its power.

Aeduan hurtled forward.

At the periphery of his rain-streaked vision, he saw a corpse. Bloodied, flattened, felled by hailstone. Then a second, seared by lightning. There was nothing he could do for them; all he could do was keep moving.

He drew in his magic. Weaker than he would have hoped, but *something*. Enough to propel his limbs deeper into the storm. Left, right, no remaining sense of which streets he careened up, only knowing he aimed vaguely toward the inn.

Right as his feet splashed over fallen wind-flags, bright bursts of color amidst the shadows, a new sound hit his ears. Or perhaps it was not a sound so much as a tremble in his ribs, coming from the north.

He glanced back, squinting against the rain and hail. Then he ground to a halt. A cyclone, black and snaking, writhed across the lake. It moved impossibly fast toward Tirla.

In moments, it reached the ships, smashing through them as easily as a cleaver through bone. It was headed this way. It would reach Aeduan if he did not move.

He ran, pulling any magic he could find. Every ounce of his witchery, every drop of blood he drove into his muscles. Faster than before, faster than any human could run.

But it still was not enough. Nothing could outpace this cyclone. It was on his heels now. He could hear it getting closer, crushing buildings one by one. Great eruptions of wood and stone, and all while the winds screamed louder.

Aeduan could not escape it. His only hope was to take cover. Something stone, something strong. He dove sideways, aiming for the nearest building. Bodies, bodies—how were there so many bodies? He reached steps leading to a front door and dropped to the ground beside them. Then he curled into a ball and covered the back of his neck with his hands.

Wind crushed over him. Water gushed into his mouth. Hail the size of bricks punched against him, and he felt two ribs break. His left finger knuckles broke too. Any moment now, the full cyclone would hit him. The building above him would topple down. He wouldn't die, but others would. Many others.

Except the attack never came.

Instead, the storm ended entirely. Between one shuddering breath and the next, the winds broke off. Hail stopped falling. Rain faded to quiet, a mere echoing throb in Aeduan's ears. *The eye of the storm,* he thought, and he unfurled, ready to resume running.

Yet as he straightened, his broken ribs numbed by the Painstone, a blood-scent rippled into his awareness. *Black wounds and broken death. Pain and filth and endless hunger.*

Cleaving.

Instantly, Aeduan was on his feet, rounding backward. He unsheathed his sword, ready to face whatever madness now approached amidst the calm. When he turned, though, he did not find a man corrupted by magic. This man, towering and pale haired, strode toward Aeduan with clarity and purpose. His eyes shone black, rim to rim, and lines slithered across his skin. Yet with each step that he prowled closer, the more the darkness shrank.

Like maggots wriggling into a corpse, the shadows vanished. The cleaving scent vanished too, until all that remained was a young man whose blood smelled of rocky shores and gasping lungs. But there were other blood-scents tangled inside him, like a knot of worms pulled from the soil. Hundreds of them, too many for Aeduan to tease apart or catalog.

He'd never faced anything like it.

"Are you the Bloodwitch?" the man called in Nubrevnan, still approaching. His now-blue eyes scraped up Aeduan. Then down. "You certainly look like him."

Aeduan sank into a fighting stance.

This only made the young man smile, a horrifying thing that stretched his face into inhuman proportions. Half his right ear was missing, blackened blood crusting the edges.

"Come no closer," Aeduan called.

"Or what?" the man drawled, though he did at least pause his advance. "Your sword can do nothing to me. You should know this, Bloodwitch. Unless . . ." His head tipped sideways. He tapped his chin. "Unless your father hasn't told you who I am."

My father. Something dark and vile trickled over Aeduan's skull.

The man laughed, a delighted sound. "I see from your face that he has *not* told you. Allow me to remedy that." The man's heels snapped together, his fist shot to his heart, and he bowed a Nubrevnan bow. "They call me the Fury. I have worked with your father for a long, long time—although I knew him as something else all those years ago. *He* still wears the same face." The grin widened. "I do not."

Incomprehensible words. They clanked around in Aeduan's mind, useless.

"Your father sent me to find you," the man went on, slinking a single step closer. "You were meant to check in weeks ago, Bloodwitch. He feared you dead, and yet . . ." The man opened his arms, thick eyebrows bouncing. "Here you are. And now it is time for us to go."

"No." Aeduan gave a curt head shake. "I have unfinished business in Tirla."

"Which is?"

"How did you find me?" Aeduan countered.

"Easily."

"And did my father tell you to destroy Tirla along the way?"

"This?" The man laughed, a throaty sound. "This is nothing, Bloodwitch. Where I travel, hurricanes reign." He spun around, seeming to take in the destruction for the first time—and it only made him laugh louder.

The darkness spread down Aeduan's neck. Voices were gathering, blood-scents too. As if people were stepping outside now, searching the streets for help. Some wailed, some screamed.

"Your father," the Fury said, stopping abruptly, "will want to know what detains you. Do not make me return to him without an answer. He won't like that. *I* won't like that."

"I will tell my father myself," Aeduan said flatly. "Tell him that I will give him a full report when I return."

"And when will that be?"

"Soon."

Doors were creaking open. Footsteps splashing closer. More screams, more crying, more desperation to fill the city. Aeduan did not want to see what the Fury would do to anyone who came here.

"How many hours?" the Fury asked. "I can wait."

"It will be days."

Anger flashed across the man's face now, and black lines hissed across his skin. "How many days, Bloodwitch? Stop evading my questions."

"I do not know."

A dry, vicious laugh, and the Fury pointed a crooked finger at Aeduan. "Then I do not know when I will return." He shrugged one shoulder. "Maybe next week." He shrugged the other. "Or maybe tomorrow—and do not try to escape me, Bloodwitch. No matter where you go, I will find you. And if your business is not complete when I return, then you can be sure I will finish it for you."

With those words, Lady Fate's knife finally fell. A downward clunking of her will like an executioner's blade. She was making Aeduan choose. Only one path lay before him now.

"It will be done," he said, because they were the only words he could say.

"Good," the Fury replied. Black crisscrossed his face. Wind rushed in. Then a flash of lightning, hot and blinding, scored down. By the time Aeduan's sight and hearing had returned, the Fury was gone.

TWENTY

✳

Time had never moved so slowly as it did while Merik half tumbled, half ran, trying to move where Esme wanted him to go, except that he had no sense of where that might be until pain arced through him.

Mind-numbing flames meant he had gone the wrong way. Moderate bee stings meant he moved correctly.

Twilight held sway by the time the Poznin appeared before him, moonlit and shadowy against the horizon. A vast, swampy river oozed between Merik and the city's fortified walls. Without human engineering and witches to hold back seasonal flows, the floodplain had grown and swallowed and consumed. Fifty years since the Republic's downfall, and nature had staked its claim. Rooftops and crumbling walls thrust up from the waters.

Merik had no idea how he was going to cross the river, and the pain jangling along his spine was not helping.

There are bridges, Esme said, tone curious. Like she wondered what Merik might do.

"But," he squeezed out, "they are all submerged."

Then find the one that is not. And with that command, the

pain reared back completely. He could think, he could breathe. He knew it wouldn't last. He knew Esme was only playing games with him—experimenting, as she'd said.

Hell-waters, though, he welcomed the respite. And this time, he would not be so foolish as to run.

Merik picked his way along the marsh, following soft mounds of earth through sluggish waters, reeds and cattails, and though he was soaked through by the time he reached the bridge, it was better than swimming.

Marble bricks lifted from the river like a sea fox coiling from the sea, still intact even if it led to nowhere. The marble had once been white. Now it was nothing more than moonlit gray with algae and dirt clotted thick. At the center, two columns thrust up with storm hounds howling to the sky. One still had its head; the other did not.

At the end of the bridge, the marshes resumed more densely. Easier to muck through—but also more crowded with the ghosts of a fallen republic. Collapsed walls, decayed wood, stairs that led to nowhere. Historians claimed Poznin had once been a beautiful, flourishing city, but now it was nothing more than a corpse picked clean by the crows.

Merik reached the fortified outer wall and clambered over a toppled section. Beyond, more water flowed over streets and bridges. This time, though, someone had assembled crude gangways connecting marshy spits to what remained of cobbled roadways. It zigged and zagged, ascended and sagged, eventually leading to the end of the floodplain, to a hill crowned by a second fortified wall.

This wall was much older. Ancient even, judging by the weathered slouch to its bricks. Like Pin's Keep in Lovats, it had stood the test of time. As Merik approached a crooked archway in the stones, his thighs burning from the climb, he realized for the first time that he was shivering. Now that no water caressed him, there was only wind to gust it dry—a wind he could not touch, could not command.

His teeth chattered and his toes had lost all feeling. Cold that burrowed into one's bones as this did was new to him.

He reached the top of the hill and shambled through the gate. A new city waited, untouched by floods, but not untouched by time. Here, oaks and maples, birch and ash thrust up through rooftops, ripped through walls, and clotted roadways with their trunks.

Ancient things made new again.

Merik thought it beautiful, until he spotted figures scattered amidst the green. At first he believed them a trick of the light, of his pain-rattled mind, but the longer he stared, the more he recognized human shapes within the forest. *Statues,* he hoped, but his stomach knew better. And as he shuffled down the hill and into the old city, his gut hollowed out with certainty.

He reached the first person. A young man made not of stone but flesh, a tattered Cartorran army uniform hanging off skeletal shoulders. His blackened eyes stared at nothing, and lines tracked across his face—lines Merik knew because they burned inside him too. He made no move as Merik approached. He made no move as Merik passed.

Nor did the next man, older and with dirt to coat every inch of him. Nor the woman after him or the little boy after her. All of them stood sentry, one after the next.

Merik was not sure when he began running again. No one hunted him, no pain lashed through him. He just knew he had to move. He had to prove to himself he was not one of these Cleaved, he was not one of these puppets. He was not poisoned like Kullen. He could still think for himself and command his legs. All he had to do was get this collar off, then he could flee too—

Merik tripped over a root. He fell to the earth, wrists snapping in a graceless fall. It did not hurt, yet a sob choked out anyway. It rumbled up from powerless lungs, and no amount of gasping for air seemed to make it stop.

It was not until a shadow slithered over the ground before him that he finally broke off. His head snapped up to find a little girl with blond braids and eyes black as midnight. She was dressed like a Northman in furs and colorful felt.

"Why do you stop moving, Prince?" she asked, and Merik knew it was not the girl speaking to him. He knew who really uttered those words.

"Lost," he croaked, and the little girl smiled—an eerie, unnatural thing that stretched her lips sideways.

"Just follow the puppets." Before she had even finished proclaiming this, bodies lumbered into view. Out of fallen buildings they stepped, and from between the trees they trundled. All ages, sizes, races assembled into a long line that snaked into the city. As far as Merik could see.

Then as one, in a chorus of voices that scraped against his skin, they sang, "Follow, Prince Merik. Follow, follow until you find your way."

Merik saw no other choice. He dragged himself back to his feet and followed.

Vivia and her Windwitches arrived home right as the nineteenth chimes were ringing. They landed at the Southern Wharf, where the main barracks and naval academy were.

"We can fly you to the palace!" the captain had roared atop her winds. "Drop you beside the gate!"

Vivia had refused, claiming she was not the one who'd drained all her energy in the flight. The truth, though, was that she had hoped to find Stix. As awkward as things were between them, Stix was the only person Vivia had to talk to. The only person Vivia *wanted* to talk to.

Stix wasn't at the school, though. Nor the barracks, nor anywhere along Hawk's Way as Vivia and a flank of four new, freshly awake soldiers strode ever closer toward Queen's Hill. She slowed on the street below Stix's apartment, briefly wondering if she ought to walk up ...

She decided against it. Vivia wanted to see her friend alone—not with this escort hounding her every move.

Soon, Vivia reached her bedroom in the royal wing of the palace, the familiar threadbare rugs and creaking floors so welcome after a day in that land of sandstone and white. A quarter clanging of the chimes after that, and she was down to her underclothes and sitting on the edge of her bed.

She stared at the Wordwitched paper. It had gotten flattened on the flight home, and now—as she unrolled it—six lines creased down the page.

Her words and Vaness's still remained, as well as a new phrase at the bottom.

Did you arrive home safely?

Vivia wet her lips. Then pressed the page upon her lap and tried to smooth out the wrinkles. Her attempts failed completely, and she supposed after several minutes that she did not really care. Vaness did not need a reply.

Vivia rolled up the letter and stowed it on a low table beside her bed. Then after whispering to her lone Firewitched lamp, she settled beneath her iris blue blankets and tried to sleep.

An hour later, when sleep still eluded her, Vivia crawled from her bed. A pen and inkpot waited on her desk, and with only moonlight streaming through a warped window to light the page, Vivia once more unfurled the letter.

I made it home safely.

She paused here, wondering what more to say. Wondering why she wanted to say more. After several minutes, the perfect sentence came to mind. She scribbled it down, and this time, when Vivia crawled into bed, she fell asleep right away.

TWENTY-ONE

※

The half-galley skipped lightly over Lake Scarza. Spindrift misted the skin around Safi's eyes. Nursemaid Rokesh had insisted she don an Adder shroud, and though the silk was surprisingly cool given how much it covered, it still stifled.

As did Habim's words upon the map.

Do nothing. We have a plan.

Well, Safi had a plan too—and she wasn't abandoning it just because Habim Fashayit had arrived. If she could actually make a Truthstone, then she could leave. No waiting necessary.

Waiting had never been one of her skills. Safi initiated; she did not complete.

And gods thrice-damn it, she was *sick* of being told what to do. At the very least, Habim could have given her more information. He had had an entire map with him, after all. How hard would it have been to offer details, so that she would not be—yet again—racing blindfolded into nothing?

Halfway through the return journey, the Tidewitches steering the ship changed course, aiming the half-galley for the main shore of Azmir instead of the Floating Palace. Safi had known this was coming. Unlike Habim, Vaness had actually *informed* her of the evening's plan.

"A birthday procession," the Empress had explained wearily the day before. "Very long, very tiresome. Yet I must do it every year." This was why Safi had been given the Adder uniform and shroud: it was one thing to claim one had a Truthwitch, and quite another to parade her before hundreds of thousands of people.

The City of Eternal Flame grew on the horizon, framed by the red Kendura Hills and whitecapped Sirmayans beyond. The golden spires that spanned across the city, one for each district, shone like torches beneath the ember glow of sunset.

A crow swooped overhead, and Safi prayed it didn't shit on her head.

"Are you ready to turn twenty-seven?" Safi asked, joining Vaness at the bulwark. "I have heard it's much better than twenty-six."

Vaness offered a sideways sigh—a sure sign she was un-*empress*ed. Though she did at least say, "When I made this same trip a year ago, Safi, there were no armies at my doorstep. And though General Fashayit might blame me for starting the war, he is wrong. The end of the Truce was inevitable. War always is. Besides," she added lightly, "by being the first to break the Truce, I can choose the terms of what comes next."

Despite her tone, Safi knew Vaness was anything *but* light and flippant. Even without her magic, ferocious truth resounded off everything Vaness did. Her ideals aligned with her actions; she demanded nothing from others she would not do herself; and she put the well-being of Marstok above everything else, even her own life.

"Well," Safi murmured eventually, "happy early birthday." And this time, she earned a smile. *True, true, true.*

When at last the ship reached the main wharf of Azmir, it did not berth, but rather coasted to a stop beside an isolated dock, where waiting sailors laid out a gangplank.

Rokesh led the way, guiding them into a long, open tent mounted upon iron struts and poles. Gold canvas and green banners flapped against the breeze, while soldiers in matching gold and green stood at attention in neat rows around it. A perfect rectangle to enclose the tent.

As soon as Vaness reached the heart of the tent, she swung up her arms. The iron lifted. Then the iron—and the tent attached—followed overhead as she glided down the dock.

Safi's fingers curled tightly into her uniform while the entire procession walked. Her calves ached to run, her knees itched to kick high. This was her first time outside the Floating Palace since reaching Azmir. This was her first glimpse of its people, its streets, its buildings old and new. Vaness had failed to mention what route they might travel through the city, and Safi hardly cared.

They could walk into a pit of vipers, and it would be perfectly acceptable. She was *out*, and that was all that mattered.

They passed ships, where sailors hollered and waved from the highest masts and more people whooped and whistled from belowdecks. Then the procession reached the main lakeside quay, where the roar of the crowds magnified to almost deafening. *Health and joy to you!* some screamed. Or the more common Marstoki greeting, *May all be forgiven in the fire!* Yet for every cry of devotion that swelled from the crowds, Safi heard just as many cries of rage.

She had no idea how Vaness endured it, and the longer they marched, the more it fascinated Safi. While Vaness's beauty, her strength, her heroism at Kendura Pass might have earned her fanatic adoration, she was still the leader of an empire. Everything she did was on display, and *everyone* had an opinion on how she should behave. Her unwillingness to marry, to smile, to bend—Vaness herself had told Safi what sort of rumors that fed.

The Iron Bitch, they called her.

That name riffled over the crowds now, flinging into the tent from all angles, echoing in a way that only truth could. Yet the people who uttered their disapproval felt it just as fervently as those who screamed their worship.

"The people have come from across the empire," Rokesh informed, slinking into step beside Safi. "To see tonight's fireworks and celebrate. Every inn within the city will be full, and every inn within twenty miles beyond."

So many people here to see her, Safi thought, *yet none who truly know her*. It must be very lonely indeed to be loved and hated, yet never seen.

The procession left the wharves and entered a main avenue of beige towers with red-tile roofs. The Merchant District, Safi learned. Beyond, shops and tents and street vendors crowded beneath white awnings. Then they crossed an intersection where one of the golden spires thrust up from the earth. No doors, no windows, only the square column racing toward the sky and capped by a flame-shaped cupola.

Safi wished she could get closer. Whatever this was made

190

of, it was not the same material as the rest of the city—not sandstone nor marble nor limestone nor granite.

Then they passed the tower and entered a new district where each building was painted a hundred different shades. "The Artist District," Rokesh explained, before they veered east into the University District, then into the Healer District. On and on, they switched back and forth through the city, covering every area. Passing every golden spire. Until at last, the buildings and towers were replaced by a long sandstone wall. Beyond, cedar branches rustled on the breeze, and a final spire reached up, up, up. The tallest spire of them all, dark against a dusky sky.

At an iron gate, the soldiers slowed to a stop, parting enough for Vaness, Safi, and the Adders to continue through. Without a single waver in the tent or in her stride, Vaness pointed a finger at the approaching entrance, and the black bars swung wide.

The tent briefly constricted inward as they squeezed through, like a cat wrinkling into a doorway. The scent of cedar hit Safi's nose, the city din quieted behind, and finally, iron bars crashed shut, closing them in.

With each step they moved through the cedars, the air seeming to tighten and coil. It pulled Safi's heart into her throat, and she did not have to ask where they were. The answer called to her, and the spire gave it away.

They were at the Origin Well of Marstok.

Yet something about the forest grated against Safi's magic as they walked on. It plucked at the hairs on her arms, and twice she thought she saw figures hiding in the trees. On the third instance, she said, "Someone is in the forest."

But Rokesh merely nodded. "They are soldiers. This area might be private, but we still take no risks with Her Majesty's safety."

Safi supposed that explained it, yet despite Rokesh's words, the fingers tripping down her spine did not go away.

After a hundred paces through the cedars and up a steep stairwell, the forest finally opened to reveal a long spring framed by sandstone tiles. Evenly spaced around the rippling waters were six massive cedars, bent and reaching for the sky. And set back from the Well, in the forest on the northern side, was the golden spire.

Vaness stopped before the water and eased down the tent. She carefully bent the poles and struts inward so the canvas creased like an inchworm, exposing them all to a purple sky.

Then the Empress of Marstok turned to face Safi.

Part of Safi was stunned this question had not come sooner—that in their two weeks since reaching Azmir, they had not visited this place before. Most of Safi, though, was stunned to be here *today*. This was the imperial birthday procession. There was no reason to travel here now.

"It is true then?" Vaness asked, observing Safi. Simultaneously contemplative and predatory. "You are half of the Cahr Awen?"

"I . . . don't know." Safi's toes curled in her boots. "Where did you hear that?"

"It is my business to know such things. And if it is true, Safi, then it is also my business to protect you. For over a century, Marstok has been the only empire with an intact Origin Well. If there are more—if there *could* be more . . ."

Safi's lungs loosened. Her shoulders drooped. For there it was, wasn't it? Safi was valuable; Safi was a risk.

"I will ask you again," Vaness continued, sharper now. Impatience flashing in her eyes. "Safiya fon Hasstrel: are you the Cahr Awen?"

Safi swallowed. She was suddenly too hot, the iron belt around her waist too tight. Without requesting permission, she tore off the Adder shroud. Air, glorious and free, kissed against her.

The truth was, Safi had no idea what she and Iseult were. According to Monk Evrane, they were the Cahr Awen—and they *had* swum to the heart of the dead Origin Well of Nubrevna a month ago, and a quake *had* shaken the land.

Monk Evrane had claimed this meant Safi and Iseult had healed the Well, and while Safi's magic had told her unequivocally that Evrane believed everything she'd been saying, her good sense had suggested it was supremely unlikely. The last Cahr Awen had lived five hundred years ago. There was no reason they would return now, and no reason they would be—out of all the people in the Witchlands—Safi and Iseult.

Not to mention, Safi had already lived her entire life with a target painted on her back. Did she really deserve a second? Gods below, she missed the easy days of Veñaza City. And gods below, she missed her Threadsister.

Her lips parted to repeat that she *truly* did not know if she was the Cahr Awen, but at that moment, a scream sundered the darkening sky. Inhuman and ear-shattering.

A flame hawk, searing like the sun, burst up from the nearby trees.

TWENTY-TWO

✳

Iseult was furious, and no amount of thinking *Stasis* made a difference. She had been so stupid. So *careless* and *loud*. She knew how to fight quietly. She knew how to approach undetected. Yet she'd charged that man like a drunken brawler in a street fight.

She had tied him up, and now he lay sprawled on the floor beside the bed, his bloodied face peaceful. Even his Threads hummed with the calm ease of a dreamless sleep. Owl had been fascinated from the moment Iseult had hauled him in, taking up sentry beside him and staring into his sleeping face. She'd made no move to touch him, thank the goddess, but there was a sunset shade of reverence in her Threads that had kept Iseult on edge ever since she'd shut—and bolted—the door.

As if she needed any more kindling for these flames.

The guest in room twelve had seen her with the body. Stupid, careless, *loud* Iseult had attracted his attention, and now it was only a matter of time before soldiers came to the door. That man was going to tell someone, if he hadn't already, and that left only one solution to this mess: Iseult and Owl

194

were going to have to leave this inn. Before Aeduan even returned.

Wildfire shrieked inside Iseult as she stuffed supplies into their packs. She did not need to see her own Threads to recognize rage and terror when she felt them.

Outside, lightning flashed. Rain hammered down.

"Different," Owl declared, the first words she'd spoken since Iseult had returned, towing a body behind her.

"Because he is Cartorran." Iseult shoved the new healing supplies into her bag. "They have different skin and hair where he comes from."

"Poke?"

"What?" Iseult glanced up and found Owl canted in close to the unconscious man, like a dog sniffing a cornered hare. Light glanced off something in her hand.

A knife. She must have pulled it from Iseult's things.

"Poke," Owl repeated, brandishing the blade. "Wake him?"

"That will *kill* him." Hell-gates and goat tits, did the Moon Mother hate her? Iseult darted for the knife. "Owl, give that to me."

The child swiped backward, laughing. First a childish squeal, then a wilder, gleeful giggle when Iseult grabbed for her waist instead. Iseult was tired; Owl was fast; and in a blur of high-pitched shrieking, she scampered for a corner behind the bed. "Poke, poke, poke—"

A knocking boomed at the door. Iseult froze. Owl froze. Then came Aeduan's voice. "It's me."

Of *course* it was him. There were no Threads—it had to be him.

With a flip of her wrist, Owl unlocked the bolt. Aeduan

strode in, drenched and splattering water to the floorboards. "There is trouble," he said, eyes instantly finding Iseult's. "You need to leave."

It was like dropping a cannonball on a frozen pond, yet instead of the ice shattering—instead of Iseult or Owl bursting into movement at Aeduan's return—the ice did not crack. Nobody moved. Aeduan's words shivered in the air and stayed there while Owl and Iseult gaped at him from the other side of the bed.

In that odd pause between Aeduan's declaration and Iseult's comprehension she realized what a strange tableau must stand before him: Iseult stooped over Owl, Owl in the corner with a knife, and an unconscious man tied to the bed mere paces away.

Then Aeduan moved, and everyone else followed. He shut the door. Owl dropped the knife. And Iseult scrambled around the bed.

"He was following me." Her words came out garbled and thick. "Th-then I thought he was going to attack, so I a-attacked him first."

Aeduan simply repeated what he had said before: "You need to leave." Then he added, words clipped and efficient, "Someone saw you attack him. Soldiers are coming to arrest you. I passed them on my return. I heard them name our room and your face. You and Owl cannot stay here, Iseult. Go to the Monastery. They will protect you."

Iseult's breath rushed out. She had known this might be coming. Yet despite that, her mind couldn't keep up. "How close are they?"

"Minutes away, at most. The damage from the storm has

slowed them. You can find horses in the stable, and I will deal with Prince Leopold."

And there it was again. The cannonball to slam down and thud against the ice. *Prince Leopold. Prince. Leopold.* Oh goddess save her, what had she done?

As if on cue, a voice thick with sleep drawled out in Cartorran, "Monk Aeduan? Is that you?"

Iseult twirled toward the man. Toward the *prince*. No more hazy Threads of sleep, but rather turquoise shock and hints of gray fear, spiraling straight into the sky.

"What is the meaning of this?" he began. Then his green eyes fell on Iseult. His expression faltered. "You."

Iseult had no idea what that meant. *You.* He had been following her, he had been crouched outside the room, trying to get in—so obviously he knew who she was.

Although, suddenly her earlier theory that he worked for Corlant no longer made sense. Suddenly, she had a thousand questions fighting for space in her brain. Why was he hunting her? Why had he carried a pistol?

No time to ask them. No time to dwell. Soldiers were coming because Iseult had been so *stupid*.

In a flurry, she finished shoving gear into their packs while Aeduan turned his attention to Owl. The girl had crawled under the bed, her Threads shining with fear.

"Take me with you," the prince said. No one listened. He strained against his bonds, body half upright beside the bed— and gaze still transfixed on Iseult. "Please," he said. "*Please,* Iseult det Midenzi. Take me with you."

At the sound of her name, cold hardened in Iseult's lungs. She paused, her pack halfway onto her back and confusion swiping across her face. Her eyes bulged, her lips parted, and with the onslaught of emotion came an onslaught of theories and contradictions.

He must be Mathew's contact and I'm supposed to meet him.

But then why was he following me? Why not go to the coffee shop?

No, he must be working with Eron fon Hasstrel. How else would he know my name?

But why would he work to depose his own uncle, then?

Before Iseult could organize her thoughts into any logical, cohesive order, Threads drifted into the periphery of her magic. Hostile, focused, and bound in a way that suggested they followed the same orders. They filed into the yard outside.

Oh, the Moon Mother hated her indeed. She should never have attacked Leopold—a thrice-damned *prince*—and she should never have dragged his body into their room.

She dropped the pack and vaulted for the lantern beside the door. A rough exhale across the flame. "Soldiers," she told the sudden darkness. "They've reached the inn."

At those words, a rattle took hold of the room. A faint trembling—so subtle at first, Iseult didn't know what the sound was. Like insect wings or ferns on a breeze. Then she realized it was the glass in the mirror, the glass in the window.

Then she realized she had spoken in Nomatsi. Owl had understood, and now the girl's Threads were pulsing brighter, and then brighter still in a terror that split the shadows of the room. All while the faint, almost invisible Threads of her earth magic tendriled outward, reaching for whatever substance she could control. First the window, then the mirror, and now the sconce that had held the lantern's flame. How much longer before her magic latched onto the screws and bolts? The bricks and the stones that kept this inn upright? Iseult had worried she'd burn them all to the ground, but it was far more likely Owl would topple them first.

In moments, Iseult's vision had adjusted to the darkness. Aeduan now knelt beside the girl. The prince still strained against his bindings, bed creaking, and beneath the shaking glass around them, shouts now trembled through the floorboards. The soldiers were inside the inn.

"I can help you." It was the prince, his voice and Threads intense with concentration. No panic here, only calm insistence. "I have a gelding in the stable—take him, and I will handle the soldiers."

"How?" Iseult asked at the same time that Aeduan snapped, "No."

"I can distract the soldiers long enough for you to get away. But you have to untie me."

Again, Aeduan said, "No," but Iseult ignored him. She had caught this man and brought hell-fire onto their heads. Maybe . . . maybe that act need not be a total waste. Especially if Leopold was the one meant to meet her all along.

She crossed the room in four long strides and glared down at the prince. Moonlight flooded in through the rain-speckled window, draining him of color. "Why should we trust you?"

"What other options do you have?" he demanded, and Iseult was inclined to agree. There was no time left for subtlety, nor time for clever word games. Iseult needed a straight answer from the prince. Now.

"Do you work for Safi's uncle?"

199

Surprise and a quick skittering of confusion spiraled through his Threads. "You know about that?"

"Iseult," Aeduan cut in, Owl clinging tightly to his leg. "You cannot trust him. *Leave* him."

She couldn't, though. Not when she had so many questions and so little time. Lips pressing tight, she withdrew the knife she'd reclaimed from Owl. She dug the blade into Leopold's lowest vertebrae, and whispered, "If you betray us, if you so much as *breathe* a word to those soldiers about where we are going, then I will burn you alive and shred whatever bits of your body remain. Do you understand?"

A gulp. A shiver of unsteady Threads. "I understand."

"Good." She hauled him upright, then cut his bindings. He stumbled into Aeduan, who caught him and slung him out the door. A shallow breath later, and the prince was gone.

The seconds slithered past as Aeduan, Iseult, and Owl waited for some sign the soldiers below were busy. The glass around them shook faster and faster. Even the floorboards trembled, and no amount of whispered words could calm Owl. Terror had sent her magic spinning out of control. Aeduan knew what that felt like.

Iseult's hand closed over Aeduan's elbow. His breath hitched.

"I'm sorry," she said. "You are ill, and now we have to run—all because I was a fool. I had no idea who he was, I swear."

Aeduan hesitated. They had come so far in this odd partnership to now be apologizing to each other.

200

He pulled away from her. "I found a Painstone at the outpost. I will be fine."

Iseult's lips parted as if to reply, but then Leopold's voice sang up from downstairs—*"Why are all these soldiers here?"*—and there was no time for conversation or explanation.

Aeduan and Iseult each carried a pack, while Owl clutched Aeduan's hand. Every shift of their belongings, every groan of a floorboard, every pause in the arguments below, sent Aeduan's pulse spiking higher. Before they even reached the back stairwell, his fingers were numb from Owl's squeezing.

Worse, she had started to cry. It was just a soft sniffle for now, broken up by muted whimpers every few seconds, but Aeduan knew a full storm might break loose at any moment. Iseult knew too, and she took the lead, whispering, "There are no Threads ahead."

They reached the first floor just in time to hear Leopold bellow, "Your superiors will hear about this!" and then Iseult was guiding them for a low door. Boot steps echoed out from the hall as the soldiers stomped up the main stairs.

Aeduan reached for the door's latch. This was a side entrance to the stable. It had to be, for he sensed horses beyond—the wild blood of freedom and open roads. But Iseult grabbed his wrist. "People. Three of them."

He flinched. Owl whimpered. How had he missed those people? How had his *magic* missed them? For Iseult was right: when he drew in a lungful of air, he could smell the faintest flicker of human blood. Weak, though, as if his Painstone were failing him already. As if his witchery were fading, carried away by a curse.

Anger rippled through him. Anger that those arrows could

do this to him. Anger that the Painstone had not lasted longer. Anger that Lady Fate had struck so decisively and so fast.

"I will deal with them," Aeduan said, the words a snarl beneath his breath. He opened the latch.

Again, Iseult grabbed him. Wariness flickered in her eyes. "Aeduan."

His anger flashed hotter. "I will not hurt them."

"It's not them I'm worried about." Her fingers tightened on his forearm. Five pressure points he wished would let go.

And that he also wished would stay.

Then Iseult did release him. "Owl, come to me."

For once, the child obeyed, and after easing his pack to the floor, Aeduan crept into the stable. Pine shavings and horse filled his nostrils. A comforting smell, were it not laced with human blood. Three distinctive scents that grew sharper with each of his cautious breaths. *Wind-flags and winter.* That came from the nearest stall, and with it the sound of water dripping down. "Damned storm," a girl muttered. Two stalls later, where the stable bent left, waited another scent. *Cinnamon and horsehair.*

But the third scent, the third—no amount of inhales was pulling the third scent to Aeduan. Perhaps the stable hand had left.

"May I help you, sir?"

Instincts laid claim to Aeduan's muscles. He spun, he kicked, his boot heel connected with a jaw. A crunch sounded, and before Aeduan could lower his foot, the stable hand crashed to the hay-strewn floor.

Blood filled Aeduan's nose. No missing it now, fresh and free. *Cut grass and birdsong. Warm blankets and bedtime stories.*

A boy. The person Aeduan had felled was only a boy, and now his jaw was broken. Pain watered in his eyes—dark eyes that held Aeduan's while his dangling mouth tried to form shouts of alarm. Betrayal. Horror.

Heat coiled into Aeduan's fists. Demon, monster. He couldn't escape what he truly was. "Stay down," he ordered before whipping away.

The boy did stay down, but distorted cries left his throat. The horses stamped and snuffed. The remaining hands hurried to their stall doors. As one, they saw Aeduan. As one, they saw their friend. And as one, their lips parted.

Aeduan stilled their blood. It was not a graceful move, nor even a powerful one. He fumbled to even *find* the folds of winter and sprays of cinnamon that made these stable hands who they were. But it was enough, and he held fast. Long enough for unconsciousness to seep in. Long enough for their bodies to crumple to the floor, one by one.

Abrupt silence, then the door clicked, and Iseult and Owl were there. Iseult stalked forward, both packs bouncing on her back as she peered into each stall. She made no move to claim a steed, though, and she made no comment on the boy with the broken jaw.

Owl meanwhile flung herself against Aeduan's leg, and almost instantly, panic took hold throughout the stable. The nearest horses started trumpeting, and some even bucked against stall doors.

"Here!" Iseult called from a corner stall, already yanking gear off the wall. "This must be the gelding. I'll tack him up—" She broke off as the black horse reared.

"Owl." Aeduan knelt beside her. Tears streamed down her

203

pale cheeks, while great hiccups shuddered in her chest. And there was no denying that the horses kicked in time to each of her building sobs. "Remember the two fish from the story I told you?" He had to lift his voice to be heard over the growing roars from the horses. "Owl, remember how they stayed strong and escaped Queen Crab? We have to do the same now. You must be strong and stop crying. Owl, can you do that?"

She wagged her head as if saying no, but her sobs did settle—and the horses did briefly calm. Long enough for Iseult and Aeduan to tack up the gelding together. Long enough for him to lift Owl, so light, so fragile in his demon arms, and drop her on the prince's fine saddle. Aeduan offered a hand to Iseult.

She did not take it. "You haven't gotten a horse." Her eyes darted side to side. She was putting it all together. "In the room, you said that *I* had to leave. That *I* had to go to the Monastery. I, not *we*."

On the saddle, Owl's crying resumed.

"I have business elsewhere," he said.

"Business," she repeated, words getting more strained by the second. "You have *business* elsewhere? Does that mean you will find us after your ... your business is concluded?"

"No." He turned away from her. The soldiers were almost to the stable, a surge of blood-scents he could not ignore, and though he could bar the door, hold it closed with his own strength, that was only a temporary solution—

Iseult's hand clamped on his shoulder. "What about Owl? What about her family?"

"I cannot help them."

A shocked laugh. Then a disbelieving, "Are you serious right now?"

"Yes."

"*No.*" She pushed in front of him. "You cannot just walk away. Not after everything."

Shouts approached: "*Check the stables!*" It was now or never if Iseult and Owl were going to escape safely.

Which left Aeduan with only one option. If the choice was slaughter or the lamb, then slaughter it would have to be. Better that than the soldiers reaching Iseult and Owl. Better that than the Fury finding them.

"I can walk away," he said coolly. "And I will walk away. We are not friends, we are not allies."

"We are—" she began.

"Nothing." He leaned closer. Their noses almost touched. "There is no we, there is no us. Do you understand? You were a means to an end, and I have found a better means."

Time seemed to slow, and during the strange lull that stretched between one heartbeat and the next, it struck Aeduan that until this moment, he had never appreciated how much feeling Iseult showed. Not until right now, when she showed none at all. The subtle movements, the tics and tightenings—how had he missed the extent of them?

And her eyes. All this time, they had held such depth of emotion, yet he had never noticed.

Until now, when the emotion had faded to nothing at all. Her face was as empty as the moon and far less reachable.

"You might lie to yourself," she said at last, voice smooth as a scythe and twice as sharp. "But you cannot lie to me."

Then she turned away, and the soldiers arrived. They burst

205

in from the back entrance, bellowing and drawing swords, pistols. Owl screamed, and Iseult swept onto the gelding.

Aeduan charged the soldiers. Eight of them. No time for magic, no time for anything but brute force and speed. He unsheathed his sword. He would hold the men off long enough for Iseult and Owl to—

The stable exploded. Wood crunched, the floor lurched. Dust and splinters rained down. The roof above was torn apart. Then fangs and fury crashed inside. Aeduan barely had time to dive away before Blueberry slammed to the earth. His wings spread wide.

Aeduan did not think, he simply ran. Wood fell around him. Horses plowed from their stalls, the latches rising one by one—as if an Earthwitch pulled the iron from afar. He passed four soldiers, men who had come in from the front. Men who now wanted to leave.

One by one, though, claws grabbed and screams ripped out.

Then Aeduan was to the stable yard, the cool air rushing over him. Horses and humans crowded for the exit. And there, galloping past the tree, its bark stark against the night sky, were Iseult and Owl.

Aeduan did not watch them go. Instead, he flipped his cloak inside out, since soldiers would now be looking for a monk, and he set off in the opposite direction. Away from the inn, away from Tirla, and away from the lamb he had never wanted to kill.

TWENTY-THREE

✳

The Adder shroud fell from Safi's fingers. She had been here before, watching as a flame hawk plummeted from the sky. As the heat roared closer and fire consumed all sight. This time, though, there was no Caden to save her, no Hell-Bard magic to cancel out the power of magicked flames.

Rokesh and the other Adders charged into tight formation around Safi and Vaness. Then everyone vaulted for the path. As they ran, Vaness flung her arms toward the sky. The folded tent whooshed by, and the hawk's screeching cry told Safi the tent had hit its mark.

They reached the path and descending steps right as Marstoki soldiers tumbled out from the forest, blades drawn to battle the hawk ...

Except their uniforms were already streaked in blood and death. *False, false, false!*

"Ambush!" Safi screamed at the same moment the nearest soldier raised his sword for an attack.

Rokesh swirled in. The soldier's blade nicked his shoulder—but not before he thrust his own into the man's heart.

One by one, the Adders clashed against the false soldiers,

formation strong. Safi and Vaness protected. Fire still crushed in from behind, though. A hurricane of heat borne on seething, magical wings.

"I cannot control the blades!" Vaness shrieked over the battle. "They are not made of iron!"

Shit, shit. This ambush was targeted and thoroughly planned—and now the false soldiers were too many to stop. An Adder to Safi's left was torn away from the formation. Then an Adder just behind.

Worse, the flame hawk had arrived.

Rokesh dove for Vaness. Safi dove for the trees. Rusty trunks and green uniforms blurred at the edges of her vision. No soldiers attacked, though. Everyone was too busy running.

Then sparks rained down. Branches ignited. And ten paces to Safi's left, the hawk swooped by. A streak of orange that razed entire cedars to ash—and entire soldiers too. Their final cries rattled in Safi's skull, somehow louder than the flames. Somehow louder than the creature hurtling by.

Safi vaulted faster. She cut, she spun, she *moved* wherever her feet would carry her. Still, no one attacked as she sprinted by. They were too occupied by the flame hawk, already blasting in again.

Yet something flickered in the farthest corner of Safi's brain. Something that said, *You're missing part of the puzzle here.* No time to consider, though. Only time to run.

She reached a fallen cedar, its branches aflame. A wall of smoke and heat she couldn't see beyond.

She jumped. She tripped, hands flying forward.

She landed on a dead man. Not just one, but a hundred. A whole *pile* of corpses waiting for the flames to consume

208

them. Freshly dead, blood still sticky, and with only their smallclothes and weapons left to them.

Metal weapons. These were the real soldiers.

Safi yelped. Then tried to rise, to scrabble desperately back to her feet. But the blood was slick against dead skin.

Flames and smoke choked in, along with flame hawk screams. False soldiers raced past, clearing the burning tree as Safi had and fleeing the flame hawk. *No time, no time.* Safi scrambled to her feet. Her bad ankle twisted, a distant pain she knew she would regret later. Assuming there was an actual *later.*

She swung her arms high and joined the racing soldiers—except she opted to run an entirely different direction. If she followed them, they would all eventually reach the sandstone wall and be trapped. If she wanted to escape, she would have to circle around.

As Lady Fate would have it, though, her plan was a poor one, for the flame hawk set its sights on her. It careened closer, screaming like the demons of the Void. Heat and noise and light.

And death, if Safi could not find cover. She needed something that would not burn. The forest fell away. Abrupt, exposing, and leading Safi right back to the Well where this had all begun.

She was left with only one real option: she dove in.

A punch of cold, a swipe of silence. Then the flame hawk reached the Well. Instantly, the waters boiled, a rush of scalding heat that shoved Safi deeper. She swam as fast and as hard as she could. Down, down, *down.*

She reached the deepest part of the Well right as the

skin-cooking waters touched the soles of her feet. Her mind wiped clean with pain. Her lips parted; air burst from her lungs in a rush of bubbles.

Then her hands touched the rock bottom of the spring.

A tremor erupted. Water blasted against her, and with it came a light so white, so blinding, she thought she had died. That the flames had claimed her soul, and this time, there would be no survival. No rebirth.

Except that two thunderous heartbeats passed, and she was not dead. Instead, she was being punched back toward the surface ... Then *above* the surface, where she found herself gulping in air and gazing at an evening sky turned to gray.

A sizzling sound behind forced her to turn. A light shone from the Well's heart—a column that seemed to whirl and writhe. So bright, Safi had to squint to see what lay beyond: the flame hawk. Its golden-feathered body hissed and smoked, fires extinguished, while the saddest whimper Safi had ever heard came from its onyx beak.

For approximately two seconds, she pitied the creature. Then its tailfeathers sparked to life, and she decided pity was better reserved for creatures that *didn't* want to eat her alive.

She paddled frantically to the Well's edge and clambered out. Sopping, she aimed toward the path ... Which was blocked by the burning wreckage of Vaness's tent. While she gaped and searched for an alternate route, a sleek black bird shot past Safi. She knew in an instant that it was the old crow. The one from her bedroom that had left her a drained Painstone.

For a single sodden breath, time blurred into a meaningless thing. The crackling flame hawk, the glowing Well, the fighting soldiers in the distance—it all became a blank backdrop to the old crow zooming by.

It flew, squawking, to the golden spire.

And *that*, Safi realized, was her protection. Lit by the Well's light, it shone like polished gold. Solid, huge, and quite inflammable.

Safi launched into a gallop—and time launched as well, suddenly feeling twice as fast. *Too* fast. She pelted past the Well. Twenty paces to the forest. Another fifty paces to the spire after that.

She reached the cedars, sparing a single glance for the flame hawk. Which was, *of rutting course*, fully ignited once more. And now bellowing at Safi with a fury that told her she was out of time. Its next attack would be the last.

The hawk took flight.

Faster, faster—Safi pushed herself *faster*. This was who she was. No looking back, no thinking. She was a bundle of muscles and power honed to move, honed to *live*. This would not be her end. She had survived a flame hawk before; she intended to survive it today too, thank you.

Gold radiated ahead. Brighter by the second. Closer, closer. And with the old crow never leaving her sight. Always, it darted just beyond. And always, the flame hawk darted just behind.

Hotter, hotter. Louder, louder.

The crow reached the spire. Safi reached the spire. She clawed for the edge, ready to sling herself around before the hawk could reach her.

211

Her footing failed. Her weak ankle snapped, and before she could catch herself, she toppled forward.

She hit empty air, no ground to catch her. Darkness engulfed her. She slammed against stone, though somehow she managed to tuck her chin to her chest, catch the impact with her shoulder, and transfer the energy into a roll.

A roll that carried her into a bright blue light.

Power crashed over her. Sudden and shocking, it stretched her and crushed her. It tore her apart and then put her back together again.

Until she rolled to a stop and stared up at a stone ceiling far, *far* overhead. Her lungs pumped, her heart pummeled, and chills rippled down her body, while her ankle throbbed with angry, fresh pain.

No memory of the flame hawk's heat lived in her veins now, though. Only ice and silence, while blue light continued to waver in her vision.

Where the hell-gates am I?

Angling a bruised arm beneath her, Safi sat up—and almost fell right back down again. She sat sprawled upon a ledge scarcely large enough to hold her, and beyond waited a black abyss of *nothing*. Somehow, in her fall, she had slipped into a cave beneath the golden spire . . .

And somehow that cave was large enough to hold the entirety of the Floating Palace. Twice.

Even as Safi thought this, she knew it was impossible. Even as her mind tried to grasp why she no longer heard signs of battle or the flame hawk, why heat no longer chased, she knew, deep at the core of her witchery, that it was because she had left the Origin Well's grounds entirely.

She had left Marstok entirely.

True, true, true.

A squawk pierced her eardrums. Safi flinched, snapping right and flinging out a hand to brace herself. It was such a long, long way to fall.

She found the crow glaring at her a mere arm's length away. It perched upon an unlit torch fixed to the cavern wall. Beside it was a door. *The* door Safi had traveled through.

It glowed blue and seemed to pulse against her, a shivering sensation not so different from the magic that thrummed inside her chest. She had to crane her neck to take it all in. Ornate carvings were etched into the granite. Ancient, Safi thought, even as they looked untouched by time.

Another squawk from the crow. But this time, Safi was prepared. She glared right back at it. "Where," she demanded gruffly, "have you taken me?"

The bird blinked. Then its beak *clack-clack-clack*ed, and she would have bet every piestra in Dalmotti that it was laughing at her.

It was as she dusted off her bloodied hands that a new light winked in Safi's vision. Red and flashing.

Iseult. Her gaze snapped to her Threadstone, dangling against her chest. It must have fallen out of her uniform during the roll, and now angry red light blinked up at her. It tossed bloodstained shadows across the cavern walls.

But did the stone blink because Iseult was in danger, or did it blink because Safi was? Safi had no idea, no way of telling. And before she could rise and try to gauge in which direction Iseult might be, the old crow made a move. Its wings swept up and it hurled itself at Safi.

She reacted without thought, shoving herself sideways to avoid it. She hit the blue light and toppled once more through the doorway.

Again, Safi was pulverized and pulled apart. Again, she was crushed and expanded while time sped so fast it stopped entirely. Then she was through the magic, striking a sharp, muddy slope. Light shone through a tiny crack above, but no flame hawk. No heat or rage.

Safi glanced to the blue light, now behind her. It glowed from an archway blocked by stones. Roots and weather had cleared a path along the bottom. Safi must have hit a crack in the earth beside the spire, slid into this hidden ravine . . . and then slid right on through that magic doorway.

She shivered. In the distance, pistols popped and people screamed, so she hauled herself up the incline, still soaked from the Well and now muddied too.

Her ankle protested the climb. It wasn't broken again, but it wasn't happy either.

She reached the golden spire. Voices were near—voices she thought she knew, even as they were swallowed by the flame hawk's roar. Then she heard someone holler in Cartorran, "*Is that all you have for me?*" and with no concern for her ankle, Safi started to run.

"*Come at me, you bastard!*"

The Well appeared through the trees, still distant and hazed by fire and smoke. With each loping, uneven step, Safi saw more. Corpses in Marstoki green. Corpses in Adder black.

And the flame hawk, on the ground and limping. Each of its hops shook the earth as it stalked toward the Empress of Marstok, unconscious beside the Well.

214

Ten paces away was a second woman, crouched defensively. No armor, no helmet, no weapons save a single knife extended before her.

The Hell-Bard Lev.

Safi had no idea why the woman was there—or *how*—but relief sent her muscles spinning faster. If the Hell-Bards were in this fight, then Safi and Vaness might actually survive.

The flame hawk lunged at Lev, beak out and neck extended. Then its body passed right over, and before Safi's eyes, Lev dissolved into darkness. Wherever the magic of the flame hawk touched her, she became a skeleton made of shadows.

A skeleton now thrusting its blade into the flame hawk's chest.

The monster *shrieked* its pain—but that was only the beginning. As Safi stumbled out from the cedars, aiming toward the fallen Empress, the other Hell-Bards—lumbering Zander and lithe Caden—charged from a different expanse of trees. They rushed the hawk from behind, and like Lev, they wore no armor, no helmets. All they had were simple knives . . .

And the power of the Hell-Bard's noose. The ability to withstand any magical attack, even a flame hawk's.

The two Hell-Bards reached the creature's tail. Then two more skeletons streaked into the firestorm. Zander attacked the wing. Caden leaped onto the beast's back. Five bounding strides and he reached the top of the creature's spine. He shoved his blade in, right where the wings met. Right where the hawk would feel it most. Such beasts might not die, but they could be injured. Safi had learned that firsthand with sea foxes.

215

The flame hawk screamed, a layered sound that split Safi's skull. That shook the ground—that shook the very *world* with its pain. Somehow, Caden remained upon the creature's back, a torch of black flame, even as the hawk attempted flight.

Stab. Withdraw. Stab. Withdraw.

Not until its massive body had cleared the trees did Caden jump. And before Safi's eyes, he became a man again. A split second later, he plunged into the Well. And a split second after that, the hawk was gone, only smoke and charred remains to prove it had ever been there.

While Lev and Zander moved to haul out Caden, Safi staggered to the Empress, who was just coming to. Her nose bled, a sign her magic had drained. And now more soldiers coalesced within the smoking cedars.

Gods below, this battle would never end.

Safi grabbed for the closest weapon: a saber off one of the fallen, fake soldiers. It was shockingly light. *Not iron*, Safi realized as she straightened. *Nor steel*. Which was why Vaness hadn't been able to control it. Whoever had planned this attack had planned it well, from the ambush to the weapons to the timing.

Safi reeled about, ready to face the next onslaught of soldiers, when Zander and Lev appeared beside her, a flanking position.

"Fancy meeting you here!" Lev grinned, her scarred face streaked with blood and ash. She snatched up two swords from the fallen and tossed one to Zander. "Come here often?"

Safi couldn't help it. She laughed, a high-pitched, almost neighing sound. And when Caden moved into position on her other side, she said, "I thought you left the city!"

"Not yet" was all he had time to reply before the soldiers poured out of the trees. This time, though, Safi's magic had nothing to say. No skittering scritch of lies, because this time, the soldiers were real. And Habim was at their head, bellowing, "Stand down, Cartorrans, or die." As one, every Marstok behind him fixed their pistols and blades upon the Hell-Bards.

And the Hell-Bards were left with no choice. Magic they could defeat. Crossbows and cold iron, they could not.

They stood down.

TWENTY-FOUR

✳

Iseult had no idea where she was going. What few Tirlan streets she recognized from before were destroyed, buildings collapsed, trees fallen, roads flooded.

Owl wailed against her, but at least she did not try to flee. She held fast to Iseult, and Iseult held fast to the horse—so well trained, so unflinching in the face of a battle crowding at their heels. The soldiers were giving chase.

"Left!" a voice bellowed, brilliant Threads approaching from her right. It was the prince, his face bloodied and bruised, atop a Marstoki army roan. "Take the left!"

"Why?" she shouted. "Where will that go?"

"Out of the city and away from the soldiers—unless you have a better plan?"

Iseult did not have a better plan. In fact, she had no plan at all. She always relied on Safi in these situations. While Safi could think with the soles of her feet and sense with the palms of her hands, Iseult only ever managed to shut down. No stasis, no use to anyone. There was too much happening around her right now, too little time to breathe. She had not even processed that Aeduan was gone. That he had *abandoned* them.

She felt trapped. Caught on some path she had never intended to take and now unable to change course. If Leopold could guide her off this trail, then she would take it. He had helped her escape the inn; she had to hope he would help her again.

Especially since alarms were sounding from nearby rooftops.

"Right!" Leopold barked next, his Threads blazing with a green so dark it was almost black. No fear or panic in him, only intense energy focused on escape.

He was as well trained and unflinching as his horse.

They sped onto a wider artery, a view of the lake opening before them. Wharves were half submerged, ships and docks smashed askew. The storm, Iseult guessed, though how it had done so much damage here while scarcely touching the inn, she had no idea.

She hugged Owl more tightly to her. They rode on.

Sometimes the lake would appear, its waters a mess of wood and debris. Other times, they would race down streets that their horses could barely fit into. Always, always the alarms blared. Even after they had left the city behind and small farms and thatch huts took hold. Even when the terrain steepened and a forest crowded in. Still, they could hear the horns crowing after them.

Iseult sensed Threads too. Occasionally, she saw the weary faces attached, brought to their doors by curiosity. Or more often by fear.

When at last no Threads grazed her awareness and they had seen no signs of habitation for several miles, she towed the gelding to a halt. A rickety bridge spanned a stream frothy with rainwater. Mist clouded the mossy clearing around it.

219

Far, far behind, the alarm still echoed, a faint call on the horizon.

Before Leopold could tow his roan to a stop, Iseult had her right leg over the saddle. She pulled Owl to the ground. The girl had stopped crying, but what replaced it was so much worse. Dead eyes and faint, shrinking Threads of numb white. She was in shock.

"Owl," Iseult said. "Look at me. Can you look at me?"

Owl could not look at her.

"What is wrong with her?"

Iseult snapped around, flames awakening. In a whisper of steel, she drew her cutlass and fixed it on the prince. "Stay where you are."

"Because I am clearly such a threat." He glared, dirt thick on his brow, while several paces behind, his stolen mare waited. Sweat glittered, a thick lather across her body. Both horses needed watering and rubbing down. "I *did* just save your life," he added. "Twice."

Iseult didn't care. Her fingertips throbbed with heat. Her mind throbbed with the voice. *Burn. Him. Burn. Him.* And beside her, Owl had not moved at all.

"Why were you there?" she asked.

"What do you mean?" Leopold frowned. "You knocked me out, so I had no choice—"

"*In Tirla,*" she ground out. Her mouth was too small. Her mind was too small. "Why were you in Tirla?"

"Again, what do you mean?" Confusion whorled across the prince's Threads. "I already told you that I am working with Safiya's uncle."

"How do I know that's true?"

"You . . . want proof?" He gaped at her.

Iseult, however, was entirely serious, and after three long seconds of only the horses' snuffs to fill the air, the prince finally seemed to grasp this.

He barked a laugh, an amused sound even as rusty frustration spiraled up his Threads. "Everything I had is back in Tirla, Iseult det Midenzi. Unless you want to return there and face all those soldiers again, then I fear you will have to trust me at my word."

She did *not* trust him at his word. She also did not know what to do. Everything had happened so fast. She needed to tend the horses. She needed to deal with Owl. She needed to interrogate this prince and figure out where she was going.

And above all, she needed to stop thinking about Aeduan. He was not coming back.

"I can see you do not believe me." The prince sighed. His breath fogged. The night had grown cold.

"Perhaps if I explained everything from the start, then that would help. Shall we sit?" He shifted as if to crouch.

"If you move again, I will kill you."

"Standing it is then."

"*Silence.*" Iseult turned away, dropping to one knee before Owl. Leopold could wait; Owl could not. The girl had not moved, her Threads had not changed. Wherever she was, it was not here. But this night—it was not so different from a night six and a half years ago, and Owl was not so different from another girl on the run, all the ties that bound her shorn without warning.

Iseult plucked a stone from beside her knee, just as Monk

221

Evrane had done on that night. Then she took Owl's hand into her own and unfurled Owl's fingers.

"Take this." She placed the rock on Owl's palm. "Look at it and tell me what you see."

Owl did not look at it, she did not speak. Nor had Iseult all those years ago.

"There's silt on it," Iseult said. "Do you know what that means? It means it's from the riverbank, but look—do you see how rough its edges are? It has never been a part of the river. And what about this." Iseult tapped sparkling flecks on the rock's surface. "Do you see the mica? It looks like starlight. You can even see the Sleeping Giant right here."

Owl's pupils shrank slightly. Her eyes rolled down to Iseult's hand.

"And what color would you call this? Gray? Or is it black? I think it's black in the sunlight, but the Moon Mother's glow makes it—"

"Old." Owl's voice rustled out, soft as the song of her namesake.

"Very old," Iseult agreed. "As old as the Witchlands."

"Older." Owl blinked, and with that movement, the first flakes of color pitched through her Threads. Cyan awareness, jerky at first, like a wave smacking against a ship. Then smoother, gentler, calm. They were not whole yet, but they would eventually build back to it.

"Gone," Owl murmured. Still she gazed at the stone. "He is gone."

Iseult did not need to ask who Owl meant, and unbidden, the muscles in her legs crumpled. She sank onto her heels. Tired, so tired.

In Tirla, back at the inn, she had not believed Aeduan when he'd said he would not be joining them. *He will follow,* she had thought while mounting the gelding. Then while riding into the yard, *He will follow.* Then again and again, her breath closing off with each beat of the gelding's hooves. *This is a joke, and he will follow. He will follow. He has to follow.*

Please, please follow.

They had left the inn, pistols firing. Final thunderclaps to fill Iseult's ears. To fill her heart. But Aeduan had not followed. He had left her, after everything. After she had saved his life, and he had saved hers. After she had cleaved a man for him.

She had gone back for Aeduan that day in the Contested Lands, but he was not coming back for her. He was never coming for her. No *us*, no *we*, only a means to an end.

"I'm sorry," Iseult said, and she meant the words as much for herself as she did for Owl.

"He will come back," Owl said, a strand of certainty wending through her Threads.

Iseult said nothing in reply. It was too familiar, that hope. That hunger. That belief that there had been some mistake, and that at any moment, the abandoner would change their mind. Aeduan would not, just as Gretchya had not six and a half years ago.

Fortunately, Iseult was saved from having to speak. First came burning silver Threads, then the mountain bat himself appeared, a silent silhouette across the moon. Before Iseult could tell Owl to keep the creature away, Blueberry had dropped into a nosedive, aiming toward them.

The horses bolted.

TWENTY-FIVE

※

When Esme sang, Merik could almost pretend he was somewhere else.

Curled beside the cold wall of her tower, with only a frayed blanket to offer warmth, he could shut his eyes and let her voice carry him away.

He did not know the song. He did not need to. As long as she was singing, he was not chained in her tower with no magic. He was not a puppet, bound to her by cleaving Threads.

She was like a sea fox, Merik decided, singing with a voice from another realm. In the stories, the sea foxes would shed their skins and lull unsuspecting sailors to the shore. Then they would drown them. A nice clean death, really, compared to this half-life Merik was trapped in.

When the last of Esme's song trilled out, a vibrato to bounce off the stones, her bare feet padded across the room. Merik was careful to keep his eyes shut, his breaths even. *I am still asleep. Leave me alone. I am still asleep.*

"I know you are not sleeping, little Prince." She sank to the stones beside him. "I can see from your Threads that you're awake."

Merik winced and opened his eyes.

She grinned down at him, her face closer than he'd realized. Then silver flashed in her hand and she stabbed him in the heart.

The shadows were not kind to Merik. They sang to him from a little girl's face framed by blond braids, and when she smiled, it did not stop at the edges of her face. It stretched beyond, off her jaw and into the air, singing and giggling forever.

Merik wanted to wake up, but the shadows wouldn't let him. There was only laughter and darkness and hate.

Merik awoke to a night sky and rainfall. He did not know how long he had been unconscious. All he knew was that candlelight flickered around the tower, and his chest ached.

My heart. He scrabbled to a sitting position and gaped down at where the wound should be. There was blood, almost black on his shirt, and there was a hole in the linen . . .

But no wound. Only a shadow-tinged pucker where the knife had gone in. And pain—always the pain.

"Fascinating, is it not?" Esme's words skated over him, and then the woman herself appeared, slinking around the wall. She wore a different dress now, honey-colored velvet as fine as any noblewoman's. It was too big, though, dragging as she skipped toward him. Clutched to her chest was the book she'd shown him when he'd first arrived. "You died, Prince Merik! And then came back to life—although not entirely. The

Threads that bind you to the Fury are still intact. It keeps you from life, but it also keeps you from death."

She dropped to the stones, her gown pooling around her. It shimmered in the candles' glow. Then she placed the book on the floor and flipped back pages, no gentleness in the movement, even when the pages protested and the binding squeaked.

"Imagine the implications," she gushed, once she'd found the page she desired, covered in hand-drawn diagrams. "Imagine the *applications*! It is very similar in premise to the first Loom Eridysi made a thousand years ago." She pointed to a sketch on the page that Merik supposed looked vaguely like a loom. "If we did not need the Fury alive, I would try other deaths. Drowning. Burning. Eventually decapitation. But I fear *that* sort of death might be too much for you in the end."

She smiled.

Merik shuddered.

"I have more work for you today, Prince." She searched her book impatiently. Merik thought he heard a page rip. Then she found what she wanted, and let the book fall open. "I need more stones like these."

He glanced at them. "Like what I found before?"

"No." She traced her finger over a stone with lines coiling around it. Beneath it, in a script that looked like old Arithuanian, were the words *Arlenni Loop*. "These will have thread wrapped around them, or perhaps yarn."

"Why do you need them?"

Her eyes thinned, and for half a breath, Merik feared he had gone too far. His muscles tensed for pain. The chain scratched against the stones.

But then a smile rippled over Esme's cheeks, and she sighed—a contented sound. "You *are* fun, Prince. No one has ever asked about my magic before. Only Iseult, but she so rarely visits anymore."

Iseult? Surely Esme could not mean the same girl Merik knew. There was no time to ask, though, nor time to wonder, for Esme had launched into a detailed explanation of Threads. She poked at pictures on the page, clearly expecting Merik to listen and observe.

"Threads," she declared, "are everywhere. They hum in the stone." She patted the floor. "In the clouds." She waved to the window. "In the trees, in the birds, in your heart." A sly smile and she mimicked stabbing him in the chest again. "All magic is nothing more than manipulation of Threads, Prince, and once upon a time, it was only the Paladins who could do so.

"Except in the Fareast, where my people first lived."

Merik frowned. "The 'Matsis?"

Her lips curled back. Her chin thrust forward. "*That* is a hurtful word, Prince."

Merik recoiled, bracing for the fire. For the pain.

"It is offensive. Dismissive of who we are. Is it really so hard for you to say the whole word? *No*-matsi. Or, as we were long ago, *No'A*-matsi."

"I am sorry," he tried to say. "I did not know—"

"You mean you did not care."

"No!" His hands rose in apology. Flames, flames, at any moment the cleaving fire would consume him. "I've never heard that before—I'm sorry."

"You *have* heard it, but you chose not to listen. All men in the Witchlands are the same." Her nostrils flared. "*Say it.*"

227

For a moment, he did not know what she meant. Then he realized. "Nomatsi."

"The right way."

Noden hang him, what had she just told him? Shit, shit. He had not listened, and she was right. In his holiest of conceit, he had chosen not to hear—

"No'Amatsi!" The word burst from his throat, surprising him and Esme too. She flinched. Then straightened, her fingers tightening to fists upon her knees. He was certain she would attack. With magic, with claws, with blades to slice open his heart.

Except she did not. The seconds trickled past with the rain, and a slow smile spread across her mouth. Then, almost lazily, she tipped her head sideways. "Good boy, little Prince. Perhaps if you can learn your lessons, then some hope yet remains for the Witchlands. Now where was I?" She cleared her throat expectantly.

And Merik's mind raced back. "You . . . you said that in the Fareast, magic is different."

"Onga. Yes. In the Fareast, anyone with training can touch the Threads of power, and long ago, the No'Amatsi people spent their lives devoted to such training."

"Why," Merik asked warily, hoping she wanted questions, "is magic different there?"

She *did* want questions. Her smile widened, and this time it reached her eyes. "It is a different goddess who sleeps inside their land, and Her will is different than our Sleeper's. Oh, I see from your Threads that you are confused. In your mind, there is no goddess—only a god, because of *course* Nubrevnans would turn a woman into a man. The very concept of a

228

woman with power is too much for your feeble minds to comprehend."

Esme leaned forward, bracing on her hands and drawing her face close to his. "You see a strong woman and deem her evil. You see a quiet woman . . . Oh wait; you do not see them at all. Tell me truly: what did you think of me when you first spied me?"

Merik's lips pressed tight. He stared down at the stone, knowing he could not argue. The Merik of a month ago would have denied her words. Vehemently. Angrily, with his Nihar rage to spiral loose on winds he claimed he could not control.

Now, he had no winds. Now, he had no lies he could tell himself. Cam had said as much two weeks ago. *You only see what you want to see.*

Just thinking of the boy made Merik's heart shrivel. His chest suctioned inward with shame. Cam had stayed beside him, even though Merik had done nothing to deserve such loyalty. He prayed to Noden . . . or . . . or to whatever power reigned over the Witchlands, that Cam and Ryber were all right.

Esme sighed, a bored sound. "We can continue our lesson later, Prince. For now, the rain has stopped." She twirled a hand toward the window. "So it is time that you travel to the next shrine."

She withdrew a key from her pocket and with deft fingers released the chain from Merik's collar. "My Cleaved will lead you most of the way, so follow the lines as you did last night. And Prince." She smiled again, dimple winking. "Do not try to run. You know what will happen if you do."

229

TWENTY-SIX

✳

It all happened so fast once Habim and the soldiers arrived—too fast for Safi to fully comprehend, much less react. The Hell-Bards surrendered. The Hell-Bards were put in chains. And the Hell-Bards were led away.

Then Safi was led away too, by Adders she didn't know and a blockade of soldiers so dense, she could see nothing beyond. For the rest of the night, she saw no one she knew. No Vaness, no Rokesh, no Habim . . .

And no Hell-Bards. She had no idea where they'd been taken; she had no idea what was going on.

Once back at the Floating Palace, healers briefly tended her ankle, then her Adder guard had her moving again. Every detail regarding the imperial birthday party the next day had to be reevaluated or rechecked. Apparently, the rebels had entered the Origin Well grounds by a glamoured gap in the northern wall, so Safi now examined every *inch* of stone in the palace for signs of similar trickery.

Nothing.

Then she was forced to meet every single soldier, servant, and Adder—women and men Safi had already evaluated.

Women and men as frustrated by the whole situation as Safi was. And while she interviewed them, the Adders checked all weapons, all tools, to ensure no iron had been tampered with.

The Adders found nothing, though, and Safi found nothing either.

It was well past midnight by the time she finished and was led to her room. Despite exhaustion tugging at her muscles and eyelids, her thoughts crackled with flame. Everything from the day collided in her mind in one massive, writhing conflagration—the flame hawk, the false soldiers in the woods, the doorway lit by magic.

Habim's secret message upon the map.

Gods below, Safi wished she could talk to Iz right now. Yet no amount of clutching her Threadstone or imagining her Threadsister's calm face made her prayers come true. Iseult, wherever she was, could not—or did not want to—dream-walk with Safi again.

At the sound of the third chimes twinkling through her garden doorway, Safi finally gave up trying to reach Iseult. She had books from Vaness's library; she had gemstones; and she still had a plan that needed finishing.

She cleared off a space on her desk and yanked off her Threadstone. Then after setting down the quartz she'd fiddled with all day, she opened a new book and set to work. *Understanding Threads* by Anett det Korelli, translated from Nomatsi into Marstoki, detailed the creation of Threadstones. How Threadwitches bound people's Threads to stones, so that lovers or family or friends would always be able to find one another. So that they would never lose those they cared

231

for most. And since Threadwitches were bound to the Aether like Safi's magic, it seemed a logical next try.

Besides, reading about Threadwitches made Safi think of Iseult—and just *thinking* of her Threadsister made Safi feel a bit better and made the fires in her mind settle.

She sank into a rhythm at her desk, fingers flipping pages. Heels drumming in time to the katydids outside. *Kay-tee-did. Kay-tee-did-did.* She even had threads exactly as the book described, and although she could not weave true *Threads* into these strands as Threadwitches did, she *could* concentrate on her power. On the warmth that sang within truth. On the claws that shredded within a lie.

Safi even recited the words used by Threadwitches to focus their magic: *Bind and bend. Build and blossom. Family fills the heart.*

Over and over, she said these words as she plaited threads of sunset pink. *Bind and bend. Build and blossom. Family fills the heart.* And she kept on murmuring until at last she'd finished braiding and at last she'd finished coiling the slender weave around her quartz. At a glance, her stone looked no different than the Threadstone Iseult had given her—except for the difference in color. In fact, Safi took great care to ensure hers looked just the same.

Yet all it took was one glance for Safi to know the two rocks were *not* identical. The Threadstone from Iseult looked and *felt* alive. Safi's Truthstone attempt, however, was just an empty hock of stone wrapped in thread.

"No, no, *no*." The words whispered out, unbidden, and she knocked the useless quartz aside. Tears prickled behind her eyeballs, and she hated it. She *hated* it, just as she hated this palace and she hated that no one had given her any sodding answers since leaving the Well.

And above all, Safi hated that Iseult was so very far away. With Iseult, Safi was brave. With Iseult, Safi was strong. And with Iseult, Safi was fearless. On her own, though, she was just a girl trapped in another country while unknown enemies tried to kill her.

Grabbing her real, heart-achingly *true* Threadstone, Safi shoved to her feet. Stars flashed across her vision. She'd sat too long, eaten too little. But she ignored them—just as she ignored the whooshing throb in her eardrums. Instead, she stumbled to her doorway and pushed out into the night.

The crow wasn't there; Safi didn't know why she'd thought he would be. There was, however, a firefly. It winked beside the telescope. Then it vanished. Then it winked again a few paces away.

When she was growing up, Habim had told Safi that children made wishes upon fireflies, and Safi supposed that if ever there was a time for wishes, it was now. So she scurried over to it, and with a swipe of her hand, caught it from the sky. It landed gently, seemingly unconcerned by her touch.

Please, Safi begged, watching it light up. Then shutter out. Then light up again, a golden flicker that turned the Threadstone still clutched in her hand to flames. *Please, Sir Firefly*, she repeated. *Wherever Iseult is, just keep her safe.*

Iseult did not feel safe.

She might have evaded soldiers, but Leopold fon Cartorra presented an entirely new swath of dangers—dangers she was not accustomed to. She could face swords and pistols, fists and flame without batting an eye. But clever word games and courtier's masks set her Threadwitch calm to reeling.

Iseult hadn't wanted to leave Owl alone at the bridge, but she had wanted to let Leopold catch the horses even less. At least Owl had Blueberry to keep her safe. If the prince decided to run off with their steeds, though, then Iseult and Owl would have no transport and, worse, no supplies.

The black gelding had bolted into the forest. The roan mare had followed, and their hooves had thrashed the underbrush and left a clear trail to follow. Leopold led the way, Iseult just behind. Her gaze never left his Threads. Her hand never left the pommel of her cutlass.

Her fingers tapped out a rhythm. Until that movement made her think of Aeduan. Then she stopped.

"There is no way the horses will return to the bridge," the prince said, tossing a backward glance. "Not so long as that bat remains."

"We must catch them first. Then we can worry about luring them back."

"Oh, we will catch them. Have no fear." Leopold strolled on, a confidence to his step. An ease, as if they merely walked the halls of a palace, not the moonlit corners of a mountain forest. "Rolf is a well-trained beast, and the mare will follow his lead."

"Then tell Rolf to go to the bridge, so the mare will follow his lead."

"He is not *that* well trained." A laugh—again, at odds with their surroundings. And this time, contradicting Leopold's Threads as well. Instead of pink amusement, they glimmered with fear. "Even the great white bears of the Sleeping Lands would not be stupid enough to approach a mountain bat."

"You're scared of him."

"You are not?"

"No," Iseult replied, and she realized it was true. In all the chaos of the Contested Lands, there had been no time to be afraid. Blueberry had attacked men who wanted to kill her, and that had made him an ally. "He will not hurt us."

"Really? Do mountain bats dislike the taste of princes?"

Before she could explain to him that Blueberry only hurt those that hurt Owl, Leopold drew up short. Iseult almost ran into him. Then she saw why: they had reached a rocky clearing, no underbrush left for the horses to trample.

"Our trail has run cold." Leopold twirled toward Iseult, Threads and expression briefly in alliance: he was frustrated. His cheeks twitched. "Any chance you can sense their Threads?"

"Animals do not have Threads." She circled around him.

"Animals do not have them," he asked, following several paces behind, "or you cannot sense them?"

Iseult wished he would shut up. "Does it matter? My magic will not help us, either way." She squinted down at the earth, turned gray beneath the moon, but even with its light, it was too dark to spot hoof prints. However, a sound bubbled against her ears. Running water. Another mountain creek.

If she were a horse who had run for an hour, she would be thirsty. And if she were thirsty, she would go to a stream free of mountain bats. In a rush of silent speed, Iseult set off across the clearing. She stepped over long shadows, then into the trees that cast them, and soon enough, Iseult found the horses. They had indeed followed the water into the forest.

235

"Rolf," Leopold said, delight in both his tone and his flushed Threads. Yet before he could cross to his gelding, Iseult drew her cutlass.

He halted mid-step. "This again?"

"This again," she replied. "At the bridge, you offered to explain everything from the start. You will do that now."

"No 'please'?" A smile on his face. Frustration in his Threads. "I am royalty, you know."

"And I am the one holding the sword."

"Ah." He huffed a chuckle, and pink amusement returned. He had liked her response, it would seem, and without another word of protest, Leopold the Fourth, imperial heir of Cartorra, began his tale.

He had a musical way of speaking. His words rolled against Iseult's skin, a perfect rhythm of sound and pause. A perfect complement to the frozen night air as he explained how he'd been working with Safi's uncle. Their aim had been to prevent Safi from marrying *his* uncle, Emperor Henrick. Then Leopold described how he had hired Aeduan under the pretense of capturing Safi, but how he had then intentionally sabotaged all travel by taking stops and even misdirecting Aeduan—all so Safi could reach safety before Aeduan caught up.

Or was *meant* to reach safety, until the Empress of Marstok had interfered.

Iseult said nothing throughout his story, carefully chewing over each assertion. They fit what she knew from Safi—and what she knew from Aeduan too—yet rather than trust Leopold more, she found she trusted him less. Throughout his declaration, he had kept a tired half smile upon his face, as if this entire situation were a game. As if he thought Iseult a pitiful child who needed his indulgence.

"And *then*," he finished with a spin of his right hand, like a minstrel taking a bow, "I stole the monk's coins and had my Hell-Bards transport them to Lejna. For you. All quite straightforward, if you think about it."

Hardly, Iseult thought. Aloud, she said: "I was in Lejna. I did not see any Hell-Bards."

"Because they were under orders not to remain, and when I arrived later, you had already moved on. I have been searching for you ever since. I was—and still am—meant to deliver you to the Carawen Monastery."

Iseult blinked. This was easily the last place she expected him to say. Back to Lejna? All right. To Veñaza City? Sure. Even all the way to Cartorra would have made sense to her. But a Monastery in the middle of the mountains was as baffling as . . .

As having an imperial prince come find her in Tirla.

"Why there?" she asked.

"Because the monks will keep you safe." Leopold said this as if it were the most obvious thing in the world. "And they will protect Safiya too, when she arrives."

Safi. For the first time since this conversation had begun, Iseult felt her calm falter. All she wanted was to be reunited with Safi. More than anything in all the Witchlands, she wanted her Threadsister at her side. For the world to feel right side up again. Safi, who was made of sunshine and laughter. Safi, who initiated so Iseult could complete. Who never abandoned her. Who was always *we* and *us* and never saw Iseult as the means, but only as the *end*.

And who would know in an instant if Leopold was lying.

"How long," Iseult said, her voice almost lost to the stream, "will it take to reach the Monastery?"

Relief rushed across Leopold's Threads. He smiled, a winning, devastating smile. "If we meet no interruptions, then we could arrive by midday tomorrow."

Iseult's fingers moved to her Threadstone. She stared absently at the prince's face, purple and puffy thanks to her pummeling. She stared at his Threads too, so desperate. So hopeful.

"If I . . . If *Owl* and I go with you to the Monastery, do not think that it means I trust you."

A pause. Wariness in his Threads, and he ran a thumb over his lower lip. Then: "What would it take to convince you, Iseult? What must I do to prove that I am here to serve you, wholly and completely? Getting you to the Monastery is my only purpose."

Iseult almost scoffed at those words. A *prince* offering to serve her. *What if, what if, what if.* Yet, perhaps against her better judgment, she found herself believing him. The fervent urgency in his Threads was real. He might change his face to suit his needs, but he could not change his Threads.

"Do that more often," she said after a while, her hand falling from her Threadstone. "Match your expressions to your feelings, and then I might start believing you. After all, trust-worthy people do not wear masks."

As Iseult uttered this last point, the prince's Threads brightened with unease. Two heartbeats passed. Then all at once, a surging, delighted warmth bolted through them—and he tipped his head back and laughed. A full, unabashed sound that sent brilliant, fiery shades of pink coursing upward.

"What is it?" she asked, her cutlass dropping an inch. "What's so funny?"

"This." He motioned between them. "It is *fascinating*. Although, I will admit that I am surprised by how easily you see through my ... Well, my *performance*." He sketched an almost mocking bow. "I suppose I shall have to either account for your magic when you're around, or else hope that you do not tell the world what I'm truly feeling. After all, charm is the only real weapon in a prince's arsenal.

"But if honesty here"—he swept a hand toward his face— "is all it will take to prove my loyalty, then you have disarmed me, Iseult det Midenzi." Again, he bowed, but this time with respect—and *this* time, his Threads hummed with raw intensity.

Oh, it was very strange indeed to have a prince say—and do—such things for Iseult. "Help me tend the horses," she muttered eventually. She did not trust him fully, but she trusted him enough to follow him to the Monastery. It was where Aeduan had urged them to go anyway; she could let a prince lead the way.

With quick efficiency, she sheathed her cutlass with a clink of steel. They had wasted enough time here. Owl was waiting. "We will have to find a way to coax back the horses without getting rid of Blueberry."

"*Coja'kess?*" he repeated.

Ah, Iseult supposed they *had* named the bat in Nomatsi. "It means 'blueberry' in Nomatsi."

"The bat's name is *Blueberry?*"

"They are his favorite food."

Another lovely laugh split the prince's lips, turning his Threads to a perfect shade of sunrise. "Did you hear that,

239

Rolf?" He patted the gelding's neck. "He's a fruit bat. I *told* you there was nothing to be afraid of, old man. Nothing to be afraid of at all."

TWENTY-SEVEN

※

Aeduan had been here before. Right here in this dark valley, hunting down a different man who owed money to a different shopkeep. It was all he had been good for back then; it was all he was good for now.

It was as if the past month, since he'd left Yotiluzzi in Veñaza City, had never happened. The past two years, even. For here he was again, mindlessly hunting. Mindlessly gathering coin. One contract, then the next. One foot, then the next. Every mark the same, every client the same, and every day that spanned before him the thrice-damned same.

He hated it. He hated how easily he slipped back into it. How the numbness seeped into his bones as he trudged onward. How already he had abandoned planning ahead. There was no ahead—only finishing this assignment, then claiming the next. On and on until the day he died.

Aeduan knew he could not avoid his father forever. The Fury would come for him. He would have to return to Ragnor's side. Really, Aeduan should just go north before that happened. Save everyone the trouble.

He did not go north.

Nor did he search for Prince Leopold, though that was something else that needed doing. He had questions that needed answering, ones Aeduan had believed important only two weeks ago.

He did not search for Prince Leopold.

Now, he didn't care who the prince was working with, he didn't care whose blood sang with frozen winters and crystal lakes. And Aeduan no longer cared who'd helped Leopold escape in the Nubrevnan jungles, stolen Aeduan's lockbox of silver talers, and then led him on a fruitless chase across the Witchlands.

If that person had not done so, Aeduan would never have joined with Iseult. He would never have found Owl, and the wish that he had made upon the fireflies would never have come true.

He was a Bloodwitch, he was a monster, and this hunger in his gut that had tried to trick him into believing he was something else—he was a fool for ever listening to it. He was good for only one thing.

Best he never forget that again.

When dawn began to stain the sky, Aeduan found the man who owed money, a shepherd with two small children and a wife sick with fever. He had bought a blade to defend his family against the raiders everyone said were coming. A blade he could not pay for.

It was so easy to frighten the man. So easy for Aeduan to send blood swirling around his eyes. To shut off all thought, all expression, all inflection. It was another man drawing his sword. Another man watching as the shepherd sank to his knees, trembling and begging for more time.

Aeduan felt nothing. He cared none. He took the only coins the man had, and he left.

On his second contract, the tier four, Aeduan felt the Painstone begin to fail.

He was supposed to report to a small iron mine in Marstok, east of Tirla. They would soon transport a shipment west; they needed protection. Likely it was not a legal delivery, or they would have hired true soldiers.

Legality mattered none to Aeduan. Coin was coin, contracts were contracts. He simply walked east, the sun rising overhead. Then burning down. It was not a hot day, but he grew hot. Miserably so. Unbearably so. Until it was too much. He had to stop beside a creek. Barely a trickle over the mountain rocks.

He removed his cloak. He drank his fill, the water gritty, and he splashed the sweat from his face. Then he sat on a rock and waited for the last of the Painstone's power to creep away.

It was worse than he expected. If he had thought that the sudden absence of pain yesterday was a clear indicator of how much he'd felt before, it was nothing compared to the sudden return of it. He had anticipated a slow cascade, like standing in a river as it slowly rose around you.

The pain was a tidal wave instead. It plowed into him, flame and violence to boil his blood. To cook off all thought, until he was nothing but shadows closing in and a body shutting down.

He collapsed into the stream.

TWENTY-EIGHT

✳

Vivia stared into her lukewarm porridge, knowing she ought to eat. Instead, her gaze shot to the empty seat beside her and its untouched porridge growing colder by the second.

It would seem Serafin was not coming to breakfast. Which could mean only one thing: he had heard about Vivia's trip to Marstok, and he disapproved.

A sigh slid between her teeth, like steam released from a bubbling pot, except that her exhale did nothing to ease the boil in her belly. She would have to deal with her father—have to apologize, perhaps even grovel. Though for what, precisely, she did not know. Sometimes, she never learned what she had done to awaken his Nihar rage.

Vivia hugged her arms to her chest. She should apologize now. Any delay and the storm would only stew and strengthen. Until eventually he would explode. Then no amount of apologies would calm him.

But what of Stix? The question tickled across her mind, and with it, Vivia found herself rising. Turning toward the door. Stix ought to be in the Battle Room by now, waiting to give Vivia her morning briefing. Surely taking a few minutes to speak to her best friend—and to bolster her resolve before facing Serafin—would be all right. Besides, she desperately wanted to tell Stix about Marstok, about the Empress, about the Wordwitched paper now tucked into her frock coat. Stix would know what to make of it all. Stix would know how Vivia should proceed.

Except that Stix was not waiting for Vivia in the Battle Room. Worse, none of the servants nearby had seen her that morning. There was no note on the table, no message sent by courier, and no sign at all that anything in the room had been touched since Vivia had last entered yesterday. And certainly no sign of Stix.

Vivia left the palace, barking at her guards to *leave her be!* before retracing her steps from the night before. No amount of knocking at Stix's apartment earned an answer, though, and the cobweb between the door and the ceiling suggested the door hadn't been opened in quite some time.

Vivia's stomach spun all the harder, pressing against her lungs now. Stix wasn't where she ought to be, and she'd not come home in at least a day. The latter part was not unusual—Stix was, in her own words, "a restless soul."

Maybe she is at the barracks.

Except Stix was not there either, and none of the sailors or officers had seen her. Nor had anyone at Pin's Keep, the Cleaved Man, or Stix's father's house on Queen's Hill. Not since two whole *blighted* days before. It wasn't until Vivia decided to sail herself out to the Sentries of Noden that she got any clue to where Stix might have gone.

Their skiff was missing. And sure enough, when Vivia questioned a fisherman named Aben—a young fellow who spent every morning anchored to the dock with his line plunked into the murky waters and from whom Vivia and Stix received regular updates on the health of the local fishes— he said, "Hye, I saw her take the boat out yesterday. Didn't say where she was going, but she looked none too pleased."

"Which way did she go?"

He waved south. "I lost sight of her before she hit the bridge."

Vivia huffed a thank-you, already scooting off. She could borrow a skiff at the wharf, and from there she could get to the southern Sentry. For *surely*, Stix would be there.

The morning shadows were long, the waters crowded, yet even with her mind racing over and over—where was Stix?— sailing came as naturally to Vivia as walking. She slipped past every vessel in the harbor before coasting onto the southern water-bridge.

The Water-Bridges of Stefin-Eckart carried the River Timetz across the valley of farmland surrounding the Lovats plateau. So high were they that clouds drifted alongside the ships fighting to enter the city. Racing to evade the war everyone knew was coming—and all in need of housing that Vivia was racing to provide. The ninth chime was already humming by the time the Sentries of Noden took shape, their weathered faces as large as warships, their stone helms adorned by plumes the size of pine trees. Long, rounded parapets jutted out in gradually widening levels from their stone-cloaked lower halves, while their towering torsos were packed with narrow windows and arrow slats. On either side of the river, where it carved into the mountains, wide inlets climbed upward, carried by magic. They carried naval vessels into a gaping hole at the Sentries' bases.

These ancient guardians of the city were also the primary home of the Royal Nubrevnan Navy and Royal Nubrevnan Soil-Bound. Brilliant blue banners hung from the battlements, flapping on the morning winds.

Vivia scarcely had to enter the hive-like hallways of the eastern Sentry before she had an answer regarding Stix. No one, military, civilian, or passing refugee, had seen anyone at all matching her description.

Stix was gone. She was missing.

As Vivia sailed numbly back, she could do nothing but stare with unseeing eyes. Even the barn swallows that swooped across her view, riding the warm currents carried up from the valley, could not distract her. They made their nests beneath the water-bridges, and normally, she and Stix would call out to them, some silly refrain about safe harbors and sprightly winds.

That thought only served to make Vivia ill now.

This was all her fault.

She had been so self-absorbed. So stupidly, stupidly naive as to think she could leave this city for a day with no consequences. If she had just stayed here, then Stix would not have left—at least not without some kind of explanation. And if Vivia had just *blighting stayed here*, then she would know where to begin searching.

Vivia suddenly knew all too keenly how Merik had felt a year before. His Threadbrother Kullen had vanished in the Sirmayans while building watchtowers, and Merik had stretched resources to obscene lengths trying to find him.

Those lengths seemed absolutely reasonable now. Paltry, even. *Now*, Vivia would do whatever it took and use whatever she could to find out where her best friend had disappeared to.

So many regrets, but she just had to keep moving, keep searching.

Stix was somewhere. Vivia would find her.

It was nearing midday by the time Vivia reached Queen's Hill once more. She was aiming for the Sotar estate at the top of the hill; perhaps the vizer himself would know where his daughter had gone. And if not . . . well, he needed to know she was missing.

She was stopped halfway up the road when a hand landed on her shoulder. She whirled around, the name "Stix" flaring through her mind—but instead of Stix's cavalier grin, a scruffy-mustached boy in royal livery faced her.

Rat, her father's youngest page.

"Highness, your father wishes to see you." His voice jumped octaves every few words. "He is in his bedroom, too weak to leave."

Vivia felt the blood drain from her face. First Stix, now Serafin . . . It was too much for one day. She shoved past Rat and charged up the crowded street. She cared none for the cries or the glares as she elbowed her way into a jog. For once, she would have welcomed her guards to help clear a path.

The King Regent had been healthy and whole only yesterday. He had bellowed with all the force Vivia had grown up with. *This is your fault. You left because you were upset, and now he's sick again. And Stix is gone too. Everything you do is wrong*. Selfish, selfish—how could she have been so thrice-damned selfish?

Vivia was panting by the time she reached the royal wing of the palace, sweating through her frock coat, her hair glued to her forehead. Rat, who had scurried behind her the entire way, now scampered in front so he could open the door.

"Your daughter—" he began, but Vivia swept into the room before he could finish.

She had expected darkness, as her father had required at the peak of his illness. Instead, she found sunlight streaming in from the ceiling-high windows. And instead of her father lying in bed, eyes closed and breath wheezing, she found him standing—not even seated in his rolling chair, but *standing* beside the blazing hearth.

He looked even better than he had yesterday. Shoulders strong, color warm in his cheeks. Even his hair seemed thicker.

Serafin did not react at Vivia's entrance, nor look away from the fire as she approached. Orange light glittered across him.

"Your Majesty," she asked hesitantly, "are you ill?"

A muscle feathered along his jaw. "Where have you been? I have been waiting for you since the ninth chimes."

"You sent no summons."

"I should not need to."

At last, he angled away from the hearth, although not toward Vivia. Instead, he crossed to his desk beneath the window. A stiffness marked his movements, and pain flashed across his face.

Vivia's chest stuttered. "Have the healers come?" She saw no signs of the amber draughts or tubs of salve they usually

249

left behind. "I will fetch them, Your Majesty." She twisted toward the door.

"Stay." Heat lightning laced the King Regent's voice.

Vivia froze.

"We need to discuss my plans for the troops."

"The . . . troops?" She angled back. "I don't understand, sir."

He snorted, a sound that suggested Vivia was being intentionally obtuse. "As Admiral, I decide when, where, and how we face this Raider King. So I have done just that." Without waiting for Vivia to respond to such an announcement, he launched into a description of his plans for advancing troops into the Sirmayans—plans he'd made with generals and lower admirals in the Royal Soil-Bound and Navy.

Plans he had apparently made over the last two weeks. Without once consulting her.

And all Vivia could do was stare. Serafin clearly didn't realize she had gone to Marstok yesterday. In fact, he seemed to have no idea she'd left the city at all.

More importantly, he was not Admiral of the Royal Forces. As Queen-in-Waiting, Vivia was the one who appointed that position. As of yet, she had named no one—and as of yet, she still wore that title herself. Meaning all of these plans he had made were both unwelcome and unhelpful.

She couldn't say that, though. Not to Serafin. Just the thought of raising such a point made her heart quake like a field mouse. Which was ridiculous, of course. Everything her father did was for her sake.

Is it, though? nudged a new voice. *Just because he says that doesn't make it true. After all, he did steal your speech—*

No, no. Vivia snapped her head sideways. She wouldn't

think like that. She had been upset yesterday because she had been surprised. She was better now.

Serafin rambled on, thoroughly oblivious, lifting papers off his desk and rattling them in the air with all the emphasis and power the old Serafin used to command.

"At their current pace, the raiders will reach our borders in four days. His Icewitches are powerful, so we will need to eliminate them first."

"Ice . . . witches?" Vivia heard how stilted she sounded, but she had no idea what her father was talking about. Nor any idea what all these papers he was shaking actually said.

And for the first time since Vivia had entered the room, her father's expression relaxed. "Of course, of course. You have not read all the missives from the watchtowers." He smiled, a warm, charming thing that was so different from the man of two weeks ago, still bedridden and scowling.

Vivia ought to love seeing her father smile like that. She ought to love seeing him stand tall and true. Instead, nausea gathered in her chest.

She swallowed. "What missives from the watchtowers? Why have I not seen these?"

"Because I am Admiral."

"I am Queen-in-Waiting. They should come to me."

"Hye, Vivia, hye. If you truly wish, I can have them sent to you. I only want what's best for you." He flashed that smile again, but now it was tinged with condescension. Like she were a child insisting on eating supper with the adults. "Your mother never did want them, though, so I assumed you wouldn't either. You are so very like her, you know."

Her mind blanked out at those words, her throat went

251

dry. She didn't want to be like her mother, with madness in her brain. She wanted to be sure and strong like Serafin.

Do you, though? the voice persisted. *Just because he has always told you that you do, doesn't make it true.* Yet again, Vivia thrust that thought aside. "What," she forced out, "do all these messages say?"

"That the Raider King has begun his advance." Again, Serafin shook papers at her. "That his Icewitches freeze the Timetz, and that his forces are vast. However, we Nubrevnans know that terrain better than he or his raiders. But I just said all this—were you not listening, Vivia?"

Hye. She had been listening, and now she had enough information to fill in the gaps and understand the full meaning behind his strategy to topple the Raider King.

He intended to send all of their forces, soil-bound and naval, to the northern borders. He intended to use their knowledge of the terrain against the raiders, stopping them before they ever reached Nubrevna. And on the surface, that strategy was a sound one; Vivia would have expected no less from her father. But there was also one gaping hole in it.

"What happens if you lose? Then there will be no soldiers left to defend the city."

"That won't happen." Serafin chuckled, a sound to make others feel small. "We will face him, and we will win."

But what if you don't?

Had this exchange happened two years ago, before the wasting disease had struck, Vivia would have gone right along with her father's plans, no questions asked vocally or internally. Right now, though, all she could see were the *holes*.

If all of their troops died, then Lovats would once more

be under siege. And while siege had always been Nubrevna's salvation during wartime, this city was not the city it had been twenty years ago. The storerooms were *not* the storerooms from twenty years ago.

Vivia knew Lovats, inside and out. From its buildings, stacked atop one another and growing higher every day, to its inner veins and passages and waterways. She had explored and studied every inch, first with her mother as a child, then on her own. And what she had learned after twenty years was that, when Jana had died, any concern for the city's infrastructure had died too.

Serafin had seen how easily the dam had broken two weeks ago, yet somehow, he still believed these walls and bridges were strong enough to hold back an army. And somehow, he believed these walls and bridges were strong enough to support hundreds of thousands of refugees.

"I have dealt with raiders before, Vivia." His patronizing smile left his eyes. "I understand exactly what awaits me at the border."

"What awaits *you*?" Now she was well and truly shocked.

"Hye. I am Admiral. That means I will lead the forces into battle."

"You aren't well enough to lead forces."

"Excuse me?" His shoulders notched up. His nostrils flared.

"You aren't well. You only just began walking without the aid of your chair a week ago. How can you expect to lead soldiers into a fight?"

"I have fought—and *won*—with worse ailments than this disease, Vivia. I fought the Marstoks in the Hundred Isles while a knife wound bled out from my thigh. This disease no longer controls me, so I—"

"*No.*" The word loosed from Vivia's throat. Too fast to stop. Too fast to consider. Then she said it again: "No. You didn't. You didn't command that battle in the Hundred Isles. You passed out the moment you were struck, and your first mate coordinated the entire thing."

Evrane had told Vivia the story long ago, before Serafin had banished his sister from the city forever.

"And," Vivia continued, "as the Queen-in-Waiting, I decide who wears the title of Admiral of the Royal Forces. And I haven't appointed you. I still remain Admiral, and so *I* will form all strategy moving forward. Meanwhile, you will cease all planning with the navy and soil-bound, and whatever steps you have taken for advancing north are now over.

"As for these messages you have been getting, that ends today. From now on, those missives will come to me. The city of Lovats and the people of Nubrevna must—and will—come first in this war."

As Vivia spoke these words, as they bubbled up from some place in her spine she'd never known existed, her father transformed. In seconds, the Nihar rage had ignited. She could see it in the rising of his shoulders, in the compression of his lips. And if she wanted to, she could still prevent it. If she wanted to, she could stop the explosion from snapping free.

All she had to do was apologize. Grovel and beg. Exactly as she'd done her entire life.

And perhaps that was what a *good* daughter would do. That was what a loving, loyal daughter would do. But maybe she wasn't any of those things, and maybe she had no interest in sharing the glory or sharing the blame.

Not anymore. Not with him.

"You are welcome to attend the High Council meeting this afternoon," she said, popping her chin high. "Your advice and experience are always appreciated, Father." Then, without another word and without a backward glance, Vivia left the royal bedroom.

No regrets, keep moving.

No shouts followed her, but they would come eventually. They *always* came eventually.

Three steps into the hallway became ten, and still no bellows sounded from Serafin's room. It was not until she turned out of the royal wing, her guards moving into formation around her, that her father's roar finally crashed out.

She merely walked onward with a new purpose in her stride. For the Raider King was on his way, and Vivia had a city—and an army—to get ready.

TWENTY-NINE

※

The Cleaved marked Merik's way. In Poznin, they lined up shoulder to shoulder, just as they had the night before, circling around trees and ponds and fallen homes. He passed city squares that had once been open to the night sky, but now were thick with oaks and beech. He saw statues choked by ivy, graveyards swallowed by thorns, and gallows reduced to skeletons by moss and rot.

All of it was overrun by Cleaved. Always the Cleaved, standing sentry with eyes that stared into nothing and faces gaunt with hunger. Merik didn't understand how they lived when clearly they did not eat, drink, or perhaps even move.

Merik himself was ravenous. Esme had offered him no food since Kullen had dropped him here, and even water had been scarce. Twice, she had admitted she perhaps ought to feed him, but both times she'd forgotten. Or perhaps her words were no more than another game, another experiment. Knife wounds had not claimed him, but maybe starvation would.

Near the northern edges of Poznin, Merik passed a half-collapsed, half-flooded building. White stone turned to brown, wood flooring had long since rotted away, and the roof had fallen in, leaving only high, crooked walls and a staircase leading nowhere. All of it surrounded a murky pool lined with cattails. Sunlight gleamed down, a beautiful view, were it not for all the corpses.

Tens of them, all ages and races, floated atop the water. And Merik couldn't help but wonder if the Cleaved had entered because they had wanted to or if the Puppeteer had commanded these deaths upon them.

Chills whispered over Merik's skin. His feet slowed to a stop. A corpse with a square shield on her back floated by. A breeze swished at the cattails.

There was something about this place. Something cool and calming that called to Merik, begged him to enter the pool and find release. Before he even realized what he was doing, he had stepped in. Ice swept against his shins. Another step, it reached his knees. Another step, it gushed into his boots—and that finally startled him back to the present.

He lurched around, panic slicing through his brain. His footing failed. He splashed into the pond. A frigid dunk that reached his chest and left him floundering amidst the cattails. *Come*, sang the water, pulling at him. *Come in and find release.*

But Merik was not ready for that kind of release. Not yet. He wanted to stay alive—very much so—and to escape by another way. *Truly* escape.

Cam and Ryber were still out there, and Merik would get back to them. And Kullen . . . the Fury . . . Merik hadn't given up on him either.

Merik floundered to his feet, water splashing and reeds slapping, and scrabbled from the water. He was running by the time he reached the shore, and he kept on running until the pond and the corpses and the waters that sang to him were well out of sight.

On he walked, freezing now with the pond's waters soaking him through. He was still damp by the time he reached the outskirts of Poznin. The moon was halfway through its descent, and open pasture spread for as far as Merik could see. Here, stone buildings remained mostly intact, only wind and storm and rot to tear away the wood.

And here, the chill wind bit twice as fiercely. These were the Windswept Plains—an ocean of grass and air currents that should have stirred at Merik's magic. Should have coaxed it to life and thrummed within his lungs.

Instead, he felt nothing.

More Cleaved awaited him on the plains, spaced out now. One every fifty paces, skeletal figures that shot up from the grass. He saw no end to the rolling hills, and no end to the Cleaved either.

Until at last, just after dawn, Merik spotted the shrine he needed nestled in the sloping lowland between two hills. Beside him stood a final Cleaved, a hulking man with tattered furs and heavy boots. He looked like a Northman, like the tribal hunters that lived on the outskirts of the Sleeping Lands, where the tundra still remained habitable. As Merik had with every other person he'd passed, he wondered how this man had gotten here. He wondered if he had any family.

Either way, the man was nothing but a walking corpse now.

Far on the horizon, smoke feathered. A village or farm, perhaps, and the urge to run that way, to beg for aid—it squeezed in Merik's empty belly. It burned inside his feet. This hunger wasn't like the pond that had sucked him in against his will. This was his brain and his body in concert, and it was the true release, the true escape he sought.

But only if he was fast, only if Esme did not follow—and of course, she would. She or the Fury would follow no matter where Merik went, and *that* truth was as guaranteed as Noden's watery end. So long as this collar bound Merik, he was Esme's favorite toy.

Merik left the Cleaved Northman behind and stumbled down to the shrine. *Please, Noden,* he begged with each step. *Please, let there be food.* It was all he thought of as he picked up speed, almost sprinting by the time the hill flattened into lowland.

The standing stone towered larger than the one from the forest, and no grass clotted its base. Only dark soil, churned by feet and hooves. Merik had eyes only for the food, though. Fruits, bread, a wheel of cheese, and even a dried pork leg . . . Merik chased away the bugs and feasted. He ate so much, so fast, that he made himself sick. Still, he kept eating, gulping and swallowing until his stomach bloated and nausea grew thick in his throat. Then, he crawled to the central standing stone and slouched against it.

He lost all awareness of time, even dozing off at one point. It wasn't until a cricket landed on his head that he startled awake. The sun had moved; the stone's shadow stretched across him. He trembled from the cold, yet Esme was not inside his mind—she had not come at all today.

Merik didn't know what that meant.

He hauled himself up, legs aching. He had a job to do,

and it was best to do it before Esme finally checked in, with fangs bared. Gemstones, gemstones, gemstones. That was what she'd wanted, so that was what he would get. By the handful, he scooped them from the dark earth and dropped them into a drawstring satchel she had given him. They glistened everywhere, all colors and sizes. This shrine was even more beloved than the last. So many offerings for a goddess Esme claimed did not exist.

Funny that Merik had not noticed how many items were here. All he had seen was the food. Now, though, he noticed dolls and bowls, flowers and rush-woven mats. And now, he noticed the knife.

It rested atop one of the smaller stones, sheathed in wood with beautifully intricate leaves carved across it.

Merik wanted that knife.

He glanced around, as if Esme might be mere paces away, ready to pounce. Ready to punish him for daring to handle a weapon.

He saw nothing within the grass. He sensed no voice inside his brain.

Cautiously, he picked up the blade by its sheath. Wind scraped against him, tugging at bright red tassels on the hilt. Then steel hissed on metal as he slid the knife free. It shone in the afternoon sun, sharp and beautifully forged. A master's weapon.

Oh, Merik *wanted* this knife.

He glanced at his boots, at the spot where his breeches tucked in, filthy but whole. Maybe he could tuck it in there, out of sight and where it wouldn't interfere with his movements. He bent and pulled his pant leg free.

A shadow lengthened over him. A shadow shaped like a man.

Merik jerked upright and spun, heart shooting into his throat. Then he stumbled back a step.

The Cleaved from the hilltop gaped at Merik, mouth working as if he wanted to speak. But of course the Cleaved could not speak, and of course, Esme must have sent the man. Merik lifted his new knife. He would kill a Cleaved if he had to; he'd done so before.

Except the Cleaved was not attacking. The Cleaved simply stood there, swaying, shivering, and trying to work his throat.

Something was wrong. Something was off.

At last, a sound like paper ripping tore from the man's lungs. A sharp breath later, the man repeated that sound.

He's speaking, Merik realized, and in that same moment, he realized the man's pupils were no longer black but iris blue. And his skin, his veins—all shadows were gone, leaving only a natural, weathered texture behind.

The man was no longer Cleaved.

Merik straightened at the same instant the man reached for Merik, beseeching. Then the former Cleaved crashed to the grass.

Merik rushed forward, dropping to the man's side. "Are you all right?" A stupid question—the man hadn't eaten in countless weeks, and he had somehow, by some miracle Merik could not fathom, come back from Esme's cleaving.

Merik left the man and clambered around the stones. The bowls he'd seen earlier had been filled with rainwater. Fresh rain, he guessed, from the storms last night. Certainly fresh enough for a dying man.

261

He found one bowl, a massive, hammered bronze creation, and, careful not to lose a drop, he staggered back to the Northman. After setting the bowl on the earth, he hauled off his coat, then his shirt. The wind attacked; his bones shook against the sudden frost. Then he got the coat back on.

After dunking a shirt sleeve into the bowl, he brought it to the man's lips and gently squeezed. Evrane had done this a hundred times when Merik was growing up. A hundred *hundred* times, bringing the sick and the injured back from the brink of death. She'd done it for Kullen too, after his breathing attacks. And every time, Merik had watched on, hands wringing and terror bright in his chest.

That same terror shone brightly now. This man had somehow survived cleaving; Merik would not let him die.

Time trickled past, moving in time to the water dropping off the cotton. Slowly, the man's shivering subsided. Slowly, he regained control of his throat, rasping strange words that did not sound like language. Eventually, the man managed to sit up.

The sun was halfway across the eastern sky.

"I cannot understand you," Merik told him after the man tried, yet again, to communicate. The man pointed as he spoke. First at the stone. Then at the hilltop.

Merik shook his head, trying Cartorran: "I cannot understand you." He tried Marstoki after that, and Dalmotti and Nubrevnan too. It wasn't until he attempted Svodish that any comprehension finally marked the man's face.

"Where?" the man asked, now in Svodish. He pointed again at the stone, at the hilltop.

"Arithuania," Merik answered.

A frown, more confusion than horror—but the horror came soon enough. "When?"

"Year . . ." Oh blighted Hell, how did you count double digits in Svodish? Merik couldn't remember, so he settled on, "Year ten and nine."

Now the shock came, and with it bile. Before Merik could grab the man and help him, the Northman lurched around and heaved. Water first, in great sprays, then dark bile, and finally nothing but choked air. By the time he finished, tears streamed down the man's cheeks, tracking pale lines amidst the dirt.

"How?" His red-eyed gaze did not meet Merik's. "Four years. How?"

Merik exhaled sharply. Four years. *Four years.* Surely the man had not been Esme's prisoner for so long.

"Why . . . heal?" Merik asked. The man had come back from cleaving; Merik wanted—*needed*—to know how.

But the Northman only shook his head. "Stop," he said simply. "Dark, then stop."

Before Merik could try to interpret this, the witch herself returned.

Where are you, Prince?

Merik spun away from the Northman as fast as he could. If Esme could look through his eyes, he did not want her to see. There was still a chance that man could flee; Merik would not let her claim his life again.

"I am at the shrine," he said, staggering toward the central stone.

Why? A flicker of lightning—a mere caress of pain through Merik's veins. *You should be back to Poznin by now.*

263

"I fell asleep," he said. "The food offerings made me sick." Panic crept into Merik's voice, his words spewing out with frantic urgency. And he let them come that way. With or without a healed Northman to hide, this was how he reacted to Esme.

Especially since the pain was notching higher now.

"Please," he squeezed out, teeth clenched. "Please, I have gathered gemstones and will walk back now—stop, stop, *stop!*"

You will run back, Esme commanded, tone dismissive, bored. *I will not be happy if you arrive here after midnight.* And just like that, her claws retracted.

"I will run," he agreed, slumping over. He had no idea how he could possibly run that far.

He would deal with that problem later.

For several long moments, Merik sucked in air. It vibrated in his lungs. No magic, only cold and the scent of rock and soil. He stayed this way until he was certain Esme was gone. He stayed this way until the Northman finally rasped, "Help."

Merik twisted toward him, assuming the man needed help. But no. He was pointing at Merik, then patting at his neck.

"Help," he repeated, and Merik realized he meant the collar.

"No." Merik shook his head. "No help for me." This man wore no collar—none of Esme's Cleaved did, save Merik. And since it sounded as if this man had no idea how he had healed, then there was nothing at all Merik could do. If he tried to leave, Esme would just summon him right back.

Shuffling back to the man's side, Merik pointed up the hill. "North." He pointed again. "Go north. People. Help you. And here . . ." Merik scooped the knife off the dirt. Its red tassels laughed at him now.

The Northman did not take the knife, though. "You." Again, he pointed at Merik. Then at his neck. "Use?"

Merik wanted to. He wanted the security of knowing he had protection, that he had some secret weapon Esme did not know of. But what would he even do with the blade? He could not attack her—she would simply attack him, *destroy him* first. And as gnarled as the logic might be, he was safe in Poznin. Right now, Esme had no desire to kill him. She needed him for the Fury. She needed him for her experiments.

Besides, if she ever turned her Cleaved army on him, a single knife would do nothing against thousands. This Northman, though—he could use it. He might even need it, trying to reach those people with the fires.

"You," Merik said again, and this time, he took the man's skeletal hand and wrapped the man's fingers around the hilt. "You."

The man's papery brow pinched tight. "What . . . place?" He motioned to the shrine, to the hill he'd come from, and then to Merik's collar. "What place?"

"A nightmare," was all Merik replied, wondering why he remembered that word yet he couldn't remember how to count. Either way, it was the right one to use here. So he said it again: "A nightmare. *Run.*"

THIRTY

✳

Stix awoke to voices. Not voices inside her head, either, but real voices attached to human throats. They were arguing.

About her.

"We can't just leave her, Ry."

"We can't wait for her to wake up either. We have a job to do, Cam. I promise, we'll come back for her after that."

"But what if she wakes up before? Or what if raiders get to her first? Please, Ry. My gut's tellin' me we ought to bring her with us."

A frustrated huff. Then a muttered, "Who's the Sightwitch here?" A heartbeat later, Stix heard footsteps approach, and when she hauled open her eyelids, light seared across her vision. She winced, arms—weak and sore—rising to block her face.

Where *was* she?

"You're awake," said a young woman with short black hair, warm skin slightly lighter than Stix's, and eyes of moonlight silver. She held a lantern high, brow tight with worry. "Do you know how you got here?"

Stix shook her head, the faintest of movements. Her brain

throbbed. Her body ached. She remembered voices … and water … and a doorway. Not much else.

"Do you know who you are?" the young woman pressed. "Can you remember your name?

"Stacia … Sotar." Her voice sounded—and felt—like broken razors. Noden curse her, where *was* she? And why did everything hurt?

"Well," the girl said, glancing behind, "she's already doing better than Kullen. When I found him, he couldn't remember his name or position or anything."

"But First Mate Ikray had already cleaved, right?" The second speaker moved into view, coppery brown skin with paler patches over his right cheek. He held a bandaged hand to his chest. "First Mate Sotar doesn't look like her magic has gone corrupt."

"It's … Captain Sotar." Stix tried to sit up; her stomach muscles very much disapproved, pushing a grunt from her abdomen. "And I'm not … corrupted."

The boy scooted closer, easing his good hand behind Stix's back and helping her to sit up. "Be careful, Captain." He offered a bright smile, so at odds with the dark and dank that surrounded them.

"How," Stix asked roughly, "do you know who I am?"

"We were in the Royal Navy, sir. Stationed on the *Jana* before …"

"Before it blew up," finished the girl. She strode closer and knelt on Stix's other side, setting the lantern nearby. Then she unlooped a canteen from her belt and offered it. "I'm Ryber. He's Cam."

Stix accepted the canteen, which only made the boy beam

267

wider. A comforting smile, she had to admit while she gulped cool water. She also had to admit that he and Ryber did look vaguely familiar.

"What is this place?" she asked, after sucking back a final gulp. "How did I get here?"

"This is the Past," Ryber responded, as if this was a perfectly reasonable answer. She pushed to her feet and seized a bulging satchel off the ground nearby. "As for how you got here, I have a pretty good guess. But we don't have time to linger, so either you get up and come with us, First Mate . . . I mean, *Captain*, or you stay here."

"Don't stay here," Cam inserted. "There are raiders behind us. We don't know when they'll get here, but you don't wanna be around when they do."

Ryber and Cam might as well have been talking to Stix in another language for how little their words made sense. "Why are you two even here?" she asked. "What *is* this place and what raiders are you talking about?"

Ryber wagged her head. "I told you. There's no time. I can try to explain while we walk, but we can't wait another second." Ryber extended a hand. "Are you coming?"

Stix didn't see many other options before her, so she clasped Ryber's hand and said, "I'm coming." Then Ryber pulled while Cam braced an arm behind. Together, they helped her stand, and Noden curse Stix, but she needed every bit of their aid.

Before she could pull free from Cam's support, her eyes caught on a low pedestal nearby. On it lay a broken sword and a broken looking glass. *Death, death, the final end.*

Gooseflesh slid down her neck, her arms. "What are those?" She took a step toward the pedestal. "I . . . know them."

"Those," Ryber said, moving in front of her, "are dangerous for people like you. Did you pick them up?"

"I . . . think so?" Stix blinked. Then rubbed her eyes. *Death, death, the final end.* "What do you mean by 'people like you'?"

"I'll explain"—Ryber laid a firm, but not unkind hand on Stix's shoulder—"once we're walking." Together, she and Cam angled Stix away from the table and away from the calls for a final, final end.

The room was an endless streak of darkness beyond the lantern, no end in sight. No change in the rough flagstones beneath their feet or the shadows wavering in from all sides.

And still Stix remembered nothing.

The tunnel beyond the low door was too thin for Cam to keep supporting Stix, so after checking she could move on her own, he moved into step behind Ryber. They vanished into the maw.

Stix took up the rear, ready to follow. Except her feet didn't quite move as they ought to.

Death, death, the final end.

She glanced back.

Figures floated behind her. A hundred of them, all shapes and sizes, suspended like dead men from the gallows. They stared at her—she *felt* them staring, even if she saw no eyes within the shadows.

They aren't angry anymore, she thought, even though she didn't know what that thought meant. All she knew was that the ghosts didn't mind if she left, so she hurried after the fading lantern's glow.

And Stacia Sotar did not look back.

THIRTY-ONE

*

*H*eat roars. Wood cracks and embers fly.

"Run." Blood drips from his mother's mouth as she speaks. It splatters his face.

With arms stained to red, she pushes herself up. She wants him to crawl out from beneath her. She wants him to escape. "Run, my child, run."

But he does not move, just as he did not move when the raiders first ambushed the tribe. Just as he did not move when his father drew his sword and ran from their tent.

Or when the raiders reached their doorway, loosed their arrows, and then his mother fell atop him. She hid him with her body until the raiders moved on.

"Run," she whispers one last time, pleading desperation in her silver eyes. Then the last of her strength flees. She collapses onto him.

"Get up, Bloodwitch."

Aeduan's ribs shrieked. Pain punched him awake. Water rushed into his mouth. It shocked. It choked. His eyes snapped

270

wide, and sunlight burned in. Water too. He must have fallen into the creek when he passed out.

He was freezing.

"Get up." The pain erupted in his ribs again. Although the touch was nothing more than a gentle toe nudging, it felt like one of Evrane's knife-toed boots. Aeduan angled his head back. A face swam into view. Brown skin, black plaits, a Carawen cloak gleaming bright.

"Monk Lizl," he tried to say, but that was not what came out. All that came out was coughing. *Speed and daisy chains, mother's kisses and sharpened steel.* Her scent was there, if weak.

She grabbed his shoulders and hauled him upward— enough for him to get his own arms under him. Enough for him to sink into a four-legged crouch. The coughing continued, although at least upright, he could drink instead of drown. One gulping splash became four; the coughing finally subsided.

Not the pain, though. Never the pain.

As if following his thoughts, Lizl dropped to a squat beside him. Dangling from a stiletto in her hand—*his* stiletto—was Aeduan's Painstone. A drained, useless chunk of rose quartz. "Want to explain this to me, Bloodwitch? I thought you healed from everything."

"I do."

She sniffed. "Then why is this creek red with your blood? And why have you not healed yet? Somehow you look worse now than when you were unconscious." She whipped the knife sideways. The Painstone flung into the woods. "You're also shivering. Thirteen years we trained at the coldest place in all the Witchlands, yet I never saw you quake."

"There are colder places in the Witchlands."

271

"Ah." She pushed upright. "Good to know you're still a contrary prick. Now get up."

Aeduan wagged his head. The forest dipped and swam. "Can't," he ground out.

"In that case"—she yanked a fat leather rope from her belt—"I will have to make you." Before he could stop her, before he could even comprehend what she intended, she had looped the leather around his neck like a hunting dog's leash.

She yanked. Aeduan moved.

He had no choice. Stars exploded across his vision, his breath slashed off. He couldn't even cough anymore, and if he did not rise, he would pass out again. So somehow, though he had no idea where he found the strength, he pushed to his feet.

The pressure at his neck relaxed.

He tried to fix his gaze on Lizl, but her face bled into the forest around them. He tried to say, *I am a fellow monk. We do not treat each other this way*, but all that came out was "I . . . monk."

"No you're not," she said flatly. Then she whistled once, and a sturdy chestnut mare ambled from the trees. Following behind on a lead was a saddled gray donkey. "Monks do not conspire with their targets, you see, and *monks* do not betray their own kind."

It took Aeduan a moment to understand those words. Long enough for the horse and donkey to approach. Long enough for Lizl to say, "Mount up." And long enough for her to tug at the rope again when he did not obey.

He grabbed for the donkey's pommel, gasping. Blinking. Then suddenly Lizl was behind him, shoving him upward. In a blur of color and pain, he climbed on. Then he slumped forward, bracing against the donkey's neck.

The rope slackened slightly, and Lizl grinned up at him. "I never thought I would see this day, Bloodwitch. *You*, trapped by *me*." She laughed, a hearty sound, before withdrawing something from within her white cloak—so clean, so unmarred.

A Painstone, new and fresh, winked in the sun. "You would probably like to have this, wouldn't you?" She glanced at it, brow knitting in mock consternation. "Why, I bet it would make you strong again. Get rid of all that torture and blood. Maybe, Bloodwitch, if you're well behaved, I will let you have it. Not your weapons, though. Those, I am keeping."

"What do you want from me?" he forced out.

"I told you already. Back in Tirla." She dropped the stone into her cloak and turned away. The rope tightened as she aimed for her horse. "I want that ransom."

"What . . . does that have to do with me?"

"Do not play a fool." She vaulted into the saddle. "I want the Raider King's head, Bloodwitch. I told you that, and as far as I can tell, there's no easier way to get it than to kidnap his son and hold him hostage."

THIRTY-TWO

※

The following morning, Safi's unknown Adders guided her to a part of the palace she had never seen before, deep within the bowels of the island. The long hall of sandstone cells stood empty, save one at the end.

"Oh gods," Safi breathed, thrusting past her Adders into the cell. The Hell-Bards hung there, bound to the wall by iron. Lev was the only one whose eyes fluttered at the sound of the opening iron gate. Caden and Zander remained limp and unresponsive.

"Lev? Do you hear me?" Safi rushed to the woman and cupped the Hell-Bard's scarred face. Two lines of salt cut through the dirt on her cheeks.

Lev's eyelids wavered up at Safi's touch. Her pupils pulsed and swayed, as if she knew Safi was there but couldn't quite find her.

"What have they done to you?" Safi whispered.

Lev laughed, a drunken burst of air. "You ... should see the other guy." It was all she got out before her eyes lolled shut again. Her body sank into the chains.

Footsteps pattered behind Safi. She whirled about to find

an Adder slinking in—one who had regularly stood sentry outside her bedroom. At first, relief dissolved through Safi's limbs. This man she knew; this man could help her with the Hell-Bards.

Then she caught sight of the poison darts in his left hand. The famed tool of the Marstoki Adders, no larger than sewing needles, with small tufts of black on the end.

And just like that, Safi remembered all the stories she had heard growing up, of Adder Poisonwitches so powerful they could corrupt a person's blood directly in their veins. Of wicked assassins who would stop at nothing to protect their empress. Of darkness and torture and pain.

"You . . . poisoned them."

The Adder bowed his head.

And Safi rocked back a step. "Will they die?"

"Pain and sleep," he said. "That is all I gave them."

"*Gave* them?" She gaped at the tear tracks on Lev's face. "That is not a gift. They saved your empress's life. Mine too, and probably a lot of other people's in Azmir—so you repay them with pain?"

No reaction in the Adder's posture. The poison darts rested unwavering upon his gloved hand. "Please step aside, Truthwitch."

"No." Safi squared her shoulders toward him. "Does the Empress know you're doing this? I cannot believe she would allow it."

"I have orders." He claimed one step toward her. "I must follow them."

Still, she stood her ground. "Whose?"

"Stand aside." Warning sharpened his tone now.

"*Whose?*"

275

"Mine." Habim strode into the cell. Startling, unannounced, and with a grim slant to his jaw. "Leave," he ordered Safi, a general through and through. "This is no place for children."

Safi did not leave. In fact, she could do nothing but stare. This was not the man she knew. On the surface, he might wear the same face, same frown. But underneath . . .

I don't know you anymore.

"Why is she here?" Habim asked the Adder.

"The Empress wants her to use her magic upon the Cartorrans."

"It will not work." Habim flipped a dismissive hand her way. "Hell-Bards are resistant to magic."

I don't know you. I don't know you. The urge to scream grated down Safi's spine. But all she said was: "How could you torture them?"

For three long heartbeats, she did not breathe. She simply held Habim's gaze, willing him to answer. She didn't care about his plan, she didn't care about their roles as court Truthwitch and Firewitch general. The world was upside down, and now *he* had to make it right again.

At last, Habim said, "I would command him to torture you, Truthwitch, if I thought it necessary."

A lie, a lie, a *lie.* Also not an answer.

"Take her away," he ordered the Adder. "And tell Her Majesty that I already have all the answers I need."

"No," Safi snarled before the Adder could move. "I won't go until I've seen them freed."

"Then you will wait a long time. *Take her.*"

The Adder advanced, and Safi dug in her heels. They would have to poison her too if they wanted her to leave.

276

Two more steps and the Adder reached her. Still she did not move—and when he grabbed her wrist, she flipped up her arm—an easy yank Habim had taught her so that no man could ever keep hold.

The Adder grabbed again, and this time, he raised a dart toward her neck—

"Enough." Habim stalked across the room, and for the first time since arriving in Azmir, his careful control frayed. Flames glittered along the tips of his fingers.

"Wake the commander," he barked at the Adder. Then, while the man slid away, Habim stared—*hard*—into Safi's eyes. "These people are not your friends. They are your enemies, and torture is no less than what they would do to you."

Habim's voice trembled with belief that fluttered warm and true against Safi's magic. But he also didn't know these Hell-Bards as she did.

She turned her back on Habim, watching in horror as the Adder pulled two darts from the back of Caden's neck. Two breaths later, Caden's eyes opened. He gasped like a drowning man, gaze flying around the room. Safi reached his side in an instant. Like she had done with Lev, she gripped his chin and held it high.

"Safi," he choked out, wobbly pupils finding hers. "Are you hurt?"

"Hush," she murmured, even as she felt her heart fishtail and writhe. "I'm sorry they did this to you, Caden. I'm so, so sorry."

"We waited for you," he murmured. He did not slur as Lev had, yet despite this small feat, he was not truly here. His mind remained trapped somewhere desperate, somewhere scared. "We waited for you, Safi, and when we saw the attack, we went in through the hole in the wall. We wanted to build wards to protect the city, but there was no time—"

"Stop." Habim's command bounced across the room. "That man is dangerous. Step away."

Safi did no such thing—and Habim's patience frayed a bit more. He stalked to her, but without pushing her aside, he wound his fingers through Caden's noose, the gold chain all Hell-Bards wore.

"What do you think this man is, child? What do you think the Hell-Bard's noose *does* to them? Whatever Emperor Henrick wants, Emperor Henrick gets. All their master must do is pull the leash, and then the dogs obey." He jerked at the chain; a groan broke from Caden's throat.

"They have no choice. Their magic—their very *Aethers*— have been severed from them and bound to the Emperor. If they disobey a command, they die. If they remove the noose, they die."

"I know," Safi said, and she *did* know. Caden had explained what Hell-Bards were. He had told her that their magics had been severed from their souls. Although, admittedly, she hadn't realized that Henrick could kill them if they did not obey.

But that doesn't change anything here.

"Tell me, Hell-Bard." Habim pulled the noose tighter, towing Caden's face up. Stretching his neck long. "What will happen to you if you return to your master without his Truthwitch? What will Henrick do to you? I have heard tales of his displeasure."

"No." Caden coughed that word. His eyes found Safi's. "That . . . isn't why . . . we stayed."

"Do not lie to her." Habim yanked at the chain. Caden hissed, eyes rolling. "If you really cared for the Truthwitch, then you would have traveled as far away from her as possible. As long as you are near her—or the Empress—then you are a liability. As long as you *live*, then you are a liability."

Tighter, tighter he pulled. Until it was too much. Safi snatched at Habim's wrist and *tugged*. "Stop, Habim. *Please*, let go of him."

To her surprise—and relief—Habim did. He released the chain. Caden's head fell back and hit the wall.

Then Habim fixed the Adder with a purposeful stare. "Finish this."

Before Safi could react, Habim swung his arms around her and hauled her toward the door.

Finish this. Finish this. It took two dragging steps and a sharp inhale before she realized what those words meant.

"NO." Safi clawed. She fought. She tried, tried, *tried* to break free, but this was the man who had trained her. She stood no chance. *I don't know you anymore. I don't know you anymore.*

Yet right before Habim could get Safi through the door, Caden's voice rang out, strong and true: "We stayed because of your uncle, Safi! We stayed because he was arrested for treason and he will hang within the week."

Habim froze. Safi froze. Even the Adder seemed stunned by this announcement. And although Safi could not use her magic on Caden, she had no doubt his words were true.

Uncle Eron. Arrested for treason. Hang within the week.

In that moment, three questions crashed in Safi's mind: How had Eron been caught? How could she save him? And why in all the sodding hell-gates did she care so much? Her whole life she'd thought she hated him. Now she couldn't even begin to conceive a world where her uncle had been taken away.

If she had thought herself helpless before, it was nothing compared to the weight that bore down now. Uncle Eron was on the opposite side of the Witchlands, and she was no more use to him than these Hell-Bards chained against the wall.

Her eyes found Habim's, certain she would find the same horror she felt reflected back at her. But all she found was flint-eyed determination.

Her stomach bottomed out. *He already knew.* Somehow, he already knew, yet he hadn't bothered to inform Safi. Nothing, nothing—he had given her *nothing*, since his arrival.

Before her ire could fully ignite, though, before screams could rip from her throat, Habim's fingers tightened around her biceps. A firm, reassuring touch that brought her back to her childhood. To the countless times he had towed her from a card game or dice match or yet another screaming match with Uncle Eron.

Uncle Eron, who had been arrested for treason.

Uncle Eron, who would hang within the week.

Habim led Safi to the cell's exit, six paces away—giving them six paces during which he could whisper without the Adder to overhear.

"Be ready," he said. "At the party, we will make our move. Be ready." Then he released her into the hall, to where her earlier assembly of Adders still stood.

The cell door clanged shut behind her.

THIRTY-THREE

✳

It amazed Iseult how much a landscape could change in a day.

Last night, there had been rowan and fir trees, nettle and grass. By dawn, evergreens had replaced the hardwoods, and the tufted grass had given way to sedge. The paths grew narrower and narrower too, until eventually they had to leave the horses behind.

"Go home," Leopold told the gelding, after removing what few supplies they had from his saddle. To Iseult's astonishment, Rolf actually seemed to understand. He turned away, and quickly vanished within the stunted pines, followed obediently by the stolen mare.

"Isn't your home far?" Iseult asked, eyeing Blueberry warily. He flew high above them, and though Owl had promised he would not eat the horses, Iseult wasn't entirely convinced.

"Quite far." Leopold smiled, his Threads flickering with matching shades of mischief. "I told you, he's a *very* well-trained horse."

Without their steeds, the group's pace slowed. Owl could not walk quickly, and the terrain grew steeper by the hour.

By midmorning, snow and ice clung to everything—to the miniature trees, to the granite rock, to old travelers' huts long forgotten. The sun glared down, melting the frosted gravel to slick scree.

Twice, Iseult fell. Twice Leopold fell. Owl, however, never fell. The little Earthwitch always knew where to place her feet. Or perhaps she simply commanded the stones to remain intact, and they dutifully obeyed.

Eventually even the dwarf evergreens trickled away. They had trekked above the tree line, where only rock and snow held court. Iseult had never seen so much snow, and she decided she didn't much like it.

It was cold, it was wet, and there never seemed to be an end to it.

She had also never been so high in her life. She hadn't known—could never have *guessed*—how vast and gaping the sky would feel at this altitude. So huge, so blue, so empty. Especially when they reached the end of their path and nothing waited beyond save a sheer cliff and a very long drop to a river.

With her back against the granite mountain, Iseult stared at the cliff ten paces away. In the last few moments, gusting winds had risen, rolling fog across the ledge like waves upon a seashore. Somehow, not seeing the precipice and thousand-foot drop only made the height seem that much more terrifying.

Owl clung to Iseult's side, little fingers fisted into Iseult's cloak and terror spiraling through her Threads, and though Iseult knew she was the second choice—Blueberry coasted on airstreams too high to see—it left a strange feeling in her chest. A warmth that wasn't quite pleasure, and certainly not love, but *something*.

Something nice that made her nose wiggle. Something nice that made her think of Aeduan, because she was, it seemed, no better than Owl for the hoping.

Leopold, meanwhile, searched the cliff for a "sky-ferry" he'd insisted would be waiting for them. Every few moments, he leaned dangerously over the edge, which made Iseult feel like vomiting and made Owl wince and whimper.

After six such instances, Leopold's Threads finally flushed with triumph and he threw a perfect grin Iseult's way. "I found it. I told you I would!"

True to his word, the prince had worn only honest emotions since last night. And despite what he'd claimed, it had not disarmed him at all. If anything, he was *more* charming when his face and feelings were in tune.

The "it" that Leopold had found turned out to be a round, flat stone that had been covered by a hundred pebbles, and after kicking the pebbles into the mist-filled canyon—which also made Iseult feel ill—Leopold began tapping a complicated rhythm with his toe. *A lock-spell*, she thought at first, until halfway through, the ferry began to appear. Inch by inch, tap by tap, it coalesced amidst the haze.

A glamour-spell. Awe washed over Iseult. Shaped like a wide river barge, the ferry was affixed to a long, rusted chain that ran diagonally up and vanished into the clouds. At the center of the ferry's deck was a steel-toothed pulley over which the chain ran.

Leopold opened his arms wide. "Did I not promise an easy route? This does all the climbing for us."

Owl was the first to speak. She tapped at Iseult's leg. "Dead," she whispered, pointing at the ferry. Tan confusion clustered in her Threads.

At Leopold's own confused Threads, Iseult translated: "She says it's dead."

"Yes, well." He shrugged a shoulder. "Wood *is* dead. But that does not make it unsafe. See?" To prove his point, he tossed the first of their supply sacks on board. It thumped down beside the pulley, and the wood creaked like a ship at sea.

The ferry itself, though, scarcely budged.

Still, Iseult and Owl did not join the prince. Iseult had no interest in peeling her back off the mountainside, and Owl had no interest in peeling herself off Iseult.

"Have you used this before?" Iseult asked.

"Many times."

"How many?"

Leopold heaved the second supply sack onto the ferry to a second fanfare of groaning wood. "I have ridden this four times? Perhaps five? Admittedly, I don't use it every time I visit."

As far as Iseult was concerned, "five times" did not equate to "many."

"And how many times have you actually visited?" she asked, even as she knew she was stalling for time.

Leopold indulged her, his grin wide. The cold air suited him. His cheeks glowed pink. "I have been here more times than I can count, Iseult. Ever since I was a boy. The new Abbot is the sixth son of a Cartorran nobleman, and the Abbot before him was the *eighth* son. Men like that, you see, are useful to princes."

Iseult did not in fact see, but she supposed she would learn soon enough what Leopold meant. No more standing here clutching Owl. No more waiting for courage to find her. After three stabilizing breaths, Iseult knelt beside the girl.

"We have to get on," she said in her gentlest tones. "I know it's scary, but we can't stay here any longer."

"Why?" Owl's Threads hummed with red resistance.

"Because it's the only way to reach the Monastery. And this"—Iseult motioned to the fog and narrow path—"isn't a good campsite for us."

"Why?"

"Why . . . what?" Iseult's nose twitched. She did not want to argue. Everything had been going so well with Owl since last night. *Please, Moon Mother, don't let it stop now.* "Why can't we camp here? Or why are we going to the Monastery?"

Owl nodded, and Iseult had to assume she was nodding at the second question. "Because we'll be safe with the monks."

"I don't want to." Then, before Iseult could stop her, hundreds of tiny pebbles scuttled across Owl's body, and within half a breath, she was hidden away.

This time, Iseult's nose really wrinkled. *Stasis,* she reminded herself, even as fire sparked in her fingertips.

"I like it here," Owl added, a tiny mouth appearing in the stones. "So I will stay."

Ah, Iseult thought, and just like that, her frustration bled away. She had heard these words before. She had *said* those words before—ten years ago. *I like it here. So I will stay.* Her mother had tried to pull her from a tree in the Midenzi settlement. It was *the* tree Iseult had always sought refuge in when the other children had turned on her.

On that particular day, Iseult had refused to come down when Gretchya called, so her mother had snipped, "Fine," before walking away. It had made Iseult's heart drop to her toes. Made her whole body feel empty. She had wanted her mother to argue with her. She had *wanted* her mother to ask why she was even in the oak tree at all.

But Gretchya hadn't asked that day, nor did she ask on any other.

Iseult wouldn't make the same mistake.

"Why don't you want to go?" Iseult aimed a taut smile at the stones.

"Dead," Owl replied.

"Yes, but lots of things are dead, Owl. The inn we stayed at was dead. The leather on the saddle you rode was dead. It doesn't mean it isn't safe."

More confusion in her Threads. Then a tiny frown.

"It's the only way we can reach the Monastery, Owl. We have to take the ferry."

"You could tell the rocks to bring you." A tremor waved across the earth. It wobbled Iseult and knocked stones straight off the cliff.

Leopold's Threads flared with white alarm.

Iseult, though, kept her face neutral and body calm. "I don't have the magic you have, Owl. Remember? Neither does the prince. So we cannot ask the rocks to carry us. We have to take the sky-ferry instead. I bet Aeduan has ridden it, you know."

It was the right thing to say. Green curiosity wavered in Owl's Threads. "Will he be there?"

Iseult scratched her nose. She did not want to lie, but she

also feared what might happen if she said no. "Maybe," she offered casually, and she supposed it might even be true. He *might* be there. One day.

The green sharpened, Owl's interest growing keener. Any moment now, she would abandon her camouflage.

So Iseult turned a cool eye toward the ferry, where the prince, to his credit, leaned against the railing and inspected his fingernails. A perfect display of fearlessness. *See?* he said with his body. *This is easy. No need to be afraid.*

His Threads, however, matched Owl's. Bright green interest, and a hint of beige anxiety.

"Aeduan grew up at the Monastery," Iseult went on. "Don't you want to see what it looks like? I know I do."

And there it was: a rumbling crunch of rocks, and soon, Owl herself appeared. The girl still shook, though, and the gravel still danced. Subtle enough to be mistaken for wind, but if the pebbles bounced higher at the Monastery ... If Owl decided to bounce *boulders* instead ...

"Owl," Iseult said, pumping authority into her tone now, "you will have to stop using your magic once we reach the Monastery. Just like Aeduan told you before we entered Tirla, you will have to keep it hidden away from the monks."

For once, the girl did not ask *Why?* But the question was evident in her wide, frightened eyes.

"Magic can always be taken away," Iseult explained. "There are Cursewitches out there who can steal a person's magic. Did you know that?"

Owl's head wagged ever so slightly. The fear pulsed brighter in her Threads—but Iseult was going somewhere with this. Following a trail Habim had once followed with her, long ago

287

when she'd been a fresh arrival in a city fraught with things to hide from.

"This is why," Iseult explained, "it is always better to do things quietly. If you hide your powers, then people will underestimate you. And if they underestimate you . . ." She pointed at Owl's chest. "Then you're the one with all the power. And you are, aren't you, Owl? You have Blueberry, and you have the stones. As long as you have that, and as long as no one knows you have them, then no one can ever, *ever* hurt you."

Owl blinked. Three contemplative shutterings before aquamarine understanding melted across her Threads. The gravel stilled around her feet.

"No one," she said softly, and Iseult couldn't help it: her lips slipped into a smile.

And her grin only widened when Owl abruptly said, "Go. Now." Then, without waiting for Iseult, she hurried for the sky-ferry, impatience bright in her Threads.

It took every ounce of Iseult's Threadwitch training not to punch the air in triumph. She had coaxed Owl all on her own. No argument, no frustrated fire sparks.

Take *that*, Aeduan.

Aeduan did not know how he held his seat atop the donkey. The world bled around him, consumed by the perpetual throb in his chest and belly. It devoured all thought, all desire, until there was nothing left but fiery talons that leached away shapes and colors. Until the whole world was gray. Gray trees, gray sky, and gray Lizl atop her gray mare.

At first, when they'd set off, aiming vaguely northwest and into the mountains, Aeduan tried to warn Lizl. He'd told her the Fury was coming for him, that the man was a killer, yet all she'd done was laugh. "I'm a killer too, and he doesn't scare me."

It would seem she had seen the Fury in Tirla. She had taken shelter from the storm and overhead Aeduan talking to him. But *not* when the man's winds had raged around him. Not when his cyclone had wrecked and ruined, nor when his cleaving magic had turned his veins to black.

So she did not believe Aeduan when he warned her, and soon, the argument was too difficult to sustain. So Aeduan shut up and turned his attention to escape—for he could not stay with Lizl. If the Fury came, she would die.

Aeduan had enough blood on his hands already.

The Aeduan of two days ago would have simply taken control of her blood, trapping her in place long enough for him to flee. Of course, the Aeduan of a *week* ago would never have been caught in the first place.

Now, he could scarcely smell her blood, much less touch it. And the more he drifted in this half-life, the more he feared it was not the fire in his veins that kept him from summoning his powers, nor the weakness as his body fought to heal.

The curse was erasing him. Drip by drip, it was draining away his magic until soon there would be nothing left. His body, he thought, might still have a chance to heal and recover. His Bloodwitchery, he feared, never would.

Eventually, even planning became too difficult to sustain. It took all Aeduan's focus just to remain upright. The roads, if they could even be called that, were slender and uneven.

Overgrown hunting paths and shepherds' trails rife with branches to poke at Aeduan's eyes and scratch apart his skin.

The donkey trundled ever onward. The sun ascended ever higher.

Once, Aeduan thought he heard a dog barking. Close, as if some farmer's hut waited nearby. It was a nice sound. A welcome respite that chased away the shadows. He liked dogs. He had liked Boots too, until the day he'd killed him. Then he'd hated Boots for dying so easily.

Now, Aeduan knew everything died easily.

"You move too slowly." Lizl's voice knifed through the fading day. She had stopped her horse. The donkey had stopped too. Somehow Aeduan had not noticed, perhaps because the leash around his neck had grown no easier. "It will be midday soon, Bloodwitch, and we need to cover more ground."

"Give me ... that Painstone," he rasped. "Then I'll move faster."

She snorted, and in an easy swoop, dismounted. Three sluggish heartbeats later, she reached Aeduan's side. "Down," she ordered, yanking at the leash—and leaving Aeduan with no choice but to obey. He tumbled from the saddle.

She sidestepped; he hit the cold earth. The impact shocked his bones, his lungs. He bit through his tongue and tasted blood. Always, always the blood. Then coughing laid claim, and shadows wavered at the edges of his vision, thicker and thicker by the moment.

This curse would kill him—and he was glad for it. If he was dead, the pain would end. If he was dead, the Fury could not come for him, and he would not need to escape Lizl to protect her.

When at last the hacking passed, a water bag landed on the dirt before Aeduan. He did not take it.

"Where . . . are we?" Eyes stinging, he looked up at Lizl.

"We're near where I was born." She unstrapped a pack from her saddle. "If you had played nice growing up, then you might recognize it."

Aeduan didn't know how to answer that. He had always played nice. It was the monster inside that had not.

He fumbled for the water bag and rocked back onto his haunches. Lizl had slackened the leash, and his gullet moved with blessed freedom as he drank his fill. A line of cool relief slid from throat to chest. Not enough to clear the pain, but something.

He sucked in a tattered breath, stoppered the bag, and threw it back to Lizl. He missed. The bag hit the earth several paces short, earning a glare. "What's wrong with you?" She scowled. "I've seen you take a sword through the gut and heal from it. This . . ." She motioned to him. "What happened?"

Aeduan's only reply was to draw in more air, his lungs rattling. There was nothing he could say that would help his cause. If he admitted he was cursed, it would only give her more power—assuming she even believed him at all. She did not believe in the Fury, so why would she believe in a Cursewitch?

"Hurt," he said eventually. "Arrows. Many of them."

She did not look convinced, but fortunately, she also did not press. "Here." Two long strides brought her to him, and she offered him a worn leather satchel. "Clean up."

291

Aeduan squinted at the brown case. A small healer's kit, he realized. Then he shook his head. "It . . . won't help. I need the Painstone."

"Well, it's this or nothing." She waved it in his face. "Your choice."

He took the kit.

By the dappled light of a turning maple, Aeduan did his best to tend his wounds. The arrow marks had worsened, the skin around each gash puffy and red while the holes themselves oozed black blood. Each touch made his teeth grind and his eyes roll back in his head. Somehow, though, he managed not to pass out.

He dabbed the final smears of a Waterwitch salve on the largest slash below his breastbone, when a question split the day: "What's it like?"

Lizl sat on a fallen tree, oiling her sword. Her cloth whispered rhythmically against Carawen steel.

"What is . . . what like?" It took Aeduan three tries to get the jar closed again. His fingers shook.

"What's it like being unable to die?"

"I can die," he answered. *I am dying right now.*

Her gaze flicked to his, unamused. "You know what I mean."

Perhaps it was her detachment that spurred him, or perhaps it was the pain and the haze and the bloodred light through a maple tree. He could not say. All he knew was that a reply fell from his tongue, raw and honest.

"It means that I forget how easy it is to kill people," he said gruffly, "so I must always be on my guard. It means I do not know what fear is, so I can never be brave. It means that

I live when everyone else around me dies. And it means"—he finally wedged the salve's cork back in—"I am not like you. Or anyone else."

Her cloth paused halfway down the blade. She considered him, eyes thinned and inscrutable.

Until at last she murmured, "No. You are not like me or anyone else, are you?" She broke the eye contact. "And it's why the world hates you. Why we will always hate you. Death follows wherever you go, yet by the grace of the Wells, you always outrun your own."

"I did not ask for this."

"No one asks for what life gives them." She sniffed and scrubbed harder at the blade. "What matters is how you use it, and as far as I can tell, you have squandered a magic that others would kill for. You ascended through the ranks faster than any other acolyte. You took all the best assignments, hoarded all the employers and coin, and the entire time, you looked down on the rest of us. We were mud for you to stomp through on your way to higher ground. You had no loyalty to the Monastery, no interest in the Cahr Awen."

For the first time since her leash had wrapped around his neck, anger sparked in Aeduan's shoulders. His fingers flexed.

Because she had it all wrong. Everything she said was backward. He had not looked down on the other monks; he had been cast aside. He had not wasted his magic; his magic had wasted him.

"Now," she went on, voice bitter as she scooped more lanolin from a tub, "it turns out you're son to the Raider King. I don't know why I was so surprised to learn this. Of course you would be loyal to a man who kills innocents and burns

293

the Witchlands—and of *course* he would breed a demon like you."

Aeduan's wrists rolled. The rage spread hotter inside his veins.

Why, he wanted to ask, should he be loyal to anyone? He had lived his entire life as a tool for others, a blade no different from the one she now cleaned. Even the Threadwitch had used him, tricking him with his own coins so he would track her friend across the Contested Lands.

Aeduan said nothing at all, though. Instead, his spine hardened and he inhaled deep. Rage was stoking his magic to life, a weak flame. Vicious and welcome within his heart. Though he was not strong enough yet to control Lizl's blood and flee, if he was patient, if he was *angry* . . .

Maybe enough of his power would return. And maybe this curse would not claim him just yet.

The Carawen Monastery was everything Iseult had hoped it would be.

It was *more* than she had hoped, because now it was real. Now it was right before her with only minutes of flying before they arrived.

The sky-ferry approached from the south, and as it creaked past peak after peak, more and more of the Monastery emerged. It was as if Iseult were peeling back a page in her old book on the Carawens, slowly revealing the full scale of the monks' home.

A black fortress clutched the side of a mountain. Imposing, impenetrable, and isolated atop its white peak. Snow-tipped trees clustered around its lower half, a dense forest that stretched into the valley below. Stone steps, ramparts, and towers fixed with trebuchets stacked their way up to the highest point of the mountain—and all around that dark stone, over it and through it, moved tiny figures in white.

They were too far away for Iseult to sense Threads, but there was no mistaking their urgency. They moved in clusters, sprinting toward the highest tower. Some drill, perhaps? Or a sudden meeting? She supposed she would have an answer soon enough.

After years of dreaming of this place, Iseult det Midenzi had finally arrived at the Carawen Monastery. It looked exactly as it had in the illustrations, except so much *more*. No painting could ever capture all the angles and shades and movement of the place.

Her chest felt so full, she couldn't inhale. The frost that had lived in her shoulders since last night thawed into something warm. Something that expanded in her stomach and pressed against her lungs ...

Laughter, she realized, and if she wasn't careful, she might actually start *giggling*. And clapping. And bouncing. And, Moon Mother preserve her, would that be so bad? She was not merely here as a supplicant hoping to train with monks, hoping to finally *be* the monk she'd always dreamed of. She was here as one half of the Cahr Awen.

Surely, even a Threadwitch could clap at that.

"See those little people, Owl? Those are the monks," Iseult murmured. The girl's Threads hovered with a pink. All her fear had whispered away, replaced by awe the instant the sky-ferry's pulley had begun its haul. No doubt it helped that the girl was certain "Blueberry would catch her if she fell," and no doubt that was true. For her, at least. Iseult and Prince Leopold, however, were on their own—and it was a long way down.

Despite this undeniable truth, even Iseult's fear had settled the longer the wood croaked beneath them without incident, the longer the chain crunched them ever onward. And she had to admit, it helped that Leopold was so calm, so at ease. If the pressure popping in his ears bothered him, he gave no sign on his face. If the wind and the cold and the endless drop-off below unsettled him, none of that showed in his Threads.

What would Safi say if she saw me like this? Iseult thought, her fingers moving to her Threadstone. A prince beside her and a mountain bat soaring overhead while she ascended ever higher into the Sirmayans.

She had come a long way from that attic bedroom in Veñaza City.

What if, what if, what if. Iseult squeezed her Threadstone tighter. Soon, she would be with Safi again. Soon, the world would make sense again. It would be right side up as it should be.

Owl's tiny voice split her thoughts. "Rook," the child said, pointing above them, where sure enough, a bird circled on the currents.

At Leopold's curious glance from the pulley, Iseult translated. He nodded, a flitter of surprise crossing his Threads even as he smiled lightly at the girl. "That is indeed a rook. They use them to carry messages outside the Monastery—*and* to spy on approaching visitors. I imagine we will be joined by monks the instant we land."

When Iseult turned to tell Owl all of this, though, she found the girl eyeing Leopold.

"Where is your crown?" Owl asked.

A valid question for a child, so again Iseult translated.

And a startled laugh split his lips. The reaction, however, did not match his Threads. They were startled, yes, but also tinged with fear. "Tell her I lost it in my search to find you."

Iseult dutifully explained, and Owl's forehead pinched, her Threads sage green with consideration. Then at last she nodded: "I will make him another," before turning once more to gaze upon the view.

Soon, the sky-ferry floated them past the final mountaintop, and the full Monastery was on display. Iseult could hardly breathe at the sight of it. Without thinking—having forgotten the height entirely—she scooted a bit closer to the railing. Owl inched forward with her.

"That tall spire there," Iseult said, pointing to a black tower twice as high as everything else, "was built a thousand years ago. And there, do you see that lower wall circling the Monastery? It's wide enough for twenty men to move side by side. *On horseback.* Oh, and look—that slope-roofed building over there. That's the great hall, where they have glass stained in every color you can imagine.

"And, oh look!" Iseult's voice came out breathy and thick with emotion—a shame to every Threadwitch in the Witchlands. "That island," she said reverently, "is where the Origin Well stands." She pointed to a wide silver streak bisecting the valley, and to a long, crescent-shaped island at its heart.

She knew from her book that the Well itself stood nestled at the southern edge, and that six downy birches stood sentry,

297

their leaves green even in winter. The Well, meanwhile, stayed frozen year round. In the summer, when the Nomatsi caravans arrived on pilgrimage, it would take them a full day of cutting through the ice to retrieve the Well's healing waters. It was only a few inches thick, but hard as granite.

"What are you telling her?" Leopold queried, moving to join them. The breeze pulled at his curls. The sun turned his eyes a sharp clover green.

"I'm showing her the Origin Well," Iseult explained, eyes narrowing at the sight of his Threads. The serenity on his face no longer matched his feelings. His earlier calm was gone, replaced by a rich yellow worry.

"What's wrong?" she asked quietly, tone intentionally light for Owl's sake.

Leopold blinked. Then grimaced. "I can hide nothing from you, can I?"

"We had an agreement."

"That disproportionately favors *you*."

"If you would simply show me your true feelings, then it would not be a problem."

"But Iseult," he countered, spreading his hands, "true feelings are dangerous. Did you not know?"

"So is trying to run from them."

"Ah." Again, he blinked, Threads doused beneath a rich, almost icy blue. As if her words had surprised him like cold water dashed against the face.

And when he looked at her again, there was something akin to respect in his expression.

"To answer your question," he drawled, cocking his head casually toward a craggy slope coming into view. It stood opposite the Monastery, and above the river snaking between. "That army of raiders has me . . . on *edge*."

Iseult followed his gaze, about to ask, *What raiders?* But then she saw, and her breath hitched. Clustered amidst the forest were hundreds of tents with a hundred more smoke spirals whipping away on the breeze—and that was only the start. Countless more spirals lifted up from the snow-covered trees, suggesting countless more tents waiting unseen.

"Why are they here?" Her voice came out shrill with surprise, prompting Owl to glance up—and prompting worry to sparkle in her Threads. Iseult forced a tight smile.

"You pose an excellent question," Leopold murmured. "For which there is no excellent answer. As far as anyone can guess, the Raider King is waiting for the river to freeze. Then he will march his forces south. And *we* will be very glad we are inside the Monastery and not down there beside them." He flashed a warm grin for Owl, much smoother than Iseult's had been.

"Can they see us?" Iseult asked.

A curt head shake. "The sky-ferry is glamoured. The monks, however, can most certainly see us, and . . ." He trailed off. Then as one, his body and Threads stiffened. "*Move.*" He flung his arms around Iseult, yanked her from the rail, and thrust her toward the pulley.

She fell to her knees beside the gears. Owl screamed. Iseult turned . . .

And she saw what Leopold had seen: a trebuchet winding back, a great ball of flame clutched in its sling. It was aimed for the sky-ferry.

Leopold pushed Owl toward Iseult, and Iseult pulled the girl close.

Crack! The massive arm snapped. Fire launched their way.

"*Hold on!*" Leopold bellowed. He dove for the pulley, swooped his arm around Iseult—who swooped an arm around Owl—and then all three held tight.

The fire roared past them. Large as the ferry, hot as the sun. Sparks sprayed onto the wood. Wind scalded against them.

The ferry whooshed sideways, pushed by displaced air. Gravity clawed at Iseult. At Leopold and Owl, but their grips held true. *Mountains, canyon, snow, death.*

The ferry swung back the other way.

And more fire ignited on the trebuchet. The ferry was closer to the Monastery now, an easier target getting easier by the second.

"Why are they attacking us?" Iseult had to shout over Owl's howls and the ferry's shrieking wood.

"No idea!" Leopold shouted back. His Threads were as pale with fear as Owl's, but green determination latticed around the edges. He had not given up yet. "Surely there is some way to turn this thing around!"

While the ferry rocked to a gentler sway, he searched the pulley mechanism, and Iseult followed his lead. Neither loosened their grip on Owl. They simply scoured and examined—and Iseult also prayed. *Please, Moon Mother. Help us survive this, please.*

"What would a switch look like?" Iseult asked.

"I don't know!"

"I thought you had been here more times than you can count!"

"But only four times on the ferry—" He broke off as the next trebuchet launched.

Fire rocketed toward them. Leopold stared. Iseult stared. Owl screamed, a sound to split mountains. A sound to summon stone.

Or a mountain bat. In a streak of fur and speed, Blueberry dropped from the sky. With his wings folded in, he dove faster than the flames.

He crashed into the fire. The ball flew off course. His flight turned to a spinning topple. No space between fire and beast. A blur of smoking flesh plummeted toward the earth.

Now Owl really screamed, but Iseult was ready this time. "He's all right." She grabbed Owl's face. Forced the girl to look at her. Iseult knew from experience with sea foxes that creatures like Blueberry were almost impossible to kill.

"Owl!" she pleaded. "We need your magic! You have to control this metal. Make the pulley stop—can you do that?"

Owl did nothing of the sort. She was crying now, a weak whimper while her Threads shriveled inward like they had the night before.

"Feel my hand," Iseult ordered, squeezing Owl's fingers. "Do you feel that? Feel the skin, feel how hot it is and how strong the muscles underneath."

Nothing. No response, no reaction, no awareness.

"And do you feel your own hand, Owl? Do you feel the way the skin and bone crush together the tighter I hold on?"

Still, Owl's Threads shrank. Breaking, breaking, breaking.

It was then that another trebuchet snapped, close enough to hear the wood punching. Close enough to hear the fire's thunderous ignition take flight.

Iseult dared not look. "The sky!" She had to howl now, to

301

be heard over the winds and flames and wood. "Do you see how blue it is? Look up, Owl, *look up!*"

To her shock, Owl looked up. So Iseult looked up too.

And at that moment, Blueberry streaked across the blue. Smoke chased behind, his tail ablaze. But he lived. *He lived.*

Color plowed through Owl's Threads. Brilliant as the mountain bat's, but with a thousand shades twirling and chasing. Too fast to read—too fast to *matter*.

"*The chain!*" Iseult screamed, seizing the moment. "Owl, please—*stop the chain!*"

The chain stopped. The pulley froze. The ferry lurched, a snapping lunge that sent Leopold sprawling toward the rail.

"Reverse it!" Iseult screamed. "Reverse it, Owl! *Reverse it, reverse it!*"

The ferry reversed.

"Faster!" Leopold now shouted, crawling back to the pulley. "*Faster, faster, faster—*"

They were not fast enough. The flames shattered against the ferry, blinding and deafening. Heat to boil the flesh off bones. The last thing Iseult saw before her world blazed to ash was Blueberry's fierce, silver Threads diving their way.

Then everything vanished beneath the pyre.

THIRTY-FOUR

✳

There is an army headed your way.

                                                    I know.

What do you intend to do?

                                        Stay alive. What else?

*Then I should inform you that I have moved ten
thousand soldiers to my borders, and I intend to
move five thousand more, once they are mobilized.
They will have a full Firewitched arsenal at their
disposal, and we are building blockades at every
road and bridge into Marstok.*

  *Raiders will not enter my empire. However, the
officers are under strict orders to allow refugees through.*

                              Why are you telling me this?

                            Why are you helping my refugees?

Because if Nubrevna falls, then Marstok will be next.

The Battle Room shook with the voices of the High Council.
Urgent, panicked, uncoordinated, and uncooperative. And
also, all male. The women who had visited for Merik's funeral
had not remained in Lovats after—for until Vivia wore

303

the crown, there was nothing to compel them to. Their fathers and brothers did not give up power so easily.

Which explained, of course, why Serafin Nihar was also not in the room.

Five of the twelve vizers wanted to face the Raider King and his armies head-on. Some variation of "We outnumber them!" hit Vivia's ears every few seconds.

Three vizers wanted to fortify the northern estates and holdings—because, of course, said northern estates and holdings belonged to their families. And three vizers wanted to attempt treating with the Raider King directly. "Surely something can be negotiated," several kept murmuring to themselves, as if by saying these words they would somehow become true.

The Raider King treated with no one, though. Vivia had tried; Vaness had tried; others had tried before them. No messengers ever returned.

Of course, for each strategic faction in the Battle Room, no one within the groups could agree on specific tactics or technique. Some wanted more soldiers, others fewer. Some wanted to attack from land, others by river.

The only point upon which all could agree was that death marched this way.

And that Nubrevna was not ready.

Vivia's own plan had earned support from only one person: Stix's father, Vizer Sotar. He approved her approach of sending a portion of the troops north, to escort refugees to safety and slow the Raider King's advance, while maintaining the bulk of the Nubrevnan forces in and around Lovats.

"What does the King say?" Vizer Quihar demanded. His

304

words boomed out, loud enough to fill the room, loud enough to shatter arguments midsentence.

Silence abruptly ruled the space. All eyes cut to Vivia.

And with those stares—with that blighted question, *What does the King say?*—Vivia felt her shoulders rise straight to her ears. Her *father* was no longer King, she wanted to point out. Nor was he Admiral.

And her *father*, she wanted to then add, had refused to attend this High Council meeting. She had gone to his room earlier that afternoon, to pay her respects—not to grovel, as she knew he expected her to do, but simply to reiterate that his wisdom was welcome. In falsely light tones, he had insisted he harbored no anger. "You are Queen-in-Waiting," he'd said. "I only act for your sake. *I* know you are strong, but the Council does not."

Then he had claimed he was too tired to join the meeting, and Vivia had recognized it all for the lie it was. *Withholding, withholding, withholding.* That was her father's favorite means of punishment, be it information he knew she wanted or his own presence when it was required. He knew exactly what Vivia needed most, and then he refused to let her have it.

And the truth of the matter was that she *did* need him here. The High Council still respected him, still trusted him. His word carried weight.

There was nothing she could do about it now, though. No more time to be wasted on begging, on waiting. If he would not help her because he was angry, then Vivia would simply have to help herself.

"My father," Vivia clipped out at last, all eyes still pinned on her, "is currently busy. As your Queen-in-Waiting and Admiral, the final decision falls to me. Not my father."

As soon as Vivia uttered those words, she regretted them. Vizer Quihar's nostrils fluttered and Vizer Eltar's eyes bulged. The room erupted once more: "You are not ruler until you wear the crown!", "Your father has fought in more battles than you have years!", "He protected this city under siege!", and "The people of Nubrevna trust their King more than some untested Queen!"

Each passive—and sometimes direct—insult Vivia bore with nothing more than a slight twitch to her eyelids and a tight smile upon her lips. Hye, her teeth were grinding, her fingers rubbing at her thighs, but none of the High Council seemed to notice. Or care.

Until Vizer Quintay piped up with, "The King will speak to the Raider King! He negotiated the Twenty Year Truce. He will negotiate something again!"

And it was the final grain of sand to flood the sea. Like her father claiming he had fought with a knife in his thigh, this was too far.

"No." Vivia's voice cracked through the room, and with that single word—with that single truth—came six jets of water. One from each cup clutched by vizers fool enough to drink near a Tidewitch.

It was just a display of magic to silence them. Nothing more. Six streams of water to shoot up toward the vaulted ceilings, circle once, and plummet back into their cups. But the room quieted once more—and this time, it was on Vivia's terms.

"How quickly you all have forgotten," she said softly,

dangerously. "It was my mother's name on that document, not my father's. For it was my mother who traveled to the original Truce Summit and signed it."

One by one, she dragged her gaze over each face in the room. Some vizers looked away. Some held her eyes, defiant. Most, though, stared back and simply listened.

"I have heard your opinions," she continued, "and I will take each one into account as I solidify our course of action. I *swear* this to you. Yet every moment we waste arguing here is a moment the Raider King gains to his advantage. Inaction will only dig our graves deeper. We must move now, we must move quickly."

She motioned to Vizer Sotar at her right, and his broad shoulders stretched broader. "Sotar here has agreed to spare his family's personal guard to help protect the northern provinces. If any of you are also willing to spare your guards, I promise that they will be put to good use."

No one raised their hand, but Vivia hadn't expected them to. They would come to her after, once they had conferred with their families and evaluated what they prioritized most: personal safety or protection of the nation. Some would choose the former, some the latter—and Vivia could guess which vizers would choose which. She would not force them either way, for there were only two outcomes when soldiers were pressed into service: desertion or death. Vivia would not risk either.

She leaned onto the table and motioned to a map of the northern lands. Small markers had been laid out according to the detailed information Vivia now had from the watchtowers.

"He has Red Sails on foot." She pointed to red tiles. "Baedyeds on horseback." These were yellow. "And then a hundred other fringe groups, tribes, and witches that have banded together. They all have something to prove to the empires."

"And they all want us dead," Sotar murmured. It was as if a great sigh settled across the space at those words. Shoulders sank, foreheads pinched, and attention latched onto the map. Bit by bit, Vivia elaborated on her plan. She indicated where specific units would mobilize, where the Firewitched weapons she had stolen would be sent, and which roads would be used for supply chains.

Any questions raised during her explanation were civil, and all protests or counter-plans were offered in polite, if urgent, tones. The frantic mayhem from before was now a low-lying tension that trembled in the air. Threads unseen, but there all the same.

At the fourteenth chimes, the High Council finally dispersed. Purpose now marked each vizer's movements as they left—Vivia just hoped it was to aid her in her strategy. She suspected that at least three of them still clung to arguments and plans of their own, but there was no time for her to fret over them. No time for her to even think.

"Vizer Sotar," she called. He paused at the table's end, and Vivia approached, smoothing at her coat front. "Have you—" Her voice cracked. She tried again. "Have you seen Stacia recently?"

His lips twisted down. "No. Should I have?"

And at those words, at that expression, Vivia's stomach turned to stone. Her mask fell away, her breath hissed out.

She had to rest a hand on the table; her shoulder suddenly ached.

"I haven't seen her," she said, her voice so distant. "She didn't come to our morning briefing today, she hasn't been at her apartment in ... I don't know how long, and she hasn't been at the Sentries or barracks or *anywhere*. I've searched and searched. All I know is that she took our skiff, sailed out of Lovats yesterday, and no one has seen her since."

Now Sotar leaned against the table. "A whole day. And you did not think to tell me sooner?"

"I'm so sorry." Vivia shook her head. "The raiders." She waved numbly at the table, but it was a poor excuse. She *should* have told him sooner. She should have reached out to him the instant Stix didn't turn up. "I know you promised your guard," she offered, "but I understand if you need them to find Stix—"

Sotar cut her off with a hand. "No matter what, my guards remain yours. The realm comes first, above all else." He offered a stiff bow, fist over heart. "I will send word to the Sotar estate. Maybe Stacia traveled there to see her mother. When I hear from my wife, I'll let you know."

For several long moments, Vivia simply watched him go. She watched the door creak open and bang shut. She watched the dust motes swirl and sway.

One shallow breath became two. Then a third and a fourth, bludgeoning faster by the second. And for once, she just let herself sink into the madness of standing still.

Because what a stupid, *stupid* little fox she had been. She should never have gone to Marstok. She should have told Vizer Sotar the instant Stix vanished. She shouldn't have lost her temper at her father, but instead found a way to ease him out of the Admiralty.

Should, should, should. Nothing Vivia did was ever right. Nothing she did was ever enough. And in the end, there was nothing to be done for it—*nothing* she could do to fix these messes of her own creation.

There was also no one to pick her up and dust off her knees. Jana was dead. Merik was gone. Her father had shut her out again. And Stix . . .

Stix was missing.

Which left Vivia all alone with the whole of Nubrevna depending on her. A little fox would never—*could* never—be enough. Her people needed a bear, so a bear she would have to be.

Vivia cracked her neck. Adjusted her collar. And then rubbed at the edges of her face, banishing away the madness. Banishing away the little fox too, into a den where no one would ever see.

No time for regrets. She just had to keep moving.

THIRTY-FIVE

❋

Safi did not care that Vaness was busy.

She did not care that a meeting unfolded in the Empress's private office. She didn't care if it was important and key to public safety. If the Adders would not take Safi to Vaness right away, then someone was going to lose an ear.

So the Adders obeyed.

Not once did Safi consider if this was what she should do—just as she would not *consider* roping herself to the mast during a hurricane. The Hell-Bards were going to die; she had to interfere before it could happen.

"Do not kill the Hell-Bards," she blurted as soon as she was in the room. "They saved your life yesterday. *Please* don't kill them."

Seventeen sets of eyes arced toward her—eight Sultanate members, eight imperial officers, and the Empress of Marstok. Though bandaged and bruised, Vaness stood at the head of the table with iron in her gaze.

"Truthwitch," she said, her voice edged with censure. "Now is not the time."

"Don't let General Fashayit kill them." Safi tried to cross the room, but two Adders peeled off the wall and intercepted her. So she stopped and simply begged, "Please, Your Majesty. Was torture not enough? Why do they have to die?"

Vaness sucked in a long, calculating breath—as did the entire room, all attention locked on the Empress. Until at last, without breaking her gaze from Safi, Vaness waved to the nearest Adder. "Bring me the Firewitch general. *Now*. And Rokesh as well."

The Adder bowed. The Adder departed.

"And the rest of you"—she scanned the Sultanate and officers—"leave."

No one dared disobey, although some glared at Safi as they exited. Others pretended she did not exist. Most simply frowned, confused perhaps that Safi held such sway.

"Adders too," Vaness commanded once the room had cleared. And as one, eleven Adders departed on silent feet.

Then the wooden door clicked shut, and all that remained of Vaness's iron melted. Her shoulders wilted. She staggered to the nearest stool. "I did not command torture." She wagged her head, urgency in her words—and absolute honesty. "Why would the general do such a thing?"

Safi didn't respond. Her voice was hooked low in her belly, anchored by surprise. Before her eyes, Vaness had transformed. She looked ten years younger—twenty years, even. As if Safi now faced the seven-year-old girl who had been thrust into power after her parents' death.

This was not the jagged grief Vaness had worn in the Contested Lands. This was something new. Something worse.

Safi hurried close, no concern over titles as she said,

"What's wrong?" And no concern over rules as she laid a hand on Vaness's shoulder.

Vaness did not pull away.

"I am tired," the Empress murmured. "I am tired and I am . . ." She hesitated. Then laughed, a harsh sound that set Safi's teeth on edge. Part fearful, part amused, and part self-loathing. "I am lost."

Safi's heart said, *True.*

"I thought having you here would fix everything," Vaness went on. "I thought you would clear the corruption from my court as easily as a tide clears the shore. But the rot is too deep, and my power too tenuous. These unknown rebels almost succeeded yesterday. Despite every precaution, they almost succeeded."

"But they didn't."

"Yet." Her head tipped back. She blinked up at the ceiling. "And who would even mourn me if I were gone? The people do not care who leads."

"The people *love* you."

"They admire me," Vaness corrected. "And the difference is an important one."

Safi had no response for this. The fact that Vaness needed comfort was more than Safi's mind could wrap around. This was not the Iron Bitch she had faced in Lejna, nor the Iron Bitch with whom she'd crossed the Contested Lands. Whatever *this* was, it was more than Safi knew how to handle. It was real, it was raw, and it was messy.

Before she could summon any sort of words worth saying, a knock sounded at the door. Vaness flinched. Safi's hand fell away.

313

"Your Majesty?" an Adder called. "The Firewitch general is here."

"A moment," she called back. Then she glanced at Safi, her face still barren and unmasked. "Tell me quickly, Safi: General Fashayit. Can I trust him?"

Everything inside Safi tensed at those words. *Can I trust him?*

All her life, lying had come so naturally to her. A skill she had inherited from her uncle. A skill she had honed under Mathew's and Habim's strict tutelage. But with Threads, with Thread-family, she had never been able to lie. *Never.* And after everything she and Vaness had endured together . . .

But does your friendship with her matter more than Habim? He was her Thread-family too. And *he* could get her to Iseult. Whatever Habim had planned, it was separate from Vaness, just as Safi's decision to come here had ultimately been separate from Uncle Eron's schemes.

And whatever Habim had planned, his treatment of the Hell-Bards was separate. She couldn't dismiss everything simply because she was angry.

If Iseult were here, she'd tell Safi to think with her brain, not her heart. So with her brain at the fore, Safi said, "Yes, Your Majesty. You can trust General Fashayit. He only tortured the Hell-Bards to protect the realm." *And to protect me.*

Vaness nodded, relief briefly towing at her shoulders. Rounding in her spine. Two breaths later, though, and she had transformed once more into the Iron Empress, her mask nailed back into place, her posture turned to steel. She pointed a serrated stare at Safi. "Let the general in, then have the Adders lead you back to your quarters."

"And the Hell-Bards? What will you do to them?"

"They will be brought to the border and sent home."

True. Safi's lungs released. "Thank you, Your Majesty. Thank you."

Vaness swatted her away. "Do not thank me for what I always intended. Simply wash up and get ready for tonight."

"Of course, Your Majesty."

Adders led Safi the short way back to her quarters. For several minutes, as they strode through the hallways, she could almost pretend nothing had changed. She walked where she was led, a troop of black around her, and she was court Truthwitch. Nothing more. There were no Hell-Bards tortured inside the island, no Habim with plans to break her free, and no Empress cracking beneath the weight of her crown.

And there was no uncle arrested for treason.

When Safi reached her door, she found Rokesh waiting. His left shoulder hunched several inches higher than the other, as if wrapped in a bandage.

"Nursemaid," Safi said. "You got hurt."

A bob of his head. "It is my job." His eyes flicked briefly sideways, and Safi knew that in that moment, he remembered other Adders. Ones who had died at the Well. Ones who had died in the Contested Lands.

He opened her door for her. It swung on silent hinges, and her room beyond shimmered in the midday sun.

Safi did not go in. "How many Adders died yesterday?"

"Seven." He offered this without inflection, without emotion. And that absence was a lie, lie, *lie.*

315

Seven women and men whose faces Safi had never seen had battled the flame hawk so Vaness could live. And a hundred soldiers had died too.

"I'm sorry," Safi said. "Did you . . . did you know them well?"

His dark eyes shuttered twice. Then a faint wrinkle formed between them, as if he frowned beneath his shroud. As if he did not know what to do with her question.

Until finally he seemed to find words. "In Marstok," he said thoughtfully, "when magic such as ours manifests, we are given two choices: enter the healing schools or become an Adder. We all choose this life, and we all choose it at the same age. So yes, I knew them very well."

Safi swallowed, suddenly struck by how *big* this was. How much space Rokesh's grief must fill inside his lungs. How much weight Vaness's doubt and exhaustion must place upon her head. And Safi had no idea how to help them.

"Magic . . . such as yours?" she asked eventually. Silly words to fill the silence. "You mean Poisonwitchery?"

A soft sigh—almost a laugh. Then a gentle shake of his head. "Waterwitch healing is what I and every other Adder is born with. But the power to cure life can also be the power to take it away. There are two sides to every coin, Truthwitch. Two edges to Lady Fate's knife. Magic is no different. It is merely what you make of it."

The truth of that statement bowled into Safi. Like lightning to a tree, it hit her with such force, her whole body snapped upright. For of *course* magic was what she made of it. And *of course* there were two sides to every coin, to Lady Fate's knife.

316

The answer to the Truthstone had been in front of Safi all along, but she had been so preoccupied by *both* sides of the coin, she had never considered she could only use one.

"Thank you," she murmured absently to Rokesh, already swirling away. But she paused after two steps, a fresh bolt of inspiration rising in her chest. She glanced back. "How do you make your poison darts?"

If he was startled by the question, he didn't show it. He simply said, "When we carve them, we tell them what we want them to be."

"I see," she said—and she *did* see. Just like Threadwitches reciting words to their stones, just like healers embedding their power into the act of creation.

Without another word, Safi left Rokesh and hurried to her desk. She knocked everything off the table. All the books with their matching covers, all the stones and threads and tools that served well for *other* witches.

Then she turned and faced the telescope outside. She had been so focused on stones because they worked for other Aetherwitches that she had failed to consider other tools. She had failed to consider that she needed to *assemble* something.

That old crow had been right all along.

Safi marched into her garden, but before she hefted the telescope high, a *clack-clack-clack* sounded from the garden wall. Chills prickled down Safi's arm as she swiveled her gaze up—and met two dark eyes.

"You aren't just a bird, are you?"

Another clack that Safi suspected meant, *No, I am not.*

"Do you belong to . . . someone?" As Safi asked this question, she realized it was a stupid one. All of this was ludicrous, actually. She was talking to a thrice-damned crow and expecting him—*believing* him—to answer.

A crow that saved your life by showing you a magic doorway.

And a crow that first suggested this very telescope to you, as well as Truthstones.

Nope. Safi was not going to talk to birds or entertain the possibility that they might be sentient. So even though its clattering laugh skipped after her, she lifted the telescope, returned to her room, and slammed the garden door behind her.

Then Safi worked. Piece by piece, she disassembled the telescope. Lenses, frames, mirrors, screws. While she turned and twisted and plied, she thought about Iseult. She thought about Habim, and she thought about the Hell-Bards, tortured and poisoned below. She thought about Vaness unmasked, and she thought about how *wrong* the world had become.

She put all her thought, all her energy, all her being into that one sensation, that one piece of her magic's power. *False, false, false. Lies, lies, lies.* She sank into the way untruths made her skin crawl and her ribs rumble. The way they pinched her spine and squished her organs. She thought of Cleaved. She thought of Red Sails. She thought of every rotten, wicked person she had ever met.

Three times, she heard the chimes clang. No one disturbed her, so onward Safi worked, following the intuition that had always guided her. And now that she followed the right path, it was as if her magic wanted this—it craved freedom as much as Safi did. It rushed out of her, filling glass and brass and screw.

Until, hours later, Safi finished.

It lay gleaming in the gauzy sunlight: a tiny spyglass assembled from the telescope's eyepiece, several interior lenses, and bits of thread and quartz.

A Truth-lens.

Then Safi staggered to her bed, her mind and body a husk, and she slept.

THIRTY-SIX

✳

The lines of the Cleaved did not lead Merik back to Esme's tower. Instead, they looped him west, up a hill clotted with forest. If there had ever been buildings here, no signs remained now.

It was sunset by the time Merik finally crested the hill, legs aching and spine stiff from too much walking. Running, too, when his body could handle it. There'd been no time to waste, so he had not waited to watch the Northman go. He'd simply pointed again, repeating the words *Go north. People help you.*

Then Merik had grabbed his wet shirt and run until his legs had given out. It had not taken long. Merik was a broken man. The Puppeteer had seen to that. Yet even if his muscles and bones might fail him, his mind was as sharp as it had ever been. Discovering the Northman had energized him. A storm of questions and implications, with one lightning bolt shining brighter than the rest.

If that man had returned from cleaving, if he had broken free of Esme's control—even if he didn't know how—maybe Merik could heal too. And if Merik could heal, then so could Kullen. So could all of these people.

That thought sustained Merik throughout the journey back to Poznin. He ran when he could, shambled when he could not, and he veered wide when he saw the gap in the Cleaved that marked the deadly singing pool.

As Merik passed the final sentry in Esme's new path up the hill, the forest suddenly opened wide. Ruby light streamed down upon a long, rounded pond, the waters still and dark. Six oaks with barren trunks and branches reached toward the sky, like corpses breaking from their graves. Though clearly long dead, they had somehow never blown over in a storm.

Not somehow, Merik realized, the longer he stared. There were no man-made structures here. No flagstones to line the edges, no monuments to worship the magic. There was only thick grass, thicker forest, and the creatures of the night whispering from the shadows.

With that thought, a memory surfaced—a skipping song Aunt Evrane had once taught him as a child.

> *Oak and grass to honor the winds,*
> *Limestone and cypress for water,*
> *Beech and granite, gifts from the earth,*
> *Cedar and sandstone for fire.*
> *Birch trees and snowfall, the birthplace of Aether,*
> *In shadowy foxfire, Void waits,*
> *While deep in the heart, where no sunlight reaches,*
> *The Giant called Sleeper awakes.*

Oak. Grass. *This* was the Origin Well of Arithuania. This was the Well bound to air magic—the Well that was the source of Merik's own power.

And it was dead. Just like the Water Well he had grown up beside, this Well's waters had stopped flowing; its six trees had dried to husks.

"There you are." Esme's voice wriggled out from the trees, and moments later, the woman herself appeared. A small path wound into the forest behind her. She wore a rich ermine cape, its hood trimmed with white velvet that glistened beneath the sun as she skipped his way.

Always skipping, Merik thought, muscles locking at her approach. *Always delighted by her latest games.* Sure enough, when she slowed to a stop ten paces away and drew back her hood, she was smiling widely.

"Welcome to my Loom." She opened her arms. "This is how I control everything. Is it not beautiful?"

Merik hesitated, swallowing on a throat that had suddenly stopped working. He saw no loom. He saw nothing, save the Well, and though it was indeed beautiful, he feared admitting he saw only grass and water and moonlight.

But then she laughed. "Of course you cannot see it, Prince. Only a Threadwitch may. Or . . ." She cocked her head coyly to one side. "A *Weaverwitch*. Now, give me the gemstones." She held out a pale hand.

Merik obeyed, fumbling the satchel from where he'd knotted it to his belt. The stones ground against one another. They had left a bruise against his hip from all the running.

"So many?" Esme said, eyes widening with hunger.

"*Onga*. There were many at the shrine." He offered her the satchel, head bowed, and with a cry of delight, she loosened the drawstring.

Her cry quickly became a snarl. "You got the *wrong ones*."

322

Eyes blazing, she advanced on him. "I told you to get the stones with thread or yarn around them, Prince, but most of these do not have thread or yarn. You disobeyed me."

"*No*," Merik breathed, hands lifting. "No, please, it was an accident. I swear it."

Esme did not care. Her free hand was already rising, already reaching toward the water. She plucked at the air like a harp.

Pain exploded inside Merik. First his skull, white and blinding. Then it lanced down his neck, into his chest, constricting his lungs and filling his organs with hot oil. He collapsed to the grass.

He screamed. He begged. He wept, but still the pain seared and slashed and boiled until all he could do was cling to consciousness.

When at last the attack reared back—a slow withdrawal that somehow hurt more than the full onslaught—Merik could do nothing but convulse against the earth. The pain was so much worse than he remembered. A day without it, and he had forgotten the full extent of what Esme could do.

Though only with her Loom, he thought vaguely, and in the back of his mind, he wondered if she had to physically be beside it to use it.

A thump sounded near Merik's head, and, neck trembling—*everything* trembling—he squeezed open his eyes to see what lay beside him. It was the satchel of stones.

"Sort through them," Esme ordered. She had not moved from her place beside the Well, and her arm was still extended, fingers ready to play again at an invisible Loom.

Which suggested she did indeed need to be near the Loom

to use it. *That* was good to know, and likely explained why Merik had not heard from her most of the day: she had been elsewhere.

"This time, Prince," she said, "do it properly. I only want stones wrapped in thread or yarn. Do you understand?"

He nodded jerkily. His throat didn't work, and his muscles scarcely cooperated as he tried to push himself up and grab for the satchel. His fingers twitched. His eyes blinked and blinked. Once he had the stones, it took him several tries to remove his coat. His shirt sleeve was still damp, and the evening's breeze was a welcome chill against the fire alight within his veins.

He spread the coat on the grass, and then dumped the stones atop it. And Esme's hand finally lowered from the Well. From her Loom.

For a time, she watched Merik separate the stones into two piles. It was slow work; he could scarcely see, even with the sunset streaming down. Thick tangles of cloud passed every few minutes, stealing the light, and often the strips of thread or yarn were so thin, they were almost undetectable.

He hated having Esme watch. At any moment, he might put a stone in the wrong pile and then she would punish him. So, though it made his throat ache and lips tear, he forced himself to croak, "Why do you need these stones? We did not . . ." He wet his lips. "We did not finish our lesson."

At the sight of her sudden grin, his spine melted with relief.

"I *knew* I could teach you!" she cried. "Oh, you are fun, aren't you?" Sweeping her skirts to one side, she sank gracefully to the grass and tucked her knees beneath her. "To answer your question, Prince, my Loom needs power, and to get that power,

I need an outside source. Magic is not infinite, you know—or *did* you know that? I can see from your Threads that you are already confused. So dull and dim your brain must be."

Esme motioned to the waters, rippling beneath a breeze. "It started with this Well. It was not completely dead when I found it six years ago. *Mostly*, but not completely. There was still enough life in it for me to cleave."

Merik's fingers froze over a red stone. Surely he had misheard.

"The death of a Well, and the birth of an army." She sighed, a sound filled with fondness and longing. "An exciting time for me. All experimental, but I succeeded—as you can see." She smiled at that.

And Merik hastily resumed his sorting. He had not misheard her; she *had* cleaved an Origin Well. Though how such a thing was possible, he could not even begin to comprehend.

As if following his thoughts, Esme said, "It requires great power, Prince. An *immense* amount of Threads to craft a Loom, and I almost killed myself doing it. Things today are not as they were in the time of Eridysi. Such power was easily accessed by the Paladins. Now . . ." She trailed off, gazing down at the grass. "Now, magic is different, so to claim enough power, I have to . . . *think beyond*." Her gaze snapped up, shooting to Merik.

He did not dare meet her wild eyes. He grabbed more stones, inspected, and discarded.

He felt her focus drilling into him, though, as she went on. "When I found this Well, I knew it could provide what I needed. I did not know the full extent of my powers then, only that I could not make Threadstones and that my *tribe*"—she spat that word—"had no need for a Threadwitch who couldn't craft them.

"It makes you wonder," she said, voice suddenly distant, "how many Threadwitches were cast out because they were like me? How many faced ruin and hate, when the truth was that they were not Threadwitches at all?"

Merik didn't answer her question, for he knew she expected none. She was, however, expecting *something*. He could feel the anticipation fretting off her.

"You . . . have no tribe?" he asked, hoping more questions would appease her.

His risk succeeded. Finally, her attention fell away from Merik, and, grazing her fingers across the grass, she stared once more at the pool. "I am amalej now. No tribe, no family, no home. And not by choice, but by force. They sent me away because I was not what they wanted me to be."

For half a heartbeat, pity unfurled in Merik's heart. To be cast out from home and family because one did not fit . . . He had felt that way his whole childhood, relegated to the Nihar lands while Vivia grew up in the royal palace.

The truth, though—the truth that he hadn't seen until it was too late—was that his family had been there all along. Evrane, Kullen, the people of Nihar, and even Vivia herself. He had just been too holy in his conceit to ever see them.

Merik's eyes slid sideways, cautious not to draw Esme's attention as he watched her. To be truly exiled, cut off from people and love—it was a fate he wished upon no one. And perhaps a person still lived inside all that hate, some of the girl she had once been.

With the glittering pool and stark sunset glowing upon

Esme's regal posture, fine cloak, and lucent skin, Merik was struck by how still the evening had become. How other-worldly, as if he floated not in nightmares, but in dreams.

"They were the first to go," Esme said, snapping Merik's mind back to the clearing, back to the lesson. She smiled serenely at him. "Every last one of my tribe. Every person who had ever turned me away, I destroyed." Without looking away from him, she reached her hand to the Well. A flick, a pull, a strum, and a rustling overtook the forest.

One by one, Cleaved stepped from the trees. Onto the grass, onto the paths, hundreds of Cleaved—and hundreds more trailing behind.

"It was worth near-death to claim them, Prince. Nothing tastes better than justice. And now I can tug at their Threads whenever I want"—she plucked at the air—"and then I can watch them dance."

No, Merik wanted to say. *Please don't make them do it.* But it was already too late: the Cleaved had started their dancing. Some clapped, some spun, some bounced and swayed, and two even went so far as to move their feet in a shambling, grotesque imitation of the Nubrevnan four-step. It was as if each Cleaved did whatever they thought was dancing.

And on and on they went, while Esme beamed and giggled and clapped a rhythm for them to move by.

Merik thought he might hurl. He had no trace of pity for her now.

"How . . . how do you do it?" he forced out, even as bile thickened in his throat. All he knew was that he had to stop this somehow, and maybe questions were the way to do it.

They weren't. She just ignored him, giggling all the louder

and clapping all the faster. Faster, faster, even as Cleaved began to topple into one another or trip over their own half-dead feet.

So Merik tried a new tack. A trick he'd learned from Vivia, so adept at handling their father. "How do you control so many, Esme? You must be very skilled."

Her hands paused. The Cleaved paused, some with legs kicked high, and others half fallen against tree trunks. Lazily, she withdrew her hand from the Loom. "I *am* the most skilled."

The Cleaved abruptly fell into stiff-backed formation. They did not retreat into the forest, though, but remained where they were with a thousand sightless eyes to gaze upon Merik.

"It is the power of the Loom, Prince. But even its gifts are finite. Which is why you must help me. Why you must *choose the proper Threadstones*." She bared her teeth. Then, in a sudden burst of speed, she folded onto all fours and crawled toward him.

Now, she did not look like a dream. *Now*, she looked like death on the prowl. Like hell-waters and Hagfishes come to claim his soul.

When she reached his coat, she scooped up a handful of gemstones bound in thread. "*These* will give me the power I need to make my next Loom, Prince. Threadwitches have bound their powers to these, and I suck them dry, like marrow from a bone. I grow stronger with each one.

"So now, when King Ragnor claims the Monastery, *I* will be ready to claim the Aether Well. And with that power, why . . ." She laughed, a bubbling, girlish sound. "Why, we will use Eridysi's doors to take all of the Witchlands. One by one, the empires will fall, and one by one, the Wells will become mine."

328

THIRTY-SEVEN

✳

B *urn them. Burn them all.*

In her dreams, Iseult stood on a battlefield thick with smoke. Massive rocks blackened the edges of her vision, and fire burned across the earth. Unstoppable. This was the Contested Lands of her memory, the Contested Lands where she had killed the Firewitch, severing his Threads and cleaving him through and through.

Burned hair and smoking flesh. Autumn pyres and mercy screams.

Ten paces ahead, the Firewitch leered at her, a skeleton made of flames. His skull grinned. Laughed. *Clack, clack, clack* went his teeth.

He dangled too, arms outstretched at his sides like a puppet awaiting Iseult's command. Shadows slaked down his frame, dark webs within the orange flames.

Unnatural flames, summoned by magic. Dominated by will.

But it was not the Firewitch who had summoned the flames this time, nor was it the Firewitch who controlled them. Iseult knew it was her own power, her own will—for she and the Firewitch were one now.

They had always been one. Set on a path toward each other. Unstoppable.

Three black lines squiggled off him. *Sever, sever, twist and sever.* They writhed across the thick, smoking air before reaching Iseult and winding around her heart. Knotted, clotted. Corrupt.

Threads that break. Threads that die.

"No," Iseult tried to say, but all that left her mouth was pluming darkness.

She stumbled back two steps.

And the dead man stumbled forward, a perfect mimicry of her movement. He cackled all the way. *Clack, clack, clack.*

"You killed me!" he cried. "And you will kill me again. Over and over, for we are bound. I am yours and you are mine."

Iseult's throat constricted. Her lungs sucked in only heat. This time, though, she managed to stammer, "I-I have to kill you. To save Aeduan. I *have* to."

"He has left you, though. And he will leave you again. Over and over, Iseult. The world will burn around you, but he will never come."

The Firewitch laughed again, a high-pitched keen like air whistling from logs trapped in a fire. Then, just like the wood, he *popped.* His Threads snapped taut, and his body snapped tall. His arms cracked backward, elbows and knees inverting. Then his mouth opened, and fire boomed out. It enveloped everything. All sight, all senses.

BURN THEM! he screamed, a silent promise that conquered every space in Iseult's mind. *BURN THEM ALL!*

The fire reached Iseult. Heat, light, and pain that shredded.

This was the end. This was her death. The Firewitch she had cleaved now cleaved her in return. She screamed too.

Except death never came. The seconds slid past, the pain slowly misted away. So, *so* slowly, much *too* slowly—yet cresting back all the same. And the fire dissolved too, white holes speckling across her vision, as if this world were made of paper and a new world were punching through. Until at last, there was nothing left. Nothing save Iseult and white flecks drifting around her.

Ash, she thought at first. *This is the end and ash is all that remains.* But then she realized it was cold to the touch. It gathered on her shoulders, holding perfect crystalline shapes.

Snow.

The nightmare was over.

Except now Iseult had no idea where she was—and now, someone new approached, appearing from the very fabric of the Dreaming. Tall, looming, with broad shoulders and hands that hung stiffly at his sides. The only part of him that looked tangible, that had shape and texture, was a silver crown upon his head.

It glittered like frostbite. He was a silver king in a world of falling snow.

Cold. Iseult hadn't realized until this moment that she was freezing. That her teeth chattered, her body shook. It was not like the fire, though—this did not hurt, this did not slay. It simply *was*.

She was tired too, and suddenly, she wanted nothing more than to curl into the frozen calm and sleep. But she forced her eyes to stay wide and her mouth to form words. "Who are you?"

No sound left her throat. No steam, either, to coat her breath. Only the snow and the cold and the king, now offering a brusque bow. He lifted his hands, black shadows trailing behind—and giving him the look of a huge black bird.

Go, his wings seemed to motion. *Wake up.*

So Iseult did, watching as the final dregs of the Dreaming dripped away. As his wings shrank inward, revealing a woman with silver hair and warm, worried Threads hunched above.

Awake. Iseult was awake, but still shaking, still freezing. She didn't know where she was. Lamps glowed so bright, they dazzled her eyes and turned the world to a mute, uniform amber. Even the glowing woman before her shone like a rising sun.

After a ragged breath and three shuttering blinks, it hit Iseult: she knew this woman. She knew the lined face above her and the silver hair.

Monk Evrane. She rubbed salves onto Iseult's arms in gentle circles. A distant touch Iseult scarcely felt. She had numbed Iseult's skin with . . . something, and Iseult's vision sharpened the longer she watched Evrane. Circling, circling, always circling.

"You are awake," Evrane murmured in Nubrevnan, words compassionate. Threads compassionate, even as her focus remained on her work. "Noden has blessed me, indeed. I never thought I would see the Cahr Awen here, in their sacred home."

Iseult's eyes stung at the sound of the monk's voice. Her throat felt stuffed full of cotton. *Evrane is alive. I didn't kill her in Lejna.* Aeduan had told Iseult this, but she supposed she hadn't fully believed him until right now.

"H-how?" Iseult croaked. She tried to sit up, but Evrane easily stopped her. A single firm hand to her shoulder, and all

Iseult could do was topple back. Her head sank against rosemary-scented velvet, and another realization swept through her: *I am alive too.*

"You are at the Monastery," Evrane explained. "In the main fortress. We were able to reach the wreckage of the sky-ferry before the others."

"Others?"

A sweep of cobalt hit Evrane's Threads. Regret. "I fear the Monastery has split into two factions. Those who support the Abbot, and the insurgents, who do not. *I*," Evrane added, "support the Abbot." Her ministrations paused. She cocked her head. "Can you hear them? They lay siege even now. Ever since we brought you in."

Iseult felt a frown hit her brow as she listened. Yes, yes— there was a distant roar, like voices shouting. Then every few moments, a boom would shudder out. More ripple in the bed than audible sound.

"Ceaseless catapults," Evrane said. "Though they have run out of pitch and use only stone now."

"Wh-why?"

A sigh. More sadness and regret in Evrane's Threads. "Because they have lost their way and forgotten their vows to the Cahr Awen. It is a wonder you did not die, Iseult. I suppose, though, that Noden protects those He needs most." Her dark eyes briefly met Iseult's, a smile flitting across her lips. Then her gaze slid to a corner beyond Iseult. "The prince came out almost unharmed. He says you protected him in the crash."

For the first time since awakening, Iseult sensed the second set of Threads inside the room. Pale with sleep, they hovered in the shadows. This time, when she tried to rise, Evrane allowed it—though not without a gentle hand to assist and an insistent, "Careful, careful."

The full room materialized around Iseult. Heavy, rich fabrics in hunter green and navy draped her four-poster bed. Curtains hung floor to ceiling beside an ornate wardrobe with a ram's head mounted to the wood above and a gold-framed mirror beside. Gold candlesticks, gold sconces, gold chandelier. Even the two braziers warming the space were painted gold.

The man in the corner, though, captured Iseult's attention. Prince Leopold slouched in a satin armchair. A sling cradled his left arm and bandages covered his hands as well as one side of his face. His Threads, faded with sleep, curled languidly above.

"He would not leave your side," Evrane said testily. "Though he did at least allow me to heal him."

"Oh?" Iseult murmured, though the truth was she scarcely listened. Her eyes racked every inch of the room, every stone and shadow. But there was no third set of Threads.

There was no Earthwitch hiding.

"Where is Owl?" Iseult turned stiffly to Evrane. "What happened to her?"

Evrane shook her head, Threads blanching with confusion.

"Owl," Iseult repeated, louder now. "She was a child. A girl. A *special* girl."

"There was no one else in the crash—"

"But th-there was. There had to be!" Iseult's words came faster, her stammer closing in.

They had lost Owl. *How* could they have lost Owl? *Moon Mother, no.*

"She was with us on the ferry, Monk Evrane. Sh-she must be somewhere!"

334

"Calm yourself." Evrane laid a hand on Iseult's shoulder.

"Was there no body?" Iseult's voice slung louder, higher. Leopold stirred in his armchair.

And Evrane's Threads darkened to mossy concern. "Iseult," she murmured, "you must calm down. You cannot heal if you are hysterical."

Iseult wasn't hysterical, though. She had lost Owl. A child she had never liked, but whom she had finally started to understand—she was out there somewhere. Possibly trapped in a war between monks . . .

If she was even alive at all.

But Iseult's voice was now dammed behind her tongue and waves of sleep were rippling down her spine. She knew this magic. It was Evrane's, meant to tow her under where she could better heal.

She didn't want to be towed under. Not yet. Not when Owl needed her. But the monk's magic was stronger than Iseult's desperation, and although Iseult tried to argue, all that came out was a distant groan.

The last thing she saw before Evrane's magic pulled her under was darkness. Shadows skating over Evrane's face, and over her Threads too.

Then darkness took hold of Iseult too, and she slept.

THIRTY-EIGHT

※

*T*wo weeks after saving Boots, the boy helps his mother tend the dog's wounds. Each day, they rub salve onto the stitches in his belly, and the boy knows his terrier is happy, even if his body aches and he will never walk or play quite the same. Whenever the boy is near, Boots's tail thumps and the boy smells flickers of contentment on the hound's loyal blood.

That monster will never get you again, the boy whispers to Boots every night, scrubbing at black, fluffy ears. *I will always keep you safe.*

He is lying, though, and three weeks after saving Boots, the boy kills him.

It happens when he is scratching at Boots's ears one night. His parents sit outside the tent, talking in the low voices they always use when they think the boy is sleeping. His mother laughs softly. She often does.

Scratch, scratch. "The monster will never get you again," the boy reminds Boots, who is curled by his side upon their mat. "I will always keep you safe."

Boots's tail thumps. Scratch, scratch.

Then stops.

336

Alarmed, the boy sits up. "Boots?" Boots does not react, and the boy realizes that the power in his veins has latched onto the freedom that thrums inside Boots.

Then it sinks into the loyalty too.

And now, Boots's blood is slowing. His heart is slowing . . . and stopping.

The boy didn't meant to grab hold—he doesn't even know how he did it. He just knows that he did, and now that the talons are in, he cannot let go.

He tries! He tries, he tries, he tries. His lungs billow. He even scrabbles to the other side of the tent and starts crying.

Let go, let go, let go, he thinks, terror tangling in his chest.

Then the boy screams, "Let go! Let go! Let go!"

His parents rush into the tent. Mother panicked. Father ready to defend.

But they can't fix this, and no matter how much the boy shouts and cries, he can't make this power inside let go.

As the boy's heartbeats judder past, he feels Boots's weaken. His mother tries to calm him. She hums, she holds, while his father tries to rouse the dying dog.

Then Boots's heart stops entirely.

Yet all the while, throughout the shrieking and the begging, the scratching and the sobs, Boots stares with loving eyes at the boy. His best friend in the entire world. Right up until the last flickers of life leave him, his tongue lolls happily and loyalty sparkles bright upon his blood.

Because he does not understand that the boy has broken his promise. He doesn't understand that the boy did not keep him safe at all.

337

And he doesn't understand that the boy was the true monster all along.

The sun had fully set by the time Lizl forced Aeduan on the move again. The salves had helped. A slice of hard cheese and harder bread had helped too. But the anger stewing in Aeduan's heart helped most of all.

Cold hardened the night. Fog rose, and they ascended ever higher until they reached a river too wide and too rough to cross. They were forced to slow and follow the rapids upstream to a stone bridge. Here, a waterfall tumbled steeply down a cliff fifty paces away, stealing the night's sounds and thickening the fog to icy mist.

Aeduan's donkey was halfway over the bridge when he smelled it: hundreds of scents, sharp and burning. Exposed to the night air. Even weak as his magic was, there was no missing the slaughter.

"People," he said hoarsely. The first word in hours. "Ahead. Fighting."

Lizl glanced back, though she waited until they were off the bridge to call, "Where?"

Aeduan inhaled, grappling at whatever magic he could find. "North," he said at last. "On the other side of the falls."

"How far?"

"I don't know." And it was true—though the old Aeduan would have known immediately. The old Aeduan would have sensed how many people there were and how many open wounds too. Now, all he sensed was bloodied turmoil and death.

Lizl squinted in the direction of the waterfall, lips puckering sideways. "I don't know this area," she admitted. "I took a shortcut to save time, but a shorter journey is not worth losing a life over. We will head south at that fork up ahead."

She kicked her mare into a three-beat canter. The donkey followed, jolting Aeduan with pain. Each impact sent fresh blood sliding down his chest. Each hoofbeat snapped the leash tighter into his neck.

They reached the fork in the road. A crack sounded. *A pistol,* Aeduan realized as more tore out across the sky. Then came screams. High-pitched and closer than he expected.

His magic rustled. It nudged, it dug. A familiar scent swelled in his veins. Someone he knew had been hit; someone he knew was dying.

"Wait!" Aeduan tried to slow the donkey. "Wait," he shouted, louder. "There's a monk back there!"

At that, Lizl reined her horse to a stop. She swiveled in her saddle, eyes immediately latching onto Aeduan's ear—onto the opal he wore. But neither his nor hers glowed, meaning no monks nearby had called for aid.

"You lie," she spat, already angling forward once more. "You try to trick me so you can escape."

"No," he protested.

"Then who is it?"

That, he could not say. It was possible he had never learned the person's name—his magic cataloged so many bloods. Some it retained, some it did not.

Before Lizl could push her mare onward, though, more shots echoed out. Closer, and with them came voices and shrieks.

A woman in Purist gray burst from the trees beside the path. Clutched to her chest was a babe, wailing. She saw Aeduan and Lizl.

She stopped dead in her tracks. "Please," she begged in Marstoki. "Please don't kill me. I beg you, please. My child—"

Her words broke off. An arrow hit her in the back. It cut through her chest, piercing her heart. Then piercing the babe. Blood cascaded into Aeduan's senses.

He stumbled off the donkey, magic grasping for the woman. To stop her blood and save her before she and her child died. He was too weak, though, and too slow—and the leather leash sliced into his neck, holding him back.

Until Lizl dismounted too, and together, they raced for the woman. Aeduan dropped to her side and stared into dark eyes. But he was too late. The last flickers of life had already fallen away. Her babe was silent, his body limp.

Distantly, Aeduan wondered if his own mother had looked the same on that night all those years ago. The arrow wound, the blood—endless blood. Aeduan had not been able to save her either.

Death follows wherever you go.

His leash yanked, forcing him to rise. Lizl dove into the woods ahead of him, sword drawn, leaving him with no choice but to follow.

He was glad for it. He wanted to follow. He wanted to kill.

They passed more bodies. Another woman, two children. Each dead, each pierced by bolts with yellow fletching. Lizl did not slow; Aeduan did not slow behind her.

The sounds of fighting drew nearer. More pistols popping

and screams filling the air. Swords clanged too, and a man's voice shouted orders. They reached the forest's edge and a moonlit massacre met their eyes. It was a Purist encampment, walls high but gate opened wide. Bodies covered the rocky earth in rows, as if people had fled in a great stampede only to be picked off one by one from behind.

Blood dribbled and drained. It was not merely Purists that tarnished the soil with red, but Nomatsis too. Different ages, different genders, different glassy eyes and splayed limbs. The blood, though, always looked the same.

A shout, and a lanky boy charged from the gate, no older than fourteen. On his back was a Nomatsi shield. He had no weapon. He simply ran.

As one, Lizl and Aeduan abandoned the trees to defend him. Yet like before, the boy slowed to a stop when he saw them, hands rising and mouth bobbing. No words, only terror.

Two arrows thunked into him. One through his ear, the other through his throat. Blood burbled from his mouth. His legs gave way beneath him.

Lizl gasped. Aeduan stumbled forward.

He stopped short, though, when the shooter strode from the woods. The man's white cloak, streaked with filth and red, billowed behind him. His eyes met Lizl's, then Aeduan's, and he nodded. "Keep herding them to me," he called, motioning to the encampment with his crossbow, "and I will take them out as they come."

Lizl blinked, confused, yet between one sluggish heartbeat and the next, the truth careened into Aeduan: he had misunderstood everything. The massacres he had found, the dying monk he had buried. He had interpreted it all wrong.

It had not been Purists and raiders against the Nomatsis. It had been Purists and raiders *with* Nomatsis.

Against the Carawens.

Aeduan turned to Lizl, words rising in his throat to warn her, to explain what lay before them. He did not need to, though, for a moment later, a girl sprinted from the encampment. Her gray gown tangled in her legs. She tripped over a corpse. She fell.

Beside them, the monk reloaded his bow.

Lizl lurched at the man. "*Stop!*"

He did not stop. The girl tried to get up, whimpering, but she had broken something. Her hands clawed, her cries lifted louder.

The crossbow cranked, a fresh bolt almost loaded. Lizl lunged. Aeduan's hands shot up.

He silenced the man's blood. It took every scrap of strength he had left, and the pain—it scorched through him. But it was enough. Enough for him to grab hold and still the man for one shallow breath. Then two.

Lizl reached the monk and knocked the crossbow from his grip.

Then the flames won, and Aeduan lost control.

The monk instantly tensed, twisting as if to attack—yet in a move too quick to see, Lizl unsheathed her sword. She had it fixed at his neck before he could fully spin around.

"Why did you do that?" Her voice was pinched and high. "*Why* did you kill them?"

"What do you mean?" the monk snarled. "Why did *you* stop me? We have orders!"

"From whom?"

Aeduan leaned in, straining to hear the answers. His heart thundered against his ribs. The shadows wavered, and his magic . . . He could no longer reach it, no longer sense blood—any blood. Not even the fallen bodies littering the earth around him.

"From the Monastery, of course." The monk's eyes darted between Aeduan and Lizl. "Who are you? If you were not sent to help, then why are you here? Are you part of the insurgency?"

"Help with what?" Lizl demanded. "What insurgency?" But the monk had no chance to reply before a new voice rang out, "Lower your weapon! We are on the same side."

As one, Aeduan and Lizl snapped their gazes to the encampment's gate. A monk towered behind the girl they had saved, his sword thrust through her back. He yanked it out. The girl spit blood. Then her body slumped among the others.

Aeduan knew this monk. This was the scent he had recognized—a man who had helped him in Veñaza City, when he'd hunted the Truthwitch. The monk's pale hair was longer now, and his leg freshly bloodied.

His sword was bloodier, though.

One by one, eleven monks joined the pale-haired man. Each carried a blade coated in flesh. After forming a line, they advanced on Aeduan and Lizl. Flecks of organ and excrement hit the earth as they walked. Twenty paces away, the lead monk eased to a stop, and the other eleven monks halted as well.

"Back away," the pale monk called. "We fight for the same side."

Lizl did not lower her sword. "You killed innocents."

343

"We killed vermin."

"They were mothers." Aeduan's voice shook, each word in his throat made of fire. He shouted on anyway. "*Children*."

"Who swear fealty to the Raider King." The monk on the end poked her sword at the nearest corpse, an elderly woman with silver hair and a chest punctured by arrows.

"Yes," the leader agreed. "And these people breed more raiders, who swell the Raider King's ranks. We save thousands of lives by destroying just a few." At these words, the outermost monks began to move—slowly, cautiously, rounding the edges of their line like wolves circling a lamb.

Aeduan and Lizl did not move.

"He"—Lizl dug the tip of her sword into the first monk's neck—"said that you have orders from the Monastery. Who gave them?"

"The Abbot, of course." The lead monk opened his arms, as if welcoming them to a party. As if they were the last to arrive, and he indulged them by inviting them at all. "These orders come directly from Abbot Natan fon Leid himself. You would defy him?"

Still, the monks inched nearer. Still, Lizl's sword held true.

"We are not *murderers*," she said, and Aeduan found himself nodding. Found his fingers flexing and readying for a fight.

One they would lose, but one worth fighting all the same.

"Whose side are you on?" The lead monk lifted his bloodied sword at Lizl. "You are clearly monks like us. You wear the cloak and the opal and you"—he aimed his sword at Aeduan—"I know. So *stand down*. Obey your Abbot's

344

orders. Or admit you are insurgents and face the holy punishment."

Aeduan's eyes met Lizl's. Hatred burned, and he knew it well. It pulsed inside his weakened veins. It wanted justice, it wanted vengeance, and it wanted blood. He so rarely let this darkness surface. He so rarely looked it in the eye and said, *Yes, today you can come out.*

This would mark the fourth time.

He would kill them all.

"*Now!*" barked the lead monk, sword curving high, and in a concerted charge, the Carawens moved.

But Lizl moved too. In a blur of speed, she slung something at Aeduan. He caught it, looped it over his neck, and the instant the Painstone touched flesh, the night sharpened around him. Blood-scents crashed against his magic, and with them came the power to control.

Lizl charged. Aeduan charged. The fight began.

With a single, fluid strike, Lizl killed the first monk. Her sword pierced his throat. In, out. Blood splattered Aeduan as he dove for the loaded crossbow. With his muscles fueled by fresh, painless power, he was unstoppably fast. He grabbed, he aimed, he shot.

Down went a second monk. A third lunged at Lizl, a fourth at Aeduan. He sidestepped, circling behind. A kick to the knee brought the monk to her knees. Then he grabbed her head and spun. Her neck snapped. He claimed her sword.

The next five deaths smeared together. Intestines and screams and blood to crush all senses. No emotions, only death. Until Aeduan found himself facing Lizl—and she faced the remaining four.

The lead monk wore a veneer of rage at the center. His head swung side to side, over and over as he growled, "You should not have done this. You should not have done this."

Muscles fueled by magic, Aeduan vaulted at the nearest two monks. His blade sliced down, then up on a diagonal and across. Wide, circular movements that would have been too slow were he not a Bloodwitch.

But he *was* a Bloodwitch, and the two monks fell a heartbeat later, ribbons of red streaking the air where they collapsed.

Aeduan rounded toward the remaining monks—except it was only the leader now, for Lizl had hacked apart the other.

"You should not have done this," he repeated. "You should not have done this."

Aeduan thrust. The monk parried, a clash of steel. Again, again, Aeduan attacked, and each time the monk defended. A good fighter—Aeduan remembered that from Veñaza City.

But good fighters did not always make good men.

Three more swipes, three more parries, and at last Aeduan caught the monk on his wrist. A spin, a yank, and he cut the man's hand from his arm. Sword and hand hit the earth.

Aeduan reared back his blade, ready to stab the man through the heart.

Lizl beat him to it. In a graceful arc that carved through flesh and muscle and spine, she cut off the man's head.

It flew several feet through the air before thumping to the soil.

Then the man's knees crumpled beneath him, blood gushing, and his headless remains toppled over. One more body to add to the mass grave. One more death to feed the night.

THIRTY-NINE

✳

Why did you lie to me?

I did not.

You said you sent 5,000 soldiers and sailors
to your northern borders. My scouts report
over 10,000 are on the way.

I did not send those forces.

Someone did.

And I can guess who.

"Who did this?" Vivia sent her gaze around the room. Fourteen officers from the Royal Navy and Soil-Bound stared stonily back. At her command, they had gathered at a long table in a fortified room at the Sentries of Noden.

No one had spoken since she had walked in. So she asked her question again: "Who did this? Troops do not move without orders, and I want to know who gave them."

A soil-bound general at the table's opposite end was the first to speak up. "We all did," she said. "Exactly as we were instructed to do." She withdrew a crumpled letter from her forest green coat and slid it across the table.

The iris blue wax had been torn, but even ten paces away, there was no mistaking the royal seal. Vivia extended a hand, lips pressed thin while she waited for the officers to hand the letter down to her.

When at last it reached her, she tore it open. And as expected, her father's handwriting glared up at her. It was a detailed missive, listing all the specifics he had described to her.

And it was dated a week ago.

"I did not give you these orders. *I*, who still maintain the role of Admiral." She dropped the page to the table. No slamming, no gales of temper. She was the bear in the forest who did not need to roar; whose sheer size and strength cowed lesser animals. "So explain to me why any of you obeyed."

"The King Regent—" a new general began.

"Is no longer in power," Vivia finished. "He is no longer Regent, and he has not been Admiral in several months. So tell me why"—she snatched up the paper again and rattled it at them—"did none of you come to me when my father began planning? Why did *none* of you think to inform me of the messages coming from the watchtowers?" Even as she asked this, Vivia knew what the answer would be.

They had not informed her because they had not wanted to.

The armed forces of Nubrevna had followed Serafin Nihar for years. Decades, even. Through war time and truce time, through battle and siege. What was Vivia compared to that?

I am Queen.

"Fix this." Another shake of the letter. "And fix it *fast*. Call the troops back, mobilize them to defend Lovats, and pray that we are not too late."

None of the officers reacted to this command. No *Hye, sir!* or crisp salutes. No apologies or explanations for why they had so easily, so willingly changed course. In fact, every officer at the table acted as if she had not spoken at all.

In that moment, Vivia realized it was worse than she'd ever feared. She had been so focused on protecting the city—she had been so intent on doing what she felt was right, on what she *knew* the infrastructure of the Lovats plateau would demand—that she hadn't seen this coming. Now, she had a full mutiny on her hands, and her own father had lit the first match.

Share the glory, share the blame.

Her confirmation came a heartbeat later, when a second admiral, black hair streaked with gray, said, "The vizers came to us an hour ago." No expression. No inflection. "Vizers Quihar, Eltar, and Quintay. They informed us that your crown has been withdrawn and the King Regent rules once more."

"Ah." It was all Vivia could say. The only sound or breath she could muster. The world had fallen apart around her and now the Hagfishes were dragging her to Hell.

It mattered none that she had stolen an arsenal of Marstoki weapons for her troops. It mattered none that she had captained a ship of her own and earned the loyalty and love of her crew. It mattered none that she had found the under-city and filled it, and it mattered none that she had been born to her title and the underground lake had chosen *her*.

When Serafin Nihar, former King Regent and former Admiral to the Navy and Soil-Bound, had beckoned, these soldiers and three vizers had answered that call.

"So," she said quietly. "You will not call back our forces to defend Lovats?"

Three officers shook their heads. Two said, "No, Your Highness," and the remaining nine simply regarded her with bored eyes.

"All right then." She pushed away from the table. "Just know that when the city of Lovats falls to the Raider King, it will be your guilt to bear—and the Fury never forgets."

No one stopped her and no one saluted when she left the room. If her threat—a promise, really—bothered the officers, none gave any indication. But Vivia knew she had spoken the truth.

Her father might be experienced on the field, he might understand wartime tactics in a way that Vivia would willingly admit she did not. But *he did not know her city*. He did not know the people crowded into the streets. He had never walked the Skulks or served the hungry at Pin's Keep. He had never ridden the waves of the Cisterns, or explored the under-city.

He was a transplant from Nihar who had married into power. Who stole speeches and titles and glory that were not his, and the right to rule did not live inside his veins.

Yet despite all that, it had taken only a few words to three vizers and a few words to the armed forces. Between one ring of the chimes and the next, all of Vivia's power—all of her plans and careful protections—had been yanked out from beneath her.

She should have seen it coming.

She hadn't, though. Not in the least.

All these years, her father had said he only wanted what was best for her, that he only cared for her sake. And all these years, she had believed him.

When she reached her boat several minutes later, her guards tried to join her. She waved them off. Then she boarded her boat, summoned her tides, and pushed off into the Waterwitched currents that led to the southern water-bridge.

She no longer felt attached to her body. No longer attached to dry land. It was not the officers who would drown—it was her. She was *already* drowning. Already sinking beneath the waves, watching the sunlight vanish, until soon, there would be nothing left but Noden's Hagfishes and a final lungful of air.

She'd done it all wrong. She had been too much like her mother, exactly as the High Council had feared. *The queen by blood*, they had said about her mother, *but with madness in her head*. They had wanted Vivia to be like Serafin, for whom command had come as easily as breath. They had wanted bluster and confidence and a rage to bend their enemies.

Vivia supposed it only made sense that the Royal Navy and Soil-Bound officers had wanted that too. Even after she had laid out the truth of the city's infrastructure before them, even after she had spent hours forming a detailed strategy for protecting Lovats and slowing the Raider King—*even after that*, a single barked command from the King Regent had sent them all snapping into line.

At some point, Vivia did not know when, tears began to fall. Hot, angry tracks that propelled her Tidewitchery faster, faster. Wind crashed against her. She dipped around ships, she swayed around ferries, she veered, she skipped, and she rode waves of her own creation.

It wasn't fast enough, though. Never fast enough. She could not outsail this shame at her heels nor the rage that she had bungled her rule *so badly*. It was not a pretend rage either, worn to win her father's approval, nor even a berserking Nihar rage that her father's family had always been so proud of.

This was a true, heart-shattering, tide-ripping *rage*. All directed inward, at the truth now laid bare before her: she was not fit to rule. She would never be the one thing she'd fought so hard to be.

She wondered if this was how her mother had felt before she'd jumped.

There was the spot, just ahead. A strip of unassuming stone on the water-bridge where her mother had finally decided the shadows were too much. That only in death could she understand life, and that Noden's court would be an easier solution than the weight of dark life spanning before her.

For thirteen years, Vivia had never looked at this spot when she sailed past. She had always fixed her gaze on the barn swallows, dancing and happy and free.

Today, she looked. Today, she slowed her skiff and stared at the gray stone, cloud-dappled and rough, while two swallows swooped past.

All this time, Vivia had feared that if she looked at this place, that if she did not turn the other way, then she would find her own feet moving toward it. That the shadows inside her would win, and the High Council—and everyone else too—would be right: she had too much madness inside her head to ever be Queen.

As a child she had tried to blame Merik for what Jana had done. Somehow, if it was *Merik's* fault, then it could not be Vivia's. And then the same fate could not befall her. The bludgeoning in her chest would not win.

She regretted what she'd said to him, but never had she regretted it more than right now. With the breeze caressing her face, with the water lapping and kind. For she felt no urge to follow her mother off the edge. She felt only the hollow grief she had always worn, and nothing—neither Noden nor time—could take that away.

It had not been Merik's fault their mother had jumped. Nor had it been Vivia's own doing. Jana had died because she had seen no other escape, and there had been no one there who knew how to help her.

All these years, Vivia had thought that she needed to be stronger than her mother, that she needed to fight the darkness to wear the crown. But that was wrong; that was her father speaking.

Jana *had* been strong—stronger than Serafin. Stronger than anyone realized, for she had lived with shadows every day and still ruled, still guided, still loved. Rather than nurture that strength, though, Serafin had nurtured the shadows. He had undermined and manipulated, just as he undermined and manipulated Vivia now.

For hye, Vivia had shadows inside her too, but they were not like Jana's. These were all her own, as unique as the foxfire arrangements that glowed beneath the city. And twenty-three years of living with them had made Vivia stronger than anyone realized.

Stronger than Serafin realized.

353

Only two weeks ago, he had promised, *Be the queen they need and soon a true crown will follow.* But now Vivia saw he'd never meant those words. He had betrayed her. He had gone behind her back and stolen the power she had worked so hard to earn and worked so hard to use with wisdom and compassion.

Yet she did not need a crown to protect Nubrevna from the Raider King. She could be the queen they needed, with or without one. Just as she could be the queen they needed, even if madness thrummed in her veins—or perhaps *because* madness thrummed in her veins.

No more backstabbing and mind games, no more seeking approval from people who thought her unqualified or unhinged. No more tiptoeing around a room because women oughtn't to run, to shout, to rule.

And above all: no more regrets.

Vivia was ready to be Queen.

FORTY

✳

Merik awoke in the night to Esme's voice. She spoke to someone he could not see, and twice, he thought he heard *Iseult, where are you? I cannot find you. Iseult?*

But it might have been a dream. Waking and nightmare—there was no separating the two. Dancing skeletons and moonlight on a magic pool. Armies of shadow and knives through the heart. They all smeared together on a canvas.

It was the cold that eventually woke Merik. Ice had spindled into his bones while he slept, and each breath felt thin and sharp. Shivering, he opened his eyes.

"Hello, Threadbrother," crooned a familiar voice. "Happy to see me?"

Merik blinked—then blinked again, until Kullen came into sharp focus before him. He leaned against the wall, arms folded over his wide chest and a foot hooked behind his ankle. His right ear was mangled and half missing, black blood clotted at the edges. Merik felt no satisfaction at his handiwork.

Frost laced the stones around Kullen, swelling and shrinking in time to his breath. Esme was nowhere to be seen. "You don't look so good," the Fury said.

Merik didn't feel so good, but he would not give Kullen the satisfaction of hearing that. He just dragged himself into a groggy sitting position and examined the mud coating his boots, the loose spot where his breeches had come untucked.

The old Merik would have fixed that the instant he saw it. Wherever there were wrinkles, he liked to smooth them out. Now, Merik couldn't be bothered. His best friend was so near in body, but in mind, he was a thousand *thousand* leagues away.

For weeks, Merik had wondered if scar tissue would ever grow atop his heart. It was bad enough to lose his best friend to cleaving. Then, he'd had to learn his Threadbrother had also become a monster. The Fury.

Now he knew this wound would stay open and raw forever. Merik *missed* Kullen. He missed his steadiness, constant as the tide to the sea. He missed Kullen's awkward grin, and the dry, sarcastic jokes he always cracked. Above all, he missed knowing there was at least one person in the world who understood him, and one person he understood in return.

But Merik did not understand the Fury. He did not know who that creature was, how he had claimed Kullen's mind and body, or how a Threadbond had saved Merik's life during the *Jana*'s explosion. Esme's magic was beyond his ken; the Fury's magic even more so.

There was one thing Merik did know, though: if a Northman could return from cleaving, then so could he and Kullen. He *had* to cling to that hope. He *had* to believe it could be true.

Kullen laughed, a harsh, crowing sound that chased away Merik's thoughts. "I must admit, Merik, it amuses me to see you this way, after all those people you put in the irons. How many was it, do you think?" He started ticking off fingers, but quickly gave up and shrugged. "The list is too long to even remember. *Discipline*, you always called it, but tell me true: you enjoyed punishing the fools, didn't you? You liked watching them writhe."

Merik's teeth ground, but he held his tongue. Even as Kullen pushed off the wall and sauntered closer. Even as ice crackled his way and Kullen declared, "I certainly enjoy watching *you* writhe. Reduced to the same fate you once doled out. How does the old saying go? You know, the one your aunt always used to say." He twirled a hand in the air. "*Whatever you have done will come back to you tenfold, and it will haunt you until you make amends. Because the Fury never forgets, Merik.*" Kullen sank to a squat, a single pace away. "*I never forget.*"

Merik drew in a frozen breath, but still he did not lift his gaze to Kullen's.

"No words for your Threadbrother? Come now. I only want to help you, Merik. I only want to *free* you. Kings should not be in chains."

At those words, Merik finally looked up. "I am no king."

The air warmed; Kullen smiled. "You could be, though. You *should* be, in fact—and trust me when I say that I know these sorts of things." Hands braced on his knees, he pushed back to his feet. "You know, all I have to do is say the word, and the Puppeteer will let you go. Just one little word."

"Then say it."

"You must first agree to join me."

"Fine." Merik bounced a shoulder. His chains clinked. "I agree to join you. Now let me go."

A laugh split Kullen's lips. The air abruptly turned to sweltering. "Very clever, but you must know I cannot trust you so easily." He wagged a finger Merik's way. "You have not been a loyal Threadbrother, and there is too much at stake to risk another betrayal."

"Then let me prove myself." The words surprised Merik as much as they seemed to surprise Kullen. Merik didn't know where they'd come from, but the quickly gathering heat in the room suggested that they had been the right ones.

Kullen's eyes thinned with thought. "And how would you do that, Merik? How can you possibly prove to me you are a loyal friend?"

Merik's pulse quickened. His impulsive words had earned him a chance—a good one that he couldn't squander. *Move with the wind*, Master Huntsman Yoris had taught him—and taught Kullen too. *Move with the stream. Too fast, Prince, and your prey will sense you long before you reach 'em.*

And as Aunt Evrane had also trained him, *Information is better earned through conversation.*

"Perhaps," he said slowly, "if you tell me what it is you aim to do, then I can tell you how I aim to help."

Kullen said nothing, and as the seconds flicked past, the room seemed to shrink, as if every drop of air was being reeled into Kullen's lungs. And as each second ticked past with no response, Merik's lungs cinched tighter and tighter.

Until at last the Fury flipped up his hands. "Why not?" he mused aloud, and Merik's breath finally released.

"It is quite straightforward." The Fury slouched once more against the wall. "I want to enter into the mountain, but my

Heart-Thread shuts me out. The entrance is magicked, and . . . Let us just say that brute force is not working fast enough. We were able to enter the Crypts, but I fear that will not get us into the Sleeper's heart."

Into the Crypts. That was where Merik had left Ryber and Cam. They must have moved on, though. Deeper inside this mountain that Merik still did not understand.

"You have seen no sign of Ryber?" he asked, careful to keep his tone casual.

"No. She and that boy Leeri went deeper into the mountain, and now they need never return. The Crypts are not the only doorway in or out."

There it was again. A reference to doorways. First Ryber, then Esme, now Kullen. "What are these doors?"

"Power," Kullen replied simply, as if this explained everything. "Whoever controls the doors controls the Witchlands. They lead all across the continent, Merik. Enter the mountain here"—he stretched his right arm long—"and come out of the mountain here." He stretched his left arm.

"Then why can't you use those other doors?"

"Unfortunately"—Kullen's nose wrinkled, arms dropping—"I cannot remember where they are. I used to know, and I *know* that I found one in the south—Ryber told me I did, but the blighted Sightwitches stole my memory. Although . . ." He flung Merik a terrible, wide-eyed grin. Then he knocked at his skull. "They could not take all the memories. Only one. Only your Threadbrother's. The rest of us are still in here. The *Fury* is still in here, and he was present on the day of reckoning."

Merik had no idea what that meant. He had no idea what

most of it meant, but as long as he could keep Kullen talking, he could keep formulating a plan. "So then," he tried, "you *do* know where the entrances are?"

Instantly, the Fury's smile fell. A wind swooped around him, vicious and cold. He began to pace.

"I know of only one." *Step, step, step, twist.* "But that wretched Eridysi made it so the door to my people only traveled one way. I cannot use it to get in. As for the other doors, I was never allowed to use them before betrayal ruined us all. And the other survivors like me . . ." He scowled, ice lancing over the stones. "They remember even less than I do. Useless, the entire lot of them. So as you can see, that leaves only the Crypts for access. Since that is the way I remember, then *that* is the way we use."

Step, step, step, twist. Step, step, step, pause. Kullen angled toward Merik. "Now tell me: what do you propose, Threadbrother? How will you help me gain what I need?"

Merik wet his lips, so dry. His throat was dry too. Distant, cursory annoyances, though. Right now, all that mattered was moving with the wind, with the stream. Prove himself; lose the collar. *Think, think, think.*

He got no chance to think, though. Not before the Fury offered a proposal of his own. "Lure them out and kill them." He spoke this almost to himself, words so faint, Merik scarcely heard them over the still-whispering wind.

Then Kullen was striding toward him, and as he sank into a squat, he repeated: "Lure them out and kill them, Merik. Then I will trust you again as my Threadbrother."

"Them?" Merik asked, even as he knew what the answer had to be. Even as he *knew* he could not say no to this

360

request—not without losing his only gift from Noden since coming here.

"Ryber and Leeri." Kullen grinned. Death gleamed in his eyes.

"But she is your Heart-Thread."

"*Was* my Heart-Thread," he corrected. "Like you, though, she has not been very loyal."

Never, in a thousand lifetimes, could Merik kill Ryber or Cam. He would kill himself before he would ever do that. But right now, it was the only thing he could say to prove himself. He would not startle this prey. He would move exactly as the wind and stream demanded.

"All right," he said, chin rising. "As you command, Kullen. I will lure them out, and I will kill them."

FORTY-ONE

✳

Something changed between Aeduan and Lizl. When the fight ended, Lizl did not draw her sword on Aeduan, and Aeduan did not attempt to flee. They simply stood there, steam coiling off the corpses and blood soaking the soil between them.

The night was suddenly too quiet.

"You did not use your magic," Lizl said eventually, small gasps to punctuate her words. Her face was marked with blood and dirt. "In the fight, you could have held them in place, but you didn't."

"I . . . only use it if I must." Aeduan gulped in air, so thick with the scent of death. "It is not honorable. Not against our own."

"What do you care about honor?" There was no venom in her voice. Only exhaustion and genuine confusion.

Aeduan offered no reply, and she did not seem to expect one. The moments slid past, both breathing. Both processing what had happened. They had fought their own people, they had killed their own people, and it had been the right thing to do.

"Are there any survivors?" Lizl asked at last, and Aeduan nodded, a ragged thing. His magic might be weak, even with the Painstone, but he could still sense four people alive within the encampment.

"We can do nothing for them," he said roughly. "They will not see us as allies." He gestured to their cloaks. "They will try to flee or try to kill us."

"Ah," she agreed, rubbing at her eyes. It only smeared more blood across her face.

"This is not the first massacre I've seen." Aeduan described the dead tribes he had found, and the dead monk who had blamed the Purists. For the first time since the fight had ended, anger flashed across Lizl's face.

No more numb shock, no more panting recovery. Her lips snarled. "Why would Natan order this?" She turned slowly, head shaking as she took in the full battle. "They said it was to stop the Raider King, but . . . but that sounds like *shit* to me."

It sounded like shit to Aeduan too. The Monastery had never interfered in war before. "I thought it was the tier ten that had drawn the monk to the Nomatsis. But now . . ."

"Now, that doesn't make sense." Lizl bent to the headless monk, and on a patch of clean cloak, she swiped her sword. Roughly. Almost violent in her movements. "It's true that all Natan cares about is coin, but how much coin can justify this? What *coin* can pay for the lives of children? I will kill him." She glanced up, pupils shrunk to pinpricks. "I will *kill* him."

Abruptly, she straightened, barking a bitter laugh. "I guess Monk Evrane was right all along. She told me that men like Natan should never lead. That he would mark the end of everything we stood for. She wanted *me* to put in a bid for the position." Lizl hammered her chest. "Fool that I was, I didn't want to be trapped at the Monastery when there was so much world to see. So much . . . so much *glory* to be had."

"This is not your fault."

"No. It isn't. It's Natan's, and he will face our justice." With a clank of steel, she sheathed her sword and turned away. "We will go to the Monastery and tell the others what he has done."

"Others already know," Aeduan said. "And others clearly approve."

"Not everyone. He said there were insurgents. They must be fighting this."

"Then why have we not heard of it?"

"I don't know." She shook her head. "Maybe it only just began. Does it matter? This must end. We swore a vow to *protect*."

"To protect the Cahr Awen, yes."

"Is that how you justify this?" Lizl reared back. "You're not hurting the Cahr Awen, so it's acceptable?"

"I am not hurting anyone."

"You've spent your whole life hurting others! How many people have you killed or maimed, Bloodwitch? How many people have you *taken* from simply because an assignment told you to?" Lizl's voice hit louder with each word. "You said you have honor, but I have seen you use your magic to kill. You said you have honor, *yet you fight for the Raider King*."

There it was again. That spark of rage to tense in Aeduan's wrists and fists. Except now, he had a Painstone. Now, he had his magic.

He could run. He need not even control Lizl's blood to

364

do it. He could fuel his muscles to a speed she couldn't follow.

But there would be no outrunning the Fury.

"You," Aeduan said, his own voice carefully controlled, "do not know me at all." Then he groped for the Painstone and eased it from his neck. Instantly, his body gave way. Fire filled his chest, his belly, his brain. He doubled over, eyes screwing shut. The stone dropped to the bloodied earth.

He hit the ground mere moments later, landing on all fours, chest heaving. The headless monk was near enough for him to smell without magic.

"What are you doing?" Lizl moved closer.

"I . . . want you to trust me," he ground out. "I did not kill these people. My father did not kill these people. Natan and the monks did that. *They* are your enemy, not me."

Lizl said nothing, so Aeduan continued: "I found the Cahr Awen. They . . . healed the Well in Nubrevna. Did Monk Evrane tell you?"

"I heard, but I did not believe." A hard exhale. Then came a swish of fabric, a clink of metal, and Lizl dropped to a crouch beside Aeduan.

And it occurred to him that he could not smell her blood. So close, but the daisy chains and mother's kisses were gone.

"It's true." Blood dribbled from his mouth. "And . . . I found half of the Cahr Awen a second time. The shadow-ender. I failed to protect her, though. I sent her to the Monastery. I sent her to the Abbot."

Lizl inhaled sharply.

"I told her the monks would help her. I told her she would be safe there." Aeduan tried to shake his head; he failed, and suddenly he was coughing.

Blood splattered Lizl's cloak, fresh and hot. Rather than recoil, she simply sat there, waiting. And waiting some more, even as Aeduan's cough sprayed wider.

"You," he forced out at last, "have to get her away from ... him."

"I," she said flatly. "Meaning alone."

Molars clenching, Aeduan dragged his face up and forced his eyes to hold hers. *Pain, pain, pain.* "I cannot go with you."

She scoffed. "Of *course* you can't. You always run away, Bloodwitch. You have since we were young."

Aeduan's eyes dropped back to the ground. The Painstone gleamed inches away. He could take it again. He could end these screams in his muscles and feel his magic thrum once more.

He did not take it.

"The ... longer you are with me," he said, "the greater the danger, Monk Lizl. The Fury ... The man who came for me in Tirla ... He will come again, and he will kill you."

"Oh?" She gripped Aeduan's chin, jerked his face toward hers. "And what does this 'Fury' want with you?"

"He works for my father. And my father wants me at his side."

"Is that where *you* want to go?"

"No," he said, and it was true. Even knowing that his father had not killed these people, even knowing that a man like Corlant had defended the Purists and Nomatsis—he still did not want to return.

Lady Fate's knife had fallen, though, and for him, there could only be one path.

"I wish I could believe you," Lizl said. "But I can't." Even as she spoke these words, her face softened. The line between her brows smoothed away. "Your skin is fire," she murmured, "and you bleed and bleed and bleed. You are dying, Monk Aeduan, aren't you?"

"Yes."

She released his chin. Aeduan's head dropped. His arms shook dangerously beneath him. If he did not move, he would fall on his face, and if he fell, he did not think he would get up again.

Lizl sensed this too, for suddenly she was there, grabbing his shoulders and hauling him upright. It took all his remaining strength not to topple backward. And it took all the focus he had just to keep breathing.

"You know," Lizl said, "I thought that seeing you like this would make me happy. I used to imagine it even, when we were younger. I imagined surpassing you on the training block, or earning more assignments, or just getting more praise from Monk Evrane.

"But I don't feel happy right now. I feel disgusted. All these years, I thought you were special. I thought you were stronger—*better* even, because your magic made you unstoppable. It turns out, though, that you die like every other man. And you are a coward like them too.

"So go. Leave me and rejoin your father as you so desperately wish to do. I do not want your weakness at my side."

In a graceful sweep, she retrieved the Painstone from the bloodied soil. Then she stalked up to Aeduan and stared down. "Just remember, you owe me three life-debts, Bloodwitch. One for the Painstone. One for the Cahr Awen. And one for not killing you right now." She dropped the stone onto his lap.

It did not touch his skin.

"And I will expect repayment, so don't die before I can claim it." Without another word, Lizl left. She stalked into the woods, away from Aeduan, away from the monks she had killed and the innocents she had tried to save.

Aeduan watched her go, waiting until she was out of sight before easing the Painstone around his neck. His hands shook. His lungs shook. Then the stone was on and the agony was tucked away, hidden beneath the lies of numbing magic.

He stood, muscles free and strong once more, and he moved. North toward the highest peaks of the Sirmayans. North toward his father.

Lady Fate's knife had fallen, and it was time to see how sharp its edge might be.

FORTY-TWO

✳

All Iseult wanted to do was wake up. All she wanted to do was stop these flames and the endless laughing. The Firewitch was there whenever Evrane put her to sleep—and Evrane put her to sleep whenever she woke up.

Iseult would have just enough time to stumble to a washroom, the curtains and ram's head and four-poster bed spinning with each step. Then she would relieve herself, drink some broth, and . . . Back to bed. Back to sleep. Back to the Firewitch's flames.

The silver king did not save her again.

Iseult begged Evrane to let her stay awake, but the words always came out strange. Garbled and small, like she spoke the wrong language from somebody else's mouth. And each time, Evrane would simply shake her head, confusion on her face and in her Threads.

Sometimes Leopold was there too, the same frown gripping his sunshine face and sunshine Threads. *How much time has passed?* Iseult tried to ask. *How long have I been here? What is outside this room? Is the battle between monks still going on?* But like Evrane, all he could do was shake his head and tell her to get some rest.

369

Finally—she had no concept of *when*, for the door never opened and the curtains never budged—Iseult opened her eyes. Evrane was not there, and no shadows trounced. No groggy magic held her under.

So she breathed, deep and full. Then she tried swallowing, amazed when she not only succeeded without coughing, but she even felt her tongue scrape the roof of her mouth. Felt her throat moving and chapped lips pressing tight.

She swiveled her head next, pleased when the room stayed mostly intact. Only slight blurring, slight dizziness. In fact, she could just make out Leopold standing at the curtains, peering outside. His Threads twined with golden worry and green contemplation. His left arm still hung in a sling.

"What happened to Owl?" she rasped. *Cartorran*. The words had come out in Cartorran, thank the goddess.

Leopold's Threads skittered with sea blue surprise. He rounded toward her, eyebrows bouncing. Relief foaming overtop his other feelings. He strode toward her, a slight limp that Iseult hadn't noticed before. Hadn't been *able* to notice. "How do you feel, Iseult? Should I fetch Monk Evrane?"

"*No*." The word burst out, overloud and erratic. Iseult might trust the monk completely and might owe her several lives, too, but right now, she did not want sleep. She wanted answers. "Don't summon her. I feel fine. Just tell me: where is Owl?"

A swallow. A wincing spiral of grief. "I do not know," Leopold admitted, reaching the bed. "Everything happened so quickly."

"Ah." Iseult rubbed at her face—only to instantly stop when her fingers met bandages. Odd, since she felt no pain there.

"Here." Leopold poured her a glass of water from a pitcher

on a table beside the bed. Though only one-handed, he remained as nimble as ever.

But Iseult waved off the drink. She did not know how much time she had before Evrane would return and make her sleep again. "I thought I saw Blueberry. When the fire hit, I saw his Threads. Could he have rescued Owl?"

"You would know better than I would, Iseult. I saw nothing beyond the flames. May I?" Leopold waved to the bed, and at Iseult's nod, he helped her rise.

This time, she welcomed the aid. No pain coiled through her, but her limbs felt made of marble. Too heavy to move on their own.

"We need to search for her," she said as Leopold's good hand slid behind her.

He huffed a laugh. Not a cruel sound, but a startled one that matched his Threads. "I will do that right after I finish lifting you . . . Wait, are you serious?" He reared back. "Iseult, there are monks trying to kill us over there"—he swung his head toward the door—"and a Raider King's vast army over there." He swung his head toward the window. "If the child lives—and I hope she does—there is nothing we can do to help her right now."

"There is always something we can do. *Always*."

At her words, slivers of rich burgundy hit Leopold's Threads. Shades of peach too. On anyone else, she would have interpreted it as tenderness, perhaps even desire. But on him . . . On him, she couldn't understand it at all.

"What is it?" she asked.

"I said nothing."

"No, but you felt something. Tell me what."

Now wheat-colored embarrassment channeled across his Threads. Then he smiled, a rueful smile that was so perfectly in sync with his feelings, Iseult found herself blinking. There was even a faint blush to warm his cheeks. "I truly can hide nothing from you, can I?"

"That does not answer the question."

"No." He ran a thumb over his lower lip, before he finally murmured, "Please, Iseult. Let a man have his secrets." Then he crooked down to grab something behind the table. "Here, I have something for you."

A clever deflection, but Iseult would allow it. There was still so much she needed to know, yet her eyes were burning more and more by the second.

"I know this is not your book precisely, but it *is* the same text. Actually, this is the original. I took it from the Monastery Archives." He slid a black leather tome onto the bed. "I thought it might prove I was telling the truth. About Eron fon Hasstrel, I mean."

Iseult glanced down at the book . . . And ice thumped into her stomach. She swallowed, feeling her face settle into a puzzled frown—and also feeling too stunned to prevent it.

An Illustrated Guide to the Carawen Monastery.

This was the same book on Carawen monks she had left behind in Veñaza City. The only way Leopold could know that would be if he was truly working with Safi's uncle.

"Likely you do not wish to read it, but I thought—"

"Thank you," she interrupted. And she meant it. Everything had been so unstable since Aeduan had left, since the crash and the dreams and the darkness. This book felt like an anchor.

And knowing Leopold had gotten it for her . . . That she could in fact trust him . . .

Iseult's breath slid out. The room was melting together; her chest felt a jumble of feelings—hot and cold alike in a hundred ways she didn't recognize.

She pulled the book closer, ready to peel it open, when she noticed a stamp on the cover. A bird with three legs and a crown atop its head.

"What is this?" Her fast-tiring gaze lifted to Leopold's. "My version did not have it."

"*That* is the sigil of the Rook King. You can find it all over the Monastery." He tapped it with his uninjured hand. "This whole place used to be his fortress a thousand years ago. Have you never wondered why the Carawen sigil is a bird?"

She had, but nowhere in her book—in *this* book—had there been an answer.

The Rook King, she thought. The man from her dream. It *had* to be, even if she couldn't explain how.

Again, she rubbed at her bandages. This time, though, she let her fingers scrape the cloth. No pain, but Leopold still grimaced and whispered, "Leave them."

"Do you believe in ghosts?" she asked, ignoring him. "Nomatsis do not, but Safi always swore they were real."

"Oh?" He blinked, pallid confusion in his Threads. "Yes, well, she *would* believe in them. The Hasstrel castle is full of ghosts. But . . . why do you ask?"

Iseult wet her lips. "So you *do* believe?"

"Most Cartorrans do. We are not a worshipping people, but we take our ancestors very seriously." He planted his good hand on the bed and leaned toward her, a frown knitting across his face. "Again, Iseult, why do you ask?"

She scratched her nose. More gauze scraped. It was one thing to ask for his insight, and quite another to tell him she had ghosts haunting her dreams. "No reason," she said at last.

His expression and Threads wore open disbelief, but he did not press her further—for which Iseult was grateful. She grew more tired by the second. Heavier, too, like a cave had collapsed atop her.

"Owl," she said, but the name came out as a long, slurring moan.

Shock brightened Leopold's Threads. In an instant, he was on his feet. "You are ill again. I will get Monk Evrane." He moved away, so fast. Too fast. Streaks trailed behind him. A hundred Leopolds, a hundred versions racing across time.

"No," Iseult called out, but like before, that was not what left her tongue.

By the time Evrane rushed in, shadows veiled Iseult's vision. Evrane looked made of darkness, black waves coiling off her.

Wings, Iseult thought before the healing magic dragged her under. *It looks like she has wings.*

When Iseult next awoke, it was to someone barking, "Get her up," in Cartorran. A man's voice attached to vague, hazy Threads.

She stretched her eyelids high. The world wheeled into weak focus. Threads, Threads, Threads—the man who had spoken, as well as two more people now striding toward the bed. Monks she did not know.

For a brief, disoriented moment, their white cloaks looked fused together, a single entity crossing the room with Threads of hostile gray and green focus. Then the white smear reached Iseult, split once more into two, and faces materialized above her.

A woman, a man. The woman seized Iseult's left arm, the man seized her right. Then, with grips that dug beneath her bandages and into her flesh, they wrenched Iseult into a sitting position and heaved her backward until her spine hit the headboard.

The world reeled around Iseult. No pain, only vertigo and confusion. Sleep still clung to her. The Firewitch still laughed in her ears.

Then the monks strode away, no longer melded into one, even as their Threads aligned in a single color: silvery revulsion. They were disgusted by Iseult's weakness. Or perhaps disgusted by the touch of her. But Iseult was accustomed to disgust and hate, and if those feelings could kill, they would have slain her a long time ago.

She drew in a long breath, relieved when she felt her lungs press against her ribs. When her vision grew clearer and clearer by the second. White moonlight slashed through open curtains. She neither saw nor sensed Evrane or Leopold nearby.

She had little time to puzzle over their absence before the third monk—the man who'd first spoken—stalked into view.

At first, as Iseult watched his Threads approach, she thought the colors blended because of her own exhaustion. Because of the shadowy sleep that refused to fully release its hold. Except everything else in the room had crystallized. She felt alert, awake. Even her muscles felt light enough to move of their own accord.

Then she realized: *He's a Bleeder.* Someone who bled from one emotion to the next, feeling each with frenetic intensity, yet never staying in one place for long. It gave their Threads a muddy weave. *They are unstable*, Gretchya had warned Iseult years ago. *Each emotion is frayed and somehow simultaneous. There is no predicting what a Bleeder will do next.*

Instantly, Iseult's body tensed. Cold shoveled through her—hard ice after so much sleep saturated by flame.

"Do you know who I am?" the man asked. He was young. Perhaps only a few years older than she. With his sallow skin and fair hair, his features bled together like his Threads, and the illusion was only compounded by the softness of his jaw and figure.

If Iseult didn't know of the rigorous Monastery training, she would have thought he'd never worked a day in his life.

He also stank of incense.

"You are the Abbot," she said. The red trim on his cloak gave it away. Then she recalled something Evrane had said in passing and added, "Natan fon Leid."

Gray displeasure darted across his Threads, somehow moving in sync with rosy pleasure too. There was red irritation as well, along with sprays of lilac hunger and orange impatience. They flitted past, quick as flies and too many for Iseult to catch.

"Your guardians"—he flung a hand toward the door—"will let no one enter. Not even me, in my own sodding Monastery. But I want to know who has brought us so low. I want to *see* the face of the woman destroying my home."

Iseult stiffened, thrown by his words. Thrown by his venom. "I don't destroy your home," she said.

He only laughed. "This insurgency wants *you*, and they will do whatever it takes to get you."

"Why?"

He did not answer. Instead, he leaned closer, his eyes scraping up and down the length of her. Violence frittering brighter with each heartbeat.

"What is your name?"

"Iseult det Midenzi."

"You are a 'Matsi."

An observation, she decided, not a question. So she stayed perfectly still. Never in her life had she felt it more important to keep her expression devoid of emotion. Her stasis unwavering and screwed tight. Natan fon Leid was the viper hiding on the forest floor; his danger lay in how plain and unassuming he appeared on the surface.

Now she understood what Leopold had meant by *Men like that are useful to princes*. The sixth son of a nobleman, he had likely been overlooked his whole life. Now, as Abbot, he had something to prove.

Iseult had no idea why Monk Evrane would support such a man. Unless, of course, the insurgent monks were even worse.

"Five hundred years," the Abbot muttered to himself, Threads jumping, bleeding, unreadable. "Five hundred years with no one, and now two Aetherwitches claim they are the Cahr Awen."

He lunged, too fast for Iseult to react. No warning inside his Threads, no warning in his body. One moment, he spoke.

The next, he had his hands around her throat and was slamming her against the headboard.

Her skull cracked. Instinct took over.

Her fists shot up, ready to punch beneath his arms. Invert his elbows and snap his bones in two. *Burn him, burn him.*

But Iseult stopped, with her fingers only inches above the velvet cover. He was not strangling her, and there were two other monks in the room—heavily armed. This was not a fight she could win. *If a man is better armed or better trained,* Habim had taught her, *then do as he orders. It is better to live and look for opportunity than to die outmatched.*

The Abbot's face loomed closer, closer. Near enough for Iseult to see the ingrown hairs above his lip. To spot individual bloodlines shooting across his eyes. And this near, his Threads bore down on her like a mudslide.

"Give me one good reason," he snarled. Spittle hit her cheek. "Give me one good reason I should not give you to the insurgents."

"Because," she said smoothly, "I am the Cahr Awen. You just said it yourself—"

It was the wrong answer. He shoved her against the headboard, cracking her skull once more. Sparks flew across her vision.

Then he tightened his grip, cutting off her air. "All I see is 'Matsi filth. You are lucky you have a prince backing you, or I would have gutted you already and hung you from the ramparts for the insurgents to see."

He released her. As abruptly as he'd grabbed her, he let her go and jerked upward.

Iseult's hand flew to her neck. *Now,* she felt pain, in her

378

throat and in her lungs. He had ripped her bandages. *Burn him, burn him, burn him.*

She could. She *should.* These monks could do nothing against flames that ate through nightmares.

"Know this, little Threadwitch," the Abbot said. "If those rebels breach our walls, I will leave you to their blades while the rest of us escape to safety."

"And if you do," she responded coolly, "then I will tell them which way you went."

He slapped her. Right across the cheek. And though she was ready for the attack this time, that didn't stop the black from ripping across her vision or the pain from whipping through her jaw.

"You are not the Cahr Awen," he hissed. "And you are not worth what the prince has promised me."

With those words to echo in Iseult's mind, he left. A sweep of white tinged with red, a blur of a hundred emotions charging and rippling and oozing free. The other monks followed, their own more muted Threads alight with crisp pleasure.

She waited until the door crashed shut behind them before she closed her eyes. Her head pounded. The skin on her neck ached where he had grabbed her. Despite that, she felt . . . fine. Strong even. Unsettled, yes, but also bursting with the need to move, like jostled sparkling wine about to burst from the bottle.

Stasis, she reminded herself. She needed to think through everything that had just happened. She needed to work through it all and formulate a plan. Pain could be dealt with later, and this wild energy could fuel her planning.

Clearly, the Abbot did not believe she or Safi were the Cahr

Awen, and clearly Leopold was paying the Abbot to protect them. Presumably he had also paid for the Abbot to retrieve Safi in Marstok. But there would be no finding Safi now, no reunion as long as the insurgency continued its onslaught.

Cautiously, Iseult swung her legs from the bed. She wore black cotton pants and a loose, matching shirt. No dirt or grime. Evrane must have bathed and dressed her. Perhaps Iseult had been awake during that process, perhaps not. For all she knew, it had only been a day since she'd arrived. Or maybe it had been weeks.

Her bare feet touched wool. Sheepskins layered over rush mats. She hadn't noticed before.

Goddess, she must have been truly ill. Evrane was right: she was lucky she had not died.

With a hand braced on the table beside the bed, she stood. The jars within Evrane's healer kit shook as she rose. In moments, her legs had remembered what standing was. Her spine too, and she straightened.

The room stayed blessedly still throughout. Even when she took three steps away from the bed. Even when she picked up speed and crossed to the window. Cold shivered off the glass, bubbles and bends warping the view of the valley far below.

There were no clouds to hide the moon. It shone, the purest of lights illuminating the valley. *A Threadwitching night*, Gretchya would have called it. *When the Moon Mother's glow washes away all color, leaving only Threads. Leaving only our work.* Back then, that work had been binding Threads to stones—or for Iseult, attempting to bind and failing.

Now, her work was observation. *Learn your opponents. Learn your terrain.*

The wide river that twined through the valley was surrounded by marsh in some spots and sharper shores in others. Islands streaked the deep, black waters, and bridges crossed, zigging and zagging toward the Origin Well on its own island, dark with evergreens. The waters north of it looked frozen.

Somewhere out there was Owl. Somewhere out there was Safi. Iseult had to find them. *Both* of them. If Iseult could get to the bridges, she could reach the Well, and from there, she could reach the northern shore by way of ice. Then it would be easy enough to follow the river east without drawing attention from either side. Yes, the raiders would be near, but dense forest stood in their way.

The only real problem she faced was how to actually reach the bridges. Monks, insurgents, fortress walls, and a sheer cliff blocked her. But the Abbot had referred to an escape, and clearly the monks had been able to leave the Monastery to retrieve Iseult and Leopold from their wreckage. That meant there *was* a way out of here. Iseult just had to find it.

She scratched absently at her nose. No bandages blocked her this time. Evrane's magic must be working. *Although the Abbot just ruined some of that,* she thought, pulling away from the window and patting at the bandages on her neck.

He had practically shredded them. Fortunately, it did not hurt to smooth them back in place. They were not the only bandages torn, though. The ones on her arms had also peeled apart. She angled her biceps into the moon's light, ready to fix those too, when she caught sight of the flesh underneath.

Smooth. Unmarred.

That . . . made no sense. She tore off more gauze, this time

381

on her forearm. But there was nothing there either. This was not new skin, pink and raw from healing. Nor was it old skin, scarred and puckered. This was *her* skin, exactly as it had always been.

No bruises, no welts, no scabs.

Iseult ripped the bandages off her other arm. Once more, the same pale, unblemished flesh met her eyes. Impossible, impossible.

She darted for the mirror beside the wardrobe, and in seconds, she had torn off every strip of gauze that she could reach. Her neck, her face, her stomach, her thighs. A white pile gathered at her feet. But each newly exposed patch of skin revealed the same thing: she had no injuries.

None. Nowhere. And Iseult knew what magically healed skin looked like—Evrane had healed her before. *This* was not it.

But there was no reason for Evrane to lie to her. No purpose in tending wounds that were not real or locking Iseult in a healing sleep. Surely, Iseult was wrong. *Surely*, she was missing something. A key piece of information that would align all the thoughts now banging around inside her mind.

The healer kit.

She spun away from the mirror, running—easily, *easily* running—to the table. She tore open the kit's latch and then dumped the contents onto the bed.

But there was nothing to see. Empty bottles, empty jars, and rolls of fresh linen. These weren't even real supplies.

"What are you doing, Iseult?"

Iseult's throat clenched shut. Moon Mother save her. In her panic, she hadn't been checking the weave around her.

Now Evrane was here, the door was creaking open, and the monk's Threads shone with alarm.

With heart-thudding slowness, Iseult angled toward the monk. *This woman saved you*, she told herself. *There must be some explanation here.* Yet when her eyes locked finally on Evrane's, she knew there was no explanation. At least none that could end well for her.

The darkness was back, throbbing off Evrane like heat waves. She was not Cleaved—this was different, this was unknown—but the monk was also not herself. All this time, Iseult had believed she was imagining the shadows, that they were from her nightmares, carried into this world by exhaustion and flames. But she was awake now, and the shadows still enveloped the woman who had saved her.

"Wh-what is wrong with you?" she tried to ask, but her words were muddled once more. Several languages all at once, or maybe no languages at all.

"Iseult," Evrane said calmly. "You are not well. You should be in bed." With elegant steps, she crossed the room. Her expression—and her Threads, too—was as serene and compassionate as Iseult had always known it to be. "You need to sleep," she went on. "Sleep, Iseult. *Sleep.*"

The shadows charged off her body, a hundred black wings taking flight. They flapped toward Iseult, then against her and over her and finally inside. A hundred thousand wings to beat within her skull.

There was no fighting it. Whatever Evrane was, she was not the monk Iseult had once known and cared about.

Iseult's knees turned to water beneath her. She fell.

And the wings dragged her down.

FORTY-THREE

✳

Safi awoke to voices in her room. Two maids had come to bathe her and dress her. Safi knew them. She had interrogated them before, and the shorter one had made her laugh.

These young women had nothing to hide, so her magic purred with contented truth at their presence. Safi let their chatter buzz around her—who had arrived for the party, who was wearing what, and how the nobility had reacted to strict security protocols.

It felt good to be clean. It felt good to have slept. And it felt good to don new clothes. Safi's silk gown was a lovely one, if impractical. Loose long sleeves, a plunging neckline, and filmy skirts that hung against her ankles. It revealed more of Safi's chest than she liked, not enough of her legs, and the sleeves would hinder her in a fight.

"But it's the latest style in Dalmotti," the taller girl insisted, which left Safi to wonder why such a gown was also popular *here*.

At least, though, it had a pocket. The perfect size for her Truth-lens, which she plunked in, her chest puffing with triumph. She couldn't wait to give it to Vaness.

384

Once the maids departed, Rokesh appeared. His shoulder was no longer bandaged, and he moved more easily as he ushered her from the room, where her Adder guards moved into formation. No one spoke, and Safi welcomed the silence.

Tonight, she would have noise enough to deal with. Tonight, she would be on full display, for every member of the Sultanate, military officer and adviser, every noble relative, and every lead bureaucrat too. *All* would be assembled in one place to gape at the Truthwitch and know they were being tested.

Safi expected to be brought straightaway to the throne room. Or perhaps to Vaness's office, or even her imperial quarters. Instead, she was brought once more into the bowels of the Floating Palace, to another part of the island she'd never seen before, a vast storage area with shelves and crates—and at the far end, a doorway that fed onto Lake Scarza.

Habim met Safi and the Adders at the door. He was in full regalia tonight, a hundred colorful sashes draped across the brilliant gold and green of his uniform. Each one for a different honor awarded to him; each one as foreign to Safi as everything else she'd learned about him in the last day. Behind him waited a long row of servants and soldiers, all with chins high as if awaiting orders.

Habim did not acknowledge Rokesh, who offered a small bow, and if Habim harbored any ill will toward Safi over the Hell-Bards, he did not show it. Instead, he gestured broadly at the room behind.

"Does all look well to you, Truthwitch?"

Safi frowned, confused, and rubbed at the scar on her thumb. "Does what look well?"

This earned her a sigh. "The fireworks." Habim pointed at the nearest crate. "Those boxes are about to be carried onto the lake for detonation, and those boxes"—he motioned to smaller cases beyond—"contain personal spark-candles for the guests. I must ensure they are safe."

Safi glanced at the boxes. Nothing in her magic reacted. No hum of truth, nor any hiss of lies either. She approached the closest crate and pried off the lid. A perfectly normal display of clay plots stared up at her, exactly as she knew fireworks ought to look.

Rokesh slid into position beside her. "Say something," he murmured, his voice rougher than usual. She glanced his way, blinking. Surprised. "*Say something*," he repeated.

So she said something. "They are safe."

"Good," Habim barked, spinning toward the servants and soldiers. "Distribute them and move to your assigned stations." He offered no more words for Safi, so Rokesh led her from the room.

Up, up, they returned the way they had come, except this time, the Adders escorted her into the main palace gardens. They hit two rows of soldiers before reaching the top level of terraces. Music lilted on the breeze, carried over murmuring voices. Some tense, some happy, all hushed and low.

Then the soldiers parted and the full gala spanned before Safi. Vaness and her own contingent of Adders waited just ahead upon a stage. Lanterns hung from decorative iron chains draped from tree to tree, and elaborate floral arrangements doused the space in rose and daylily.

Six musicians performed on the level below the Empress's, flutes and harps and a single, hollow-throated drum. And on the lowest level waited the guests. A sea of figures, dressed in their finest. Silk and satin and velvet and taffeta twirled across a dancing circle surrounded by ornate iron posts with Firewitched flames.

The guests were nothing compared to what waited beyond the Floating Palace, though, for the lake was covered in boats. White-masted or with oars extended, nets flapping or with sailors crawling, no matter the ship, they were all kept at a distance by prow-to-prow naval ships. The Azmir shore, meanwhile, writhed like an anthill. Hundreds upon thousands of Marstoks gathered to watch the imperial fireworks take flight.

The attack on the Well had kept no one away.

Vaness turned at the sound of Safi's footsteps. She glowed at the center of her stage, her gown a fiery red crepe fit for the Empress of the Flame Children and Chosen Daughter of the Fire Well. Her hair, coiled atop her head like a torch, was woven through with matching ribbons, while her manacles had stretched into thin bands spiraling up her arms. Instead of iron at her waist, she now wore a belt of gold.

At the sight of Safi, her chest deflated ever so slightly. A subtle exhale of relief, and Safi couldn't resist tossing her a grin. Vaness waited until Safi fell into place just behind her—and then for Rokesh to fall into a matching place on her other side—before she turned to face the crowds.

Before she turned to face the tens of thousands of Marstoks who loved her, yet didn't know her at all.

Vaness lifted her arms. The people of Azmir roared. It was a sound to topple storm clouds and swallow thoughts. The noise bellowed against Safi, gyrated in her lungs, her legs, her skull. So many people, so near and so far, all screaming their approval—and all of them screaming true.

No sign of disapproval now. The Azmirians wanted to be dazzled, they wanted to be entertained. So Vaness gave them what they asked for. Her wrists flicked up, her fingers pointed to the sky with palms out . . .

Three bursts of light zoomed into the sky. Then they detonated, a thousand shooting stars streaming down. Explosive *cracks!* followed a heartbeat later—and somehow, the crowds roared all the more.

Safi wanted to roar right along with them. It was an endless thunderstorm of colored light that swelled and skated. Sometimes, mere bursts of brilliance to fill the sky. Other times, elaborate pictures of battles and cities and forests came to life in an explosive tableau. One after the other, a spectacle like nothing she had seen or heard before, and with Safi in the best possible seat to witness it—the Empress's own patio.

She was also in the best spot to constantly assess the party below. She couldn't help it; something felt *off* about the assembly. Something scrubbed against the back of her neck—something that wasn't her magic. Yet no matter how hard she scrutinized, all that swept against her was truth; all that bubbled in her belly was honest conversation and delight.

It was as a row of firework soldiers marched across the black sky, their reflection moving serenely on the lake below, that it finally dawned on Safi: what she was witnessing was impossible. Everyone lied. There was no escaping that fact, yet Safi sensed no falsehoods from the people below.

The ceaseless tide of lies that crashed within truths was gone. Completely vanished.

Gods curse her, what had Safi done? Clearly, she had used up her magic on the Truth-lens. Only half, though—the half that recognized deceit. The half that she had chosen to imbue into the glass. She didn't understand how this was possible. Her magic simply *was*. It existed inside of her, always present, always responding.

Until right now, when it didn't anymore.

She fumbled for the Truth-lens. Though she had not wanted to show it publicly, not before giving it to Vaness, she had no choice now. She had to know if it worked—she had to know if she could *get her magic back*. But when she shoved her hand into her pocket, her fingers did not touch metal.

Her fingers touched paper. With a slackening jaw, she gaped down at a spark-candle upon her palm. Almost the same shape, almost the same weight. Someone had switched them out.

The question was who—and why and *when*? She spun away from the horizon, away from the fireworks. Someone would have needed to get very close to trade items without her sensing.

Her eyes landed on Rokesh, ten paces away. He gazed steadily back. He *watched* her, and she suddenly remembered how he'd placed his hand upon her elbow in the storage room. The lightest of touches, but enough distraction for him to have snagged her Truth-lens and replaced it with a spark-candle.

It made no sense, though. There was no reason for him to want it, no reason for him to *take* it. All he'd had to do was ask. After all, she had tested Rokesh. She knew him to be true. *Unless he isn't any longer.*

Earlier, she had noticed his injury was gone. Then in the

storage room, he had commanded her to say something—and she had. Without thought, she had obeyed.

And then there was the glamoured hole at the Well. Glamourwitches were *not* common, nor Dalmotti silk gowns with a pocket *just* the right size for a spark-candle.

Then there was the simple truth that Habim had always said since his arrival: "We have a plan." Not *I*, but *we*.

With your right hand give a person what he expects. With the left hand, cut the purse.

Rokesh unsheathed his sword.

And Safi screamed, "*Mathew, don't!*"

FORTY-FOUR

✳

The Fury made short work of the chains that bound Merik to the tower. The collar, though—that required Esme's magic to open. So Kullen hauled Merik outside, and they took flight.

It was glorious. Even if it wasn't Merik's magic to carry them, even if he had a collar around his neck and cleaving magic to pump in his veins. Flying, however brief, made him feel whole again.

Not even two full days had passed since the wind had lashed his face and blustered beneath his feet, yet it felt like it had been centuries. Below Merik, moonlight washed the lost city of Poznin in silver. From above, it looked different. Alive and dreamlike. Ancient things made new again, and even the endless Cleaved looked fresh, whole beneath that glow.

The journey ended all too soon, and the forest around the Well clustered thicker and thicker. Then the Well itself appeared, a tiny figure in ermine standing at its side. Her eyes were closed as the Fury landed, her arms extended while she worked at her Loom.

She did not react when Kullen and Merik arrived, nor when Merik's knees buckled from impact and he hit the grass on all fours. And she did not react when the Fury barked, "Puppeteer." Her fingers kept on strumming and twining at invisible Threads.

The Fury lost his patience in an instant. "Puppeteer!" he called louder, still to no avail. So he launched once more into a prowling pace. It flattened the grass in a crooked line, and with each step, he picked at the scabbing on his mutilated ear.

He also muttered to himself: "Thankless tasks, *thankless* tasks. I am no tool. I am the Fury. I was there on the day the Six turned, just as he was." As Kullen walked, black lines slithered across his face. Shadowy snow fell.

He reached the end of his line and pivoted. *Pick, pick, pick.* "That will change with you at my side, Merik. Unlike you, the General is not a king, and once I find the blade and the glass, then I won't need him. Or any of them." Now his glare turned to the Puppeteer, and he stalked right up to her.

Then he lurked over her, staring down while snow fell and darkness webbed across him. "Six turned on six," he sang, "and made themselves kings. Five turned on one and stole everything."

The Fury remained that way, humming rhymes, while Esme continued her focused work at the Loom. And the Fury remained that way as Cleaved slowly emerged from the forest, one by one, to flank the Well.

Merik hardly noticed them. His blood had rushed to his head from the flying; his ears had popped; and the energy from his last meal had already worn off. More importantly, his mind was snagged on what the Fury had said—on the fact that no one wanted the same thing. Hye, they all wanted to enter this mountain, but Esme wanted the Wells. The Raider King wanted the empires. And the Fury wanted a blade and a glass, and then Merik at his side . . .

That was valuable information. People with different aims could always be pitted against one another.

When at last Esme's eyelids rolled up, her head swiveled to face the Fury. "What," she hissed, "do you want?" Before Kullen could answer, her eyes caught on Merik several paces away. Rage snarled across her face. "How dare you bring him here." She shoved past the Fury, voice lifting as her arm lifted too. "Go back to the tower, Prince! I command you!"

Merik's whole body tensed, shoulders rising to his ears. Pain—he *knew* the pain was coming.

"No." The Fury clamped a hand on Esme's shoulder. "He comes with me."

Esme jerked free. She looked fit to destroy Kullen. Her fingers had curled into claws at her sides. "I am not done with him."

"He is not yours to play with. Release his collar."

"He *is* mine. Both of you are." Again, her arm levered high as if she planned to use her Loom.

But the Fury only laughed, a mocking, chesty sound that echoed across the water. "You cannot control me, Puppeteer. And you cannot hurt me. My power is too immense for your magic, as you well know."

"I do not need to control you, because I can control *him*." Her fingers moved, and Merik moved with them.

It was not as if he wanted to; his feet simply walked toward the Well, and there was nothing he could do to stop them.

393

Cold splashed against his feet, then his ankles, then his calves, and no matter how much he spun his torso or tried to twist back, his feet kept striding. He even stretched and spun his arms, grasping for the shore, but it did nothing. Step, step, step. Splash, splash, splash.

And now it was the Puppeteer's laughter that echoed across the waves.

Hips, waist, chest. Cold squeezed the air from Merik's lungs, and soon only a few steps remained before he would be fully submerged. His breath had turned staccato. "Please," he tried to say, but the sound was instantly swallowed by a gathering storm.

The Fury's storm.

"*Enough.*" The Fury rounded on Esme. "Release him."

"No." She stood taller. "I want to see what happens if he drowns. Will he come back from such a death, I wonder?"

Merik's feet took another step. Water lapped against the collar, against his neck.

"Do you want to enter the mountain or not?" the Fury demanded. "The prince is my key inside."

"Is he?"

Another step. The water reached Merik's chin, even with his head tipped as high as it would go. And now water slapped against him and choked down his throat, carried by the Fury's building winds.

"He has agreed to lure the Sightwitch through the mountain door. Release him."

"The mountain door?" Esme hooted a laugh. "You have not even *reached* the mountain door! Your soldiers still fight the monsters of the Crypts!"

The sky overhead turned darker with each passing, spluttering breath. No more moon. Only hell-waters and ash.

"Leave," Esme ordered the Fury, shouting over the growing storm. "Or I will drown him."

"He is not the only reason I am here—" Merik did not hear the rest of the Fury's words. A wave crashed into his ears, into his mouth. By the time he could hear or breathe again, Esme was responding.

"I told you," she spat. "He is not so easy to find as the others."

"Why?"

"He has no Threads. He is outside the world's weave."

"Impossible. Do not lie to me."

"He was born in the sleeping ice. You, of all people, should remember that." A withering tone had taken hold of Esme's voice, and finally—*finally*—the storm reared back. Less wind, fewer waves. Holding his breath, Merik lowered his chin and twisted his face toward the shore.

The Fury looked puzzled. The shadows on his skin, the snow and the winds—they had faded. "You have found him before."

"Because he was with others I knew." Esme gave a dismissive flick of her wrist. "He is no longer."

"The General will be displeased."

"Then tell him to come here and say so himself."

"Oh, *I* see." Kullen's head fell back, and he cackled at the sky. "That still bothers you, does it? You are still bitter he did not bring you with him."

"*No.*" The word cracked out, and with it, a pain lightninged through Merik. His back arched. He gasped for air.

Then it was over, as fast as it had come.

"The King," Esme snipped out, "will bring me to him once he opens the doors."

"Is that what you tell yourself?" The Fury clucked his tongue. "A lovely delusion, Puppeteer, except he already got what he needed from you. He got *me*."

A pause. Stillness and silence softened around the Well. But it passed in an instant, and Merik had just enough time to suck in air before the storm tore loose.

First came all-consuming pain. His muscles locked; his throat screamed.

Then came waves. Wind too, and the sudden hammering of rain. He could not breathe, he could not see. No screaming, only choking and convulsing.

Finally, his feet moved. He stepped below the surface. Three long strides while cold and darkness shuttered over him, stealing sound. He exhaled, bubbles charging out even though he needed to conserve air. There was no conserving anything here. No thinking, no moving. The only thing he could do was drown, electrified by Esme's cleaving while the last of his life drained away.

Merik lost consciousness, there beneath the waves. He couldn't say for how long. He could not say how many lungfuls of water he inhaled. All he knew was that the final sparks of pain towed him into Hell ... Then he came back into his body, and he was on all fours upon the shore, vomiting.

He was mid-heave, bile-laced water gushing from his throat onto grass, when he realized he was awake. He was *alive*.

Esme sat several paces away. Her prim pose was a lie; her tight smile a painted mask. Her fingers yanked grass from the earth. Fistful after fistful, she wrenched up the blades and then dropped them at her feet.

Blinking, Merik scanned the forest and the Well, searching for the Fury, but the man was nowhere. Only the usual Cleaved remained, standing guard as always. How long had Merik been underwater? How many times had he drowned?

"No gratitude." Esme ripped up more grass, smiling a flat-eyed smile at Merik. "They have no gratitude for what I do, Prince. No understanding of the difficulty. They come to me, they demand I find people, and then they leave again. *No gratitude.*"

It was similar to what the Fury had mentioned, and even in his drowned misery, Merik had enough sense to tuck away that information.

"He has no Threads!" she went on. "I can only find him if he is near Iseult—not that I have told *them* that." Another fistful of grass. "She is mine. Not theirs. And you are mine, Prince. *Not theirs.*"

Merik forced his head to nod and throat to wheeze, "Yours," before his lungs started seizing again. Dry heaves shook through him.

Esme, however, stopped her grass-shredding, and when she cocked her head sideways, the anger had dimmed in her yellow eyes. "So you will *not* help the Fury enter the mountain?"

Merik had to wait until his stomach stopped shuddering, his throat stopped coughing. Then he eked out, "No."

"Then why did the Fury say such a thing?"

Move with the wind, move with the stream. "Because he wants to frighten you. You are the Raider King's favorite."

397

Her flat smile faltered. "And why do you think that, Prince?"

"Because it's obvious." Merik sucked in a broken breath, forcing his exhausted eyes to hold Esme's. "The King sends the Fury on menial errands. Fetching other people? That is the job of a page boy."

Her nostrils flared. Her lips twitched—the hint of a real smile in her eyes.

"You, however, have an entire city. You have an entire *army* at your command, while the Fury commands no one."

It was the wrong thing to say. Her face fell. She wrenched up more grass. "But he *does* command an army. He leads the Raider King's southern assault upon the Sightwitch Sister Convent. And once they enter the mountain, he will use the doorway to enter Lovats and claim the hidden Well that should have been mine."

Merik's stomach hollowed out at those words. *The doorway to enter Lovats.* Noden, no.

"The Fury's soldiers will stream into the city from the underground, and then *he* will win all the glory." Esme's lips curled back. "All while I am stuck here, winning nothing. Just *waiting* for them to find the doorway that leads to Poznin."

Noden, no, no, no. The world wavered and blurred around Merik. His home was in danger. Never had Lovats fallen, even in the worst of wartime. The Sentries and the water-bridges had always protected it.

But if soldiers attacked from within—if they used these magic portals and poured in from the underground . . .

Merik's retching resumed. Bile splattered the grass.

Vivia had planned to lead refugees into the underground. They had thought the newly discovered ancient city a miracle, a space to house all the homeless and hungry and lost. Now the homeless and hungry and lost would be the first to die.

Merik had to stop that. He had to lose this collar, no matter the means, and he *had to stop that*.

"I never should have cleaved him," Esme went on. "Not before I made a second Loom. If I hadn't, then *I* would be the one now leading the march—"

"*Do it.*" Merik's voice graveled out, desperate and wild. "Do it. Beat him to the Crypts, and use me to lure out the Sightwitch. Then I will kill her, and you can go inside *before* the Fury does."

Esme eyed Merik askance, as if she thought through what he'd just said. As if she played it out, step by step, and—

"Yes," she breathed. "Oh, yes, yes, yes. You can fly me there, Prince. And then you can trick the Sightwitch from her hiding place and kill her while *I* deal with the monsters of the Crypts. I know how to control them—it's in Eridysi's diary. Yes, yes, *yes*! I will lead the advance into the mountain before the Fury can, and then the Raider King will see how much he truly needs me. And *oh*," she sighed, "if we are so near to the sleeping ice, perhaps it will suck him in. Eliminate the Fury and all of his memories for good."

In a lurch of speed, grass flinging around her, Esme pushed to her feet. She was grinning now, an exultant expression with cheeks flushed and eyes aflame. In three skipping hops, Esme reached Merik. Her fingers gripped and tugged and twirled around the collar, as if she teased apart a braid of Threads he could not see. Her eyes flicked quickly side to side. Her heels bounced and her cheeks scrunched with a grin.

Then the collar gave a soft hiss, like steam leaving a kettle.

The wood clanked apart, two halves that toppled toward the earth. Neither Merik nor Esme tried to catch them.

Merik grasped for his magic while Esme's hands shot toward the Well. "You are mine, Prince. You know what pain awaits you if you disobey."

He nodded. "I will not disobey." Then, to convince her fully, he bowed his head. "Command me, Puppeteer."

She giggled, and Merik used the moment to inhale as deeply as he could, fumbling, fumbling. His magic was in there—he could feel the faintest spark alive within his lungs. But it was weak. It was tired. It did not want to wake up.

That was all right, though. He knew that if he fled while Esme was at her Loom, then she would lash him with pain unimaginable. And if he fled at *any* time, the Fury would sense the magic and return. Merik would simply move with the wind and the stream, allowing his magic to rebuild with each careful step.

His plan, however, was short-lived. For as he lifted his face to watch Esme, still bouncing and laughing and thoroughly absorbed by her dreams of glory to come, a figure darted from the forest. It moved quickly through the lines of Cleaved, immobile and unresponsive to this living person in their midst.

The Northman, his red-tailed knife in hand, vaulted across the grass and stabbed Esme in the back.

FORTY-FIVE

※

Pain clogged Aeduan's veins by the time he reached his father's encampment, a sign the Painstone was almost depleted. He had jogged most of the way, only slowing when terrain or humanity required it. Four times, he had come upon battles in action—and four times, it was his ears that had warned him of what lay ahead. Not his magic.

Which was one more reason to return to his father. With his father, he could find Corlant, and if Corlant had indeed cursed these arrows, then Corlant could also cure him.

At least so Aeduan hoped.

He had known this might be coming, of course: the end of his power, the end of being a Bloodwitch. But caring had seemed an impossibility before. Loss was such an abstract thing until one was pressed beneath it and forced to stare into her dead eyes.

So Aeduan ran faster, pushing the limits of what the Painstone and his magic could still provide, and avoiding battles as they came. Nubrevnans and Marstoks, Baedyeds and Red Sails. Blood and death and violence that he could no longer smell.

401

He hit the first outskirts of the encampment as the moon began its descent. Snow fell, a fresh dusting atop the perma-frost. The air nipped at Aeduan's face and fingers. He had grown up in this cold, but years away had erased the memory of how it needled into one's bones.

Thousands of Nomatsis, Purists—and anyone else on the run—were nestled into these snow-glossed spruce trees. A lesson in efficiency, with hundreds of makeshift homes hammered into whatever space the land allowed. Smoke trickled up in pale mists from the loose-woven Nomatsi tents, and in darker ribbons from the sharp-sloped tents that Sirmayan natives and Northerners favored. Frequent camp-fires, frequent families.

But no soldiers, no raiders. These were the people displaced by war, not the ones who fought in it. Occasional sentries armed with bows and spears were the closest Aeduan ever spotted to fighters of any kind. Yet he'd seen his father's ranks before, tens of thousands of women and men who sought the end of imperial whips—and tens of thousands of raiders, too. The skirmishes Aeduan had encountered coming here only accounted for a fraction of those soldiers, which begged the question of where the rest of the forces had gone.

As Aeduan strode through a cluster of Nomatsi tents, two older women tending a central fire caught sight of him. Terror widened their eyes. They darted for children nearby, herding them frantically inside.

And Aeduan realized a step too late that he had forgotten to turn his Carawen cloak inside out. In his rush to get here, he had not considered how he might be received. After all, in the past no one had given him a second glance—and some had even recognized him as the Raider King's son. Now, though, white cloaks were the harbingers of death.

But it was too late to turn the fabric inside out, and now a Nomatsi huntswoman charged his way, a square shield on her back and bow drawn.

Aeduan's hands lifted. "I'm not here to hurt you—"

"On your knees!"

He lowered to his knees. The huntswoman reached him, and in quick, practiced movements, she slung a rope from her hip and bound him. Aeduan didn't resist. He couldn't, even if he wanted to. His magic was too frail—it took him three rib-stretching inhales to even sense a glimmer of this woman's blood-scent, so there could be no controlling it to escape.

There would also be no healing from any wounds she might try to inflict. Not merely because his magic failed him, but because the Painstone was fading fast. A subtle burn throbbed louder by the second, as if fire ants crawled beneath his skin. As if they gnawed and stung and singed ever closer to the surface.

"King Ragnor," he tried to say. "I am his son."

The woman ignored him, and now other Nomatsis crowded in. There was hate and fear in their eyes. Well deserved, and he knew there would be no convincing them that *he* was not like other monks.

How could he have been so foolish? Exhaustion and pain had leached him of common sense.

A second huntswoman appeared, carrying a canvas sack. She moved for Aeduan, clearly about to yank it over his head, when a voice rang out. "Wait!"

It was a woman's voice, thin and aged, but instantly, the

Nomatsis nearby fell silent. Then the speaker herself hobbled into view, and Aeduan understood why. Beneath a heavy fur, she wore faded Threadwitch black—making her the leader of this tribe.

Frostbite scars marked the folds of her inscrutable face. She was old, she was tired, and she was used to having her own way. When she came to a stop before Aeduan, she stared down with the same unabashed emptiness Iseult always wore.

"You are a monk." She spoke Marstoki, clearly assuming Aeduan would not understand her native tongue.

But he did, so he responded in Nomatsi, "I am. And I am also the Raider King's son."

No change in her expression. No reaction at all.

"Is it true?" She switched to Nomatsi. "Is Dirdra truly at the Monastery?"

Aeduan frowned. Then shook his head. "Dirdra?"

"A child from my tribe." At Aeduan's continued frown, she added, "She is an important child, stolen by raiders. And now we think to be stolen again by the monks."

Owl. She had to mean Owl.

Aeduan drew in a long breath, grappling for whatever Bloodwitchery remained inside him. It made his lungs burn and his skin scream, but he held tight. And he grasped and he fumbled and he reached until . . .

Summer heather and impossible choices. This was the woman he had been following. The only survivor from Owl's tribe. Finally, he had found her, safe beneath the banner of the Raider King.

Aeduan's lips parted to tell her he had saved Owl before, and that if she was at the Monastery, he would save her again, but before the words could rise, a wind burst through the tents. Strong enough to knock over people, strong enough to sputter the massive fire.

Then small cries sounded, and the Nomatsis scrambled for safety. Not the huntswomen, though, and not the Threadwitch. When the Fury stalked into their encampment, they only straightened their spines and glared.

"What have we here?" the Fury asked, moving past the fire. Snow swarmed around his head, kicked up around his feet. "I hear a monk has arrived in the camp, and it turns out to be the General's son. I must admit, Bloodwitch, I am half tempted to leave you here after all the effort I wasted trying to find you." He came to a stop, hands gliding open. "But unfortunately, time is of the essence with the coming assault."

"You cannot have him," the Threadwitch said in broken Arithuanian. There was iron in her posture. Ice in her gaze. "I am not finished with him."

"I'm afraid you very much are." The Fury flicked his wrist.

And wind slammed against the Threadwitch. It knocked her to the earth, snapping bones, and before the huntswomen could draw their bows, the Fury had smashed them aside as well. Then he strode to Aeduan, gripped his shoulder, and hoisted him to his feet.

Aeduan tried to turn to the Threadwitch, tried to tell her, "I do not know where Dirdra is, but I will find her again." Except wind roared in, thick with snow. It was too loud to shout over, too wild to see beyond.

Two heartbeats later, Aeduan and the Fury took flight.

*

405

Endless flames and inescapable laughter.

Over and over, Iseult died on this battlefield. Over and over, the blaze engulfed her and pounded her ordinary heart to dust. But even in death, there was no relief, for death only brought more hell-fire and cackling.

There was the Firewitch she had killed. There was the Firewitch she was going to kill. She was his, and he was hers until time ended and the Moon Mother released them all to eternity.

She tried to beg—always she tried to beg—yet all that ever came was a muffled, echoing roar. As if another woman screamed and that woman was buried deep beneath a mountain.

Over and over. No end, no beginning.

And no warning, just like before, when the new world seared into hers. Iseult wept at the first holes rending through the battlefield. Hot tears on a face that was charred to nothing.

One by one, the flames flickered away, and one by one, gray shadows and frozen winds swept around Iseult. Still she wept, a hiccupping, silent sob on a body crumpled to the snow.

She had no idea how long she stayed that way. All she knew was that eventually her tears subsided, replaced by chattering teeth and shaking bones.

The silver king had arrived.

One moment, Iseult was alone. The next, she sensed him—and on the third moment, she saw him too.

He was more solid tonight. Where Iseult had imagined his back hunched, she now realized he simply wore thick furs atop his shoulders. And where she'd thought him stiff, she now saw he was tensed. Defensive even, as if he worried Iseult might attack.

His crown glittered as brightly as before, and its icy shimmer shone over dark hair, olive skin. That was all Iseult could see, though. No eyes, no mouth, just a blur where his face ought to have been.

"Are you the Rook King?" She was surprised by how clear her voice rang out across the gray. More musical and crystalline than in real life. After so long without words, she almost cried again at that sound.

The King bowed his head.

A *yes*, Iseult had to assume. "But how are you here when you died centuries ago?"

Again, he bowed his head, silver crown glinting. But Iseult's question demanded more than that for an answer . . . Although, she supposed, with no mouth, there could also be no words. Whatever questions she flung at him, they would have to be answered by a simple yes or no.

All right. *Think, Iseult, think.* She didn't know how much time she had before the Firewitch returned. Ask the important questions first.

"Did you help me escape the Firewitch?"

A solemn nod.

"Can you help me escape him again?"

He opened his arms, shadows streaming like feathers beneath them. It meant nothing to Iseult . . . unless . . .

"You don't know?"

Nod.

"What about Evrane? Can you help me escape her?"

This time, he nodded once before bowing low, like a knight offering fealty to a queen. Then his arms lifted high above his head, and the landscape changed.

First came a stone wall behind the King. Then shelves beside the stones. Then books on the shelves and a rug beneath their feet. Item by item appeared, and a room assembled around Iseult and the Rook King.

"What is this place?" Iseult asked once the room was finished. Though they had left the snowscape, Iseult still trembled with cold.

The King said nothing. Gave no indication he'd heard her question. Instead he moved to the edge of the room, to where the two walls met in a narrow gap between the shelves. Here a plain wooden chair rested beneath an unlit iron sconce. He glanced back at Iseult, blurred face briefly marred by two dark eyes. So dark they were almost black.

His gaze stayed fixed on Iseult as he motioned to the wall. A flick of his hand, shadows trailing, then two more flicks, and a doorway appeared. Gone were the shelves, gone were the stones. Now, only a low arch descended into darkness.

The Rook King waved again. The stones and the shelves returned.

"What is it?" Iseult asked, even as she knew that he could not answer. She looked back to his face, but his eyes were gone once more. Everything was gone, actually—all of his features had blurred together like water dropped on drying ink.

Iseult stepped toward him. *Think, Iseult, think.* "Your eyes come and go. Do you have a mouth too? Can you make one form?"

His hands shot up, palms encased in shadow. A warning for her to stop walking.

Iseult stopped.

Then slowly, arms still outstretched, he shook his head. No

mouth. No answers. Yet as Iseult watched, a shadowy third arm slid out from his shoulder. It snaked across the space toward the nearest shelf, before stopping beside a plain leather tome.

One moment, the book was there. The next moment, it was not.

"The Carawen book," Iseult breathed. "The one Leopold took from the Archives. That's where this doorway is?"

The Rook King bowed, and the shadow arm dissolved to nothing.

"But I can't go in." She shrugged helplessly. "I can't wake up. Evrane keeps me asleep with some . . . some dark magic."

A pause. The Rook King's chest expanded, as if he inhaled. Then his eyes returned, winking into place beneath dark brows. He strode toward her. His left hand swung up, but this time, instead of shadows, there was only light. Bright shards like crystallized fog.

Iseult tried to rock back, but her feet were rooted. Her hands too. Even her head. All she could do was watch as he loped closer.

Then he reached her. His hand touched her face and cold stabbed through, stealing her breath. Claiming her mind. Frost and moonlight and a Dreaming drained dry.

GO.

The command filled her top to bottom, more urgent need than actual word. Go, go, go—now it is time to go.

When Iseult woke up, a sputtering second later, there was no magic to hold her down. No shadows to flap and crow. No Evrane either.

Iseult was free.

And it was time to go.

FORTY-SIX

※

The Sotar family house stood proudly on White Street, halfway up Queen's Hill and surrounded by a limestone fence with iron bars. Orange trees and jasmine grew thick within, and at the sight of Vivia and her guards, the two Sotar soldiers within immediately opened the gate.

The conversation Vivia was planning to have, however, was a private one, so she left her personal guards behind and marched to the front door alone. There a page boy also hastened to attend to the Queen-in-Waiting.

Except I am Queen-in-Waiting no longer, Vivia thought. She didn't know what she was. Princess was the person from before. Captain was too.

She supposed it didn't really make a difference.

Vizer Sotar met her in a bright sitting room with worn chairs and even more worn flooring and curtains—of which Vivia approved. The Sotar family might produce the most wealth in the nation, their lands insulated from the poison and flames of the war, but they also put more into their own people than anyone else.

"I have not yet heard back from my wife," Sotar said upon

410

entering the room. He strode into the sunlight, matching Vivia's stiff pose beside the garden window before offering a bow.

"That isn't why I'm here." Vivia turned to face him. She wore no mask now; she was neither bear nor Nihar. She was simply Vivia the little fox, and she hoped that would be enough. "Did you know that my crown has been reclaimed?"

Sotar frowned, as if he'd misheard. "Reclaimed?"

In quick, efficient tones, Vivia explained what she had just learned at the Sentries. No tears. No emotions. No madness. With each word, Sotar's mouth slackened more and more.

By the end, he had to place a hand on the windowsill to steady himself. "The bastards." His eyes met Vivia's. "Your Highness, I *swear* I did not know any of this. Quihar, Eltar, and Quintay worked without approval of the other vizers. They did the same with your mother, thirteen years ago."

Of course those vizers had done the same; Vivia didn't know why she was surprised. And suddenly, she had to wonder if her father had been behind that move too. If *he* had been the reason the High Council had declared Jana unfit to rule.

Either way, it did not change Vivia's current situation. If the High Council was not unanimous in its support of Vivia as Queen, then she was not allowed to lead. The power returned once more to the Regent.

Yet just because she had lost the loyalty of three vizers, fourteen officers, and her own father—that did not mean there weren't people who supported her. There were many, and she knew if she called them, they would come.

"You must go to the other vizers," Vivia said. "I trust your ability to gauge where their loyalties lie. Gather those who still support my rule and ask them to provide not only their guards, but anyone able and willing to fight. I will press no one into service, but we need *every* person we can find to protect the city."

"Hye." Sotar nodded firmly. "It will be done."

"I will assemble my own crew. I led many on the rivers and seas of Nubrevna, and I trained with many before that. There are a core group of soldiers I trust, and I will ask them to find others."

"We can meet here." Sotar opened his hands to the room.

But Vivia shook her head. "No. There might be nothing legally preventing us from meeting, but my father will notice if we assemble somewhere so prominent. And . . ." She sucked in a steeling breath. "And I do not trust him not to act against us again." *Against me.*

Sotar's face tightened. A compassionate wince that cut straight to Vivia's heart. He knew how much this hurt her; he also knew there was nothing to be done and no time to dwell. They had been betrayed, Vivia most of all, and now the only path forward was to minimize damage and minimize death.

Vivia tipped up her chin. Pulled back her shoulders. She was her mother's daughter. She could do this.

"We will meet at Pin's Keep, Vizer Sotar. At the twenty-second chimes. Bring the High Council members who still support me, and I will bring the soldiers. Together, we will craft a new strategy."

Now it was Sotar's turn to inhale deeply. To draw back his shoulders and lay a fist over his heart. Then he sank into a bow, deep and true. "I am yours to command, my Queen."

412

Chills trembled down Vivia's arms at those words. No one had ever called her "my Queen" before. No one had ever offered her such genuine respect and such real approval. She had wanted this from her mother, but her mother had been filled with too many demons of her own.

So Vivia had turned to her father. She had scraped and begged and apologized, and every now and then, he had dropped scraps for her to devour. But Serafin, she saw now, respected no one save himself, and his approval was only given so long as it did not affect his own self-image. He wanted all the glory, none of the blame.

"Thank you," Vivia told Sotar, and she meant it. "I will see you and the other vizers soon."

Then Vivia Nihar, rightful Queen of Nubrevna, Chosen of the Void Well, and Little Fox of Nubrevna, returned once more to the crowded night.

Safi lunged in front of Mathew. He wouldn't hurt her. Her body knew that, even if her mind had yet to fully fathom that he was here. She reached Vaness before the blade could connect, forcing Mathew to spin away. To swipe up the sword at the last second.

It still hit Vaness. A slice across her face.

The Empress did not move, though. Did not even flinch.

"What are you doing?" Mathew cried. His voice, that was *his* voice—how had Safi not noticed earlier? How had she not noticed the lightness of his eyes and lashes? *Because Mathew and Habim gave you what you expected to see.* And now they were cutting the purse.

Mathew twirled sideways, a graceful swordsman, and planted two paces away. Safi twirled with him, keeping her body between him and Vaness.

Still, the Empress did not react behind her. None of the Adders did either, or anyone in the crowds below. Everyone watched the fireworks cascading above. Blissfully oblivious.

It was then that Safi realized Vaness wasn't bleeding. Safi had *seen* the blade connect with flesh, but no blood streamed down her face.

Glamour. The Empress must be hidden beneath a glamour made to look just like her.

Weasels piss on Safi, she should have seen this coming. Uncle Eron had used the same plan in Veñaza City: glamour the party while an attack ensues. Which meant there was a Glamourwitch somewhere near, and likely the same one they'd used before.

If Safi had had her magic, she would have sensed this coming. For that matter, if she'd been paying *any thrice-damned attention*, she would have spotted the signs. This was why the false soldiers hadn't attacked her at the Well. This was why, when Safi had first interrogated Habim, she had sensed him lying.

Habim hadn't merely heard of a plot to overthrow the Empress and claim the throne, he had *created* it.

Habim, Mathew, and Uncle Eron. Three men Safi had known for nineteen years, but never truly known at all. And now her body was all that stood between the Empress of Marstok and death.

"Step away," Mathew hissed. He advanced a step, Adder blade raised in warning. "Why are you interfering, Safi?"

"Why are *you* attacking?"

414

"Because this is the plan. The one we have all worked for. You know that."

"No, I don't. Because you and Habim have told me nothing!"

"Then we will explain after." Mathew circled the Empress; Safi circled too. "Now is not the time for this—"

"Explain after what? After the Empress is dead? How will *that* bring peace to the Witchlands, Mathew?"

"By eliminating someone who wants war! She broke the Twenty Year Truce, Safi. She *caused* this war to resume."

For half a heartbeat, Safi believed him. After all, it was what everyone always said, including the Empress herself. Vaness had landed forces in Nubrevna, canceling the magic that bound her to the Twenty Year Truce—and therefore the magic that bound all the other nations and empires as well. So yes, she had caused it.

Yet as each of these thoughts speared through Safi's mind, she realized her chest hadn't buzzed with truth at Mathew's words, her magic hadn't twinkled and sung.

Which meant he was lying.

Safi's gut flipped. A great downward drop that yanked her lungs straight to her toes. She felt like vomiting. Or shrieking. Or even demanding that Mathew tell her it wasn't true—that *they* hadn't somehow coordinated the end of the Truce, the resuming of the war.

Somehow, though, Safi managed to do none of those things. Somehow, she managed to channel Iseult's stasis and sink more deeply into a defensive stance. "It was you who ended the Truce, wasn't it? I don't know how, but it wasn't the Empress who did it at all. It was *you*."

Mathew's eyes shuttered within his shroud. A pained wince

415

that cut straight to Safi's heart. *True, true, true.* "I told you," he said gruffly. "In Veñaza City, I *told* you there were big wheels in motion—"

He did not get to finish. At that moment, the glamour wavered. Ever so slightly, as if the entire world blinked, and for half a breath, the real world tore through.

It was so much worse than Safi had imagined. There was the Empress, standing in exactly the same place but with blood gushing down the right side of her body. Behind her, twelve Adders lay dead, every one of them impaled on their own swords. It was Lake Scarza, though, that made Safi gasp and rear back—and made everyone in the crowds do the same. A collective cry of horror that rippled outward while the world they saw was briefly replaced with another.

Military boats aflame and sinking. The wall of soldiers now a wall of corpses. Smoke and fire and explosions erupting in time to the fireworks.

Then the glamour snapped back into place. The ships floated once more. The soldiers and Adders stood sentry. And Vaness did not bleed.

It was too late, though. The mistake had been made. People knew they had been duped.

"Safi!" barked a new voice. Habim leaped onto the terrace, Firewitched pistol in one hand, sword in another. He moved into position beside Mathew. "Stand down, Safi. Do not ruin this. I realize you care about the Empress, but—"

Safi laughed. A surprising burst of sound that shut up Habim and made Mathew flinch. A fuzzy, burgeoning thing that could not have been more at odds with the crowds panicking below or the fireworks still detonating.

416

"Do not *ruin* it?" she repeated. "I already thought I had! All this time—ever since Veñaza City, I thought I had ruined your precious little plan. I thought I had made choices that were wholly my own, and sent Uncle's scheme spinning through the hell-gates.

"Now I see I was nothing more than your puppet. I suppose you knew about the engagement to Henrick all along. You *knew* I would end up in Marstok. And I suppose you thought I would help you here tonight, didn't you? Well, you're wrong. Because I won't."

"The Empress isn't what you think she is, Safi—" Habim began.

"That is rich coming from *you*, General."

"She is what her parents taught her to be, Safi. She will only lead Marstok into more war."

"*No.*" Safi hissed that word with all the conviction she could conjure. Then she spat it again, harder: "*No.* You're wrong. You don't even know her, Habim."

"We are running out of time," Mathew warned. He stood taller now, with Habim at his side. Two Heart-Threads doing what they believed was right—and what Safi might have believed was right too, if she hadn't seen behind Vaness's mask.

"Do not make me compel you," Mathew warned. "I did so with the Empress, and I will do it to you too."

"You already have!" Safi laughed again, a ridiculous, high-pitched sound that screeched inside her skull. Mathew must have commanded Vaness not to move, so she could stand there and take a blade through her belly. Now, he would do the same to her. "You bewitched me in the storage room earlier, Mathew. And you bewitched me a month ago in Veñaza City."

417

His betrayal had cut deep then. Now, it severed her heart entirely.

All her life, these men had been there. To scold and to teach and to tend her wounds from another sword lesson gone wrong. They were not evil; Safi knew that as surely as she knew that Vaness was not evil.

They were merely wolves in a world of rabbits, who had forgotten that rabbits were important too.

Safi had no doubt that Mathew, Habim, and Uncle Eron *believed* in their cause—she also had no doubt that it had begun as good and true when they'd first started scheming twenty years ago. But along the way, they had become exactly what they hated.

True.

And now it was up to Safi to remind them that rabbits mattered too.

True, true, true.

She slipped her hand into her pocket. "You say that Vaness is what her parents taught her. Well, I am too, Mathew and Habim. You both showed me right from wrong, and you gave me a conscience.

"I love you," she finished, "but I will not help you."

She yanked the spark-candle from her pocket and threw it at the men who'd raised her as a daughter. "Ignite," she whispered, already spinning away. Already slamming her body into Vaness and sprinting like the Void was at her heels.

Thank the gods, Vaness was small. And thank the gods, Mathew and Habim had trained her for exactly this moment, when she would have to lift a compelled Empress onto her shoulder and make a run for it.

As she'd expected, the spark-candle was no spark-candle at all. An explosion cracked behind her. Mathew roared her name—roared a command for her to stop. And she would have followed the command too, unable to resist such Wordwitched power.

But she was to the garden's edge and he was too late.

She and the Empress toppled over and plummeted toward the lake.

FORTY-SEVEN

✳

The Fury flew them down the mountainside, a sharp descent that made Aeduan's ears ache and lungs compress until they were lowering again. No light shone on the forest below, and no amount of squinting through the winds revealed any landscape beyond. All he knew was that they were nearer to the valley that separated Ragnor's mountain from the Monastery's.

And all he could assume was that the Fury was bringing him to his father.

They lowered into a clearing surrounded by evergreens. One pine spired above the rest, twice as tall, twice as wide. Snow sprayed wide, carried on the Fury's winds. It gathered in a circular bank around them.

Aeduan's knees almost gave way upon the landing—and his teeth gritted against the sudden surge of pain. His Painstone bore only flickers of magic. He had, at most, an hour before the curse regained its full control.

At most.

"Hurry," the Fury ordered, impatience thick in his voice as he left the clearing, and in his posture too. Eyes glittered within the trees, watching Aeduan and the Fury as they passed. Soldiers, Aeduan realized by the weapons in their hands and at their hips. They lurked in the darkness, some sitting, some standing, and all clearly waiting for a signal.

Aeduan had found his father's forces—and an attack must be imminent. There was only one target this way, though: the Monastery.

After passing rows upon rows of archers at work crafting arrows with the practiced speed of the battle-worn, and then passing Baedyeds on horseback, their steeds draped in camouflaging white cloth, the Fury led Aeduan to a round-roofed tent. Light shone from cracks in the hide walls and a hole at the top. Voices wafted out; smoke did not.

Which meant this was the command tent. Ready to be moved at a moment's notice. Ten women and men hovered nearby, varied in their skin and clothes, because Ragnor had chosen a personal guard from each faction he commanded. They scowled as the Fury passed, but none tried to interfere.

Then the Fury shoved into the tent, and immediately, all voices silenced. Aeduan followed a heartbeat later. Orange light washed over him, bright enough to steal his sight.

Gradually, four figures materialized, poised around a long table covered in maps. On the left was a woman with skin as dark as the night's sky and white hair piled atop her head. She held a pipe in one hand, extended mid-gesture before Aeduan entered. A jade ring glinted on her thumb.

Beside her stood a man with serpents tattooed across his brown face and the gold serpentine belt all Baedyeds wore. On the table's right was a Threadwitch, tall with wide-set green eyes that glittered in a brazier's glow.

At the head of the table stood Aeduan's father, the Raider King of the North.

Ragnor det Amalej.

He was not a tall man, shorter than Aeduan by half a head, but furs added breadth to his shoulders. Beneath them, he wore the same high-necked black silk he always wore. Silver streaked his hair, more since Aeduan had last seen him. There were more lines around his eyes too—eyes of pale hazel beneath thick lashes.

Age, height, and eye color. The only differences between father and son.

"Leave us," Ragnor said, and his three commanders instantly obeyed. The Baedyed and the Threadwitch ignored Aeduan as they strode by, but the white-haired woman paused her saunter just long enough to give him a thorough once-over.

And just long enough to murmur, "Blood on the snow." Though if she directed these words at him or at herself, he could not say. Then she was gone, and the Fury swiveled to follow.

"Wait," Ragnor ordered in Arithuanian.

The Fury obeyed, spindling toward the table. The tent was too small for him; he had to duck beneath struts, and once at the maps, he twitched and blinked and fidgeted like a leopard trapped within a cage.

He bore no sign of cleaving darkness, though. No shadows or cruelty or anything beyond blond height, blue eyes, and a mangled ear. Snow flickered around his head. He bowed.

"General." It was the wrong title, but Ragnor did not correct him.

"Find Corlant. Bring him to me."

The Fury straightened. "What about the attack on the Crypts? I have a new strategy for entering the door—"

"And this errand will not detract from it."

The Fury's face tightened. Snow swirled faster around his head. "But it will. I lose precious time with the Puppeteer. She fights me at every turn."

"Then you will have to fight harder."

Another tightening. Another swishing of snow. "And what if your soldiers reach the Monastery before I can break the Crypts?"

"Then so be it." Displeasure hardened Ragnor's tone. "Why do you argue with me, Bastien? Go to Esme, have her find Corlant. Then fetch the priest and return him here. These are your orders."

For a long moment, the air in the room stretched long and tight. A bow being drawn. Until at last, the Fury loosed it.

"I do not like Corlant," he spat, and at that declaration, frost erupted across the floor. It crackled over the rushes and climbed the walls. It crunched on Aeduan's boots. "This iteration is an abomination, and you know it. Kill him and be done with it."

"We need him. A babe is no use to our cause."

"Nor are raiders! They will turn on us—and on each other at the first gleam of gold."

"We have opened our arms to all, and that means all." Ragnor's voice had turned lethally low, unimpressed by the Fury's ice. "Now leave. This argument is over, and I will hear no more on the subject. You have your orders. Follow them." Without another word, Ragnor turned his back on the Fury and focused on the maps before him.

Black lines laced over the Fury's face. The snow around his head turned to shadows, and the frost at his feet turned to darkness.

Then his whole body tensed, head cocking sideways as if he heard something far away. Two breaths before his face relaxed, the shadows dissolved. He sighed audibly, a smile even towing at his mouth.

The Fury left in a slice of cold and wind.

Aeduan approached the table, approached the bloodied iron and sleeping ice that marked his father's blood. The frosted baby's breath and bone-deep loss. Even as weak as Aeduan was, his father's scent was too familiar to ever lose—and too strong to ever evade. It called to his magic, a brief spark of power muffled by the curse's pain.

His father had already sent for Corlant, so Aeduan would deal with the poison in his veins when the man who'd caused it arrived.

As Aeduan skirted the table, a map of the valley came into focus, recently drawn, with the river's current flow and the islands marked. Coins were spread across the eastern hillside, denoting troop placements. Ragnor offered no expression when Aeduan came to a stop beside him. He simply assessed his son.

There was a stillness about the Raider King. A thoughtful calm that suggested that he always knew the best course of action and that he had, in his quiet way, thought through all possibilities before landing on the best outcome for everyone. No words were spoken without a pause, no choices ever made without great deliberation. This moment was no different.

"Son," Ragnor said eventually, using Nomatsi.

"Father," Aeduan replied. Two years of saying that word, yet it still tasted so strange.

"It is good you arrived when you did," Ragnor said. "I did not want to begin the assault without you." He bent over the map.

"You plan to attack the Monastery?"

"We have already begun." His father pointed to silver coins placed atop the river. "Icewitches," he explained. "From the Herk-hül tribe in the north. As we speak, they freeze the river so our troops and cavalry may cross." He waved to bronze and copper coins. "The horn for the attack should sound at any moment."

"Many of your soldiers will die."

"Yes," his father agreed.

"The Monastery is built to withstand years of siege. Decades, if needed."

"Yes," his father repeated. "But what is it that I always tell you?"

Aeduan swallowed, fingers tapping at his sword pommel. "That the empires have grown lazy and unambitious."

"And the monks have fared no better. They have gone to war amongst themselves, never suspecting someone might be waiting for such an opportunity." With curt efficiency, he pulled a second vellum map from a stack beside the table. Two steps brought him to a clear expanse, where he unfurled it.

Despite dirty edges and faded ink, the layout of both the Monastery and its surrounding grounds was unmistakable. Large portions of the building were absent, though. The forge and mills were in the wrong place, and there were inconsistencies in the landscape. Trees where there should have been a stream, rock where there was now forest.

Sweat broke out on Aeduan's brow.

"This is the fortress as it was a thousand years ago," Ragnor said. "When it still belonged to kings. This cave here"—he tapped a shaded circle at the base of the cliff—"leads to a tunnel. It was once used for escape. Today, it has been left forgotten—and left open."

"How do you know this?" Aeduan asked. The curse was working quickly, constricting at his insides. Cording around his bones.

His father did not answer, and Aeduan had not expected him to. After all, this was not the first time Ragnor had said something that came from another age. Often, he referred to histories as if he had been there. Legends as if he had faced them.

Aeduan knew his father had been a soldier for some nobleman in these mountains. That he had met Aeduan's mother, and they had joined a passing Nomatsi tribe. Yet soldiers did not speak of long-dead kings, and tribesmen did not know of castles built a thousand years ago.

"What I want to know," Ragnor continued, "is what awaits at the end of this tunnel." He traced a line up the cliff, under the Monastery. It forked halfway up, one line aiming to a spot beyond the Monastery, the other tracing toward a second circle in a long, rectangular room marked *Chapel*.

It was not a chapel now. "That is the main library," Aeduan said. "There is no door in that corner there. Only wall."

"I expected as much, which is why I have a Stonewitch to handle it. Is the space guarded?"

"No."

"And the layout?"

Aeduan hesitated. The sweat on his forehead was now sliding down his jawline, and pain sent heat waves floating across his vision. "What," he began after a long inhale, "do you plan to do inside?"

"Justice. The monks have slaughtered our people, and I will not leave that unanswered."

"So you will slaughter them in return?"

"Do you care?"

Aeduan's pulse echoed in his eardrums. He thought of Lizl. "Not all monks know of these attacks. They do not all deserve to die."

"Perhaps not," Ragnor admitted. "But if we try to separate the good from the bad—these so-called 'insurgents' from the others—then too many of our own people will die in the process. Remember: it is always easier to kill ants in the mound than spread out upon the field."

He did not wait for Aeduan to respond to this before he pushed away from the table and returned to the first map. For the Raider King, once a decision had been made, the conversation was over. It was not cruelty that made him act so, but simple logic. The transaction was complete, what more was there to say?

In the past, Aeduan had liked it that way. Simple, clear. He was given orders. He followed them. Coin and the cause, coin and the cause.

Right now, though, as the tent began to dip and sway around him, he found his father's expectations rankling. Scratching atop skin made of flames.

"There will be two main groups," his father explained while Aeduan shuffled toward the first map. "Foot soldiers, cavalry, and archers will launch a frontal attack as soon as the Icewitches have finished their work. Then a small group— which you and I will join—will enter through the cave." He dropped a wooden coin atop the Monastery. "Once we are in the library, then the foot soldiers from the frontal assault will follow." He pushed the other coins toward the cliff where the cave awaited. "By dawn, the Monastery will be ours and the Cahr Awen will be eliminated."

The Cahr Awen eliminated.

Cahr Awen.

Eliminated.

And just like that, Aeduan understood why his father truly wanted to enter into the Monastery: he wanted Iseult. He wanted her gone.

It made no sense, though. "Why?" The question croaked out, surprising Ragnor. Aeduan did not withdraw it, though. "Why do you want the Cahr Awen?"

His father considered him, frowning. Never had Aeduan pressed him for deeper explanations, never had he required more answers. But now, Aeduan did not merely want them. He *needed* them.

His father seemed to understand, for the lines of his face abruptly smoothed, and he held Aeduan's gaze a beat longer than was comfortable.

"You . . . have her eyes." He turned away, lips compressing. Lines returning. "Perhaps, though, it is time I explain what your mother wanted—"

A horn, deep and distant, bellowed out. Three short blasts, followed by a fourth long drawl.

Ragnor's demeanor turned to stone once more. He was not a father, but a king. "Remove your cloak. A spare fur is in that trunk." He jerked his head toward a shadowy corner. "Take it and your blade. Then meet me at the tallest mountain pine. We ride out when the second horn sounds."

A flap of tent and a gust of wind marked the Raider King's exit.

Aeduan was alone.

Alone, yet no longer unsure. He had been wrong back in Tirla. Lady Fate's knife had not yet fallen. *Now*, it hovered above him. *Now*, the edges gleamed, ready to draw blood.

With pained care, he peeled off his old cloak. Blood-streaked and shredded, the white salamander fibers had carried him far. He had lived inside this cloth for three years, believing it would protect him. A wall against the flames.

But walls hadn't saved his mother. They hadn't saved the woman and babe dying on the forest floor. And this cloak had not saved him from a curse borne by Nomatsi arrows.

The cloak pooled around Aeduan's feet, and it was done. He turned his attention to his chest, to where the Painstone made a small bump beneath his blood-crusted uniform. No matter how hard he strained, how deeply he inhaled, he could not feel his heart pumping just below it. He could not sense any of his organs or any of his blood.

He was alive, but he was empty. The curse's work was complete.

There was nothing he could do about it either. He had

429

known this moment would come, and caring now seemed impossible. If he had truly wanted to stop the curse, then he should have made different choices, should have followed different paths.

He was a Bloodwitch no longer. He was a monk no longer.

He was man, just a man.

It would have to be enough.

Iseult stood half crouched beside her bed, breath held as she stared at her Threadstone. It blinked, insistent and inescapable.

Safi was in trouble. And judging by the stone's brightness, Safi was far away. *Very*.

Even if Iseult could escape this Monastery, she would be too late. Safi needed her now. Safi's life was in danger *now*.

Her gaze flicked to Leopold sleeping in his armchair. Was he the enemy or her salvation? Could he help her reach Safi or would he slow her down? Lips parted and head tipped to one side, he looked young. Just a boy, innocent and dreaming. Even in the dim moonlight, he shone bright as sunshine, his Threads spun from gold. His promises spun from charm. Iseult so desperately wanted to believe he was on her side, but even she was not so fanciful a fool.

Not after what she had seen tonight.

Evrane, the Abbot, the Firewitch forever cleaving, the shadows that flew on black wings. *No one* could be trusted but Safi.

And Safi was leagues upon leagues away, her life hanging on a knife's edge. Each second Iseult stood chained by indecision

430

was a second lost forever. Another moment in which Evrane might return, or the Abbot. Another moment in which the insurgents might finally break the fortress walls, or the danger that threatened Safi might overwhelm her forever.

Trust Leopold or leave him?

He was a prince; he had connections; he knew the full reach of Eron fon Hasstrel's plans. He was also Iseult's only way of reaching the Archives—at least without losing her way.

But Leopold might be working with the Abbot. Or with Evrane. Or both. He might lead her straight into their clutches, and there would be no way of knowing what he intended until it was too late. Iseult had no weapons to defend herself. No strategies for evasion.

She also had no time, no *time*. She had to decide now.

"Wake up." Her voice split the room, clear as in the Dreaming. Commanding and pure.

Leopold woke up. A jolt in his body and across his Threads. Then confusion as Iseult stalked over. Three long steps. Her shadow stretched over him. "You said you were here to serve me, Prince. Wholly and completely. So prove it. Lead me to the Archives."

His mouth bobbed open. "Iseult—"

"Now." With her command came fire. Full force, no reining it in. Small sparks ignited in the air. *Pop-pop-pop.* Bursts of light and sound.

Leopold recoiled, his Threads shocked clean, all the way to their stormy core.

"I will burn you," she repeated. "Unless you lead me to the Archives. Now."

He nodded, gliding to his feet with surprising grace.

Astonished he might be, but he did not seem unsettled—and he neither argued nor even questioned how Iseult had commanded flames. He had been unflinching in Tirla; he was unflinching now.

"If you want to see the Archives, then to the Archives we will go—but first you need shoes." He moved toward the wardrobe. With his good hand, he swung it open, revealing a pair of boots and his own beige wool cloak.

A second cloak waited too, fur-lined and white as the moon outside. Shining and ready. The uniform of a Carawen monk. All her life Iseult had wanted to wear one. All her life, she had wanted to be part of this shining order that accepted new members without prejudice.

Lies, lies, all of it lies. Aeduan had warned her in the Contested Lands, but she hadn't wanted to believe him. Now, though, she saw this cloak and wished it was *his*. Broken and bloodied. Safe and familiar. She wanted that over this fake piousness and false purity.

This was her only option, though, so Iseult slipped into it.

"Why . . . the Archives?" Leopold asked between grunts as he fought to pull on his own cloak with only one arm. "What's there?"

"A way out of the Monastery."

A burst of turquoise surprise. "How do you know?"

"Go." She pointed at the door.

"Iseult, I don't understand—"

"Let a woman have her secrets, Leopold. Go." She spoke that word with all the force of the Rook King behind her, and without another word of protest, Leopold nodded.

And Leopold went.

The hall outside Iseult's room was empty, the windows boarded and sconces unlit. The stones shook every twenty paces, and the impact of catapults thundered louder and louder. Leopold led her down stairs, across intersections, and past countless doorways.

Four times Iseult sensed Threads approaching, and four times, all it took was a whispered word of "Monks ahead." Then Leopold towed her into a small alcove or empty bedroom, where they would wait in silence—Iseult's heart would jitter against her throat and Leopold's Threads would turn muted gold with anxious caution. Then the Threads and the monks attached would move out of range, and Leopold would once more lead the way.

By the time they reached the Archives, the ground rumbled beneath their feet, shaking Iseult's knees and clattering her teeth. The walls under siege must wait just beyond the library's vast space, and like the halls from before, the windows were boarded and sconces dark. Huge sandbags had been placed in front of the windows too—only visible because a faint streak of light still crept in at the very top.

It revealed high ceilings and rows upon rows of bookcases. Little else, though. Nothing specific.

As if following her thoughts, Leopold hurried to a nearby sconce, fumbled a small candle from within the glass, and whispered, "Ignite."

A tiny flame awoke.

"Where do we go?" he asked, voice low. Face glittering behind the fire.

"The farthest corner," Iseult answered, and yet again, the

prince took the lead. No questions. Only obedience, his green Threads focused on escape.

Down aisles, around shelves, they moved ever closer to the corner.

They were halfway there when the door to the Archives heaved open. A scream of hinges, a groan of wood. Then Evrane's voice coasted across the space. "Iseult! Where are you?"

No, no, no. Iseult grabbed Leopold's cloak. "Run."

Unflinching, unquestioning, Leopold ran. The Firewitched flame guttered and flared, but it did not wink out. Their footsteps pounded on flagstones, an easy sound for Evrane to follow—and not just Evrane. There were other Threads too. Other monks, merciless and hunting.

And the Abbot, bleeding, blending, slithering this way. "We had an agreement!" he shouted. "You promised me an army, Prince!"

An army? Iseult had no idea what that meant, and she had no time to dwell on it either. They were almost to the farthest corner, almost to the Rook King's secret door.

Then they skittered past a final row of shelves, and the stone corner flickered before them. No archway, though, and no exit.

The floor quaked, and voices escalated from beyond the wall—voices of the insurgents. Iseult sensed Threads too, frantic and furious. The attack was *right there.*

Leopold rounded wide eyes on Iseult. "What next? I see no escape."

Iseult saw no escape either. And now Evrane was declaring from across the room, "It is not safe for you to roam the

Monastery, Iseult. You are not well. You must come back to me so I may heal you."

No, no, *no*. There had to be a way out of here. What had the Rook King shown her? *Think, Iseult, think.* She could follow the cool course of logic wherever it led, even without a pause or time to breathe.

A stone wall. Shelves. Sconces and a wooden chair. It looked exactly as it had in the Dreaming, except this was real. This was right before her.

Another *boom!* rattled through her knees. She and Leopold were surrounded on all sides.

"Iseult," Leopold murmured, and now white panic shivered across his Threads. "Please say you know what you are doing."

She ignored him. She ignored the approaching Threads and drumroll of feet, she ignored the Abbot bellowing about payments and bargains and tier tens betrayed. And she ignored the shockwaves raging through the foundation.

Iseult was stasis. Iseult was ice.

A stone wall. Shelves. Sconces and a wooden chair. Each item perfectly still. As calm as Iseult was amidst all this chaos.

But they should not be still. Everything else shook; they should be shaking with them.

Iseult dove forward, shoving past Leopold. She smacked her hands on stone. Cold, rough, real. But also frizzing with magic. This wall was a lie. This wall was not real. It was bewitched, like the sky-ferry, and all it needed was the right combination of taps.

Or three flicks of a feathery wrist.

Iseult knocked three frantic times, and in a whoosh of

charged air, the entire corner disappeared. Before her yawned the arched doorway.

This time, Leopold was the one to grab Iseult by the cloak. Awe, relief, and explosive surprise shaking across his Threads. The verdant focus was back too. He bolted into the darkness, and Iseult flew just behind. Once on the other side, though, she paused long enough to angle back.

Three flicks of her wrist, and the wall reassembled. Then she and Leopold ran.

Thank the Moon Mother he still held the candle, for otherwise, they would have scrambled in total darkness, missing where to duck and twist and crawl around stalagmites. The insurgent attacks thundered through the rock, but Iseult heard no pursuit and felt no Threads chasing from behind.

Eventually, they reached an opening in the tunnel, where a small cavern spanned upward and the path split in two. One route angled sharply up. The other angled sharply down.

Leopold slowed to a stop, panting. The flame's light sputtered, casting shadows on the dark walls.

Shadows that looked like wings. Shadows that sent chills trilling down Iseult's spine. Where had the Rook King led them? She forced herself to look only at the prince, though. At his Threads, burning and vibrant and true.

"How," he said between harsh gasps, "did you know about this?"

"You would not believe me if I told you." She fought for rough breaths of her own. Too much time in bed without a proper meal had stolen her energy. "We need to keep going."

436

He straightened, eyes thinning and Threads tanning with suspicion. "Why? Why did we need to leave, Iseult?"

Iseult didn't answer. There was nothing she could say that he would believe. *Evrane is possessed by darkness and imprisoning me in sleep. Oh, and the ghost of the Rook King showed me how to break free.* Iseult hardly believed it herself.

"It wasn't safe there," she answered. "And since Safi cannot come, there is no reason to stay. You have to trust me."

He chewed his lip, expression and Threads wary—though now sage consideration spooled around the tan. Then all at once, a sharp column of fern funneled through. He had come to a decision.

"I trust you," he murmured. "But which way do we go?" Swinging the candle away from her, he peered first at the ascending path, then the other.

"Down," Iseult said, and she plucked the candle from his grasp and took the lead. She had no idea if *down* was actually the right way to go, but it seemed the logical choice. The valley was below them, so surely aiming that way would eventually take them where she wanted to go.

Or maybe it would lead them straight into hell-fire. Iseult really had no idea. The Rook King had only shown her the way out of the Monastery, not the mountain.

The sounds of the insurgent battle faded the deeper they went, and Iseult took this as a good sign. The rock formations smoothed out too, and the air turned colder. A sharp bite that she hoped meant winds ahead.

Then she felt actual wind against her face, crisp and frozen, and gradually, light began to suffuse the stone. Iseult's gait quickened. Even drained as she was, she had done it. She had gotten away. Whatever Evrane had become, whatever the Abbot had wanted, and whatever the Rook King truly was—none of that mattered.

She had escaped, and now she and Leopold would find Owl. Then they would find Safi.

The tunnel's end gaped before them, gray and frozen. A Threadwitching night, the light bright enough to send spots skating across Iseult's vision as she approached.

She was running now, Leopold's footsteps pumping behind her. Marshy shoreline waited just ahead. So close.

They reached the exit. They hurried through.

And that was when Iseult sensed the Threads. That was when she saw the people fifty paces away. Twenty figures in heavy furs crouching amidst the frozen reeds, all bound by faint blue Threads. People with the same magic, working together. They gaped at Iseult and Leopold, their Threads shifting to a uniform glaring surprise.

Except for one man. The only man standing separate from the group, he had not noticed Iseult or Leopold skittering to a halt upon the shore. He held a large curved horn to his lips, and a fraction of a heartbeat later, the horn sounded. A clear, startling call. Three short blasts.

At the fourth long drawl, the twenty others shot to their feet, axes and blades thrust high. Then they roared, Threads blaring to violent steel, and charged right for Leopold and Iseult.

FORTY-EIGHT

✳

The Northman's blade punched through Esme's chest. Blood sprayed. He yanked back. She fell, gasping. Shocked. Silent.

Merik lunged forward, unsure why he felt the need to catch the Puppeteer before she hit the ground. His body acted without thought. He pulled her into his arms; her blood gushed across him.

"The Loom," she choked out. "Bring me closer to the Loom."

Merik did not bring her closer to the Loom. "You must stay still," he said, but she fought him then, clawing and coughing: *Loom, Loom, Loom.*

The Northman lunged, his arm reared back to stab her again.

"No!" Merik dropped Esme roughly to the ground. He snapped tall and raised his hands. "No hurt!"

The Northman frowned. Blood dripped from his knife, brighter than the tassels. "Help," he said, clearly confused. "Help. Go." He waved to the trees. "Help."

On the grass, Esme began to weep. Blood—there was so much blood. "Loom," she whispered again, clutching at Merik's leg. "Bring me to my Loom."

Still, Merik did not bring her to the Loom. He knew, viscerally and logically, that this was his chance to flee. That this was a gift from Noden not to be tossed away. Yet for some reason, his feet felt rooted to the spot. His eyes rooted on a dying girl beside him.

Blood, blood. There was so much blood, and Merik felt no triumph at the sight of it. No relief at Esme's face, taut with pain, or at her chest shaking while she tried to breathe.

He felt only pity. There might still be a person inside all that hate. After all, she did not bleed so differently than he did.

Nubrevna. His homeland flickered through the back of his mind, and with it came the memory of crowded streets and soaring bridges where ships sailed home. It was the one place he had always believed in, the one thing that had always made sense.

Letting the Puppeteer destroy it, letting the Raider King or the Fury destroy it—that did not make sense.

Esme might bleed as he did, but so did everyone else around them. All these Cleaved, all these people who had once had lives and families and loved ones of their own. She had destroyed them, just as she would destroy Nubrevna too.

Unless Merik did something to stop it. He would not kill her. Esme had cleaved Kullen; she might end up being the only way to *un*-cleave him too. Merik also had no idea what might happen to her Loom or to her Cleaved if she died. What if they died with her?

That was a risk he couldn't take. And with that thought, he finally moved. With gentle hands, he carried Esme to the

440

Well, to her Loom. She gasped, she convulsed, and her blood sank deeper into the grass. He could do nothing to heal her, but maybe her Cleaved could.

Merik turned to the Northman. "Go," he said. "Now we *go*." For of course, if Esme's Cleaved could save her, they could also hunt down Merik.

The Northman did not argue. He let Merik wrench him around and haul him toward the main path, and when Merik pushed into a run, he also kicked up his knees. Their feet thundered down the hill, over variegated shadows cast by a bright, oblivious moon in a bright, oblivious sky. Trunks streaked in the corners of Merik's vision. Cleaved, too, immobile without their Puppeteer to guide them.

Merik didn't know where he was going—away, away. That was the extent of his plan. Away from the Well and Esme, and once his magic felt strong enough, away from Poznin entirely.

They reached the bottom of the hill. Moonlight beamed over them and streets snaked off in different directions. Merik slowed to a stop, already panting. He leaned on his knees while the Northman did the same, and swung his gaze in each direction.

Right would lead to Esme's tower. Left to the river. Straight to the Windswept Plains.

The plains, his magic murmured, and he felt himself grin. On the plains, there were other people. And on the plains, there was *wind*. No, he was not yet strong enough to fly, but soon. Beneath these gulps of air, the power sparked hotter.

He straightened, hand rising to point . . .

His eyes caught movement in the trees. Figures were shambling this way. The Cleaved were shambling this way.

Shit, shit, *shit*. Esme was working faster than Merik had anticipated. Too late now to stop her, though, and what was it Vivia always used to say? *No regrets, keep moving.*

Merik grabbed the Northman's shoulder, and he got moving. *"Run."* As one, they launched into a sprint.

The Cleaved didn't like this, and their half-dead legs picked up speed. They tumbled from the forest, and then from buildings too. Body after body, filling the streets. Gathering into a stampede that swarmed at Merik and the Northman from all angles.

They pushed themselves faster.

Down streets and over walls, around fallen statues and through tree-choked squares, Merik and the Northman drove their legs. They leaped, they slid, they barreled around anything that blocked their way.

Until Merik and the Northman reeled onto a wide avenue, free of trees. Swallowed by grass. The ground shook beneath them. The grass stalks rattled and swayed.

And now a hundred more Cleaved chased from ahead. There was no exit. They were cut off from all sides.

The Northman's pace faltered, but Merik gripped his arm and pulled him on. They could not stop. They could not slow.

Merik had a hundred paces to find an escape—or else he had a hundred paces for his magic to return. It unfurled more with each razoring breath. Ninety paces. Eighty. Sixty paces, and Merik could see black eyes. Fifty, and the shadows that lined Cleaved skin came into focus—

There. A toppled building on the right. It hid an alleyway clotted by saplings. The trees would slow Merik and the Northman, but they would slow the Cleaved too.

He hauled the Northman into the slip of space between ruins. Leaves and branches slapped against them. They zigged and zagged and did not slow. Not when the earth shook so hard it knocked rubble loose from buildings. Nor when flesh slapped against flesh and saplings crunched behind.

They reached the alley's end. A new road, a new expanse—and more Cleaved. But Merik knew this road. He had walked here only last night, and straight ahead would lead to a pool filled with corpses.

A pool that had sucked him in. A pool that might suck in others too.

If he and the Northman could get into that water and reach the stairwell at the back, then maybe the Cleaved would pour in behind them. Even if the water did not kill them, it would at least slow them. It would at least give Merik the time he needed to reclaim his breath.

And reclaim his magic.

Then he saw it. The cattails and the murky waters and the floating bodies, so calm beneath the night sky. He plowed directly for it, praying the Northman would not argue or slow.

More Cleaved streamed along the corners of his vision. He dared not turn his head to look at them. If this pool did not save him, then he was out of options.

"*Swim!*" Merik roared at the Northman, pointing ahead. Then he reached the cattails. His feet squelched in mud.

Instantly, the pool's power rushed against him. *Come,* it sang. *Come in and find release.* This time, he was ready for it, though. This time, Merik knew to fight.

He splashed onward until the water reached his knees. His thighs. Then he launched into a dive, the Northman just behind.

His head crashed beneath the surface.

The power of the pool grew tenfold. A chorus that vibrated in his brain, crushing and creeping into every crevice, every memory.

Come, come, and find release. There were the water-bridges and the white-sailed ships. *Come, my son, and sleep.* There was Kullen chasing crabs beside the shore. *Come, come, the ice will hold you.* And there was Merik's mother, tired and sad, while she read to him about Queen Crab and her treasures.

Merik swam deeper. His legs propelled him, his arms pulled.

Come, come, and face the end.

A faint blue light glowed from a stone wall at the bottom of the pool. Corpses, some pale and fresh and floating, others rotten and sinking, blocked it. They had tried to reach that light; they had failed.

Merik would not fail.

A body slammed into him. The last of Merik's breath burst from his lungs in great, blinding bubbles. And suddenly he realized his chest was on fire. His skull. His eyeballs, his very mind.

He was drowning.

Arms fished around him, tugging him toward the surface, and he did not resist. Seconds later, he and the Northman broke the surface. But there was no respite here. The water churned and splashed as Cleaved poured into the pool, ten at a time, row after row, tumbling, toppling, grabbing.

444

Merik's plan had worked too well.

He led the way, swimming for the stairwell. Corpses bumped and sloshed against them, but he kept going—and the Northman kept going just behind. Until at last, they reached the first steps.

Merik hauled himself up.

The step crumbled beneath him, dropping him back into the water. Knocking him against a dead man and tangling him in the corpse's long black hair.

The Northman tried the next step, but it too collapsed beneath his weight. And now the pool was filling at a rate that would soon leave Merik and the Northman cornered. Trapped. They could not tread water forever, and the Cleaved could not keep rushing in. Eventually, the pond would fill and then Cleaved who still lived would simply walk across the bodies.

The water seethed around Merik. Corpses bumped against him, and the Northman splashed and sprayed, trying over and over to reach higher stairs.

This was it—this was the best Merik was going to get for time. If he couldn't make his magic work now, if he couldn't coax it back to life, then this was the end. Not just for him, but for the Northman who had come to save him.

And for Nubrevna, exposed and unready for the Raider King's attack.

Merik wasn't ready for that end. He closed his eyes.

Come, the water sang around him. *Come and find release.* There was power in that water. Where it came from or what it meant, he couldn't guess. But the magic was there all the same.

Listen, he told the spark in his lungs. *Listen and see.*

All his life, Merik had been a weak witch. Barely able to earn his Witchmark as a child, he had disappointed his father. Disappointed himself. Only when his temper flared did he ever seem to have any power.

The Nihar rage, his family called it.

But in anger there could be no listening. In rage, there could be no sight. And in fury, there could be no understanding.

Esme had been right—just as Cam had been right. Merik saw what he wanted to see. He told himself he made all choices, good and bad, to help Nubrevna as if this somehow justified his willful blindness. As if this somehow vindicated his dependence on blood-boiling rage.

And Safiya fon Hasstrel had been right too: Merik loved to feel needed. It did give him purpose—and it also gave him *excuses*.

For almost two days he had lived without his magic inside him. For almost two days he had moved where someone else willed, and he had seen with eyes unclouded by wrath. Words had freed him from Esme's collar, not anger. And it was not anger—or even magic—that would free him from this pool filled with corpses.

Listen and see. Listen and see. The spark in his chest thrummed louder. The waters sang and pulled. The power at work here wanted him to reach that blue light. It wanted him to travel through. It wanted him to embrace the full magic that waited on the other side.

Merik's eyes snapped wide. Water rocked and crashed against his face. A woman's dead eyes stared into his. There were too many bodies now, splashing and piling and raising the water with each second.

He inhaled as deeply as he could, a desperate gasp with no grace or ease, but it was enough.

Wind rushed in.

A second breath, a second gale. Three breaths, four, ten—the winds writhed in stronger, wilder. Water spun and corpses spun too. Until at last, enough air cycloned around Merik for him to finally make his move.

He flung up his hands. Air rocketed beneath him, beneath the Northman. They shot up from the waves.

Merik flung his hands down.

Water and bodies and Cleaved ripped backward, away from Merik and the Northman. Away from the blue light still glowing below.

Power, power, power.

This was what magic was meant to feel like—this was what it had always wanted to be. No Nihar rage to fuel it. No dark magic from the Fury to taint it. If only Merik had listened sooner. If only he had bothered to see.

"Down!" Merik warned. Then he punched his winds toward the blue light below, and he and the Northman flew.

In seconds, they landed before the blue light and the stone wall that surrounded it. Behind them and above, held back by a wall of winds, the water waited. The Cleaved struggled and clashed.

"Go," Merik told the Northman, pointing at a doorway made of blue light.

But the Northman took no steps forward, and Merik supposed he could not blame him. So he took the enormous

447

man's hand in his own. Then he towed him toward the light.

"We go," he said, attempting a smile. "We go."

Together, they stepped through the doorway.

Together, they entered the mountain that everyone wanted to claim.

FORTY-NINE

※

*S*tupid as it might seem, Safi always told Iseult, *stupid is also something they never see coming.* Except this time, there was no Iseult to save Safi's hide. To complete what she'd initiated. It was Safi and only Safi flying straight down toward Lake Scarza with Vaness right beside her.

The lake swallowed them. Light and heat tore against them—boiling in its ferocity, curls of flame to claw beneath the waves—and with no glamour to hide the sinking naval ship right before them.

Beside Safi, Vaness jolted to life. Mathew's control had ended, and the Glamourwitch's magic too, so there was no missing the blood pluming around her.

Safi frog-legged to her and then propelled them both toward the surface. Vaness tried to swim, to help Safi rise, but her legs tangled in their waterlogged gowns, which then tangled Safi too.

Safi pushed on, though, and she pushed through. Even as heat and light off sinking boats made it impossible to see where they were going. Even as her lungs ached from a breath held too long and the world heaved from the pressure gathering in her ears.

At last, Safi's head broke the surface, and Vaness burst up beside her. But Safi had no idea where to go now, or what to do. They were caught between ships aflame and an island overrun by the enemy.

Vaness took charge. Despite the jagged wound across her face, she raised a single, weak arm upward.

A rope of iron shot off her wrist, looping around Vaness's waist, around Safi's. Then it yanked them toward shore.

"*Hold on!*" Vaness screamed.

Safi held on. The rope hauled them through smoke and bursts of fire, past ships and corpses, over waves building higher with each new explosion upon the lake. Vaness knew where to go, though, and eventually, both women were pulled beneath the surface once more.

Water and darkness rushed over Safi. The iron rope cut into her hips, her belly. She couldn't see, couldn't gauge where they traveled. All she knew was that it was *down* and that her lungs howled.

Then her trajectory changed. No more flying forward. She was abruptly jerked *up*, and somehow, the water charged even harder against her. She couldn't think. She couldn't move. Her fingers brushed rough metal, and she prayed it wasn't a sinking ship.

Safi erupted from the water. Carried by iron, carried by magic, she hurled from the darkness and rammed onto a narrow lip of stone. Gasping, coughing, squinting.

"Sewer," Vaness said eventually, between sputtering breaths of her own.

Well, that explained the smell. It also explained the rounded shape of the tunnel overhead, and the constant current of water rushing past. As Safi's eyes adjusted, she spotted a single lantern flickering nearby, a single ladder moving into a new tunnel above.

It was the blood that caught Safi's attention, though. It dribbled in spurts from the top of Vaness's forehead down to the edge of her right jaw. A deep wound had rendered her right eye completely useless. The Empress clutched it, still breathing hard.

The stone lip around her was already stained red.

"We need to wrap that." Safi scooted toward her, reaching for her sleeve so she could tear it. Vaness moved faster, though.

"Wait," she panted. Then her iron rope transformed, slithering inward before expanding and sharpening and splitting in two. In seconds, the iron became scissors that Vaness used to snip off a piece of red skirt.

Safi gathered up the crepe. It wasn't clean. Not after the dunk in sewage. Nor was Vaness's wound. But it was the best they could do, given the circumstances.

"I'm sorry," Safi said while she wrapped the fabric around the Empress's head. Over and over, tighter and tighter. "I'm so, so sorry I couldn't stop the attack."

"I watched it, you know. I watched the entire thing unfold, but I could do nothing."

"Because you were Wordwitched." Shamed fire burned in Safi's shoulders. In her belly. She should have seen this coming. *Why* hadn't she seen this coming?

"You know the man who did this to me." A statement, not a question.

And Safi couldn't lie. "Yes. I know him, and General

Fashayit too. They raised me, and I'm *so* sorry I didn't tell you. You trusted me, and I failed you." She tied off the red crepe. Then with all the truth she could summon, straight from the heart of her magic, she said: "I *swear* to you, Your Majesty, that I did not know what they had planned. I thought Habim had come to the city to take me home. Nothing more. Had I known they planned to ... to ..."

She trailed off. She couldn't say the word "assassinate." She couldn't believe the people she'd loved—her *Thread-family*— were capable of such a thing.

Vaness watched Safi. Her left eye blinked and blinked. Her chest trembled. No expression, though. No hint as to what she might be feeling. Until: "I believe you." She looked away. "I heard what you told the men. And ... Well, I suppose people do not jump off cliffs for just anyone."

"No," Safi replied, a taut chuckle beneath that word. "They don't. *I* don't."

As Safi uttered these words, Vaness changed. Between one moment and the next, the Empress went from injured and weak to poised and unharmed.

"Shit," Safi whispered. "You're glamoured again."

No change of expression hit the magicked Vaness, but Safi heard her gasp. She heard her gown rustle too, as she frantically examined herself.

All Safi saw, though, was a cool, collected Empress staring straight ahead. And if *this* glamour had returned, then the others must have too. Which would make this escape much, much harder.

"Hell-Bards," Safi blurted at the same moment Vaness said, "The Cartorrans."

452

"They can see through this," Safi went on, and at the glamoured Vaness's nod, she asked, "Where are they now?"

"Only a level above." The false Vaness pushed gracefully to her feet.

Then the false Vaness tumbled into the wall, and Safi realized she was barely clinging to consciousness. Safi slid an arm behind the stone-faced Empress. "Hold on to me," she said. Then together, they walked to the ladder. Together, they ascended—Vaness first, in case she lost her strength.

It felt like a lifetime climbing those rungs. And the higher they moved, the more sounds drifted down from above. A rhythmic *boom!* that could have been fireworks, or could have been explosions. And a roar that sounded like the water in the sewer had felt. Like wind on a storm-crossed day.

It wasn't until they reached the small hatch that would eject them into the palace that Safi realized what the sound was.

Fire.

Everything from the escape in Veñaza City was being used again. Glamours and distractions, soldiers with shifted loyalties, and fire—*lots* of fire.

Heat pressed against them through the door. "We should turn back," Safi called, but either Vaness did not hear, or Vaness did not care. With her magic, she melted apart the door.

And the heat and roar doubled.

Vaness crafted a shield—a tactic she had successfully employed twice with Safi. Of course, both times there had been somewhere for the smoke to go. Now, there was nowhere except around the iron barrier as Vaness and Safi climbed into and then across a room thick with flames.

Or maybe they were in a hallway. Or maybe it was a closet. Safi had no idea what was around them. Her eyes streamed. Her throat and lungs spasmed, and she only kept going because Vaness did. When they reached a stairwell not consumed by flames, though, Vaness sagged into Safi.

No warning, since Safi's magic was still half missing and she only saw a perfectly poised Empress. Again, she helped the woman ascend, this time up low steps clogged by heat and smoke.

They reached the next level, and a familiar sandstone hall met Safi's eyes. However, now it burned, and now, there was no one alive.

Vaness came to the same conclusion. She shook her head, expressionless, and shouted, "They cannot have survived this!" She tugged at Safi to continue rising.

But Safi didn't move. In Veñaza City, Habim had started the fires in the walls. *A Firewitch's flames were magic.*

"Release their restraints!" she called. "They could still be alive—*please!*"

A nod. A choking cough from a mouth that did not move. Then Vaness lifted an arm. Her wrist tipped upward, and together, she and Safi waited. Safi squinted into the flames while the glamoured Vaness appeared to do nothing at all.

Two charred breaths later, shadows appeared. Black and skeletal and moving this way.

Safi whooped. She couldn't help it. The Hell-Bards were alive. Habim hadn't killed them. The flames hadn't ended them.

Zander stumbled from the fire first. His golden noose glowed. His face was red with heat. Then Lev raced out behind, and finally Caden staggered out last.

"Fancy meeting you here," Lev said between coughs, but Safi just grabbed her arm and roared, "*Come on!*"

Without being asked, Zander scooped up Vaness and tossed her over his shoulder—which meant Vaness's injury must be grim indeed. Safi couldn't see it, though. Not so long as the glamour ruled and her magic failed.

Together, Safi, Vaness, and the Hell-Bards ran. Up stairs that boomed beneath their feet in time to explosions that definitely weren't fireworks.

"Wait!" Safi screeched as they charged past a hallway. She recognized it. It led to the storage room filled with fireworks, and at the end, there was access to the lake.

"Your Majesty." She pushed in close to the Empress draped over Zander's massive shoulder. But Caden shook his head. "She's out."

"I can wake her," inserted Lev. "It won't be pretty, though." Safi nodded. "Do it."

"All right, Domna, but later when she wants to kill me, you tell her it was *your* idea." Without preamble, Lev stabbed her finger into Vaness's injured eye.

And the Empress awoke shrieking.

It was horrible to see, horrible to hear—an expressionless face emitting a sound of absolute, bone-rattling agony. But Safi needed Vaness awake, and pain was a better alternative to death.

"A boat!" Safi flung her voice over the screams, over the flames. "Is there a boat beyond this storage room?"

"*YES!*" Vaness screamed. Then Lev released her, and the Empress toppled limp against Zander's shoulder.

Hollering for the Hell-Bards to follow, Safi shot out of the stairs and into the hall. Caden stayed close at her side, while Zander followed with the Empress, and finally Lev took up the rear. They crossed the hall and no one stopped them. No soldiers or fire appeared.

They crossed the storage room, and still no one interfered. They crept past crates of spark-candles—except they weren't spark-candles at all. Which meant as soon as the fire chasing behind them reached this room . . .

"Faster!" she urged, and the Hell-Bards obeyed.

They reached the doorway at the end. As she'd seen earlier, it led to a cavernous boathouse that opened onto the lake. Naval vessels appeared to float harmlessly, but Safi knew, even if her magic did not, that it was all a lie. The battle echoes spoke otherwise.

And there, at the end of the boathouse, was a ship. Small, flat-bottomed, clearly meant for transferring goods off larger vessels, it was the only option, so without discussion, everyone aimed for it. Caden and Zander maneuvered Vaness in, then Safi followed while Lev untied the boat.

"Oars," Zander said. "These aren't going to get us far."

"Not with what's out there." Caden stared at the lake, face screwed with concentration. Whatever he saw, Safi couldn't.

"Guide me." A ragged voice listed up from the Empress. Safi hadn't realized she was awake again, and when she looked down, she only saw closed eyes and peaceful sleep.

But then Vaness tried to rise—and Zander helped her into a weak, slumping seat that even the glamour could not hide. "Tell me where to go," she repeated, "and I . . ." A shaking breath. "I will send the boat where you command." As if to prove that she could, she knocked her wrist sideways and the boat slithered away from the dock.

"You're not well," Safi protested, but at the same moment, Caden declared, "Forward." Then his eyes met Safi's, holding hers in that grim, unrelenting way he had. "It's our only chance, Safi."

She knew he was right. Smoke now plumed from the storage area. Any moment, the flames would hit. The explosion would tear the flesh from their bones and boil it straight to the Void.

So without another word of protest, Safi reached down, gripped Vaness's other hand in hers, and said, "Forward."

FIFTY

Aeduan went to the clearing with the tallest mountain pine. There his father waited, a group of women and men clustered to him, and twelve horses stamping and snuffing just beyond.

Ragnor met Aeduan's eyes amidst the throng. He nodded, and Aeduan thought he almost caught a smile on the edge of his tired lips. Approval, maybe. Or relief.

Two years ago that would have given Aeduan pause. Even two weeks ago, it would have stopped him in his tracks and warmed the blood in his veins.

Now, Aeduan felt no blood in his veins. Now, he smelled nothing of his father—no baby's breath or bone-deep loss.

All Aeduan felt was a faint constriction in his lungs. Regret, he supposed, that it had come to this. After all, his father was not a bad man; his father's cause might even be just.

But one need not be evil to become it.

His stride did not slow as he passed his father. Already, his gaze skipped ahead to the twelve steeds intended for Ragnor's small group. The black on the end—ears back, her hooves light upon the snow—she had energy to do what Aeduan needed done.

"Aeduan?" his father called.

Aeduan ignored him. He went to the mare, young and impatient. He had not taken the fur from the chest; his wounds still bled, and he did not want the added layers to confine him. He *had* taken his sword, and he now adjusted it to avoid hitting the mare as he mounted.

"Aeduan?" his father repeated, distress in his tone now. Distress on his face when Aeduan finally looked at him.

"I am sorry," Aeduan said, and he meant it. Then he kicked the horse into a gallop. He and the mare shot off into the trees.

Voices chased behind. Cries of warning, of surprise, of danger if Aeduan did not slow. But Aeduan did not slow, and in seconds, the people were gone.

His father was gone. All he heard was the thunder of the mare's hooves, the spray of snow and soil as she galloped faster, faster. This speed in terrain unknown—the horse might throw a shoe or twist a leg, but he could not slow. Lady Fate's knife was coming.

Around trees and ever farther down the hill, Aeduan and the mare moved. Past more soldiers, past snowdrifts and tents. All he smelled was the cold of the night and the sweet musk of a horse on the move. Until at last, they reached the end of the descent and the valley opened before them.

The river, a frozen expanse of white, shone beneath a full moon. And far, far on the other end, Aeduan could just make out the Monastery, a dark bird roosting upon the cliff.

Below it, dead ahead, were figures. His father's Icewitches, he presumed. He dug his heels into the mare's ribs, leaned forward, and she pushed into a gait that practically sang. She ran with joy, with energy in her muscles and speed in her heart. No concept of what lay ahead, only the purity of this moment with a flat path and no obstacles before her.

Something flickered at the top of his vision. A bat-shaped shadow crossing the moon, vast and quick. When Aeduan glanced up, though, he saw nothing.

It wasn't until they were a hundred paces onto the frozen river that he realized they were no longer alone. It was the trebuchets that told him. The hiss and burn of fire propelled into the sky. It launched across the river from the Monastery, and when Aeduan turned his gaze to watch it land, he caught sight of the raiders.

None of their blood-scents swept against him, no noises hit his ears over the mare's four-beat, snow-churning gallop.

This was his father's distraction. Thousands of raiders flooding from the trees south of him.

Not fast enough—Aeduan and the mare were *not fast enough*. He pushed her harder, and she obeyed. Sweat lathered on her, despite the cold. She was obedient, though, and she was ready.

She galloped on.

More fires erupted from the trebuchets. They crashed to the ground south of Aeduan, balls of orange light that drew his eyes, even as he tried to focus forward. There were figures ahead—two people who were not part of the Icewitches. They sped toward Aeduan on foot.

Later, he would wonder how he knew it was her. Later, he would question if maybe his magic had been there all along and the silence of her blood had called to him. But in that moment, all he knew was that it was Iseult running toward him. It was Iseult fleeing the Icewitches.

And he had to reach her first.

Fire shot from the Monastery and roared toward Aeduan. He veered the mare left. Heat and black light screamed past.

It hit the ice.

This time, though, the dark flames caught and spread and ate. White, alchemical hearts beamed bright. Wider and wider it grew in a way that only seafire could.

The mare panicked.

Two more trebuchets launched, both aimed at Aeduan. As if the Monastery had decided that he, the lone rider, was the greatest threat in the valley. Furious flames that wind could not snuff, and that water only coaxed higher. Aeduan smelled raiders roasting alive behind him. He felt the heat on the ice expanding.

A wall of fire to hold him in, and no salamander cloak to protect him.

Aeduan yanked the mare left, then right before two volcanic *booms!* shuddered through the ice. The seafire crashed down. Heat stormed against him—and now the mare truly panicked. She reared. No more joy, no more energy. Only terror as the black flames crushed in. And Aeduan saw no choice but to punch his heels into her ribs and drive her even faster.

He could see Iseult now. A Carawen cloak flapped around her, and the man beside her wore beige. But Aeduan had no attention to spare for that person. All he saw was the Threadwitch, a beacon of white amidst the eternal flames.

He should never have abandoned her.

He should never have let her go.

Another trebuchet fired. Aeduan estimated its trajectory. He swerved the mare with time to spare.

But arrows loosed a half second behind the seafire. A hundred longbows aimed by a hundred monks. They did not see one of their own riding toward them; they saw a raider and they aimed to kill.

Aeduan could evade the seafire, but he could not evade those arrows. They rained down, blacking out the moon.

Then they hit their mark. Aeduan. The mare.

Countless wounds to rip them wide. To stop them where they ran.

The mare screamed, a sound that broke Aeduan's heart even as the arrows shredded that organ in two. Then the pain he knew so well filled him. The pain he had felt a thousand times over the course of his life, but that tonight, he could no longer heal from.

The mare went down.

Aeduan went down with her.

He tried to pull free. He dragged and heaved and clawed at the ice winged in flame, but the mare pinned him down. She screamed, a shrill sound that no animal should make. That Aeduan wished he could end, wished he had never caused in the first place. She tried to rise, but arrows covered every inch of her. Her belly, her back, her eyes.

And there were almost as many in Aeduan. He could not see, he could not breathe. He was trapped beneath the mare while smoke choked into his throat and his life bled out upon the ice.

It wasn't enough, he thought before he died. *Being a man wasn't enough.*

Iseult saw him die.

She watched the arrows hit him and the flames consume. She watched his black horse fall, and she watched him fall with it.

And she knew in that moment that logic didn't matter. Nor escaping the raiders, nor even preserving her own life. What mattered was the Bloodwitch named Aeduan.

This would not be his end. Not for the man with no Threads, the man who had held her gaze without fear, who had saved her life from Cleaved and raiders, from rivers and soldiers.

From the day she had stabbed Aeduan in the heart, that heart had become hers—and she would not let this be his end.

Leopold shouted for Iseult to stop, but he could have been a million leagues away for all she heard. For all she cared. Instead, she pushed her limbs faster. They had cut away from the raiders, and though the raiders gave chase, the trebuchets distracted and blocked.

Iseult's lungs burned. Her legs tired beneath her, and smoke tidaled in. Such trivialities she could ignore, for who needed breath, when one had power? Who needed sight, when one had Threads? She turned her mind inward and whispered, *Come. Now is your time.*

Instantly, the Firewitch awoke. Elated and alert, he slithered to the front of her mind—and then he laughed with glee at the battlefield spanning before him.

Death and flames and smoke for the claiming.

Yes, Iseult told him. *You will take that fire and you will swallow it. It is yours. It is mine.*

She flung up her arms and screamed, "COME." Then Iseult dropped from a sprint to a jog. From a jog to a walk.

She entered the fire.

It pulled her in, a lover's embrace while the Firewitch squealed and laughed. This was his home, and this was Iseult's home now too.

Heat seared against her. Smoke clawed down her throat. She welcomed it. She was one with the Firewitch, and he was one with the flame. Where she commanded, the flames moved, and with each long stride that she advanced, the flames skipped aside.

They loved her, but they dared not touch her.

Then at last, she saw Aeduan. The seafire licked across him; his black horse burned.

"*Stop*," she ordered the flames, and the flames obeyed.

He was dying and bloodied. Broken and burned. She crouched beside him, cradling his head in one hand, resting fingers to his throat with the other.

There was no pulse.

No pulse, no life, no Bloodwitch named Aeduan.

No.

The word slipped from her throat. A raw, distant thing.

No.

He could not be dead. She would not *let* him be dead,

and she would not let this be his end. Not after what had happened in Tirla. Not after *everything* that had passed between them.

She dug her hands beneath his shoulders and with a strength she did not know she possessed, she pulled.

Iseult pulled and pulled and *pulled* until eventually, his body tore free from beneath the mare. The flames caressed her. Hungry and wanting more than Iseult would give. *Not now*, she told them. *Not now, not now.* And they listened, a cocoon to hold her while she strained to lift Aeduan higher.

She tried. Four times, she tried to get him onto her shoulders. He was not so heavy, not so large—but limp and unresponsive, he was dead weight she could not carry.

On the fifth try, she found that she was crying. She did not know when the tears had begun, and now that they'd started, there was no stopping them.

Do not cry, the flames whispered, and inside her, the Firewitch whispered too: *Do not cry, Iseult, do not cry. The fire eats what it wants, so you must do the same.*

Oh, she thought. *I see.* And in that moment, it was true. Power was Threads, and Threads belonged to her. All she had to do was take them.

So she did. She sucked in power from the heat, power from the black flames, and power from the man she had cleaved in the Contested Lands. She focused it into her muscles. Into her legs and arms and back . . .

On the sixth try, Iseult hefted Aeduan up high enough for her to stand—and on that sixth try, she got him across her shoulders.

Then she walked. One hobbling step turned into two, then three. She left the dead horse behind. She crossed the seafire.

She did not know where she was going. She could not see beyond the shadowy fire and moonlight. Yet something stirred inside her. A string winding tighter and tighter—but only so long as she walked in this one, true direction.

She planted one foot in front of the next, following that string, until at last, she left the frozen, burning river behind. Until at last, her feet landed on solid, craggy earth.

Ahead of her, through the smoke, was a fir tree. Somehow, despite the chaos and the fire, it seemed to shine. Green and healthy and strong. A hand beckoning her onward, so onward she moved.

Iseult's strength was flagging, though. Without the flames to fuel her here, she was just a girl. Just a girl with a man upon her back and tears—inexplicable, unwelcome tears—still sliding down her cheeks.

Threadwitches do not cry, she thought as she hauled Aeduan ever onward. *Threadwitches do not cry.*

The pines thickened around her, as did the sense of life that breathed here. Even in the dead of night, birds chirruped. Snowdrops bloomed.

Then the conifers cut away, and she reached the Origin Well of the Carawens.

Six downy birches shivered on the smoke-charged breeze, oblivious to the fire and explosions raging so near. The ice stretched between them, glimmering beneath the moon. Where the river had shone white, the Origin Well simply *shone*. As if it bore a light of its own. As if it sensed Iseult near and now it listened, it waited, it welcomed her approach.

The Aether Well, some called it. The spring to which Iseult had always believed her magic was bound. Now she knew better. Now she knew she was bound to the Void, and cleaving and Severed Threads were all her future had ever held.

But she was also the Cahr Awen. She *believed* that, even if the Abbot did not, and if anyone could save Aeduan, then it was she.

Iseult reached the edge of the Well, where a fringe of snow hugged the ice. Two steps out and her knees finally gave way. She collapsed, dropping Aeduan onto his back beside her.

The frozen Well did not shudder, it did not break. She knew, of course, that the surface was hard as stone. She *knew* it took the Nomatsi pilgrims an entire day to carve through. She didn't have an entire day, though. Eventually, the battle would spread. Eventually, Aeduan would no longer be savable— if he was even savable now.

She had to believe that he was. That he always had been.

"Aeduan," she panted, turning toward him. So many arrows, so many burns. And still no response.

No, no, no.

She freed his sword from its scabbard and staggered several paces away. She would have to carve open this ice. Somehow, she would have to reach the waters below before the battle reached them.

Surely if Iseult could walk through fire, then she could tear through ice.

She gripped the pommel with two hands and lifted both arms high. Then she slammed the blade into the ice. *Crack.*

Again. *Crack, crack, crack.* Over and over, she pushed all her strength into the sword, into the ice. And over and over,

467

she failed. The Well would not break. The healing waters would not come to her.

While behind her, Aeduan's body cooled, his soul drained. And behind them both, smoke clotted. Explosions boomed.

Iseult was out of time; she was out of patience. The tears still trailed down her cheeks. Where they came from, why they flowed, she did not know. Nineteen years of holding them in, she supposed, and they had finally flooded over.

And in that instant, it hit her: *Threadwitches might not cry, but perhaps Weaverwitches do.* She was going about this all wrong. This ice was frozen by the Well's magic. It was bound to the Aether and unbreakable by mere sword and strength.

She flung her blade aside. It clattered to the ice. She wiped the tears from her eyes and dropped to her knees. When Esme had first shown Iseult how to cleave, the snapping of Threads had felt like a misstep on a frozen lake. Well, here was her lake. Here was power she wanted to command.

She punched the ice. Her knuckles shrieked. Her wrist screamed.

She punched again, again, ignoring the blood on her knuckles, the shockwaves in her wrist. She switched hands, switched arms. Again, again, again.

Black lines spiderwebbed out.

So Iseult punched faster, harder, and the lines cut wider, fatter. *Sever, sever, twist and sever.* She alternated hands. *Threads that break, Threads that die.*

The ice bowed beneath her. A fracture ripped out. It split the air. It split her heart.

The ice tore open.

Iseult and Aeduan fell.

The water shocked the breath from Iseult's lungs, shocked the thoughts from her brain. For several eternal seconds, she sank. Lost in the warm, churning waters of the Origin Well. Then blood wisped across her vision, and she remembered where she was and why.

Aeduan.

Iseult turned, pulling herself through the waters, vibrant and alive. *Aeduan, Aeduan.* It was the blood that guided her. A trail that wound to him like a Heart-Thread.

He was sinking, eyes closed. Blood streaming upward, a hundred strands to unravel toward the surface.

Iseult reached him. She slid her arms around his waist. He *burned.* Hot as the fires she had carried him through, except these flames felt like they roared within.

Iseult swam, pulling Aeduan with her. When Evrane had healed Iseult in Nubrevna, she had sent Iseult to the heart of the Well—so to the heart Iseult now kicked her legs and swept her arms. Darkness ruled the deeper she moved. Darkness and pressure and the heat of Aeduan's touch.

Iseult's lungs shrieked. She wanted air. She wanted light. She wanted life. But here, in the shadows of the Well, she wanted Aeduan more.

Two more kicks, and her fingers sensed bubbling water. Then her fingers touched rock. The source of water, the source of magic.

Power washed over her. A light flared. Blinding in its brightness, and the waters surged against her. Deafening in their strength, they thrust Iseult back toward the night.

Yet in that moment, as Iseult held fast to Aeduan, as she

squinted against the brightness and *willed* his eyes to open, she saw red. Scarlet and true and spooling around them.

Red that was not blood. Red Threads that led from her heart and ended inside of his.

Impossible, she thought.

Then Iseult's air ended. The world went dark.

FIFTY-ONE

✳

Never had Pin's Keep been so quiet. Never had Vivia felt so many eyes upon her inside these stone walls. This was her haven. This was her den, and this moment was worse than the opening of the under-city. Now she had to lead. Now, pretty speeches wouldn't be enough.

She stood at the front of the main space, atop a footstool so she could scan and assess. Count and quantify. Before her stood soldiers, sailors, guards, and anyone who was willing to defend Lovats and defy Serafin Nihar.

There weren't many of them. Three hundred, Vivia estimated, and they were woefully underarmed and underarmored. She still had time, though, to find more fighters and equip them as best she could. The Royal Navy and Soil-Bound forces her father had sent north would slow the Raider King, even if Vivia did not believe they could stop him.

Noden curse her, she'd thought her list of tasks long yesterday. Now it ran for two pages, scribbled quickly onto a paper taken from her office overhead, and as she scanned the main room, she continued scrawling more. No real order to the list; simply what came to her as she assessed readiness.

Whetstones. Fletching. Lanolin. Boots. Painstones. Gauze. On and on and on.

Once she had finished her furious writing, she stepped off the stool to hand the list to Vizer Sotar's head guard, an older woman with a sharp chin and sharper eyes.

Except before she could touch down, the earth jolted. A hard heaving that shuddered through the Keep, through Vivia's knees. Her arms windmilled. She fell toward the shaking wall—and a second judder hit. Then a third and fourth, closer together until everything simply shook.

Then as fast as the quake had come, it quelled. A slow dissolution of movement that eventually ended in calm. Not without damage, though. Already, Vivia heard shouts from the Skulks. Shouts from the cellar of Pin's Keep.

And for half a breath, all Vivia wanted to do was scream. Did she not have enough to do? Had Noden and his Hag-fishes not already dragged her people *far enough* beneath the waves?

Then Vizer Sotar's head guard was there, helping Vivia to rise. Dust coated the woman's face. The whole room had clouded to gray. "The under-city," Vivia said. "We must check the under-city." She did not wait for an acknowledgment before turning toward the next person within reach—Vizer Sotar himself. "The streets," she barked at him. "Get people into the city to check for damage—"

"*Sir!*" A voice slashed through the room, high-pitched and strained. Then louder, "*SIR.*"

Vivia turned, terrified by what such urgent shouts might mean. Terrified what damage this person would report to her. What she found, though, was a boy staggering her way.

472

Familiar and young with dark eyes bulging and dappled brown skin flushed to russet.

She knew him . . . She *knew* him, but Noden save her, she couldn't recall from where.

"Sir," the boy repeated once, stumbling right up to Vivia. He was covered in white dust, as if he'd just come from the underground mid-quake—and he was unconcerned by the guards moving to stop him.

"Sir," he said once more, and this time, he doubled over.

Vivia lurched forward and caught him before he could collapse. His skin was damp and chalky.

"First . . . Mate," he panted, dragging up his gaze to meet Vivia's. Even his lashes were thick with dust. "I mean, *Captain* Sotar . . . sent me."

Stix. Vivia's breath hitched. Cold doused her. "What is it? Where is Stix?"

But the boy only shook his head, a desperate movement. "It's the . . . the raiders, sir." He coughed, one hand clutching tighter and tighter onto Vivia's arm.

And distantly, she realized the whole room had fallen silent again. It was as still as the open sea before a storm.

"The raiders . . . are coming," the boy finished at last.

"I know," Vivia tried to say, but the boy shook his head harder.

"And they're coming through the under-city. *Soon*, sir. So you gotta . . . you gotta empty it. And then you gotta defend . . . the door."

Now it was Vivia's turn to shake her head. The boy made no sense. Where had he even come from? "What door?" she asked. "And where is Stix?"

"*The* door," the boy insisted, voice pitching higher. "Underground, sir. I'll . . . I'll show you." He pulled away, already rising and turning, as if to race for the cellar.

And that was when Vivia noticed the bloodied bandage on the boy's left hand. That was why she knew him. He had been with Merik in the under-city. *Cam*, Merik had called the boy—though Vivia had foolishly mistaken him for a girl two weeks ago.

Yet that didn't explain how Cam had ended up with Stix. Nor where Stix was now—nor what *any* of what the boy was saying actually meant.

Before she could press him or even stand to follow, he added, voice low and private, "I was supposed to tell you somethin' else, sir. Something to make you believe Captain Sotar really sent me and that raiders are really coming. She said, 'Noden and the Hagfishes ought to bend to a woman's rule.'"

At those words, a dullness settled over Vivia. An icy, seeping weight that numbed her limbs and brain. *So this is what drowning feels like*, she thought, and now she knew that she'd reached the last of the sunlight, the last of her air.

FIFTY-TWO

✳

Merik's body was pummeled, his mind stretched long, his magic shrunk down to a pinprick yet somehow inflated to enormity at the same time.

Then he returned to himself and burst into a new world. Underwater, dark and cold. No chance to summon winds here, only swimming, aiming for a surface he hoped he would find.

Four kicks became ten before his head finally broke free. He gasped and spluttered, spinning around to search for the Northman in this dim world lit only by blue light off the door.

Water swept against Merik's legs, and three rough breaths later, the Northman splashed up beside him.

"Where?" the Northman coughed.

"I do not know," Merik replied, and it was mostly true. Hye, he knew he was inside of a mountain with magic doorways that somehow connected to the mythological Sightwitch Sister Convent. But this explanation was far beyond his ability to articulate in Svodish.

Hell-waters, it was beyond his ability to articulate in Nubrevnan.

In fact, his mind couldn't seem to pin down the layers of

it all. He might have heard about it from Esme and the Fury, but he had not truly *believed* such a thing existed until right now, when he was actually there.

And even right now, with a blue door glowing at the bottom of a pool, he still wasn't sure he believed it. But as Evrane used to say, *The shark will eat you whether you acknowledge it or not.* And if Merik were facing a shark right now, his aim would be trying to escape it.

No Cleaved might be coming through the door yet, but that didn't mean they wouldn't. And there was still the issue of the Fury and the Raider King finding these doors soon.

Merik swam toward a hazy ledge five strokes away. After hauling himself out, he pulled the Northman up beside him. Already, he shook from the cold and the Northman's furs dripped and splattered—but that was a remote distraction. What mattered was what lay beyond: a cavern, large enough to hold the city of Lovats.

It was large enough to hold the entire plateau actually, and somehow this basin of water was nothing more than a shelf hugging the cavern wall. Merik inched closer to the edge, peered down . . .

And for the first time in his life, vertigo engulfed him.

Ever since his witchery had awoken in him as a child, heights had never bothered him. But this was no mere drop-off. This was staring into another universe. Into the very heart of Noden's court.

Merik sucked in a long, girding breath before pulling his gaze back up—and then up and up and up. Lights flickered across the cave, as well as other blue glows. And then, high at the top of it all, was a stretch of ice, almost like a bridge.

"Up," Merik said, pointing toward the nearest ledge. One of the other blue glows had to be the door Merik needed to reach Lovats, and the only option before him was to try every one and see where they took him—and then, of course, pray to Noden that it didn't eject him somewhere worse than Poznin with the Puppeteer.

At the Northman's nod, Merik closed his eyes and called his magic to him.

He expected resistance. Underground, there was little air and no winds. And underground, there could be dangerous consequences if one tried to manipulate the air too much. Air currents led to storms, and storms in small spaces were never good.

Merik's winds came easily, though. A huge rush that punched into him and the Northman. They both toppled backward, but before they could fall into the water, Merik swirled his winds behind them. Beneath them.

Power, power, power.

Merik and the Northman flew. It was as natural as breathing—Merik couldn't believe how easily the power came to him. And it wasn't the Fury's magic channeling over their bond either. Those winds were cold and vengeful. *These* winds sparkled.

It was the only word he could find to describe the feeling. This sense that the glimmering galaxy below somehow fed his lungs and carried him faster, higher, stronger than he had ever managed on his own.

They reached the first ledge, where a second blue door glowed. It was identical to what he'd seen submerged in Poznin. "Wait," he told the Northman, and he moved toward it.

But the Northman did not like that command. He shook his head and hurried after Merik. Two bracing breaths for each of them. Then together they stepped through, and like before, Merik felt compressed and elongated, paused yet pushed along. Then he and the Northman were out the other side.

Wind and night kicked against them. Pine trees shivered. Merik's eardrums instantly swelled, as if he'd flown too high too fast, and a full moon shone down.

This was *not* Nubrevna. Merik gripped the Northman's forearm and hauled the man back through the magic door.

Crush, stretch, stop, and move. They stumbled onto the ledge they'd just left, both men panting. "Cold," the Northman said, and Merik could only nod. He motioned up. Then once more, his winds twined beneath them and carried them high.

The next door, on a ledge scarcely large enough to hold them both, ejected them into a ditch. A narrow slope cutting upward toward a crack in the earth, and the scent of cedar and stale smoke hit his nose.

This was not the Lovats under-city either.

Back into the cavern they moved, and on to the next ledge, the next door. This ledge, next to the cavern's falls, was slick with water. The Northman slipped; Merik's winds caught him—but not gracefully. He shoved the man through the glowing blue . . .

And once again, cold snapped against them. This time, though, there was no wind. An icy staircase ascended before them, and Merik and the Northman quickly skipped up. All they found, though, was a vast, flat expanse of nothing. Moonlit and white. Shimmering and lifeless.

"Sleeping Lands," the Northman said, and there was fear in his eyes as he backed down the stairs. "Death," he warned. "Death." Then the Northman rushed back through the magic doorway.

Merik hurried after. He had heard of the Sleeping Lands—of course he had. It was an uncrossable frozen wasteland that sucked in unprepared travelers. Only the Nomatsis . . . the No'Amatsis, rather, had ever managed to cross it.

Once more, the door's magic pummeled against Merik. This time, though, when he toppled through and landed inside the cavern beyond, something was wrong. When he inhaled and called his winds, they came—and they came strong. With power, power, power for the taking.

But there was cold slithering beneath them. Icy rage that Merik recognized in an instant.

"We must hurry," Merik said. Nubrevnan words useless to the Northman, but all he could manage. In a burst of strength and momentum, Merik flew them to the next door, this one tucked at the end of the cavern.

This door did not glow, and when he stepped inside, no magic battered against him. He saw only shadows. Next door, next door—they had to reach the next door before the Fury came. Before the Fury could lead the Raider King here. And this doorway was near, connected to the current ledge by stairs.

But the mountain shook. So hard, it flung Merik to the ground. So hard, it flung the Northman off the ledge.

Merik threw out his winds, catching the Northman and ripping him back to solid ground—solid ground that still quaked. Rubble fell. Dust plumed. And as Merik and the

Northman stood there, gripping each other and waiting for the tremor to slow, cold twined into Merik's lungs. It plucked at his breath.

Power, power, power.

Then came the darkness, undulating and frozen. It rippled around Merik and the Northman, and both men wrenched toward the doorway they'd just abandoned. Dust clouded its dark gullet now.

A figure formed.

"Why do I hold a razor in one hand?" he asked. *"So men remember I am sharp as any edge. And why do I hold broken glass in the other? So men remember that I am always watching."*

The Fury stepped from the shadows. Cold billowed off him in vast, violent waves. He was his namesake; he was fury through and through.

His blackened eyes met Merik's. "Where are they, Merik?" he asked. "What have you done with my blade and my glass?"

The Fury attacked.

FIFTY-THREE

✳

A rush of scalding air hit the boat as Vaness sailed Safi and the Hell-Bards onto Lake Scarza—and as she sailed them into a battle only the Hell-Bards could see.

The heat swept Safi's hair from her face, stung her cheeks with invisible embers she couldn't spot, and set her lungs to choking. All while the boat dipped and shuddered, guided by Vaness's magic, which was guided by Caden sitting at the helm.

They aimed for shore.

Not fast enough, though. Not before the explosion ripped loose through the Floating Palace. A sudden visceral surge that *battered* into Safi. She heard nothing else, she felt nothing else. The firestorm ripped against her, lived inside her, and breathed with her dry lungs.

Then the glamour fell. Just a flash like before, but enough for Safi to see the full extent of the battlefield.

A ship splintered in half burned just ahead, great plumes of smoke given to the sky. Blood stained the water. Sailors clung to debris. Charred corpses floated by.

Habim had always said war was senseless, yet he had caused

so, so much senseless horror here. *This* was what Uncle Eron's scheme had done, and it was not peace in the Witchlands.

Vaness's bandage was soaked through now, turning the red crepe to almost black while more blood oozed from her nose.

Then the glamour winked back into place, and false peace shrouded Safi's vision once more.

"*Right!*" Caden roared. The boat veered right. "Sharper!"

"Oh gods, *sharper!*" screeched Lev.

And Vaness's hands wrenched sharper. So hard, they almost flipped. But Zander clung to Vaness, and Lev clung to Zander—all while Caden and Safi simply clung to the boat. Ash flew into Safi's mouth. Her eyes burned with unseen smoke.

Then the boat heaved back the other way, and so the other way they all flew. Back, forth, back, forth. On and on, side to side while Caden shouted directions and Vaness obeyed.

Three more times, the glamour fell, and three more times, Safi saw wreckage and death and blood smearing from the Empress's nose. Then they left the glamour behind entirely. Between one breath and the next, Safi could see again. The Empress could see again—and abruptly, she sat taller.

The boat hurtled faster, sheering atop the waves. The lake crawled with ships fleeing the glamoured battle behind, but Vaness swerved and skipped and carried them ever onward.

Until quite suddenly, there was nowhere left to go. They were almost to shore, the quay zooming in fast. Vaness did not slow, though. If anything, she pushed the boat harder. Even when Caden roared for her to stop and Lev screamed, "*You're going to kill us!*"

Vaness only flung her arms higher and aimed straight for

the road, where thousands of people poured by. Blood streaked off her face. It hit Safi's cheeks—not that Safi cared. All she saw was death propelling toward her, made of stone and bodies and pain.

Now Zander was shouting too and Safi also joined in, but still Vaness did not listen.

They reached the stone lip onto shore.

The boat lifted from the lake, water spraying and people screaming. Then the boat landed, a crash that shocked through Safi's bones.

For several resounding seconds, everyone sat there in gaping shock. Not just Safi, Vaness, and the Hell-Bards, but all the Marstoks who'd fled the boat too. *Everyone* stared, breathing hard and trying to grasp what the rut had just happened.

But the moment of recovery was short-lived. Pistol shots rang out, and when Safi turned, she saw another ship plowing this way, packed fore to aft with soldiers. They fired their weapons into the sky, a warning for people to clear—a warning that people obeyed with frantic shrieking.

Leaving only Safi, Vaness, and the Hell-Bards sitting in a boat on dry land while they waited for death to reach them.

"So," Lev piped up, "I guess it's fair to assume those Marstoks are *not* on our side?"

"No." Safi swung out of the boat. "*Run.*"

The Hell-Bards did as ordered. Again, Zander slung Vaness onto his shoulder, and Vaness uttered no word of protest. Her nose still gushed, her face had lost all color, and now her crepe bandage leaked blood down her face. It sprayed against the street in time to Zander's leaping stride.

They cut off the quay onto a side street, barged through

an intersection, and then shoved onto a wider thoroughfare. Crowds clotted thick against them; pistols chased from behind. No slowing, no looking back. They pushed and ducked and fought their way through the throngs.

Two streets later, though, Lev hollered over the traffic, "Where are we going? We need a plan!"

"You think?" Caden called back. "I don't want another Ratsenried any more than you do."

"We had a plan in Ratsenried," Zander inserted. "It just didn't work."

"Because it was *your* plan!" Lev began. "Hell-pits, if you'd just let me—"

"*Shut up!*" Safi snatched Lev's arm. "All of you, *shut up* and follow me!" As before, the Hell-Bards obeyed, and at the next intersection, Safi angled left. West, toward the mountains.

She had a plan. Oh, it was slapdash and Iseult would pick it apart in seconds, but it was *something*. Act now; consequences later. Plus, it gave her a place to run toward and easy landmarks to follow: the golden spires. One after the other, she found them above the buildings, above the crowds, and one after the other, she tracked them toward the heart of the city. Toward the largest spire of all.

"Yesterday," Safi shouted to Lev, the closer they got to the final spire, "how did you get into the Origin Well? Where was that hole in the wall?"

"Why?" Caden demanded, eyes widening as he pushed around a woman with a squalling child.

But Lev—blessed Lev—simply barked, "Shut up, Commander. She didn't ask you." Then she pointed north. "The hole was that way!"

So Safi went that way. Four more streets and two more turns, she spotted the wall. No longer glamoured, but *very* well guarded. The gaping, crumbling hole revealed cedars and shadows.

"Vaness!" Safi called without slowing her stride, even as the twelve soldiers spotted their approach. Even as two on the right unsheathed their blades.

"Yes," Vaness slurred. A snap of her fingers ...

And the two blades turned molten in the soldiers' hands. They screamed. Their blades fell and Vaness snapped again.

Every piece of iron nearby melted. Anything that it touched caught fire. Sheaths, uniforms, people. Burning flesh, burning hair—it all sizzled into Safi's nose as she sprinted by. Then they were to the hole in the wall. Then they were *through* the hole in the wall and tramping into a blackened stretch of charred forest.

Soon, they reached the tiles surrounding the Origin Well, and Safi risked a backward glance. Maybe there was time to heal Vaness before ...

No, there *definitely* wasn't. Hundreds of soldiers poured into the Well grounds, and if Safi and the Hell-Bards didn't move fast enough, those soldiers would see exactly where Safi was running to.

"*Faster!*" she screamed, her feet slamming onto the tiles. The waters rippled and hummed beside her. Then she was past, the Hell-Bards at her heels, and charging once more into the cedars—not blackened. Good cover for what she was about to do.

They reached the spire.

Safi cut left.

And there, hidden within the dirt and the rocks and the trees, was the crack in the earth she remembered. "Down here." She scrabbled toward it.

"Domna," Lev warned behind her. "This seems like a *very* bad idea."

"Just trust me!" As she'd hoped, the blue light shone before her. She scooted toward it, scree slipping beneath her ankles, and the closer she inched, the more magic pulsed against her skin.

True, warm, happy magic that strummed in her heart. That beckoned her to enter. Yesterday, she'd fallen through. There'd been no chance to feel this magic. No chance to revel in its power or analyze what it might mean.

Lev crawled down behind her, and when Safi glanced back, the Hell-Bard's mouth hung open, her eyes huge and glowing in the light.

"*This* is your plan?" Lev asked, voice barely a whisper.

"Yeah." Safi grinned. "Follow me."

She stepped through.

FIFTY-FOUR

※

*H*eat roars. Wood cracks and embers fly.

"Run." Blood drips from his mother's mouth as she speaks. It splatters his face.

With arms stained to red, she pushes herself up. She wants him to crawl out from beneath her. She wants him to escape. "Run, my child, run."

But he does not move, just as he did not move when the raiders first ambushed the tribe. Just as he did not move when his father drew his sword and ran from their tent.

Or when the raiders reached their doorway, loosed their arrows, and then his mother fell atop him. She had hidden him with her body until the raiders had moved on.

"Run," she whispers one last time, pleading desperation in her silver eyes. Then the last of her strength flees. She collapses onto him.

The six arrows that pierced her body slam into Aeduan. Pain and punctured breath and blood, blood, blood. Always the blood.

He is pinned by cedar and corpse. His mother is dead.

And now there will be no running. Now there is only flame. He begins to cry.

*

487

Aeduan watched himself. He stood where the raider had stood when he loosed the six bolts into Dysi's back. He stood at the mouth of their tent—except there was no tent now. No walls or battle raging in the tribe. All that surrounded him was fire and shadow.

Over and over, he had died that day. A thousand times until the rain had come and Evrane had found him. The arrows had bled him. The fire had burned him. Yet always, he had come back. Always he had snapped awake to find his mother's dead face above him while the flames and smoke bore down.

Death follows wherever you go, yet by the grace of the Wells, you always outrun your own.

It was true. Always, Aeduan had outrun death, beginning on this day fifteen years ago.

Except there was one thing Lizl had gotten wrong: it was not grace that had saved him. It was a curse. All he had wanted that day was to die and stay dead. All he had wanted was to join his mother and escape the flames forever.

But death had refused to claim him. Aeduan's magic had healed his wounds while his mother's body had kept away the full brunt of the fire's force. Until she was nothing more than a charred husk, and the arrows in Aeduan's body had burned away to white-hot heads buried inside his chest.

Eventually, the rainstorm doused the flames. Eventually, only damp smoke remained, and Evrane's gentle face and gentle hands found Aeduan among the debris.

Every night, he relived that attack in his dreams.

Never before, though, had he hovered outside like this.

488

Never before had he watched his mother die or his own wounds ooze blood upon the floor.

Now, he stood at the edge of the scene, observing while the boy died without him beneath a burning sky. He watched his mother's flesh sizzle and smoke. He watched the tears slide down his broken cheeks, evaporating instantly with the heat. He watched his young skin sear, only to heal as fast as it could be blackened.

He watched the life leave his body, only to return a moment later. Again and again.

He watched the fletching in his mother's back catch fire. Six bright bursts of light before the shafts caught fire too. Down they burned. Through his mother. Into him.

Still he healed. Still he sobbed. Still he died.

But this time, Evrane never came for him. The rainstorm never broke.

It took Aeduan a long time to notice that the memory had changed—that it wasn't adhering to the truth of that day fifteen years ago. The truth of what happened every night when he dreamed.

Evrane should have come by now.

For the first time since awakening in this memory, Aeduan turned—as if he thought he might find Evrane behind him. As if she might be stuck, waiting for him to stand aside so she could move within.

There was no one there, though. Of course there was no one there, and all he found was more fire. More smoke. More shadows and more pain.

He was alone in this nightmare. There was no Evrane. There was no escape. There was only the darkness and himself.

He turned back to the child. He turned back to the boy he had once been. He did not see a demon. He did not see a monster.

And in that moment, Aeduan understood: it was not just that he had wanted to die forever that day. He *had* died. The child inside him had burned away alongside his mother, and since then, though he might have existed, he had never truly lived.

Now nobody came for him in the nightmare because that was the truth of it. No one *had* come for him. Evrane might have moved his mother's corpse off Aeduan, she might have tended his wounds and taken him to the Monastery, but she had not saved him.

All these years, he had blamed himself for what had happened. If he had just fought, if he had just reacted, then his mother would not have died. Then he would not have been trapped beneath her; his tribe would not have burned.

It was as if by blaming himself, he had given the death meaning. He had given it a reason—and that reason was his own existence. His own failings and weakness and monstrous, Void-bound magic fueled by blood.

But there was no reason. There never had been. He was just a child, trapped in the wreckage of war. He had not done this, he had not caused this. Yet he had lost his life to it all the same.

Now no one could save him but himself.

Four long steps carried Aeduan to the boy. He stared down into his own face, half hidden by the charred remains of his mother. Dysi had been beautiful in life. Now she was nothing more than a smoldering corpse and a handful of memories.

With careful hands, Aeduan gripped her arms to move her. The instant he touched her, though, she crumbled into black nothing and whispered away. So he sank to a crouch beside the boy—beside himself—and he gazed into ice-blue eyes.

Aeduan had never gazed into his own eyes before. They swirled with red.

"Run," he told the boy. "Run."

"I can't," the boy said.

"You can," Aeduan replied. "We can. Together."

Heat roars. Wood cracks and embers fly.

He is pinned by cedar and corpse. His mother is dead.

But he is not supposed to die with her. She had told him to run, so running is what he needs to do.

He pushes upward, a scream ripping from his lungs. Up his scorched throat and out across the fire. Push, push—his mother is heavy, but he cannot let the loss of her hold him down.

His screams pitch louder, his muscles labor and groan. The wounds in his chest stab deeper and the flames score at his cheeks.

Then he is up. His mother falls stiffly to one side, leaving his legs free. His path is free too, a clear gap in the flames, and winding through that trail is a single red line. Feathery and fine, it reaches into the boy's chest.

It is shrinking fast, though. With each heartbeat that passes, with each flame that claws at him from all sides, the line shrivels inward like a string that has caught fire. Or like a thread burning to dust.

The flames cannot have this thread, though, for though blood might burn, the boy's soul will not.

The Bloodwitch named Aeduan runs.

FIFTY-FIVE

※

When Aeduan's eyes opened again, light flared around him, as if the night had turned to day. As if he had somehow fallen into the heart of the sun.

Waters streamed, obscure and blinding . . . and then morphing into a face.

Iseult.

She hung suspended in the water, eyes closed. Hair floating around her face, a halo of night to encircle the moon. The white Carawen cloak undulated behind her, heavy and wild. No bubbles left her nose or mouth.

Instantly, panic laid claim to Aeduan's muscles. He grabbed her, one arm looping around her waist. Then he released the clasp at her neck.

The cloak fell beneath them.

He kicked for the surface, strong and fast and desperate—and it was as if his blood had waited for this precise moment. As if this was all it had ever wanted to do. His magic ignited within him. It spurred his muscles to a speed and power no man could ever match, and he flew toward the surface with Iseult at his side.

The Well had healed the curse, just as Iseult had promised. Then it had brought Aeduan back from death and returned to him the one thing he had spent his whole life hating. He'd had it all wrong, though. He saw that now.

Being a Bloodwitch did not mean he could not also be a man.

He towed Iseult toward the night, and a moment later, they crashed above the surface, cold and jarring. Aeduan grabbed for the nearest expanse of ice and held on, tugging Iseult tightly to him so she would not drift away.

Light and steam rolled around them, erasing the world. Blending it into a featureless expanse. He saw no one else. He heard no one else. For all he knew, they were the only people left alive in this battle.

In the entire world.

"Iseult," he tried, willing her to wake up. "Iseult, Iseult, Iseult." He could not stop saying her name, even as it came out in short, shallow bursts. Even as he searched for a way out of the water, a spot to gain purchase on the ice. Her name simmered from his chest and would not stop.

"Iseult, Iseult, Iseult."

She had saved him. One more life-debt he owed her, except now he saw it did not matter. It had never mattered. Not since she had stabbed him in the heart beside a lighthouse. Not since he had given her his salamander cloak and told her *Mhe varujta.*

"Iseult, Iseult, Iseult."

He could scarcely see her face through all the light and steam. He needed to get them out of this Well. With one arm, he pulled himself—and Iseult too—along the jagged ice.

He knew this went beyond life-debts, and that this fear

anchored in his chest went against everything Aeduan had ever wanted to be—against everything he'd ever believed himself to be.

There. His fingers hit a ridge he could hang on to.

"Iseult, Iseult, Iseult."

He grabbed hold. He pulled. His fingernails carved into ice. His forearm strained. A cry broke from his chest, and he could no longer say her name. So he thought it instead. *Iseult, Iseult, Iseult.*

He kicked his legs. The water pushed and his magic sang. Soon, his biceps cleared the ice. Then his head. Then her head too.

Iseult, Iseult, Iseult.

Now his chest was out of the water, and with one final kick, he wrenched his whole torso free. It was not graceful, nor gentle. Iseult's body scraped against the ice, but she was high enough that he could release her for half a heartbeat.

Aeduan pulled himself the rest of the way onto the ice, then he scrabbled around to haul her out beside him. Steam coiled off her body. Off his too, and the cold of the valley gnawed deep into his bones.

"Iseult." He uttered her name again, hoarse and low. Again and again and again.

She was warm to the touch, and a pulse fluttered at her neck. She breathed. Shallow movements in her chest that meant she had not drowned.

In a vague corner of Aeduan's brain, he supposed the Cahr Awen could not drown—not here. When they had been in the water, he had felt sentience. Oneness. Completion. He had no doubt now about what Iseult was.

Aeduan ran his hands down Iseult's wet arms, down her wet legs, checking for broken bones. For anything that might explain why she would not wake up. But he found nothing. Everything he touched was intact, though growing colder by the second.

"Iseult, Iseult, Iseult."

She and Aeduan had survived the cleaving Adders in Lejna. They had survived raiders and the Amonra. They had survived a Firewitch and the Contested Lands and weeks of survival in the Sirmayan Mountains.

He could not lose her now.

It was as Aeduan pressed his fingers to the back of Iseult's neck, searching for some damage to her spine, that her body tensed beneath his.

He stilled, waiting. Staring.

Then her back arched, face tipping up. She gulped in a single, wheezing breath before her body relaxed beneath his. She opened her eyes.

Golden eyes streaked with green. The only eyes that had ever met Aeduan's without looking away.

His heart fluttered at the sight of them. His whole body did, a strange feeling of relief and confusion. He tried to pull back, to give her space, but in a movement too quick to resist, she gripped his collar. She yanked him down. His elbows gave way. His chest landed atop hers. Their faces were only inches apart.

Iseult, Iseult, Iseult.

The ice was cold against Aeduan's hands on either side of her. Wind furrowed into his wet clothes. Water dripped off his face. A drop landed on her cheek and slid sideways. He wanted to brush it away, but he was afraid to move. Afraid that if he did, she would remember who he was. She would recoil and retreat.

And she was so close now. He could see every line of her. The way her jaw sloped to a pointed chin. The way her lips parted to reveal the edge of teeth, a flicker of tongue. But it was her eyes that held his attention—that had always held his attention. Her pupils pulsed in time to her breaths. Her ribs did too, battering against his.

He did not know how he had ever thought her plain.

Iseult's fingers curled more tightly around his collar. She tugged him closer, until their noses almost touched. Already, hers had turned pink with cold. Her cheeks too.

Iseult, Iseult, Iseult.

Her abdomen contracted beneath his. She curled toward him until she was so near, her breath whispered against his lips.

"Aeduan," she began. "I—"

The light within the Well winked out. No warning, and abruptly, the forest coalesced around them—as did smoke and fires . . .

And faces. A hundred soldiers stepping from the northern trees.

Aeduan shoved to his feet. The night air froze against him. "Get behind me," he told Iseult, even though she was already behind him, already on her feet and sinking into her own defensive stance.

How had he missed the raiders approaching? The Well's power must have interfered with his witchery. Now, though—now there was no mistaking the onslaught of bloods, as diverse as the faces that matched them. And at the fore was frosted baby's breath and bone-deep loss.

The Raider King, his father, strode out from the shadows.

"Aeduan," he called, coming to a stop at the Well's frozen edge. "Give me the girl."

No, Aeduan wanted to say, but before he could respond, a new blood-scent whispered against him. *Crisp spring water and salt-lined cliffs.* He had just enough time to whirl about before Evrane stepped from the trees on the opposite side. Behind her came a hundred monks with blades drawn.

For half a breath, relief rolled through Aeduan's muscles. Evrane had saved him; she was on his side; she would protect Iseult. Except Iseult was shaking her head. "No," she murmured. Then louder, "No, Aeduan. She is not who she seems to be."

Aeduan had no idea what those words meant, but he did not question them. If Iseult did not want to join Evrane, then he would keep Evrane away.

His veins hummed with power. His muscles with strength, and his heart with magic. A coruscation in his blood, bright as the light off the Well had been only moments before.

"Aeduan." Now, his father pleaded, a flash of desperation to sparkle across his blood. "You know what this is. You know that I need her." He lifted a single hand, not quite beseeching. Not quite demanding, either. "Give her to me, son."

"No, give her to me," Evrane called. "The Cahr Awen has come to save us, Aeduan. Remember your duty."

I do, he thought, and in that moment, it was true. He turned to Iseult. "Take my hand," he said, and without hesitation, she twined her fingers into his. Her golden eyes held Aeduan's and did not look away.

She trusted him. She had claimed his Aether, and she

would guide his blade. She was the dark-giver, the shadow-ender, and he would not betray her. Not again.

Aeduan inhaled deep, quieting his mind and stilling his body so his witchery could rise to its maximum power. A thousand blood-scents crashed against him, and a thousand more trickled and skipped beyond that.

All were his for the taking. All were his for the controlling.

But Aeduan already had enough blood on his hands, and as far as he was concerned, death did not have to follow wherever he went.

Not anymore.

Aeduan's hand was warm in Iseult's. Despite the cold wind scratching at them, despite the water burrowed deep within her clothes and bones.

"Follow me," Aeduan told her. Then he walked toward the cedars, so Iseult walked too.

"Aeduan, what are you doing?" Evrane cried. "Give me the Cahr Awen! You *know* the vow."

"Blood runs deeper than any vows," shouted the man with the raiders. He looked like Aeduan, except older. And except with Threads—dark green with command, but also flickers of white fear and blue loss.

"Aeduan, please," the man begged, and the fear and grief flashed brighter.

The same white panic soon hit Evrane's Threads. "Aeduan!" she screamed. "Where are you going? *Stop!*"

Aeduan did not stop. Nor did Iseult. They were almost to the edge of the Well.

Anger erupted in Evrane's Threads. "*Catch them!*" she barked at the same instant the man ordered, "*Stop them!*"

With those words, every figure, every set of Threads around the Well launched into action. A vast swarm that would reach Iseult and Aeduan in seconds.

Iseult's heart guttered. Her muscles tensed, ready to flee, but Aeduan only squeezed her hand tighter, his pace steady. His pace calm.

Iseult had once thought Aeduan carried himself as if he came from another time. As if he had walked a thousand years and planned to walk a thousand more. Now, though, there was a new stillness about him—and suddenly a thousand years seemed a very short time indeed for a man with strength such as his.

Aeduan and Iseult left the ice; their sodden boots sank into snowdrifts. Two monks bore down, Threads blaring with focused blue and violent gray.

Then the first monk reached them. His sword swung back. His sword swung down ...

He froze. Midstride with his arm high, his mouth wide—and only two paces away from carving through Iseult.

Then the second monk reached them, her knives extended and Threads frantic and shaking.

She froze too. Then the third monk behind her as well, and then two raiders closing the gap on the left. One by one, every person that came near enough to attack stopped dead in their tracks.

And Aeduan showed no reaction at all, no change in his purposeful, forward stride through eternity.

He guided Iseult into the cedars. Ruddy trunks and

glittering needles, so surreal and vivid amidst the smoke pluming ahead. Amidst the figures charging in from all angles.

Still, though, Aeduan did not rush. His eyes swirled red. His breaths were even and pure, and Iseult could feel his heartbeat thumping through his grip. *Blood. Witch. Blood. Witch.* A beat to walk by.

Every step brought more people rushing in. Monk and raider. White-cloaked and fur-clad. All with the forest green Threads of people on the hunt—until they reached Aeduan and Iseult. Then, as their bodies locked into place, a uniform brilliance overtook all other shades: shock. Only hair and cloaks and beards moved then, shivering on a cold breeze.

And their eyes moved too. Countless eyes to slide sideways. Watching, furious and powerless.

Iseult had not known Aeduan could hold so many people at once. She wondered if he had known either—or if he would ever be able to do it again.

They broke from the trees, and the island ended. A battle spanned before them, raging across the frozen river. Raiders and monks caught in combat. A seething mass of bodies and Threads, crammed wherever seafire did not rage.

As far as Iseult could see, there was no way through the chaos. She felt no affinity for those flames, no desire—or ability—to control them. The Firewitch trapped within her had gone silent. Released, she supposed, by the magic of an ancient Well.

Iseult turned to Aeduan. Behind him, raiders and monks stood stiff as stone, a trail of statues through the trees. A silent tribute to the flames' howl and the screams of the fighting, of the dying.

501

A deep breath swelled in Aeduan's chest. He rolled his shoulders. Just once. Then he lifted his free hand, arm trembling. His eyes screwed shut, and like a wave lapping against a sandy shore, Aeduan's power rippled outward. Swords paused mid-thrust, shields stilled mid-defense. Blades stopped, embedded in flesh, while faces went rigid, trapped in agony or anger or surprise.

And on that wave rode a tide of shock. In moments, the weave of the battle shone brighter than the moon.

Aeduan's eyes opened. There was no white left within them, no blue, only red from rim to rim.

"Now we run," he told Iseult, a ragged sound against a battle suddenly silenced. Only the flames sang now.

"Yes," Iseult agreed. "Now we run."

She squeezed his hand.

Aeduan led the way, a snaking path across the ice, between the flames. Around frozen fighters—and corpses too—they twisted and raced. Black smoke burned Iseult's eyes. Heat blasted against her, and in the back of her mind, she wondered how many times she and the Bloodwitch named Aeduan had raced together like this. Through hell-fire and beyond.

The longer they ran, though, the more people began to move. As if trapped in quicksand, a subtle inching forward.

Aeduan was losing control. So Iseult ran faster, and Aeduan ran faster beside her. Soon enough, the heat reared back, and through the smoke, a dark cliff face appeared. At its base, surrounded by frozen marsh, was a shadowy door.

Iseult tried to stop at the sight of it, but Aeduan tugged her on. His breaths were rough and erratic now. His eyes had darkened from red to rust, like blood drying upon a blade.

502

"That goes to the Monastery, Aeduan!" She had to shout over the seafire.

"It also goes outside," he shouted back—or tried to, but like his breathing, his words were weak, unstable. "There is . . . a fork."

Yes, yes. Iseult remembered that split in the tunnel. She and Leopold had chosen down . . .

Leopold. Goddess, where was he? She had left him without thought upon the battlefield, and she had not considered him since.

"If we go right at the split," Aeduan continued, "then it will lead us beyond the Monastery . . ." His voice faded, and Iseult flung a backward glance, worried his exhaustion had finally caught up to him.

It had. The battle moved faster now, a thousand figures slogging through mud and writhing this way. Still, Aeduan ran. Still, he held Iseult's hand tightly and did not stumble.

Above, she felt silver Threads blaring. *Blueberry*, she thought hazily. The bat was near; Iseult prayed Owl was not. Before she could search the sky for the creature, though, a new set of Threads cut into her awareness. A shivering, melting, dangerous set that bled from death to hunger to pleasure to rage.

The Abbot.

Iseult snapped her gaze forward once more, to where Natan fon Leid emerged from the cave's entrance, sword in one hand and buckler in the other. His Carawen hood was towed up, a fire flap fastened—but Iseult didn't need to see his face. She knew those Threads. She knew that cloak too, with its red trim.

Aeduan's hand lifted. He reached for the Abbot, stride slowing ever so slightly. His hand shook.

Nothing happened, though. The Abbot did not freeze; no shock overwhelmed his bleeding Threads. Instead, he laughed.

"Salamander fibers," he called. "A trick I learned from you, Bloodwitch. Now give me the Cahr Awen." His Threads wore sky blue calm, as if he intended to wait patiently. As if all he had requested was a bit more salt for his lamb.

Which was why there was no warning before he rushed at them. Far quicker than his bland shape had suggested; he was still a fighter trained by the Carawens.

Aeduan barely swept back in time. Iseult had to yank him and shove. Their hands released. They evaded.

Behind them, the battle picked up speed. Threads shifted this way, and it was only a matter of time before Aeduan lost control entirely. He could not fight *and* hold the raiders and monks. He could barely keep standing and hold them too.

Burn them, Iseult's heart said, and this time it was not the Firewitch speaking. She knew what to do here. She had done it before, and she did not need flames to do it. A different kind of fire lived inside her: the power that broke through enchanted ice and Origin Wells.

She lifted her arms, fingers stretching wide. Just as Esme had shown her. Just as she had done before in the Contested Lands.

But when she reached for the Abbot's bleeding Threads, Aeduan lunged at her. "*No.*" He knocked her arm, and in that same instant, the Abbot's sword whistled through the air. Right where Iseult had been.

A wisp of cold wind brushed against her. Then Aeduan

was hauling Iseult backward, sideways, out of reach. Until they were the ones standing before the cave—and there was no missing just how fast the battle was thundering toward them now. Half-speed, if not more.

"Run," Aeduan commanded, pushing Iseult behind him. "Run and do not look back."

"I can cleave him," she tried.

"Can ... but should not. You do not want his mind inside yours."

So Aeduan had figured that out then.

"I will handle Natan."

"No." Iseult gripped his forearm. "Come with me. I didn't save you so you could die again."

"I will be right behind," he said, and she realized there would be no changing his mind. So she nodded and patted the bloodied coin beneath her shirt. "Find me."

"Always," he promised, and for a brief pause in the chaos, he looked into her eyes. So pale, so blue. When she had seen those eyes in Veñaza City, she had thought they were the color of understanding.

She had been right.

"*Te varuje,*" she told him. "*Te varuje.*"

Then Iseult did as Aeduan had ordered, and she ran.

FIFTY-SIX

✳

The cavern had changed since yesterday. An ice-bridge now spanned overhead, cold coiling off it, while a harsh wind blustered and kicked.

How wind could build underground, Safi had no idea, but she suspected it wasn't natural—and that it had something to do with the voices filling the darkness far across the cavern. Distant, echoing sounds that tangled inside her gut. That seemed to call to her, even as she knew such a thing made no sense.

Nothing in this place made sense.

Beside Safi, the Hell-Bards tried to catch their breaths while Vaness lay limp upon Zander's shoulder.

"You know," Caden said between gasps, "we have a saying in the Ohrins. *Over the falls and into the rapids.* That's what this feels like, Safi. Where the hell have you taken us?"

"I too," Lev panted, raising a hand, "would like an answer to this question."

"Magic," was all Zander offered, his mouth agape as he ogled the blue-lit door.

"I don't know," Safi admitted. "I found it by accident while

I was evading the flame hawk, and now . . ." She shrugged, a helpless gesture—because really there was nothing else she could say.

"Well, where does it go?" Caden squinted into the darkness, inching closer to the cliff's edge. "Those soldiers will find us eventually, you know. Assuming they aren't already on their way. We need to get moving."

"Magic," Zander repeated, louder now, and pointing at the door. "*Magic*."

"Yeah, Zan." Lev patted his shoulder. "We know."

Wind thrashed harder, pulling at Safi's hair, and the distant voices pitched louder—loud enough for her to catch a single word: *Threadbrother*.

Safi snapped her gaze toward it, straining to see, straining to listen. Because that word had been shouted in Nubrevnan. And it had been shouted in a voice she knew. *His* voice, even though he'd died in an explosion two weeks ago—

"Safi," Caden said. "Are you listening?"

It can't be, she thought, head shaking. *It can't be him. Merik's dead, he's dead*. And yet, that voice had sounded exactly like she remembered from the *Jana*. Just like she remembered from that night on a dusty road.

And these winds—could they be his?

"*Safi!*" Caden clapped a hand on her shoulder. She flinched. "We need to follow this bridge." He dipped his head until his eyes bored into hers. "We can't stay here."

She blinked, confused now. Lost, even. She had been so certain that voice belonged to a dead man.

"Bridge?" she murmured at last, gaze finally latching onto Caden's.

"That one." He pointed straight into the crevasse, and when Safi followed his finger she saw only shadows.

While far, far below, a galaxy swirled.

"Magic," Zander repeated once more, and for the first time since stumbling through the doorway, he moved, striding right off the ledge and into the abyss.

Safi lunged forward to grab him, but she was too slow, and . . .

And Zander didn't plummet to his death. Instead, he marched right across the cavern while Vaness bounced upon his shoulder.

"Another glamour," Lev explained, moving to Safi's side. "I bet you're getting real sick of those." Then with a rakish grin, she too strutted onto invisible nothing.

"Stay close," Caden murmured, and his fingers laced into Safi's. "This bridge is narrow, and it's a long way down."

Merik met the Fury head-on. A collision of winds, a clashing of magics. Cold and ice-bound against stars that now sang inside his blood. The two winds plowed against each other . . .

And stopped. A wall of noise, a wall of storm.

"*Run!*" Merik bellowed at the Northman on the steps behind. A refrain he'd yelled so often to this man—but that had never mattered more than it did right now. "*RUN!*"

The Northman ran, vanishing from Merik's peripheral gaze.

Does he have them? Kullen's voice raged atop his winds— or perhaps he only raged it inside Merik's skull. Either way, it jolted the gale in his favor. A sudden *lurch* of shadowy power that thundered against Merik.

He skidded backward. His calves hit stairs, and his balance was thrown. He fell. Winds pulverized him, and suddenly Kullen was there, sweeping past in a swirl of shadows that aimed for the Northman.

Merik did not think, he did not evaluate. He *moved*, flying full force toward Kullen. And right as Kullen landed—right as the Northman flung himself through a glowing doorway that led only Noden knew where—Merik blasted into him.

He tackled the Fury in a graceless tangle of limbs. Together, they keeled over the edge, tumbling into the chasm below. They spun, they fell, and for several eternal heartbeats, gravity gripped harder than any magic or any storm.

Then Kullen's frozen winds pummeled in, and Merik's swooped in just behind. Now, they shot back up toward ledges, toward glowing doorways half masked by dust.

Where are they? Kullen's words severed into Merik's brain. *Where have you put them?*

"Put what?" he tried to scream, but there could be no out-screaming this storm. And there was no out-flying Kullen either. Every flip Merik attempted, Kullen flipped faster. Every evasion, every sweep, Kullen was there before Merik could twist away.

You took the blade and the glass. But I will get them back, Threadbrother. You cannot hide them from me.

The Fury grabbed, his magic clawed. Twice, ice-fingers scraped at Merik, sharp enough to cut. Cold enough to cauterize. First his face, then his chest. And twice, it would have been Merik's throat if he hadn't punched his winds between them.

The harder Merik flew, the harder the Fury flew to catch

him—and the more winds they sucked in, forcing the air to thicken. Ice-laden, yet hot with rage. Snow streaking, yet charged and building.

Then lightning cracked. Near enough to singe Merik's skin. To judder electricity through his chest and veins. And bright enough to startle both him and the Fury.

Merik used that moment. He used the spots flashing in his eyes to thrust away. Aimlessly, yet with every piece of power inside—and inside those stars spinning far below.

It worked. Merik launched high, he launched fast. Kullen *roared* after him, a bellow to rupture Merik's skull. A scream that set off more lightning, more winds. But Merik had the momentum he needed, and he catapulted up, up. Away, away.

And as he flew, he ransacked his mind for something—*anything*—that would help him. Kullen thought Merik had stolen his blade and glass; there had to be a way Merik could use that. Especially since as long as Kullen was here, he wasn't letting the Raider King inside . . . and that meant the Raider King wasn't reaching Lovats.

But Merik couldn't distract Kullen forever.

Merik's winds zoomed him to the ice-bridge. Cold quivered off it—different than the ice of Kullen's storm. It seemed to hum, it seemed to sing: *Come, come, and find release.*

It was the song from the pond filled with bodies, firmer here. A mother urging her child to bed.

Merik's flight slowed. The refrain thrummed louder. *Come, my son, and sleep. Come, come, the ice will hold you.*

His gaze traced the bridge across the dark expanse to where it fed onto a ledge with a tall door, half choked by more ice.

Come, come, and face the end.

Before Merik could fly that way, before he could fully answer that call, Kullen's voice shattered across his brain: *AND WHO ARE THESE INTRUDERS?*

Merik flinched, a twang of his muscles that drowned out the ice, drowned out the song. He looked down, fearing he'd find the Northman. And sure enough, there was movement surging within the storm—colors that were not lightning. Figures that were not the Fury.

But they were not the Northman.

Four people ran across the cavern, somehow sprinting above the galaxy despite no stones to cradle their feet.

Even with his eyes streaming and lightning flashing, even with the ice to chorus and call, Merik recognized one of those figures the instant he saw her. That golden hair, shorter now, and that loping stride.

But she died, he thought, heart tightening. Mind reeling. *She died in an explosion two weeks ago.*

Then a second thought hurled in: *And so did you.*

In an instant, Merik pulled in his winds.

And Merik flew to her.

FIFTY-SEVEN

※

Vivia led the way to the under-city. Cam leaned on Vivia, his bandaged hand clutched to his chest and words tumbling out, incomprehensible and disjointed. Vizer Sotar followed just behind, lantern in hand. He did not believe Cam, but he also had not refused Vivia when she had asked him to join.

"Ryber and me," Cam explained, "found Captain Sotar in the mountain. Or maybe the captain found *us*—I don't know, sir. She was following Eridysi's blade and glass. The ones that call out to people like her, see?"

Vivia did not see at all, and Sotar cleared his throat in frustration. The limestone tunnel descended steadily; the foxfire overhead shone green and bright.

"So Ryber took the captain with her into the tomb. It's the fastest way back to the Convent."

"Tomb?" Vivia asked. Then a second question hit her. "What about Merik? Where is he? You left the city with him two weeks ago."

Cam grimaced, and behind them, Sotar's pace stuttered—for of course, he didn't know Merik still lived. *No one*

512

in the kingdom knew that. They all believed he'd died in the *Jana*'s explosion.

"Merik was with us," Cam admitted, "but we ... we got separated. He ain't dead though," the boy added hastily. "I just know it in my gut that he ain't dead."

In your gut? Vivia wanted to demand—just as she wanted to demand more information on where Merik and this boy had been or how they'd gotten separated. Now wasn't the time, though. Not with Vizer Sotar right there and a city to defend.

So Vivia returned to the early trail of information. "You mentioned tombs, Cam. Where? Whose tombs?"

"At the Sightwitch Sister Convent." He spoke as if this explained everything. "Ry said the ice tombs were the fastest way to the surface, so she and Captain Sotar followed them up. They're going to destroy the standing stones, see? Then, once they break 'em, the mountain will collapse and the magic doors'll stop working. After that, the Raider King won't be able to reach Lovats. Or anywhere else."

Vivia's forehead wrinkled. A squishing frown between her brows because all of this was *absurdity*. Magic doorways and standing stones and the convent from a long-lost order—it was madness. Something out of one of her mother's dreams. Yet, as Cam kept speaking, kept explaining all these impossible pieces as if they were real, Vivia started to wonder if maybe ... just *maybe* it was true.

If the Void Well could live inside Lovats, maybe there were other hidden wonders out there too.

"But," Cam finished tiredly, "just in case Ry's plan doesn't work, she and Captain Sotar sent me here. To warn you."

"Just in case," Vivia repeated, and this time, she glanced back to Vizer Sotar.

His nostrils were flared, his head shaking a warning.

They reached the end of the tunnel, where the doorway framed by Hagfishes waited. She shoved inside, and a young father with a babe in his arms bowed crookedly at Vivia's entrance. Then other people along the narrow limestone street caught sight of her. Hesitant smiles flashed, curtsies and bows, and more fists over hearts than she deserved. Most, though, slept at this hour. Oblivious and thinking themselves safe.

Vivia's teeth ground. If Cam spoke the truth, then every one of these people was at risk—and with each step, Vivia felt more and more inclined to believe him. Cam's story might be fragmented and wild, but he had spoken words that only Stix could know.

Noden and the Hagfishes ought to bend to a woman's rule.

"That way," Cam murmured when they reached an intersection, and Vivia walked faster, towing Cam along where he pointed. Three more intersections and they reached a narrow tunnel at the edge of the cavern. She'd seen this space before, but it led nowhere, so she and her workers had left it alone.

Now, though, she followed Cam inside, and when they reached the stone end, Vizer Sotar stepped closer, lantern light spraying over it. A rectangle as tall as Vivia, framed by a hundred tiny boxes with diagonal lines.

"This is it," Cam said, and he patted the stone with his unbandaged hand.

"This," Sotar said flatly, "is a wall."

And Vivia was inclined to agree. It was as if someone had started a door here, but then given up.

"No," Cam insisted. He turned earnest, pleading eyes on Vivia. "The door only goes one way, sir. You can leave the mountain to come here, but you can't go back through. The original Six made it that way for safety. I *swear* this is where I came in."

Only goes one way. A breath hissed from Vivia's lungs. What the hell-waters was she doing here? She wasn't really going to trust a boy she barely knew just because he'd quoted something Stix had said . . .

Was she? *Could* she?

"Please, sir," the boy whispered. He laid a hand on Vivia's sleeve. "You gotta believe me."

She turned and met his eyes. Sincere, innocent eyes—no shadows, no deceit. Merik had trusted this boy, and clearly Stix had too. And if Stix had truly sent Cam here because she believed that Vivia and Lovats needed warning, then Vivia couldn't risk ignoring him. No matter how impossible his tales of magic doorways and Sightwitches might seem. Vivia would rather empty the under-city and be hated than lose hundreds of lives.

She turned to Vizer Sotar, and said, "Evacuate the under-city."

He reared back. "You cannot be serious."

"Do it," she countered, fidgeting with her cuffs. "Then evacuate the entire plateau, Vizer. Or at least try to. I want every wind-drum in the city pounding."

Sotar's mouth bobbed open. Then shut. Then: "Please reconsider, Your Majesty. To empty the city would take—"

"Every woman and man inside Pin's Keep," she interrupted. "I know exactly what it would take, and I also know exactly what's at stake if we choose to ignore this boy. If he's right, Vizer Sotar . . . We cannot risk that. Now go. Please."

At that name, Cam suddenly straightened. His eyebrows suddenly jumped. "Oh. It's *you*, sir. I'm so sorry—I didn't realize, or I'd have told you sooner. The captain also had a message for you." A solemn bow to his head. Then: "She said she's sorry she missed your birthday yesterday. Next year, she swears you'll go to the Cleaved Man."

It was like watching a wind change. One moment, the sails caught the breeze and Sotar's ship flew. The next moment, he was dead in the water. His shoulders deflated, his eyelids fluttered shut. "I hate the Cleaved Man," he said under his breath. "And she blighted well knows it. But she makes me go every year, all the same."

Vivia inched closer to Sotar and, just as Cam had done to her, she laid a hand on the man's sleeve. "You know what we have to do."

"Hye." He nodded slowly, almost to himself, and when he opened his eyes again, it was to offer a slow salute for Vivia. "It will be done, Your Majesty. We will evacuate the underground and the city."

"Thank you." She swallowed. Then she smoothed at her shirt, her coat, and said, "Also, I want you to bring me every witch in the city, Vizer. We need to block this doorway, and we need to block it fast."

FIFTY-EIGHT

✳

Te varuje.

I trust you as if my soul were yours.

Aeduan had never thought he would hear those words spoken to him. Not since his mother had died. Not since he had learned he was a demon—and that all demons died alone.

Te varuje.

Iseult vanished into the darkness of the cave.

And Natan bellowed his fury. The layers of his blood stank with it. The cackling laughter and mountain cold, the endless hunger and bloodied knuckles.

Aeduan had only two paths before him. He could fight Natan and let the battle overwhelm him. Or he could hold the battle and let Natan kill him. Both choices ended in his death, both choices ended in Iseult with danger on her heels.

And both choices would come to pass if Aeduan could not maintain his grip upon the battle. The Well's power was fading fast from his blood.

Iseult, Iseult, Iseult. She was all that mattered. He just had to buy her enough time to get away.

Natan charged—and Aeduan was ready. For a stuttering

517

heartbeat, he shifted the balance of his magic. Away from the battle, he pushed power into his muscles. Enough to duck beneath Natan's blade. Then to swoop up against his arm and knock the buckler from his grasp.

It fell to the snow.

The raiders and monks on the river lurched forward. A heaving *push*, like an avalanche about to break. Thousands of fighters ready to destroy.

As Aeduan swung the buckler off the snow, Natan heaved again at Aeduan, strong and fresh and ready. He might have lost his buckler, but he was still a Carawen. Prepared for anything.

Aeduan deflected, buckler wrenching high—and arm juddering with the impact.

The battle jerked closer.

Another attack from Natan, and this time, when Aeduan blocked, Natan laughed. A crowing, vindictive sound. The same mocking laugh he'd flung at Aeduan every day when they were children. "I can keep going forever, Bloodwitch. But how long will you last, I wonder?"

Natan swiped, he swung, he sliced. Aeduan dodged, parried, and ducked, but each move was slower than the last. Each attack a hairsbreadth closer to connecting.

Then Natan drove his sword into Aeduan's heart, cutting it in two. He wrenched the blade out, and like ice melting, Aeduan's magic gave way. The battle slipped from his grasp. Noise battered against him, sudden and focused and plowing this way.

Natan jolted at the sudden upheaval. He glanced behind.

And Aeduan moved. He tackled Natan to the ground,

sword flying wide. They rolled across the snow. Aeduan's heart gushed, spraying Natan in red, but already the wound healed. Whether Aeduan wanted it to or not, his magic knit his heart back together.

And without that magic to push his muscles faster, he stood no chance. Natan grappled atop him, and no amount of bucking his hips or straining would get Aeduan free.

So he stopped fighting. He lay back on the snow, blood sliding down his chest—a distant pain, just as the snow beneath him was a distant cold—and watched as Natan laughed at him. Watched as he unfastened a cleaver from his baldric.

"I never thought to see you this way," Natan said, echoing what Lizl had uttered only yesterday. But unlike her, he savored this moment. "I imagined it so many times, carving your head from your neck. And now here we are.

"You were always the best fighter—always claiming the best assignments—but who is the Abbot now? And who is the one about to die?"

As Natan spoke, as Aeduan lay there limp and gasping while blood-scent after blood-scent careened his way, his magic sensed a new blood shimmering above the rest. *Speed and daisy chains, mother's kisses and sharpened steel.* It came from the cave, and it was not alone.

"How does it feel, knowing I will kill you?" Natan continued. "Knowing that your magic cannot save you now?"

She was so close. Almost here ...

"I will do the same to that girl, you know. The 'Matsi smut claiming to be the Cahr Awen. I will carve off her head too."

Then Aeduan saw her, a vague figure coated in ash and blood.

"And you cannot stop me. You cannot kill me—"

"No," Lizl snarled behind him. "But I can."

Her sword burst through Natan's chest. The exact reverse of what Natan's had done to Aeduan—into Natan's back and out through the heart. Then just like Natan, she wrenched her blade out again.

Natan's body toppled sideways, still spurting and warm, and Lizl offered Aeduan her hand. As she helped him rise, he spotted a new streak of blood on her cloak. It trimmed the edge, a perfect mimicry of what every Abbot wore—and of what Natan would wear no longer.

Behind her, a hundred monks thundered from the cave.

"Now you owe me *four* life-debts, Monk Aeduan!" Lizl lifted her voice above the raiders and the other monks barreling this way. She shoved Natan's blade into Aeduan's hand. "And a fifth one for this sword, plus a sixth for the rebels I've brought to save you."

Then she turned to the monks behind her, pumped her free hand to the sky, and roared, "*For the Cahr Awen!*"

The insurgents charged. A snarl of bodies and blades and blood that pumped with purpose. They rumbled past Aeduan, shaking the earth and the frozen reeds. And for a century, or perhaps only moments, he stood there, watching them leave while his heart stitched itself back together. While his blood—gradually, gradually—pumped stronger and his witchery finished what it had begun.

Once it was done, his lungs breathed fully. His heart boomed strong, and for the first time in his twenty years of existence, Aeduan knew who he was and what he had to do.

He straightened.

He joined the fight.

For the Cahr Awen.

Iseult's footsteps echoed off the tunnel walls. Her breaths carved in and out. Steady. Trained for this, and bolstered by the power of the Well.

She was running. Again. Always running. The light from the valley, from the moon, showed her the way, but when a bend in the tunnel stole that, she walked with arms outstretched. Straining to remember what had been here when she and Leopold had come this way.

Leopold, Leopold. She had left him. Curse her, she had left him and that guilt would crown her for the rest of her days— as would leaving Aeduan. Every few seconds, she looked back, praying she might see his face in the darkness. Praying she would hear Threadless breaths and know he had arrived.

But he did not come, and she kept moving. Until faint flickers of light glowed ahead, spurring her faster. She rounded a bend, reaching the fork in the path from before.

She slung to a halt. Even staggered back two steps. On the ground at the center was a candle—*the* candle Leopold had carried. Thanks to the magic within, the wax had not melted. The wick burned strong.

It was the bodies, though, that made Iseult's heart drop low. Raiders and monks were locked in place, not so different from what Aeduan had done, except these people were held by stone. As if hewn from the tunnel's granite, yet more real than any sculptor could ever produce.

Owl. Iseult had no doubt. The girl had been here. Both forks in the path, the one toward the Monastery and the other to the unknown beyond, were filled with stone fighters.

Threads skated into Iseult's awareness, stunned and horrified. Confused and even relieved. Then a voice came, authority strong in her command: "*Continue on!*"

Iseult bolted for the tunnel out of the Monastery. She snagged the candle as she sprinted past, and right as the first Threads barreled into the cavern, she dove onto the ascending path. More stone monks, more stone raiders. She dipped and spun around them, accelerating even as the tunnel's incline sharpened.

Then it became stairs, and though her breath scorched in her lungs, Iseult hopped them two at a time. The air sharpened, and frost glistened on the walls. The steps, though, were now layered in gravel. A clear line upward—as if an Earthwitch had come this way.

Iseult pushed her body even harder, and soon, moonlight and winter washed against her. She sprinted the final distance into the night.

Snow-dipped fir trees surrounded her. Wind kicked, and the first tendrils of dawn reached across the sky. Even here—wherever *here* might be—the sounds of battle and fire sang. Distant, though. Too far to sense Threads, too far for Iseult to even pinpoint a direction.

Except there *were* two sets of Threads near enough for her to feel, and they waited straight ahead. One set radiated brilliant green with the power of an Earthwitch, and the other bore a heart of churning, stormy blue.

Iseult reached Owl and Leopold in seconds. They waited

ahead beside two piles of boulders, and at the sound of Iseult's feet, Leopold whirled about. Then his Threads ignited with such pure relief, it hurt Iseult's eyes. Meanwhile, Owl's Threads tinged pink with delight, while the girl herself, filthy with dirt, grinned ear to ear in a way Iseult had never seen before. Such happiness. Such warmth.

Iseult almost wept at the sight of her.

No, she *did* weep. Tears flecked from her eyes, and she realized she had been wrong before. Back at the sky-ferry. The warmth in her chest *was* love, for this strange child who was not a child at all.

"You were slow," Owl said, and before Iseult could process what that even meant, Leopold reached Iseult. Without warning and with one arm in a sling, he pulled her into an embrace. She was so startled, she did not resist it—and his Threads, such icy relief, such sunset happiness and mossy concern, briefly veiled the world around them. "I lost you on the river," he said. "I could not find you, and I thought it was all over."

No, Iseult thought, pulling back. *I left you.* She would confess that to him later, though.

"We have to go," she told him in Cartorran. "Raiders and monks are coming this way . . ." She trailed off as the meaning of the scene suddenly sifted into place. Owl. Leopold. Together with two heaps of stones behind them.

"What are you doing?" She put the question to Leopold first, then in Nomatsi for Owl.

And Owl was the one to answer. "Leaving," she said simply. "I know the way." Then she turned to the smaller stone pile and levitated a boulder. It crashed onto the other pile with such force, the ground shook. Snow fell from the trees.

"The bat found me," Leopold explained. "I was surrounded on all sides, and he scared them off. Then Owl was there, and I followed her." He shook his head, incredulity in his Threads and on his face. As if he still did not understand what had happened or why.

Crash, crash. Rocks gathered. Owl's Threads shone. The wind blew on and on.

"What is she, Iseult?" Leopold asked, watching the girl. "She is no mere child."

"No," Iseult agreed, but she had no answer beyond that. Owl was special, and that was all she knew.

"This way," Owl interrupted, and in a burst of stone and speed, she launched the final boulder away, revealing a hole in the earth like a bear's den that emanated blue light.

Before Iseult could stop her, Owl smiled again—a flash of pink amusement in her Threads—and crawled into the hole. The blue light swallowed her.

And Iseult, with Leopold just behind, pitched in after her.

FIFTY-NINE

✳

Lightning dominated the darkness. Safi's eyes sizzled. Her heart fried, and each breath tasted of burning death. But she and the Hell-Bards did not stop running.

It didn't matter that Safi couldn't spy the path beneath her feet, it didn't matter that all she saw was a storm-spun galaxy far below—and it didn't matter that this unnatural storm clashed harder and harder by the second. The Hell-Bards ran true, and not once did Caden let go of Safi's hand.

Until suddenly he did. Until suddenly he had no choice because the earth was shaking and tearing Safi from his grip. A great sideways crunch that sent the bridge lurching.

And sent Safi flying headfirst into the darkness.

She screamed, a sound lost to the winds. A sound swallowed by the eternal *crack!* of lightning. Or maybe it was the mountain still breaking that stole her voice. There was no telling what crashed around her, no telling what death might hit her—or when or where or how.

Then her body slammed against something solid. Something frozen. Except she wasn't dying and her life wasn't

525

sapping from her veins. Instead, strong arms were flinging around her and a man was bellowing, "*HANG ON.*"

So Safi hung on, even as her mind fought to catch up. Even as her eyes fought to see and her fingers fought to hold true. She had no idea who she was pressed against. All she knew was that he held her tight and that he *soared*.

Winds charged beneath them. They rocketed up, up while the storm pressed down. The squall tried to squash them and boil them and keep them from rising.

Then lightning slashed. A mere arm's length away, so bright that the world turned to day. And so bright that, even as her eyes winced shut, Safi glimpsed the face before her.

Impossible, she thought at the same instant that her magic screamed, *True!*

And he must have glimpsed her face too, because his magic skipped a beat. Their flight faltered. The world dragged, and in that space between frenzied, storm-swept breaths, Safi saw everything she needed to see.

For the first time in a month, she *saw* Merik Nihar. She *saw* the man she had believed to be dead.

Angry red scars webbed up the side of his face, crawling above the hairline. Eating into his shorn, dark hair. Half an eyebrow was missing, and he'd lost weight. Gaunt bones poked against scorched cheeks, while strange shadows undulated beneath his skin.

But it was *him*. Safi would know Merik's face anywhere. She would know his eyes anywhere. *True, true, true.*

Then time and storm plowed into them. Safi lost all sight, all sound. Static expanded inside her, scratched against her skin. Merik's flight resumed.

Higher they hurtled, while the storm thrashed against them. Frozen, relentless, alive. And the earth trembled too—a bass vibration that chattered in Safi's lungs and sent rocks coursing by.

When at last their ascent slowed, Merik's winds dumped them roughly onto a crude staircase carved into the mountain wall. The storm still raged, and the stones still quaked. Safi could barely keep her knees steady beneath her as she clutched for a handhold against the side of the cavern.

Merik braced himself on the step below hers, one arm against the rock. The other still looped around her waist. He gazed up at her, his eyes as brown as she remembered, even in this lightning-lit world. He was alive. He was right here.

"How?" she tried to say at the same instant he said, "You *died.*"

She shook her head, a frantic movement that matched the wildness in his own shaking head. Yet before she could ask, could move, could do anything but stare, a voice carved through the storm. Made of ice and nightmares, it sang, "*You cannot run forever, Merik. Wherever you go, I will find you.*"

Then wind pushed against Safi. It kicked at the snow and weaseled beneath her clothes, like hands fumbling, searching—

"Go," Merik said. He released her and pulled away, and new winds—strong and true—gusted. "Go," he repeated, louder now. Eyes wide and pleading. "Safi, please. Go." And before she could stop him, before she could beg him to stay or explain or at least tell her how to find him again, he launched into the darkness.

She watched Merik leave. Watched him shrink until he was nothing more than a shadow. She watched lightning and cyclones steal him away. And she watched until falling rocks forced her feet to move.

The staircase was collapsing beneath her. Booming eruptions of noise and dust that punched upward, punched nearer. Soon, she would be standing on thin air.

So Safi spun on her heel and ran. Her hands grabbed at the higher steps, the only thing she could do for balance. The only thing she could do to hang on while hell-storm and earthquakes pummeled against her.

Boulders fell. Scree shattered. Safi's knees rolled and her ankles popped. Until abruptly, the stairs ended. Her hands met empty air, and a ledge stretched before her.

"SAFI!" roared a voice she knew. Then a second voice, "Safi, faster! Safi, this way!" So that way Safi charged, dead ahead to where two figures materialized in the shadows and a blue light glowed.

She reached Caden, who grabbed one arm. Then Zander, who grabbed her other. Together, they heaved her toward the doorway.

Safi had just enough time before tumbling through to look back. Just enough time to search for one final glimpse of Merik.

It wasn't Merik she saw sweeping by, though. It was an old crow, black and sleek, winging through the storm.

Then blue light frizzed over her, time stopped, and Safi and the Hell-Bards were transported far, far away.

Merik did not watch Safi leave. He couldn't. The Fury was almost to her; Merik had to keep him away.

And now Merik also had a plan.

It was neither cohesive, nor perhaps even possible—but it was the only option before him. The only thing he could do that might calm the Fury once and for all.

"*Do you want these?*" Merik bellowed, pumping all his magic into that sound. "*You'll have to come and get them.*" Then he lifted two jagged rocks, remnants of the mountain that he hoped, from afar, might look like the Fury's missing tools.

Like a razor in one hand, and broken glass in the other.

A screech ripped across the cavern, borne on lightning. Swollen by the storm. It slashed over a mountain that would not stop its quaking. Then the Fury himself appeared within the squall.

Merik moved. He zoomed toward the ice-bridge, fueled by starlight and a need to protect Nubrevna, no matter the cost.

And also fueled by the lure of a mother's call and by a sleeping ice Esme had said would suck you in.

As Merik had hoped, the Fury followed him.

Merik reached the ice-bridge. His feet touched down, and instantly, the song bombarded him, sentient and hungry.

Come, come, and find release. Come, come, the ice will hold you.

Good. Merik hoped it would do exactly that.

He ran. His heels hammered, ice crunched, and all around him, thunder clapped and crazed.

Then the Fury landed. "*Where are you going?*" he bellowed. "*That way will not free you!*"

Merik sped faster, legs careening and arms swinging. The door was near enough for him to see details in the wood, to spot a key-slot with ice spindling through.

"*Stop!*" Panic laced Kullen's voice now. Static too, that

529

crackled in the air and stabbed at Merik's skin. "*Stop!*" Kullen pleaded. "*Do not go that way!*"

Merik reached the door. He reached the ice, and, twisting sideways, he flung himself through. Instantly, the song magnified. Tenfold louder, it throbbed in his lungs, compelling him instead of crooning. Tenfold stronger, it jittered in his teeth and rooted in his heart.

As Merik wiggled and squirmed, straining to squeeze through a narrow passage that glowed blue with an inner light all its own, ice crunched outward. It poked. It grasped, fingers that wanted to hold him still.

Come, come, and find release. Come, come, the ice will hold you.

"Not . . . yet," he gritted out, and with a final shove, he toppled into an open space.

But like everywhere else in this mountain, the ground shook—though instead of rocks to tumble down, it was ice. Boulders and debris that shattered on impact and filled the air with crystal mist.

He stumbled forward, arms blocking his face while he squinted into this frozen room. Shaped like a seashell, it spiraled upward with hundreds of doors branching off, each one clogged with ice.

All except for a single door high above.

Come, come, and find release. Come, come, the ice will hold you.

Merik inhaled. Ice razored his throat and lungs, but with it came a wind. With it came power. Like the starlight from the cavern, but stronger—and tinged with something sharp. Something savage.

"*Stop*," Kullen commanded, pushing into the room. And it was the strangest thing, seeing the Fury afraid. The shadows pulsed inward and blue flickered around his eyes.

Then Merik moved. Before Kullen could see he held nothing but two stones. Before more ice could fall and stop him from fleeing forever.

His winds vaulted him high. Up three spirals, he zipped and swirled. Ice meteored down. Lightning scorched upward. But Kullen and his magic were not fast enough. Merik reached the open door and soared in.

What he found was a tomb—he knew that truth as soon as he burst inside, for already two shadows hovered inside the ice wall. Small, child-sized figures sucked into this eternal, sleeping ice. Between the two shapes were two empty holes, man-sized and waiting.

Merik strode toward the one on the right. Three long paces, and the closer he came, the more the ice crackled outward. Clawing and hungry. *Come, come, and find release. Come, come, the ice will hold you.*

But Merik did not step into the hole. Not yet.

His blood roared in his ears. His muscles shook and his belly spun—and it was not because of the mountain. It was because Merik knew what he had to do.

Then the room darkened, as he'd known it would, and shadows skated across the trembling floor. Even though Merik was ready, even though he was waiting, nothing could prepare him for the Fury's attack.

It railed against him, a battering ram of winds that crunched Merik's spine before slinging him around to face the entrance. To face Kullen stalking just outside.

"Give me my blade," the Fury ordered through the tomb's entrance. "Give me my glass."

Merik opened his hands. Empty now, for he'd left the rocks in the collapsing spiral. And as he'd hoped—as he'd *expected*—the Fury's temper took hold. He charged into the tomb, a berserking streak of winds and shadows and raging, blackened snow. He slammed Merik against the ice, first with magic.

Then with touch, with a grip that cut off Merik's air and silenced the magic in his veins. "What," he hissed, "have you done with them?"

All Merik could do was laugh at that question. At the beast before him. A breathless wheeze that rattled in his chest because Kullen was gone. Merik saw that now, and it made the next step—the final step—so much easier.

For at least in all his mistakes, Merik had gotten one thing right: one for the sake of many.

Kullen's grip tightened. Sparks flickered over Merik's eyes. No breath, no thought, and that was all right; he didn't need them anymore. All he needed were his muscles and a few more seconds . . .

Merik flung both his arms backward, into the nearest tomb. Into the waiting ice. His hands pressed against it, instantly numbing. And instantly singing, *singing* that song that never ceased.

Come, come, and find release.

Then the ice erupted. It raced up Merik's arms, a climbing, heaving, frantic thing that hit his shoulders, then leaped across to Kullen. Shadows froze in midair.

Come, come, the ice will hold you.

Kullen gasped, as if plunged into a winter sea. Still the ice groped and expanded. It glazed over his chest before raking down his legs. Then it sliced over Merik's back, and down Kullen's too.

When it reached their throats, Merik finally looked into Kullen's eyes. His *real* eyes, no longer black. No longer lost, but merely blue and sad and true. His Threadbrother's eyes.

"I'm sorry," Kullen croaked.

And Merik wanted to say the same thing. Never had he wanted anything more. Kullen was here. He was *alive*. And there was so much Merik needed to apologize for.

But the ice had covered Merik's mouth now, and all he could do in that moment was blink—again and again, fluttering away thick tears building on his cheeks.

"I'm sorry," Kullen said once more. "The raiders made it into the mountain."

Then the ice covered Merik's tears. The ice covered Merik's eyes.

Come, come, and face the end.

Merik and Kullen slept.

SIXTY

※

It all happened so fast. Safi's mind and body were pulled apart, then reassembled. And before her thoughts could catch up to her muscles, she was plunged out the other side.

She toppled into Lev's waiting arms. Cold, damp night brushed against her.

A heartbeat later, Caden and Zander toppled out too. Zander, though, wasn't well. His right hand and wrist were bloodied and smashed. Knuckle bones glistened in the moonlight.

"Oh gods," Lev breathed, moving for him. "That needs tending."

For several seconds, while the Hell-Bards moved to a fallen oak, Safi spun and spun . . . And kept on spinning, searching every beech and pine and shadow for a fifth person. A river churned nearby, more sound and vibration than anything she could see. And then there was the doorway, glowing and glaring beside a pile of rocks as tall as she.

Somewhere within all this fog and mist coiling from the trees—somewhere in that craggy rise of earth beyond, there had to be a fifth person.

But there wasn't. No matter how hard Safi stared, she couldn't find Empress Vaness.

"Where is she?" Safi rounded on the Hell-Bards. "Where is Vaness?"

No one looked Safi's way. Lev's grip was strong at Zander's back. "Hang on," she kept murmuring. "Hang on, Zan."

Meanwhile, Caden hastily bound the ruined hand in a shredded shirt sleeve, completely oblivious to Safi's panic. "This wound needs water," he told Zander. "And a healer. All the bones are broken, and with this much exposed—"

"*Where is Vaness?*" Safi's voice slapped across the forest. Petulant. Terrified.

Lev finally looked away from Zander. She bit her lip and shook her head. "The Empress fell, Domna. Right before we got through. Zander tried to reach her, but he . . ."

"Too late," Zander finished, and the pain flinching across his face was not just from his wound. Tears squeezed from his eyes. "I tried. I swear, I tried."

Safi's magic told her the man spoke true. She also knew that he needed help—soon. But right now, Vaness was trapped inside a collapsing cavern, and until Safi found her, all other concerns were meaningless.

She dove back toward the door. The blue light wavered. Caden and Lev screamed at her to wait. She didn't. She shoved into the doorway.

And Safi slammed against solid stone. The force of the impact flung her back. She crashed to the earth ten paces away. It punched the breath from her lungs. The world darkened and spun, and power buzzed in her chest, throbbed along her skin.

535

"No," she groaned, blinking at the moonlit sky. "No, no, *no*." She pushed upright, determined to try again.

Lev dropped to a crouch beside her. "It doesn't work, Domna. I already tried. The magic won't let us back through." She offered Safi a hand, but Safi didn't take it. She couldn't. All that running, all that escape and violence and flame . . . and for what? Vaness still hadn't made it in the end.

No, no, no. Safi couldn't believe it. Not after everything, Vaness *couldn't* be gone. She *couldn't* be dead. Not her too.

But Merik still lives, her brain reminded her—though even that seemed impossible now. Had she really seen him? Or had he been an apparition made of lightning and snow? Even if he had been real, even if he did still live, he was also trapped inside that mountain.

No, no, no.

Lev moved away, and Safi simply sat there, staring into the trees. There were mountains beyond, vague silhouettes against a darkened sky. Clouds wafted across the moon. The creatures of the night hesitantly resumed their song.

Safi didn't cry. She almost wished she would. Tears seemed appropriate after everything. Habim and Mathew, Vaness and Merik. And Rokesh too, for she had no idea what had happened to him. Likely, he was as dead as all the other Adders, and didn't *he*, her Nursemaid, deserve tears?

But no tears came. All Safi could do was breathe and keep on staring.

And all Safi could do was tap. Her left hand, filthy and cold, would not stop this steady rhythm against the earth. Faster. Faster. A roiling, building beat.

"We can't stay here." Caden's voice drifted into her aware-

536

ness. So far away, and yet she knew he was right there, kneeling beside her. *Tap-tap-tap.*

"I think we're in the Ohrins, Safi. Near the Grieg estates. I know that river."

The Ohrins and the Grieg estates. The literal opposite side of the Witchlands from Marstok. Oh gods below, what were the chances? So many impossibilities all colliding in a single night. Safi didn't doubt Caden was right, though. Those trees, this cold and mist—she had spent her childhood in these mountains.

"Grieg has men who patrol," Caden went on. "If they find us, they'll bring us to him, and if that happens, then you won't stay free for long."

No, Safi thought. She wouldn't. Dom fon Grieg was one of Emperor Henrick's favored noblemen. One look at Safi, and he'd send her off to Praga . . .

Her spine tensed at that thought. She sat a bit taller. *Tap-tap-tap.* Then she turned and looked in Caden's eyes. The blue door scarcely glowed now, a mere halo to frame his tight-lipped face.

"Good." Safi let that word drip from her tongue. It tasted like metal. Then she said it again, harder, "*Good.* Let his men find us. Zander needs help, and a man as rich as Dom fon Grieg will have the best healers in the Witchlands."

When Caden gave no reaction beyond a creasing frown, Safi held out her wrists. "Here. I'll make it easy, Hell-Bard. Tie me up and walk me straight up to his castle."

"What?" Now Caden recoiled, shooting a worried glance Lev's way.

"You heard me." With Caden's help, Safi pushed to her

537

feet. The forest blurred and swayed. Then she held out her wrists again. "Bind me up and bring me to his castle."

"Domna," Lev warned now. "Did that magic mess with your mind?"

Maybe it had. Safi didn't know, and she didn't much care. *Tap-tap-tap* went her heel, and she knew what she had to do. As clearly as if Iseult had made this plan and whispered it in her ear. *Initiate, complete.*

Zander was the first to figure it out, even half-conscious and pain-wracked. "She . . . wants to save her uncle," he rasped.

"Exactly." Safi flashed her most cavalier grin. "The giant has the right of it. So, Caden, I'll say it one last time: bind my wrists, walk me to that castle, and turn me in. Because I have an emperor to marry, and I don't think Zander here can stand to lose much more blood."

Vivia stared out across the under-city. *Her* under-city. As empty as the day she'd found it, but now instead of dust and cobwebs and foxfire there were clothes and blankets and favorite dolls, forgotten inside homes or on limestone street corners.

It felt like defeat.

Hye, Vivia knew this was the only option before her, the only way to save her people. And she knew this was what little foxes did when their den and kits were threatened: they fled.

Still, it felt like she was handing the Raider King a gift. *Here is my city, cleaned and emptied just for you.*

The streets of Lovats must look a hundredfold worse than this. Boats crammed the water-bridge aiming south, and people were being led out of the city on foot into the farm-lands and valley below.

It was not an official evacuation. Already, the King Regent had moved to counteract Vivia's work, but he was too slow, too late. The wind-drums had pounded the alarm: raiders were coming. People fled.

Vivia just hoped her father and his officers would believe it too, and that they would order the troops back this way.

The second chimes ought to be ringing, and Vivia was now the only person left in the under-city. She had sent every one of her volunteers away, including Cam—though the boy had tried to stay. Such loyalty, such honest goodness. If . . . no, *when* they survived this, Vivia hoped the boy would stay.

She glanced behind her, at the barrier erected by the only witches able to help—two Plantwitches and a Stonewitch. Roots and rock knitted together to form a wall that would, if these raiders really were coming, slow any forces entering the magic doorway.

Perhaps it will all come to nothing, Vivia thought, turning away from the door and stepping into her under-city with foxfire to light her way. *Perhaps Stix and this Ryber girl will destroy the magic doorway.*

Or perhaps there is no magic doorway at all.

Vivia was almost to the exit from the under-city and slipping the barricade key from her pocket when her feet stopped. Her hand stilled.

A thunderclap boomed across the cavern. Then a second thunderclap and a third, as if someone knocked at a door. With fire-pots.

Finally, a fourth explosion tore out, and this time, wood

539

splintered, stones flew, and the ground tremored beneath Vivia's feet. She didn't have to turn to know what had happened. She didn't have to *see* to know the doorway's barrier had been destroyed. That raiders were entering the city.

A city that wasn't ready. A city that needed more time. *Her* city.

Shouts trickled into Vivia's ears, Arithuanian words. And Marstoki too. Then footsteps scraped on limestone, and she knew raiders stomped this way. In a matter of minutes, they would reach her and this wooden barricade. In a matter of minutes, they would reach the other blockade to Pin's Keep. They would make short work of it, just as they had before.

Soon, all of Lovats would be overrun.

But when a little fox finds her den and kits threatened, when she finds that her escape routes have failed, then she turns back. Then she *fights*. And a captain always goes down with her ship.

Vivia's hand fell away from the key, and without a second thought, she abandoned the door and strode for the heart of the under-city. To the same spot where she had saved Merik's life two weeks ago, to a square where the limestone ground just happened to be at its thinnest.

Vivia did not need a crown to protect Nubrevna from the Raider King. She had never needed a crown, because she had something far, far more powerful.

She reached the center of the square. Green shadows skipped around her. Footsteps hammered close, and voices chased. But she could not be rushed. This would require power. This would require trust.

She dropped to one knee and planted both hands on the

stone floor. Her fingers splayed wide. Then she closed her eyes, and Vivia Nihar *connected*. She reached until her magic brushed against water. She reached until she sensed every drop that flowed through the plateau, that snaked through vast tunnels and hidden arteries. It punched through the Cisterns and trickled down limestone walls. It swept over the creatures of darkness and treasures hidden away.

All of that water—so, so much water—was bound to a lake lit by foxfire. To the Void Well that answered to Vivia and Vivia alone. Its waters sang within her blood, and just as the roots of the Well stretched everywhere, Vivia's magic stretched with it.

Come, she commanded the water and the Well. *Come to me.*

The water and the Well obeyed. Small rivulets at first that climbed and curved, that converged and magnified. Higher, higher, stronger, stronger.

Distantly, Vivia heard war cries approaching. Distantly, she felt stampeding feet upon the stone. But it was the water that told her exactly where these raiders were—small vibrations and shivers. Hundreds upon hundreds of intruders vaulting this way, and more pushing in through that impossible, magical doorway.

They were almost to Vivia's square.

Come, she urged the water. *Faster.*

The water came faster, vast rivers now that rocketed toward the surface. Toward Vivia.

The raiders came faster too. They had reached the square. They had seen her, and even as connected as she was to the waters and to the Well, there was no missing the roars that bellowed nearby.

541

Come, she thought again, but this time she did not address the water. This time, she lifted her chin and opened her eyes—and *this* time, she addressed the men charging toward her. Baedyed and Red Sail. Furs and beards and black silk and tattoos. A mass of violent hunger.

Come.

For half an eternal second, she almost imagined she saw what they saw: a woman waiting for her death. Submissive and weak and bowing to the force of masculine rage. But men had ruled the Witchlands long enough with only bloodshed and chaos to show for it. It was past time Noden and the Hagfishes bent to a woman's rule.

Vivia erupted to her feet, and the water erupted with her. Two geysers that punched through stone right as the first raiders entered the square.

The water destroyed them.

It tore them from their feet with the force of a tidal wave, and as Vivia's arms flung high, the water flung high too. It carried bodies, it carried weapons. Then it tossed them wide in a cascade of snapping spines and shattering skulls.

More raiders hurtled in behind the first wave. They tried to circle around the geysers, around the bodies crashing down.

Vivia twirled, and the water twirled with her. It whipped outward, splitting into a hundred limbs that moved as she commanded. That lashed and struck and yanked men low. The water was an extension of her body, of her mind. It wanted what she wanted—it wanted its home empty and safe.

Vivia lost all concept of time. She lost count of how many people she felled. The water measured time by drought and flood, it measured life by wave and erosion. It had no interest in humanity, no concern if blood stained its soul.

The water gathered and built and rose, and the higher it climbed, the stronger Vivia felt. Still the raiders charged; still she slashed and slew. Free, alive, *unstoppable*. No fetters to hold her down, no masks to hold her back.

Until her water suddenly hit resistance. Until it suddenly reached a body that would not yield, that would not bend.

Vivia startled back into her mind. Her water whips stilled. She gasped, stunned by the water's icy claws—by how high it had flooded around her. All the way to her mid-thighs and still rising. Bodies floated by, some twitching, some choking, but most unmoving and dead.

More raiders still came too. Vivia heard them splashing and shouting.

It was the person standing before her, though, that seized Vivia's attention. A figure in a sodden gown swayed in the water, and on either side of her were two iron shields that had stopped Vivia's attacks.

The Empress of Marstok's chest quivered in time to desperate breaths. Black coated half her face. She stared at Vivia and Vivia stared at her.

Then as one, they started running. Toward each other. A slogging, slow stride through water and corpses.

They reached each other, and the Empress of Marstok collapsed into Vivia. Her skin was frozen to the touch and it shone a sickly green beneath the foxfire. The black on her face was, Vivia realized, crusted blood.

No time to ask how Vaness had gotten here. No time to prop her up and keep fighting the raiders. Now the men were pouring into the square faster than Vivia's waters could attack—faster than she could keep track of.

The water, though, did not need her anymore. It had answered Vivia's call, and now it reigned supreme. A frothy, rising mass that would soon be too high for the raiders to defeat.

So, without another thought, Vivia let her water whips fall. Then she gripped the Empress of Marstok tightly to her—she was so small, so broken—and together, they drove through corpses and water.

Together, they left the underground. Together, they ran for the night.

SIXTY-ONE

✳

Storm and stone, lightning and earthquakes. Iseult's body was a conduit for noise and electricity. Wind seared against her, rain flayed her skin. She held Leopold, and he held Owl. Their Threads shone, two beacons to guide Iseult home.

She knew that having a child lead her through the end of the world was as impossible as walking through blue light and ending up inside a nightmare. But there was also no other alternative. To release Leopold was to lose her way, and to release Owl was to lose the only anchor they had inside this chaos.

There was no sight in this tumult, no sense of up or down. At any moment, Iseult expected the ice-slick stone beneath her feet to crumble away.

But the ground would never betray an Earthwitch, and Owl led them true.

Once, Iseult thought she heard voices. She thought she saw Threads cresting through the fray, an army of people far, far below. It could have been a mirage, though. Shadows shaped like humans dancing in a storm.

Boulders crashed around them. Never did they hit Iseult or Leopold, though, nor their strange, icy bridge. Always, Owl flicked them away as easily as a girl tosses toys—and for a dragging moment between steps, Iseult wondered if Owl had ever had toys. She did not seem like a child now.

Moon Mother's little sister.

"This way," Owl called, more a trembling in the stone than actual words, and Iseult realized they had reached a doorway where weak light shimmered through the chaos. It was small, though, and shrinking inward by the second.

Just as she had done above the Monastery, Owl scrabbled through without waiting for Iseult or Leopold.

They followed—of course they followed. Anything to escape this maelstrom. Iseult crawled through first, using Leopold's grip to drop to her knees and squeeze through. She was battered, she was beat, she was pulled and compressed and broken in two.

Then she keeled out the other side, where cold air and blessed silence dashed against her. Owl squatted just ahead, her Threads a swirling array of pleasure and Earthwitch power. Still on all fours, Iseult dragged herself toward the child . . . then collapsed atop silty, damp earth. Two heartbeats later, and Leopold landed beside her.

Iseult and the prince sucked in gasps. His Threads radiated with the same wonderment and horror that Iseult felt. Her muscles twitched as if lightning still clashed. Her ears echoed and droned.

"What was that?" he rasped, pushing himself upright with his good arm. "By the Twelve, Iseult, what *was* that? And what is she?" He edged a wary stare toward Owl, his Threads briefly glimmering with distaste. Or maybe it was disgust. Or just continued horror.

Iseult was too sapped to interpret anything anymore. "I think that the more important question is, where are we now?" They had definitely left the Monastery. It was cold here, but not frozen—and water rushed nearby.

Threads hummed nearby too.

"People," Iseult said at the same time Owl chirped, "Finished, finished, finished." Now Iseult was the one to eye her warily. Owl had changed since leaving the mountain. It was as if, after leading them through a world caving in, she had abruptly reverted back to her childish self.

She even drew figures in the soil with a finger—all while singing, "Finished, finished, finished."

"You stay here," Iseult said slowly, directing her words to Leopold though her gaze never left Owl. "I'll go see who's out there. Maybe they can help us."

"Or," he countered, "you stay here, and I go check."

Iseult glared sideways. "We have no weapons, Prince, and last I checked, I'm the only one here with a magic that can hurt people. Well," she amended, "there's Owl. But . . ." She waved vaguely.

And Owl smiled up from her drawing. "Finished, finished, finished."

"We could all go?" Leopold suggested, Threads shriveling inward with discomfort.

"And then all risk getting hurt? No." Using her hands, Iseult hoisted herself to her feet. The moonlit pines and beeches briefly hazed together—then quickly slid apart once more. "I can creep up and observe them without being seen. I'll be back soon."

Leopold's only response was a dissatisfied grunt, but he

didn't argue. He was the one with a crown here, but Iseult was the one with the power.

Soon enough, she was tiptoeing into the trees. The landscape reminded her of the Sirmayans, of the forests she'd journeyed through over the past month. This was different, though—and she couldn't say how she knew, she simply did.

And all of it was so, so different from Veñaza City. *What if, what if, what if.*

The Threads brightened ahead, and soon Cartorran voices rippled into Iseult's ears, tense but not angry. A discussion, she decided, or a debate, for concentrated green wavered across their Threads.

Three of the people, though, had odd Threads. It wasn't obvious from afar, yet the closer Iseult sidled, the more she noticed black tendrils writhing in their hearts.

Severed Threads, she thought. Except . . . not. It was unlike anything she'd ever seen, anything she'd ever been taught.

Iseult would have continued to study them, to evaluate safety and intent, but two footsteps later, she was close enough to distinguish individual words. And to hear a voice she had feared she would never hear again.

"Weasels piss on you," said the only speaker without the darkness in her Threads. "I know more about these mountains than you, Caden. After all, who's the domna here?"

"You do realize what my last name means. *Fitz* Grieg?"

A pause. Then: "You bastard!" Safi cried, and a sound like punching filled the forest. "You are literally a bastard! Why the rut didn't you tell me?"

"It's implied in the name! I'm sorry if you were too dense and self-absorbed to notice."

Iseult couldn't believe it. Her hand shot to her throat, to the Threadstone. Then without a single thought, a single precaution, a single lesson Habim or Mathew had taught her, she broke into a run.

The underbrush thrashed and slapped. She almost tripped on a root. Her elbows cracked against trunks, and ahead, four sets of Threads flashed bright with alarm. Then voices lifted too, and Iseult knew that they heard her—that they were drawing weapons or getting ready for an attack.

But Iseult didn't care. Her heart was so big, she thought it would pummel through her rib cage. And like before, tears had started to fall—these tears she understood, though. These tears she welcomed.

She reached a clearing. Four shadows glowed in the moonlight, arms high and stances ready. But Iseult had eyes for only one person. How had she not recognized her Threads sooner? So vibrant and alive.

"Safi," she breathed, a whisper of sound. Then again, "*Safi.*"

And that was all it took. Her Threadsister's hands fell. "Iseult?" She gaped. Then without waiting for a reply, she charged forward and tackled, arms grabbing and laugh burbling out. "It can't be, it can't be."

Never had Iseult been squeezed so tightly, and never had she squeezed so tightly back. *What if, what if, what if.* None of those speculations and daydreams mattered now.

Because now Iseult was back where she belonged. Initiate and complete. Threadsisters to the end.

And together once more while a sky sang with stars and a child whispered, "*Finished, finished, finished.*"

*

Stix did not remember picking them up.

In fact, she remembered very clearly doing as Ryber had ordered and leaving the items behind.

Death, death, the final end.

Yet somehow, here they were, resting upon a broken slab of granite. Ice covered the soil, the remnants of a standing stone. Already, it melted, shrouding the dawn in thick, white fog.

Stix walked slowly, each step cautiously placed as she approached the granite. Each inch examined with squinting eyes. She and Ryber might have successfully destroyed most of the standing stones to which the mountain's magic was bound, but there were still raiders inside that mountain, inside the Crypts leading to it, and inside these woods nearby.

Then Stix reached the two items she knew she had left behind.

A broken sword lay on the right, only its hilt and cross-guard fully intact, while a jagged slash of blade still razored out from above. A hole opened inside her belly at the sight of it.

Death, death, the final end.

Beside the hilt rested a square frame with a handle for grasping. It reminded her of a small mirror her older sister had loved, yet where that glass had been reflective, this glass was clear—and it was shattered, too. Only a few shards still clung to the frame.

Stix reached for the handle. Like the blade, this device sang to her. Though it hummed not with death, but with answers. This plain, broken glass was a way for her to see. *The* way, if she was willing to peer inside.

Carefully, she glanced back to see if Ryber watched. To see if Ryber would, once more, warn her to step away.

But the Sightwitch Sister was too absorbed by recording in her diary what they had just done to the stones, had just done to the mountain. She didn't notice Stix creeping away.

Carefully, Stix picked up the broken glass. Carefully, she looked through.

The world fell away.

Stix was no longer beside the standing stones. She was now surrounded on all sides by thick forest and white-capped peaks. Snow fell, and nearby, a river churned. On a stone bridge spanning its dark waters, a man in black furs strode her way.

On his head shone a silver crown. In his hand gleamed a silver sword.

Then the Rook King fixed his gaze on Stix. "It will all be over soon," he said before his blade arced out and crashed against her neck.

Only as the sword cracked against stone did she realize she was locked in place. Only when it cut through the rock—three swings it took him—did she realize she was encased in granite.

Then blade bit into flesh.

She died.

SIXTY-TWO

✳

The blood looked fresh in the snow. It had wept, it had oozed, and now it was trapped in time by ice and cold. The frozen river would accept no offering of corpses; these dead would stay here for months, until next year's summer thaw.

So many blood-scents to mingle against Aeduan's magic, so many dead for his gaze to drag across. Aeduan had not killed these monks and raiders, though. While he had fought to protect the Cahr Awen, to give Iseult time to flee, he had taken no lives.

Death did not have to follow wherever he went. Not anymore.

He turned away from the battle. Some people still fought, far across the valley, while others simply moved through the corpses and gathered their dead. And in some spots, seafire still licked and reached for the sky.

Aeduan left it all behind. There was one blood-scent he had to follow, one promise he had to keep.

He tracked the scent through a tunnel in the mountain, where stone men waited. Grotesque creations Aeduan didn't look at too closely or consider too deeply. At a fork in the

552

path, the scent veered right—so to the right he veered as well. Up, up, until at last he reached a forest above the Monastery.

The full moon streamed down, a shimmery glare upon the snow. Footprints traced forward, the right size to have been hers.

Strong, the scent here was strong: Aeduan's own blood, bright and fresh and laced with fireflies. She must be near, the one who wore his coin. The one who'd carried him, when no one else could. The one who'd shown him that only he could save himself.

The conifers parted. Here, more footprints stamped and splayed—and more blood-scents too, from two people Aeduan knew.

He rushed forward. The tracks and the bloods moved into a small ditch just ahead. He reached the edge and strode in.

And then he stopped. For the path went nowhere. Before him was nothing but a stone wall, and resting atop the snow was a gleaming silver coin.

Aeduan had not known he held his breath until it slithered out. He had not known his heart pounded so hard until it skipped a beat—and the world skipped a beat with it.

For Iseult had lost her silver taler. She had lost the only means Aeduan had of finding her. *He* had lost the only means he had of finding her.

With a stiff bend, he scooped the coin off the snow. Cold and wet, the double-headed eagle stained in blood grinned up at him. Laughing, he thought; and for half a stuttering breath, he wanted to fling it back to the ground.

But he didn't. Instead, he furled his fingers inward and turned away from the strange, blank stone. Then he climbed back into the clearing, back into the moonlight.

For the first time in his life, Aeduan was free to move of his own accord. No cloak bound him, no contracts held him, and no leash locked him in place. Even vows he'd meant to keep were now lost to a wall of stone and snow.

He was a tool no longer. He was a blade no longer, to be wielded by others or brandished by Lady Fate. He was Aeduan. Just Aeduan, and he could choose whatever life he wanted. He could go wherever his will might lead.

He already knew exactly where that was. Not a place, but a person. Not a job, but a promise. And not an obligation, but a desire. He might not be able to follow her, but there were other ways than blood to find people in the Witchlands.

With that thought to guide him, he eased the coin into his pocket. Two rolls of his wrists, a crack of his neck, and the Bloodwitch named Aeduan set off into the night.

FIREFLIES

✳

*H*e does not hear her coming; he does not smell her. It is not until she is upon him, while he washes at the spring, that he realizes she is near.

He left her at the campsite with the child and the mountain bat. She stood watch while he scouted ahead, exactly as they have done each night for the past week while traveling together.

"You're hurt," she says, and he spins around to face her. Were he not injured, he would have attacked her—startled into action. But he is injured, and he is slow.

"Let me help," she offers, striding toward him. The moon, a growing crescent, beams down from a sky dappled with stars. It turns the blood on his chest to black.

He does not know why she helps. He also does not pull away.

She reaches him, and though he wants to recoil, though his fingers tap against his thighs, he holds his ground. He lets her lean in. He lets her brace a hand on his shoulder and grip the first of six arrows poking from his belly.

A parting gift from a Nomatsi road just north of here.

"Why is it," she asks softly, long fingers furling around the first shaft, "that I always seem to be pulling arrows from you?"

She yanks. He coughs. Blood pours.

Five more times, she repeats this, and he can practically see her calculating the life-debts between them. He would have healed from these wounds on his own, though, so as far as he is concerned, this counts for nothing.

"At least this time," she says when she is done, a pile of red fletching at her feet, "you waited until you were here before removing them. The cuts will heal cleaner because you let me do it."

This is not how his magic works. Not at all, but he also does not contradict her. Instead, he says, "You are an expert in Bloodwitches now?"

"No." Her lips sketch a smile. "Just in stubbornness."

"It takes it to know it."

Now her smile widens, and for some reason, his heart hitches at the sight of that. And for some reason, he likes that he can see the tips of her white canines. He doesn't think he's ever seen them before.

"I could not sense you coming," he tells her, gaze flicking away from her mouth. Back to her yellow eyes. "Did you remove the coin?"

"No." She pulls back her collar to prove this, but he finds he is not watching the silver taler or the leather strap it is bound to. Instead, he finds he is staring at her collarbone. At the small hollow along the base of it.

Her pulse flutters.

"It must need more blood," she says eventually, startling him back into the moonlight.

Their eyes meet. Hers seem closer now. The air seems smaller. He does not breathe. She does not breathe.

Until, suddenly, it is too much. He backs away two steps and blurts, "I am leaving soon. So you need not worry that I will hurt you."

He does not know why he tells her this. He had not planned on letting her know. Then again, he had also intended to leave last night. And the night before. And every night since they had found that child in the Contested Lands.

He had yet to actually follow through, though.

"You would have left without saying good-bye?" she asks.

And he counters, "You would have cared?"

She does not respond to this. She simply stares in that inscrutable way of hers while heat gathers in his shoulders. On his cheeks, too. This is not the response he had hoped for from her; he does not know what is.

Without warning, she swoops down and reclaims an arrow from the spring's rocky shore. Then she takes a single step toward him, and though he wants to back away, he resists. Even as she closes the space between them. Even as she reaches for his arm.

With a touch light as snowfall, she laces her fingers around his wrist. Then she lifts his hand.

At first he thinks she is trying to read his palm like some Sightwitch from centuries past—just as his mother used to do. But then she lifts the arrow, and before he can stop her, she rakes it across his skin.

A soft pain lances through him. He hisses, and blood pools.

Then her free hand moves to the silver taler at her neck. A yank, a snap. She places the coin atop his palm.

Already, the cut is healing. Already the blood clots and the rough skin knits itself back together—but not before a smear of blood can mark the coin's surface. A fresh spray of red to sink into the grooves of the silver eagle.

557

"You want me to be able to find you?" He can scarcely hear his own voice. It is caught somewhere inside his chest.

But she hears him. "I don't want you to kill me. Assuming we ever meet again."

"Ah," he murmurs, although "ah" is not the word he truly wants to say.

Two breaths later, she plucks the coin from his palm, careful not to get blood on her own skin. Then she offers him one of her sly, subtle smiles—only visible if you know what you are looking for.

He knows what he is looking for.

"Also," she adds softly, "I want you to be able to find me."

Without another word, she turns and walks away. His heart thumps unevenly inside his chest. His lungs swell against his breastbone, as if there is something he ought to say. Something he wants to say before she is gone.

In her odd, perplexing way, he thinks she might be asking him to stay. No one has ever asked him that before.

No one. Ever.

But he does not speak, and he does not follow. In seconds, the forest welcomes her. The night turns colder. Yet all the while, he stands there, as rigid as the earth beneath his feet.

And all the while, he watches, moment by moment, heartbeat by heartbeat, as the cut on his palm closes until nothing is left but dried blood with a circle missing at its heart.

ACKNOWLEDGMENTS

Whitney (Ross) le Riche, this series would never have reached readers if not for you. Thank you for taking a chance on my complicated fantasy. Thank you for being my champion in-house and on the page. Thank you for being a friend through some tough years. I miss you.

To Rachel: *Tu me manques.* I said that for the last book, and I mean it still. You have been a brainstorm buddy, a critique reader, and such a true, true friend. When next we meet IRL, the Thai dinner is on me.

Diana, thank you for pulling all-nighters alongside me. Thank you for taking the helm and steering this new ship into the surprise deadline storm. It has been a real pleasure to work with you, and *boy*, am I proud of how much we accomplished in such a short time. Go team!

For Joanna Volpe, Suzie Townsend, Hilary Pecheone, Pouya Shahbazian, Devin Ross, Mia Roman, and Abbie Donoghue: I don't know what I would do without you all. I think I say some iteration of that with every book . . . because it's true. Thank you! For reading, supporting, and providing. Love you all.

559

Alex, I owe you so many thank-yous for tirelessly enduring my long, convoluted explanations of the Witchlands. Thank you for brainstorming, thank you for listening, and thank you for always being there.

Sam(antha) Smith: thank you for all your endless support and patience. You're awesome, and I'm so grateful to work with you.

Cait Listro and Melissa Lee, I love you ladies. You cheerlead when I need cheerleading and critique when I need criticism. Thank you, thank you, *thank you!!*

To Holly Black, thank you for helping me find the theme in my series that I couldn't see. You literally saved this book with a single afternoon of chatting.

And I owe so, *so* many thanks to all my other friends who helped me survive this book's creation: Erin Bowman, Leigh Bardugo, Victoria Aveyard, Amie Kaufman, Courtney Moulton, Elise Kova, Robin LaFevers, Jenn Kelly, Rae Chang, Kristen Simmons, Shanna Hughes, Karen Bultiauw, Kelly Peterson, and oh dear, I'm sure I'm forgetting someone . . .

To Alexis Saarela, Kristin Temple, Lili Feinberg, Zohra Ashpari, Lucille Rettino, Eileen Lawrence, and Kathleen Doherty, and all the incredible faces behind the scenes at Tor and Macmillan: thank you for putting up with me for all these years. I could not be more grateful to be part of your family, and I hope you all know how much I appreciate and rely on you.

To my family, Mom, Dad, David, and Jennifer—thank you for being there during a rough time. Thank you for always being there, actually, and always being my number-one fans.

And to Seb . . . Well, what can I possibly say to convey my

560

gratitude? Most people would have lost patience with a spouse like me, but you are a truly wonderful, giving, eternally patient soul. Thank you and *je t'aime*.

BUT WAIT, THERE'S MORE!

Read on for a deleted *Bloodwitch* scene, and continue for a sneak peek at the next novel in the Witchlands series

※

Reaching the Well of Nubrevna took time. Though Stix had her Waterwitchery to sail her straight down the Timetz, the whispers did not like that she was leaving Lovats.

She departed before midmorning in a narrow, sharp-bottomed skiff that she could maneuver easily through the river traffic that clotted the waters near the capital. It felt good to move. To summon her powers. Like liquid filling a glass, it was a charge that flowed into every inch of her body.

For the first hour, as she navigated her way across the Bridges of Stefin-Eckart, past the southern Sentry of Noden, and around the mass of refugee ships waiting to enter the city, Stix wondered why she hadn't done this sooner. Skating down the cold river dissolved all the knots in her belly in a way that even the underground had not.

She should have just sailed and sailed and avoided that limestone darkness entirely.

The second hour, the voices erupted—but now they were no longer whispers. They were screams, and they wanted blood. Stix knew it was the second hour because the eleventh chimes rang out from a low shrine squatting near the river's muddy shore. She knew it was the second hour because she thought, delighted, how much time had passed without any murmurs from the back of the skull.

Then they careened into her, so hard and so loud a scream of her own burst from her throat. Her magic snapped off. The skiff cut to a stop. Stix doubled over, scarcely aware of how much the vessel now dipped and waved with her movement.

She thought she had been stabbed in her gut, and it took three damp-eyed checks to confirm that no, no blade was lodged there. Meanwhile, the voices—so *many* voices—screamed all the louder.

Somehow, though sweat gushed off her and unconsciousness waved at the edges of her sight, Stix summoned her magic once more. And she kept on sailing.

Faster now, sucking in every drop of power with no concern for how it might weaken her. She was already weakened, and all that mattered was that she did not stop. Later she would marvel that she hadn't turned around and sailed back—hadn't given in to the absence of pain that would have awaited her if she'd simply returned north. But her body and her magic knew that north was not where answers waited. Only south. Only at the Origin Well.

She lost all track of time. It was only as the sun was several hours past its zenith, when clouds began to tumble in and the air to cool, that Stix realized the voices had faded. The pain, too. In fact, each mile she rushed down the river, they receded more. Even the exhaustion she should have felt after using this much power was nowhere to be seen. She felt strong. She felt sure.

This was the way she *had* to go.

At sunset, she reached the Hundred Isles. At moonrise, she reached the shore closest to the Water Well. It took some navigating. Now that she had arrived, now that the whispers and the pain had settled into almost total silence, exhaustion reared its ugly head. Suddenly, the crashing rhythm of the waves seemed impossible to control.

And had salt water always been so buoyant against her magic? It was like trying to wrestle butterflies.

The full moon glittered on the rounded stone gravel when at last Stix hauled her skiff ashore. The plateau upon which the Well waited hunched like a massive tortoise against the night sky. A strong breeze, smelling of fish and cedar, gusted against her. Every few minutes, it carried clouds across the moon and turned the world to dark.

"Well, shit," Stix said once she had the skiff firmly out of the sea's reach. Then, as she plopped onto the ground and tried to catch her breath, she said it again. "Well, shit."

Now that she was here, she had no idea what to do. She'd drained the last of her drinking water an hour before, and all food had been eaten as she'd sailed. She supposed she ought to ascend the plateau, and examine the Well up close—a healed Well now, if the rumors were true. But where her vision was poor during the day, it was almost useless at night. Shapes blurred together and no amount of squinting would break them apart.

Besides, the angle from Stix's dream had not been *at* the Well, but beside it. . . .

Stix rubbed at her eyes. Her skin was crusty with salt from the sea's breeze. She wished she'd brought more water.

It was then, as she sat there wondering if maybe she ought to sleep in her skiff until sunrise, that she realized she was no longer alone. Four people approached from the jungle.

Had Stix not been so drained, she would have noticed them sooner. Her magic would have *made* her notice. After all, the human body was made almost entirely of water, and where there was water, Stix sensed it.

The jungle had confused her, though, with its succulents packed full of moisture and its insects brimming with life. It was a soothing blanket of power to thrum behind Stix while she scrubbed and scrubbed at eyes that refused to work properly. Not until the people had crept from the jungle's edge did she finally realize they were there.

And not until one shouted, "Do not move or we'll shoot," did she realize they must have bows.

Stix did not move. "I'm with the Royal Navy," she shouted. "First mate to Vivia Nihar."

"Right," barked a woman. "And I'm the Empress of Marstok."

They all laughed at that.

"Stand up slowly," ordered the first voice. An older man. "We don't want trouble."

Really? Stix wanted to retort as she pushed to her feet. *Then why corner me with bows?* As she turned to face them, eyes screwed so tight she could almost, just *maybe* make out four figures . . .

The clouds parted. The moon shot down. She saw them: two men, two women, one with a crossbow and the others with swords undrawn.

Stix moved. A single inhale, and her magic surged and the

568

water around her *moved*. Not from the sea, but from the beach. Shards of water that cut up, that cut high.

On her exhale, they heated to boiling.

It hurt. Not just the women and men, but Stix, too. A thousand stings on exposed skin, like a jellyfish had sucked her in. It was over in an instant, and after—*after*—was the part that mattered.

Steam blanketed the shore.

Stix ran.

She heard the crossbow bolt *thwang!* and she sensed a figure charging to her right. But she easily swirled away. No one could see her, yet she could feel each of them. Once she hit the jungle's edge, they started to shout behind her.

"Where did she go?"

"Find her!"

"We need to alert Yoris!"

Within moments, they were out of earshot and the steam was left behind. The scrub was thick, and in the darkness, Stix missed roots, vines, branches. She tripped three times and her blood roared in her ears. There was no path to follow—at least none that she could find—but Stix quickly found she didn't need one.

Come, the whispers sang. *Come this way, keep coming.*

Twenty steps became forty became sixty until at last, the cedar and the vines gave way to a shadowy stone wall.

And to a shadowy stone door.

Come. Come this way, keep coming.

It was identical to the door in the underground, but where that one had been incomplete, this one gaped open. Shadowy save for the faintest blue light that hummed around its edges.

Come this way, keep coming.

Without another thought, Stix went. She went that way, and kept going.

She stepped through the door.

Turn the page for a sneak peek
at the next novel in the Witchlands series!

Available February 2021 from Tor

BEGINNINGS

✳

he Rook watches from an oak branch.

His feathers rustle. His beak clacks. It has been a long time since he saw the Sun and the Moon come together.

It has been even longer since he saw them heal a Well.

A hundred people attend, arranged in stiff rows around the wide pond. Some have weapons, most have uniforms, and all have bored scowls. Behind them, long dormant beech trees stand sentry. Six—always six.

Snow fell in the night, a light dusting that has turned the pine forest to fragile white. But it never touches the Well, nor the mossy flagstones surrounding it, nor the beech trees waiting to come alive.

The Sun, with her shorn golden hair, and the Moon with her shorn black hair, wear matching brown shifts that come to their knees. The Sun is annoyed and does not try to hide it; the Moon is impassive, all her feelings and thoughts kept tucked away behind lucent nothing.

She reminds the Rook of someone he knew long ago. Someone who broke the world just to make it new again.

Both girls are clearly cold. Both shiver and bounce, breaths fogging. A stone overhang lurches above the Well, blocking what little light the true sun gleans at this early hour.

The girls are trapped in shadow.

When at last a round man with furs nods for them to begin, they do not hesitate. A single glance passes between them, a hint of a smile on the Sun's face, then hand in hand, the Sun and Moon dive into the cold, dark Well.

Soon, all that is visible are their legs, flashes of pale skin that wink beneath fresh-churned froth. A flicker of pale hands, a shimmer of toes.

Then they vanish entirely, swallowed by the Well.

Several moments pass before a graceful man with hair the color of sunrise begins to prowl along the Well's southern edge. Back and forth, back and forth, always staring into the depths with an intensity no one can match, not even the Rook. The rotund man snaps at him to stop; the graceful man ignores him.

That one has never been good at listening.

Then it happens: a gentle boom, so subtle one might think it a trick of the mind. A heartbeat that has pulsed too long. A tremor in the muscles, not the earth.

But the Rook has seen this before. He has felt it before and watched as ripples tore out across a pond. Perfect, concentric rings to lap against a Well's rim.

The graceful man smiles.

Then a second boom breaks loose—strong enough to shake snow off the trees. Strong enough to rattle in the Rook's hollow bones.

Suddenly, none of the people surrounding the Well are bored. None of them are scowling.

The graceful man cries out—a whoop of joy—and his arms

fling wide. Triumphant. He twirls to face the other man. Yet as the turns, his eyes briefly catch on the Rook's. If he is surprised to see the bird, though, he does not show it.

"It is done," he declares, advancing on the round man. "The Well is healed."

The round man smiles. A slow thing that makes his dark eyes gleam with hunger. And not for the first time, the Rook is reminded that there are no creatures in the Witchlands as insatiable as men.

"His Majesty will be pleased," the man begins, but then a splash steals the rest of his words. The girls have returned.

The Sun appears first. Initiate.

The Moon follows next. Complete.

They both gasp for air, paddling clumsily for the Well's edge. Cold has leeched color from their skin, save for a painful pink along their noses. Two uniformed guards await them with thick blankets.

The Sun reaches the rim first, and after the guards haul her free, she turns back to help the Moon. Not because there aren't men to aid her, but because this is who she is. Who they both are: inseparable and true.

And the Rook nods at that. Clacks his beak too, just for good measure.

Because everything has happened as it ought, and now it is time for him to leave. He has orders to follow; his detour here certainly wasn't one of them.

But the Rook feels that he deserved to see the Sun and Moon united. A reward for all his centuries of devoted focus. After all, there are still pieces of humanity twinkling inside him. Tiny slivers that like rewards for a job well-done.

And tiny slivers that like chocolate and sweet jams, too.

With a flap of his glossy wings, the Rook bursts off the oak tree. The branch shakes, snow flutters down, and soon the discussions of two men accustomed to power fade from the Rook's hearing.

CHAPTER ONE

*

S he knew she was walking into a trap. She had seen their tracks twenty paces before, just beside that bend in the road, and she had sensed their Threads even sooner.

Maybe, if she wanted to, she could avoid them.

But she didn't want to. She was hungry. Winter's cusp had left nothing to forage on this side of the Ohrins, and what little she had managed to gather had all been given to her companion.

A tiny companion now waiting in a hollowed-out beech with a weasel who wasn't really a weasel.

When she was fifteen steps from the closest soldier, she stopped and planted her staff in the mud. It was roughly hewn hawthorn, taken off a corpse two days before.

Hawthorn, the hill folk said, was good for warding off nightmares. So far, she hadn't found that to be true.

The closest man's Threads hovered green with concentration. He was poorly hidden behind an alpine rhododendron, and even if his Threads hadn't given him away, the footprints speckling the narrow road would have. Muddy from yesterday's rain, it was grooved so deep from travel that it was practically a ditch—which meant all these men waiting in the forest brush had higher ground.

Not that it would help them.

"I know you're there," she called.

As one, bright alarm punched across eight sets Threads, each in comparably poor hiding places.

"And I have nothing of value," she continued. Her voice was rough with hunger. She thought she might pass out just standing here. The world had been a sickening spin for days now. If not for the Threads, she would never have been able to focus on these men.

Or on the one man, now stalking toward her down the path. A Hell-Bard. She didn't need to see his scarlet uniform to know that. The shadowy twirl at the heart of his Threads gave him away.

"We were warned about you," he declared, pausing twenty paces away. Near enough for her to spot the ruddy nose of a man who drank too much. He smiled. "You don't look like a threat."

"Oh, but I am." She lifted her left hand and flipped it his way. "Do you know what this means?"

He didn't answer, but fresh concern rippled across the hidden soldiers' Threads.

"And do you," the Hell-Bard countered, drawing a gold chain from beneath his collar, "know what this means?"

She laughed at that—a dry, starving chuckle. "I guess they didn't tell you, then, did they?"

His eyes thinned. He took the bait. "Tell me what?"

She lowered her own collar, revealing what she knew to be a vicious black line across her neck. And from that line came countless jagged offshoots, crawling up and down her pale skin.

"They noosed me, too, Hell-Bard." She let a dramatic beat pass. Then added, "But they failed."

The Hell-Bard swallowed now, his weight shifting. His Threads flickered like a stormy sky from bluish surprise to gray fear to iron violence.

He would attack soon. So would the soldiers in the woods. Bushes shifted; branches snapped. These men did not like feeling afraid, so they would end her and be done with it.

She sighed at that. She was tired, she was hungry, but she was not weak.

"You have two choices," she offered them. "I will cleave you or I will you kill you. There is still a chance at life if you choose—"

"Nommie filth," the Hell-Bard said.

And inwardly, she smiled. Yes, she thought, grateful he'd said that. Grateful he'd made it clear exactly what he was made of.

It would make this next part so much easier.

Or rather, it would make the nightmares so much easier. After all, she had already decided to kill them; now she simply had a good reason.

The man's blade whispered free.

He attacked, charging with sword arm high. Foolish. Easily dodged.

Men always did underestimate her.

When he reached her, she swept easily sideways, planting her heel on the path's inclined side. She launched up, a brief boost of speed and air. Then she twirled past him, her staff extended.

It cracked the back of his head, right where spine meets skull. Not hard enough to kill him, nor hard enough to knock him out. Just enough to send him to his knees and buy her the time she needed.

Because she wasn't done with him yet. She still had a use for his corrupted soul.

As seven more soldiers charged toward her—none of them noosed and none of them well-trained—she grabbed the closest man's Threads. Just a simple reach, a simple grasp.

They were slippery and electric. Like river eels made of lightning.

She brought them to her mouth and chomped down. A single, fluid movement that that had become as natural to her as swinging her staff. All she had to do was yank and bite. Yank and bite.

The man began to cleave.

He was not a witch, so no wild winds or vicious flames ripped loose. But he didn't need such powers to cleave. There was magic in everyone in the Witchlands, and now it burned through him.

He was a pot boiling over; the Threads that bound him to life had come unmoored.

He screamed, a sound of such agony it stopped every soldier in their tracks.

It did not stop her, though. She knew that sound, and she knew the pain that came with it—for she had felt that pain when the noose had cinched into place.

Had almost cinched into place.

She did not let the man cleave fully. Instead, she wound her fingers more deeply into his shredded Threads, and though it sent lightning through her veins, she hung on.

And she commanded.

"Kill them," she ordered.

So the man did. He killed two of his fellows—vicious, bloodied attacks with teeth and clawed hands—before a third man finally brought him down.

She was ready for that, though. She was waiting for it. This was not her first fight, and it would not be her last. With a yank and a bite, she cleaved a second man. Then a third, even as the raw power in their Threads made her fingers shriek. Made power and pain judder straight into her soul.

The first time she'd done this—cleaved someone and held on—she'd fallen over. The second time, she'd been smart enough to hold onto a tree. The third time, she'd had the staff.

Soon, her three Cleaved had burned through themselves, leaving empty, blistered husks on the road, framed by the tarry oil that their blood had become.

Steam coiled in the air.

Slowly—her head still throbbing with power, but her fingers finally free—she approached the only man still alive. The only man with Threads still aflame.

He was pinned to the mud, his own gold-hilted blade stabbed deep into his stomach. It had shoved there by one of her Cleaved.

He would die slowly from that wound, and, contrary to what Hell-Bards wanted the world to believe, they could die.

She came to a stop before him and gazed down. She would take that blade once he was dead; it was too nice to leave behind.

"Nommie bitch," he said, blood spilling from his mouth.

"That's not polite," she replied. She knew what she must look like, towering over him with no expression and a teardrop scar beside her eye.

She knew because she had seen that face in her dreams—in their dreams. They would not let her forget, no matter how fast she ran.

She knelt on the mud beside the Hell-Bard. His chest shuddered. He tried to pull back, but there was nowhere for him to go. He was a dead man in more ways than one.

With no gentleness and only speed, she grabbed the golden noose at his neck. Instantly, power slammed into her.

It was like touching Threads, but instead of heat and thunderstorms, it was cold—the purest cold she'd ever felt. Cold she could only endure for a few, determined heartbeats.

"I'm . . . coming for you," she gritted out. Ice collapsed her lungs. Wrung out her spine. "You cannot hide from me. You cannot . . . stop me."

Then as quickly as she'd taken hold, she released the noose. Cold scattered. Her lungs and spine released.

"You spoke to him," the Hell-Bard rasped. Shock wefted through what remained of his Threads. "How?"

"You know what I am," she told him. "You just didn't want to believe it."

"Yes," he said on a sigh.

"I did try to warn you, though." She unsheathed a rusted cleaver at her hip.

"Yes," he repeated, and this time resignation swept across his Threads. A beautiful rose red to match his blood.

Which was good. There was no sense in fighting the inevitable. She knew that better than anyone.

"May the Moon Mother light your path," she told him in Nomatsi, pressing the blade against his throat. "And may Trickster never find you."

Then she sliced into his flesh. Deep enough to slash the artery; deep enough to end him quickly.

Blood burbled. His Threads faded. She did not sit and watch, though—not like she'd done before, back when she'd still bothered with respecting the dead.

Instead, she pushed to her feet and heaved her rusted, bloodied cleaver into the forest. It vanished in the wintery underbrush. Then with one foot on the Hell-Bard's chest, she wrapped her fingers around the sword hilt . . .

She yanked the blade free. A fine weapon, even with all that blood. She would clean it as soon as she had the chance.

She took the man's sheath next, and after fastening it at her hip, she swept a final, disinterested glance around her.

At the road, sunken like a frown into the mountain. At the eight corpses with steam clawing off their bodies. So much blood, so much Cleaved oil.

She'd told herself at the last fight that she would find a cleaner way to do this. If not for her own eyes, than for whoever had to find it.

Perhaps at the next ambush she would finally succeed. Or at the ambush after that—because there would be another ambush. Many of them. Just as eventually the Emperor's army would catch up to her from behind, and she would kill, kill, kill.

Her stomach growled, an earthly reminder of why she had come here. Of why she had wanted to kill all these soldiers in the first place.

Even Puppeteers had to eat.

So after reclaiming her staff, she hauled herself off the muddy road. Then Iseult det Midenzi stepped into the forest in search of food.